Gabriel

Paul Cartmell

To Helen,

Really hope you enjoy
any little tale, and
can't wait to hear
what you think !!
All the very best!
Bron/Paul
May 2014

Paul was born in Northern Ireland in 1970.

He has been a peace-worker, army medic, teacher, computer geek, musician and writer. He lives in Cornwall with his wife and two lurchers.

There is little space on his sofa.

Paul Cartmell is a pseudonym.

Praise for Gabriel from Amazon:

"This is a fast paced, well written thriller with some wonderfully emotive characters. Couldn't put it down!"

"What a fabulous first novel! Great story, characters that stay with you, tension, drama and a generous sprinkling of humour. I can't wait to read more from Paul."

"I was gripped from the first page and couldn't put it down until the end. I hope there are enough characters left for another book!!"

First published in 2013

ISBN-13 978-1493559077

Published by Paul Cartmell

www.paulcartmell.com

To my wife, Katina, who is much hotter than Zara.

Prologue

"Ready to rock and roll, Marty?" The man looked up from his lab book and held up a single finger.

"Give me a minute, Brad." He continued to make a few notes in the book.

"No problem." His assistant smiled revealing his perfect white teeth, and battered a few keys on his computer.

The laboratory was a large room, airy and bright although it was deep in the university basement. The side benches held all kinds of equipment ranging from ultra-modern monitors, the university screen saver creeping across their huge screens, to an antiquated set of balances screened in a teak and glass case. White boards and posters covered the walls, the boards filled with tightly scrawled equations and diagrams, the posters a mixture of safety and evacuation instructions and tongue-in-cheek de-motivational pictures from across the Internet.

"All good here, Brad. All set?" Marty asked, putting his pen down and looking at Bradley.

"Yeah, all done. One of the thermistors was down, but I boosted one from Spencer's lab."

"Spencer let you?"

"Spencer doesn't know. He's off for a few weeks up north. He has some cabin in the Rockies. Christ alone knows what he does there."

The door to the lab opened and one of the campus security guards entered.

"Af'noon, doctors. Y'all seen Miss Carlton around?"

"Hey John," said Bradley. "Haven't seen her today." He glanced at Marty, who shook his head. "What's up?"

"Nuthin. Visitor at reception for her. Ah'll try paging her again. You boys send her my way if she drops by?" John was a huge black man with a ready smile and a wrinkled forehead. He was instantly likeable, although Marty had doubts about how useful a security guard he would be. The man must weigh at least twenty-five stone and seemed constantly out of breath.

"No problem, John." The big man tapped his eyebrow in salute and left through the other door.

"I think this'll be it for today. I've got shitloads of reports to write up later." Bradley nodded, and crossed the room to a set of long stainless steel tables surrounded by high safety glass screens. At one end stood a metal framework studded here and there with various sensors, cameras and complex circuit-boards, flashing LEDs hanging off them like industrial Christmas decorations. Surrounding the frame were ribbons of cables and leads, all channelled along metal struts before terminating in a nondescript grey box. A fat cable emerged from the other side of the it, coiling beneath the table and into the back of a computer on top of which sat a battered looking monitor and keyboard, the keys faded and pale from use.

Hanging forlornly in the middle of the frame, surrounded by more electronics, hung a joint of raw meat. Occasionally a bead of pale liquid would drip off, splashing sadly onto the metal. Probes and wires studded the meat giving it the appearance of a post-apocalyptic pomander. The sort of thing Lady Gaga would stick in her mulled wine.

Bradley walked to the opposite end of the tables where more equipment was set up. Connected by an array of power supplies was a device like a fat torch with a grey plastic moulding instead of a lens. Various warning stickers adorned the side of its casing. Bradley took a notebook from his pocket and fiddled around with some dials and switches on the rack beneath it.

"It's setting four dash seven today, right?" asked Bradley.

"Yes. Two millimetre penetration."

"Gotcha." He adjusted several more switches, walked back to the other end of the table, and tapped a few characters into the computer. "Ready when you are."

"Alright. Give us a twenty second count." Bradley hit return on the little computer and the figures 20.000 appeared on the screen, the numbers spinning as they counted down. Bradley pushed the safety screen into position around the apparatus and wandered across the room to where Marty was checking his watch and scribbling into the lab book again.

15.000

He pulled a wheelie chair from beneath the bench and sat down in the Christine Keeler pose, legs on either side of the backrest, arms resting on the support cushion.

"You up to anything fun later?" He tapped the backrest with his fingers, absently watching the little screen count down.

12.000

"Not much. Too much work to do." Marty took his ruler and underlined his notes.

9.000

"I, my friend, have got a date..." Brad smiled slyly.

"A night with your Seven-of-Nine poster isn't a date, Bradley," chuckled Marty.

6.000

Various lights blinked to life in the rack of equipment, and a low hum filled the room as the power supplies switched on.

"Let's just say Big John isn't the only one who has business with the delicious Miss Carlton," said Bradley, beaming.

4.000

"Stacey? You're joking!" Marty stared enviously at Brad, who continued smiling broadly.

"Oh yeah. The delectable Miss Carlton. Ribs. A few drinks. Maybe more." Bradley tapped the back of the chair even faster.

2.000

"Ten dollars says you're back tomorrow with a black eye. She does karate." Marty sighed.

The humming noise increased slightly, and a little LED on the side of the torch device began to flash.

0.000

For an instant there was a slipperiness around the room as the microwave beams ionized the air, the little screen filling with readings from the probes around the joint of meat. A tiny wisp of smoke drifted from it, attracting Bradley's attention.

"Hey." He pushed his chair alongside Marty, both watching the puff of smoke drift toward the ceiling. "That's new."

Then the pork exploded into flame.

"Jesus Christ!" Brad jumped back, tripping on the chair and stumbling into the side bench. Marty stood staring, his mouth agape. The pork was fully alight now, temperature probes falling from the roasting meat onto the table. Boiling juices sizzled and poured out of the flesh. Above the apparatus, black smoke tumbled across the ceiling.

Marty ran to the wall and triggered the fire alarm, adding the shrill siren to the sound of roasting meat. Brad dashed through the smoke to the rack of equipment. He tried flicking switches before shrugging and pulling the main cable out of the socket. The lights on the equipment blinked out.

Something shoved Marty in the back, pushing him to the side, as Big John stormed past clutching a huge metal fire extinguisher like it was a child's toy. He stopped a few metres away from the fire before blasting the joint of meat with foam. A few seconds later the flames were out, the table and equipment looking like they were coated in melted marshmallow. John turned to the scientists and grinned broadly.

"I got some jerky sauce in ma locker."

---oOo---

Book One. Bad Parenting

Chapter one

"You can call me Mr Gabriel," said the stranger, his back silhouetted against the sunlight pouring in through the French windows. "This is my colleague, Ms Nadir." He gestured to a young Indian woman who I hadn't noticed, perched comfortably on the edge of the sofa, leafing through one of my old photo albums. She flicked a little wave with her fingers as I instinctively dropped my keys into the bowl on the coffee table.

My coffee table. In *my* house. With two uninvited strangers standing in it.

"Oh." The sound had left my mouth before my mind shifted into gear with a dozen retorts, none of which made it to my tongue. I guess our lives are like that. Funnier and more heroic when edited later.

My head was spinning, never having walked in upon a burglary before, and certainly never having walked in upon such a debonair couple of burglars. Weren't burglars meant to be pasty-skinned skeletal buggers, with bloodshot eyes and wandering teeth? I felt underdressed.

The figure turned to me, revealing a broad, square-jawed face. In his early to mid forties, he was handsome, fit and wholesome, like the hero in a 1950s B movie. His salt and pepper hair was casually cut, a few fronds hanging down above his eyebrow, and he wore a dark suit, cleanly styled, his white shirt open at the neck. Leanly muscled, with smooth tanned skin, Gabriel was a little over six feet tall. That made him one six-pack, healthy colour and a few inches in height better looking than me. An Abercrombie and Fitch catalogue made flesh. He smiled with perfect white teeth and sparkling blue-grey eyes, and raised his hand disarmingly. But I noted something hard behind his expression. Not threat as such. More like a certainty within him that he never need threaten. He just *did*. And if I was stupid, I would be next on the 'to do' list.

My eyes flickered toward the hallway as I considered dashing from the living room and careering into the street shouting 'help' before Gabriel could reach me.

He read my thoughts.

"There's no need for that, Mr Devenish," he said. "We're not here to get all gnarly with you." There was a twang of the southern states in his voice, but there were other accents too. They hadn't quenched the American one completely but they diluted it enough to make it less of a drawl. He seemed full of confidence. Full of control.

In contrast, I felt like I was about to pee myself.

"What's going on here?" My voice squeaked a little at the end, which did little to project the calm machismo I was aiming for. God, I loathe myself sometimes. "Are you the police?"

"Good Lord, no," said Nadir with disdain. She was wearing a neat fitting dark suit with a patterned purple blouse. Small and leanly built, her cascade of lustrous black hair was tied neatly into a ponytail.

I noticed that the buttons on her blouse were struggling to contain a striking figure. Even in times of imminent danger the libido never ceases to amaze me. Maybe that's why hanged men are said to sport impressive erections. Perhaps they spotted someone pretty in the crowd.

My musing was interrupted by Gabriel walking toward me, his square-toed ankle boots clicking across the parquet. His gait was smooth and fluid, but I noticed the slightest hint of a limp as he moved, a subtle stiffness as though he had been sitting with his legs crossed for too long. I realised he was already much too close and I had few options except finding out what they wanted. Unless, of course, I could turn back time a few decades and spend most of my younger years learning a variety of lethal martial arts.

Gabriel extended a perfectly manicured right hand. "I apologise for taking the liberty of waiting for you inside but it's important that we speak with you." He stopped before me, hand outstretched. "And it looked like rain," he added with a shrug.

He paused, his eyes flickering once from my own to his offered hand. That uncomfortable moment, when a response is expected.

I responded.

I'm not generally a very tidy person, but I have managed to keep the majority of my little Oxford house relatively neat. The downstairs living room even has a few houseplants and a brightly painted rustic bowl on the coffee table where I keep loose change, keys, and the normal rubbish which somehow finds its way into the pocket each day.

I moved my arm to take Gabriel's hand but, at the last moment, I grabbed the bowl and flung it, coins and all, as hard as I could at his face, while turning to dash into the hallway.

The bowl didn't reach him, and I didn't reach the door.

Still smiling, he flung his arm up like it was spring-loaded, slapping the dish off to the side and deftly avoiding its contents which clattered uselessly against the windows. With the same hand, as part of the same movement, he grabbed my arm and held on tightly. Squeezing.

I stopped in mid-dash otherwise he would have dislocated my shoulder. The dish smashed pathetically against the far wall.

"I guess that's an understandable response, Mr Devenish," he said, squeezing harder, his eyes sparkling with amusement. "I think, though, you should sit down before you break something. We're not here to hurt you," he said, hurting me as he squeezed more tightly. It's remarkable how much pain develops from merely applying pressure to a limb. He guided me to a chair and I sat down, massaging my arm when he released it. "My colleague makes a fine cup of coffee. I suggest that we have a cup whilst we talk." Nadir stood, regarding me for a moment.

"It's not instant, I trust?" she said, her voice elegant and smooth, her midnight eyes searching mine. I shook my head while rubbing and stretching my arm. "Milk? Sugar?" I stared at her, pale faced and shocked. "Black, then." She went into the kitchen.

"Let's have a chat while we wait, Mr Devenish. Or can I call you Wolf?" I was about to answer when he shrugged and interrupted. "Actually, forget that. We'll go with Mr Devenish. Wolf is a dumb name, FYI." He winked at me. I was racking my brain for any reason why these people were in my house, thinking through the last few weeks to see if I had pissed anyone off more than usual.

"Is this about... are you here about that Jesus story?" I asked. It was Gabriel's turn to look puzzled.

"The Jesus story?" He crossed himself and pointed to the ceiling, an eyebrow raised.

"No... no... I'm working on a story about Jesus College. I thought you might be here about that."

"Oh, I gotcha." He waggled his finger at me like a schoolmaster. "Have you been poking your little English nose in where you shouldn't, Mr Devenish?"

"No." I paused. "Well, perhaps." I relaxed a little knowing that they weren't two heavies coming to warn me to leave the Rodney story alone. "I'm a journalist and I was digging around in something. I thought perhaps that, well, you were here to tell me to stop digging."

"Sorry, Mr Devenish, but the shade of magnolia on your wall interests me more than your work." Gabriel shrugged. "Apologies, buddy, but there you have it." A big smile. "Couldn't care less about what you do for a living."

"So who the hell are you?" I asked, beginning to get my composure back. "And what the fuck are you doing in my house?" His eyebrows raised slightly as I swore. He seemed amused, like a spider threatened by a foul-mouthed fly.

"Yes, of course." He smiled again, teeth glistening. "Well, I've told you who we are, and I've told you that we're in your house because we need to speak with you."

"You couldn't make an appointment?" I muttered.

"We're not that kind of operation, Mr Devenish," said Nadir, back from the kitchen carrying a tray of steaming mugs. She handed me one.

"So what do you want with me?" I asked. Gabriel paused a moment.

"We need to talk to you about your son."

"My son?" Relief bubbled up within me. They'd got the wrong person. "I don't have a son." I sat back on the sofa, the germ of a smile growing across my face.

"Ahhh," said Gabriel, a disappointed glance at his colleague.

"He doesn't know," she said.

My smile died half-formed.

---oOo---

The human jaw is firmly attached by muscles and ligaments to the base of the skull. The shape of the joint determines how far we can open our jaw, which isn't very much compared to, say, a shark, a Tasmanian tiger, or Jim Carrey.

I was trying to outdo all three of them.

"I told you he didn't know," said Nadir, but Gabriel shrugged and scowled.

"You should close your mouth, Mr Devenish. I can see your liver from here." Gabriel switched focus back to me. "Now, let's have a chat about this son of yours. This chip off the old block that you don't know you have."

"I don't have a son," I said. "And before you start breaking my arm again, I think you've made a mistake. I think you've got the wrong person. Hundred percent."

"Oh, so you're hundred percent certain you don't have a kid, Mr Devenish?" asked Gabriel. I nodded.

"Not ninety-nine?" He held his finger and thumb close together.

"One hundred percent. I don't have a son." He stared at me for a moment, his grey-blue eyes sparkling with humour. A crack of doubt opened within me. "Alright, perhaps ninety-nine percent."

"Drink your coffee, Mr Devenish," said Gabriel, reaching for his mug and taking a sip, savouring the flavour. "It is very good coffee, you are exactly the person we wish to speak to, and you do have a son." He raised his palm to stop further interruptions. "In fact, some might say that you not knowing that you have a kid could be seen as bad parenting on your part." Big smile again. "But hey, who are we to judge? We just broke into your house."

"I prefer to say 'introduced ourselves to your hospitality', Mr Devenish," said Nadir. Gabriel raised his mug to her in approval.

"I don't have a son," I repeated. "I have no children." I tried to sound convincing, but his constant gaze, amused grin, and the delicate way he supped his coffee was making my certainty wilt away.

The issue which was worrying me was the *extent* of my various sexual relationships. Don't take me the wrong way. I wasn't that awful when younger. I had my share of girlfriends, some of whom became lovers, and I had also enjoyed a strange evening with a guy called Terence at a festival near Leeds. But I was very careful to avoid any unintentional consequences, both the milk-drinking, crying kind, and the pus-weeping, painful kind.

"This is nonsense." I was growing cross. "You break in here, almost break my arm, steal my coffee, then tell me that I have a child? It's bollocks." I stared at each of them in turn with my best 'enough is enough' glare. Gabriel maintained his smile, but an impatient flintiness crept into his eyes, and I noticed muscles tensing beneath his jacket.

"Do you remember a woman called Zara Moore, Mr Devenish?" asked Nadir. I shook my head. "That's surprising, really, as we've established that you used to be quite good friends back in the late eighties."

She extracted a small notebook and produced a photo of a woman in her early middle age. I didn't recognise her straight away. "This is Zara Moore, Mr Devenish," she said. I took the picture from her and looked more closely. Perhaps there was something. A look about the eyes. Something in the way she captured attention. She was a good-looking lady, that much was for sure. Far too good looking for the likes of me. Could I have been that lucky once?

"You *hung out*, Mr Devenish," said Gabriel, sneering, "and it seems that that wasn't all you let hang out."

"I don't think I recognise her..." I waited for Nadir to respond but Gabriel, muscles still bubbling away beneath the suit, seemed to be losing patience.

"Oh for Christ's sake... we do *not* have time for this," he muttered. He snatched the photo from my hand. "This," pointing at the picture, "is the girl that you, what's that phrase, *made love* to sometime in nineteen eighty-nine!" He threw the picture at me.

"Do you remember now?" asked Nadir, tapping a finger against her bag.

"Twenty years ago... how the hell am I meant to remember what I did twenty years ago?" I asked.

"I remember twenty years ago very clearly, Mr Devenish." Gabriel smiled generously. "I remember twenty years ago being smart enough to wear condoms, asshole."

"Well, I'm afraid that a hangover wasn't the only remnant of those parties," said Nadir. She produced a 6" by 8" photograph from her bag and tossed it onto the coffee table. It was an image of a tall, slightly awkward-looking, dark-haired man smiling uncomfortably for the camera.

"This is Martin Moore... your son," she said, calm and professional. I picked the picture up for a closer look. It was hard to see any family resemblance... hold that thought. Five minutes ago I had no son. Now I was looking to see if he had my nose. I placed the photo back onto the table.

"We did the math. We have the evidence. And guess what, Mr Devenish?" said Gabriel, picking up the photograph. "This is the result of that little summer of love." He flicked the picture at me. "So there you are. You've got a son, he's just turned twenty-three and, in a bizarre freak of genetics, given that you're a useless hack and Ms Moore is a free-spirit who lives on a canal boat selling bits of hedgerow to imbeciles, he's a post-graduate researcher in America. Do you follow me so far?"

Somewhere in the dark recesses of my mind where my memory used to live, there was a bell ringing. Zara. I *did* remember a Zara. But, surely I would have remembered *doing* a Zara. Had I been that bad when I was younger? Possibly.

The story Gabriel was telling me was starting to make just a little bit of sense.

"Right." I paused, trying to remember back to that hectic summer. "Okay." Gabriel watched me with interest, the flicker of laughter still dancing around his eyes. "You seem to be fairly certain that this Michael bloke..."

"Martin," said Nadir. "Martin Moore."

"Right. Martin. You seem certain that he's my son." Gabriel continued to stare, and I sensed his impatience growing again. "Supposing that's true, then what do you want from me? Do you just want to tell me what a bad father I've been? Fine. I get you. Of course I'll have to try and track this Moore woman down and sort this out, but I don't see how it's any of your business, or how I can be any help to you."

"May I use your bathroom?" asked Nadir. I nodded, and pointed her upstairs. Although Gabriel was staring right at me, I found my eyes drift and follow Nadir as she left the lounge. Well, follow Nadir's pert bottom, neatly outlined beneath the expensive fabric of her skirt. Gabriel leaned forward, close enough for me to notice his scent, a clean smell peeking above the tang of his mint and coffee breath.

"Okay, Mr Devenish. In a way we're trying to help you. Help you build the family bonds that you should have built before." He leaned back again, smiling. "But we need you to help us in return. Your son has started a research career in the University of New Mexico, but he's under a lot of pressure at the moment. Working with some serious people. And, since his mother is still living on a boat in the South Downs and hasn't spoken with him for two years, she's not really being very supportive of him."

"What's that got to do with you?" I asked. Gabriel's expression flickered once again. He alternated expressions all the time, from joviality, to murderous intentions, to tightly controlled calmness. He had more mood swings than a maternity ward.

"It has everything to do with us, actually, Mr Devenish. We solve problems for people, and Mr Moore has a problem. One which you can fix."

"We? You and Nadir?" Gabriel's eyes widened, and he shook his head slightly.

"Did you spend your schooling finger-painting in the corner while the other kids learned to read and write, Devenish?" he said. "Of course me and Nadir, you moron."

Nadir reappeared from upstairs. I glanced at her as she sat down, and couldn't fail to notice that she wasn't at all bad looking from the waist up either. *Focus, Devenish, focus.* "Who do you solve problems for?"

"People who pay us to solve problems," said Gabriel. He picked up the photo of my son and pointed to Martin. "This is the problem we have to solve. In fact, annoying as you are, and you are very fucking annoying, Mr Devenish, this is one of our more pleasant jobs." He paused. "Definitely less messy, anyway." Nadir shot him a hard look which he returned. "What? It's true, isn't it?" She sighed and turned to me.

"Your son did very well in Cambridge University," she said, kindly. "First class honours in mathematics and physics."

"I must remember to buy him a card or something," I muttered, trying to lighten the mood. Gabriel quashed my levity with a vicious glance.

"Indeed." I couldn't read Nadir. Her eyes said that she found me interesting, but her body language didn't back that up. She was being pleasant to me because she had to be. Had I met her on the street she wouldn't spare me a second glance.

"Yes, he did very well in his studies, and has a prestigious postgraduate position in New Mexico in an interesting and useful area of physics. It's his current work that concerns us." She put her notebook back in her bag. I fancied I saw the glint of something dark and metallic in there too.

"Have you heard of Los Alamos laboratory in New Mexico?" Gabriel asked, waiting for a response from me. I said nothing. "The Manhattan project?" I sat still. "Top secret military experiments in the heart of the New Mexico desert?" Nothing. "Okay. I'll give you a clue. Your son works in UNM. The University of New Mexico." Again I said nothing. "God, you are obtuse, Mr Devenish, and you call yourself a journalist. Los Alamos is an American Department of Defence establishment. Can you guess which university Los Alamos often works with?"

"The University of New Mexico. Of course. So Moore works for the Americans, now?" Gabriel nodded and continued.

"Your boy's working on a postgraduate research programme through the university. He is developing equipment of a sensitive and downright scary nature, based on research he completed during his degree. In short, your son is a genius, which is amazing given that he has fifty percent of your genes. He has been vetted by just about everybody. FBI, your MI5 and 6, the CIA, the Department of Homeland Security, and half the cast of *Sesame Street*. He checks out clean."

"Good for him," I said.

"Yes. Good for him." Gabriel grinned. "Then we found out about you." His smile widened. "How do you think we found out about your existence, Mr Devenish?" I shook my head.

"DNA," said Nadir. "Of course Mr Moore's DNA was run against a number of DNA databases as a normal precaution and, on this occasion, a near-match was found."

"Now, who do you think would be on a DNA register, and be very closely related to Martin Moore, Devenish?" asked Gabriel, with a sneer.

"Ah." Fuzzy as my memory was, I did remember a visit some years back from two charming law enforcement officials. They were interested in seeing what herbal remedies I had been using, perhaps because they had a sick relative or something. They also took me to their place of work, asked me lots of questions, took my fingerprints and rubbed a small cotton bud around my mouth. Later that day they let me go with a warning that if they found me with the same herbal remedies again they would return to repeat the performance, albeit for a considerably longer time.

I nodded, embarrassed.

"Bingo, Mr Devenish," said Gabriel. "So, we have a very important young man working in a very sensitive organisation, and suddenly a near-match pops up on a criminal DNA database. You imagine both our surprise and that of Mr Moore when we found this out."

"Okay. I think I understand now. So you had to get me vetted too?"

"Yes," said Nadir.

"So... what do I need to do to get this vetting sorted out?" I asked.

"Oh, nothing, Mr Devenish," said Gabriel. "They've already done it. Now, I wouldn't go all Californian and tell you that you checked out bright and shiny, because you didn't. In fact, from what we've seen, you're a useless bastard who I wouldn't trust to babysit my cat never mind keep a state secret. The scary, unsmiling men with the buzzcuts, however, don't think you're a threat. But they let your son know about you, and now he wants to meet."

"Why didn't the people he's working for just contact me directly?" I asked. Gabriel looked at Nadir, then at me, then at Nadir once again, before reaching across the coffee table and slapping me sharply across the head.

"That direct enough for you, buddy?" said Gabriel.

"Point taken." I flicked my hair back across my forehead. "What if I don't want to meet him, or this Moore woman? I've got rights, you know." Gabriel laughed suddenly, the sound empty of mirth.

"You don't *want*, Mr Devenish? You've got *rights*?" he said, imitating my accent. Nadir looked nervous. His laughter died and he leaned close to me, his voice dripping with venom. "You will do exactly what we fucking tell you to do. We clear?"

"Easy," said Nadir, putting her hand on Gabriel's wrist. "Mr Devenish asked a fair question."

"Fuck his questions," Gabriel spat. He turned to me. "Devenish, if I wanted to I could remove all record of your existence from every database on the planet. All that would be left of you would be some bills that don't match any account, a few speed dial numbers to a dead phone line, and a bit of overturned soil in a forest somewhere. So don't get carried away about rights." He sat back on the sofa, thankfully out of slapping range. "However, supposing that you actually have any rights in the first place, and supposing we choose to give you those rights, in this case your rights are of less importance than what Mr Moore wants. If he wants to meet his father, he shall meet his father. If he wants us to buy him a house looking over the sea, we shall buy him that house even if we have to build it first. If he wants to have Led Zeppelin play in his front room, then play they will even if we have to dig the fucking drummer up and work him like a puppet." He paused. Sighed. Turned to Nadir. "This isn't what we do."

"Calm down, Gabe," said Nadir. "And calm down Mr Devenish. Nobody is going to hurt you, but we do need you to go and meet your son. And, before that, you should probably meet the mother again. Explain what's been going on. Perhaps apologise for not knowing about Martin." She pulled an envelope from her bag. "Your son is very important to many people, and he has asked for our help to reunite him with his father. Because he's important to us we are making every effort to do what he wants. All we need is your co-operation."

"What do you say, buddy? You'll take one for the team?" Gabriel winked at me, suddenly calm again, but his face was taut, his jaw clenched.

"Tell me what you want me to do." Gabriel looked at his watch while Nadir explained.

"We want you to fly to New Mexico in a week and meet your son. We'll work out all the arrangements. All you have to do is be on the plane. Before that, of course, you might want to meet Zara Moore again..."

"Hey, about that. Does she know about me?" I asked.

"That's for you to find out, I'm afraid, Mr Devenish," said Nadir. "All we know is that she has the father listed on the birth certificate as unknown. Oh, and Martin Moore's original name was Stardust Moore, but he changed it."

"You're kidding me..." Nadir nodded, somewhat sadly. "Does she know who he works for?"

"Yes, she does," said Gabriel, "but I guarantee she won't breathe a word of it to you when you meet her. The security people fed Moore a cover story to give to her, something about a top secret project to detect alien signals from space. She lapped it up, and even if she did tell some of her filthy friends about it one evening after smoking too many buttercups or whatever it doesn't matter. It's all bullshit." Gabriel spread his hands wide, the magician at the end of his trick. "Besides, I've got a ten buck bet with Nadir that she'll punch you in the head when you meet her." Big grin. Psycho.

"Alright... I'll do as you ask," I said.

"All you need to know is in this, along with a phone to keep in contact with us," said Nadir, passing the envelope to me. "We've included train tickets to the South Downs for three days from now, plane tickets for next week, including transfers and a hotel. You'll find that they're all in order, and we've also cancelled any appointments for you during the time you're away. Your US visa exemption is also here."

"My appointments? You cancelled my appointments?" Christ, even I barely looked at my diary. When I missed appointments clients were usually great at reminding me. Sometimes they would shout so loudly they barely needed a phone.

"Yeah, we did. We cancelled your two appointments in seven days. Keeping busy, dick?" Gabriel didn't seem to like me much.

"So," continued Nadir, "all you need is right there. Keep the phone charged and with you, and follow the instructions carefully. There'll be no need to tell anyone else about this meeting, and no need to tell anyone about us."

"Otherwise..." Gabriel winked, then stood. Nadir gathered her things and joined him next to the sofa. "Till next time, chief," he said.

Nadir paused for a moment before offering her own hand. "I know this is a shock, Mr Devenish, but do as we ask and everything will work out fine. Trust me." She followed Gabriel into the hallway.

"Hey," I called, as Gabriel opened the front door. "What is Martin Moore working on?"

"Oh, that," he said lightly. "Oh I really don't think you need to have any more secrets for one day, Mr Devenish. You've seen my face, had a conversation with me, hell, we even shared a cup of coffee together, and most of the other people I meet in my line of work stop breathing before we even reach the coffee stage. So count your blessings, and don't ask me, or your poor son, any more stupid questions? Have a nice day, Mr Devenish." The door clicked shut and they were gone, leaving me to collapse on the sofa with the envelope and the empty mugs, the only evidence they were ever here.

---oOo---

Chapter two

Outside Gabriel and Nadir sat in their rental car.

"Do you think he'll do as he's told?" asked Gabriel.

"I don't know. I imagine so." Nadir put the key into the ignition and started the engine.

"Do you think I scared him a little?" he said, grinning.

"I think you were losing it a little in there, Gabe. What's your problem with Devenish?" She was angry with him.

"Oh, the guy just pisses me off. There's something about him." Gabriel reached behind his jacket and produced a burnished, dark grey automatic pistol. Smoothly, he removed the magazine and emptied the chambered round, placing it back into the magazine. He checked the chamber and released the action with a gentle click, slotting the magazine back in place. "He's one of your classic idealistic losers. He thinks he's a good guy, a great guy, running around the world righting wrongs with his stories and his cock. But when you take a closer look, you see he's just as bad as the rest of us."

"Really?" said Nadir pointedly. "As bad as the rest of us? Really, Gabe?" She looked at the gun in Gabriel's hand. Dull metal, thoroughly cleaned and oiled, but well used. "Do you think he would ever do half the shit we've done?"

"Of course he wouldn't. The guy doesn't have the balls. He lives in a fucking dream world, where life is all about deep, meaningful conversations at parties, and everything's so hopeful and loving and soft and sexy. But the world isn't like that, is it?" Gabriel slipped the weapon back into the belt holster under his jacket.

"He's a journalist, Gabe. He must have seen what the world is like by now."

"Journalist my ass," snorted Gabriel. "Let me tell you something about Devenish, Nadir. He's going to be trouble. People like him never do as they're told. Why? Because he thinks he's so much smarter than everyone else. Because he figures that everything has a loophole, and that he's the one to find it. He thinks that he's invincible, and that *bad things* don't happen to people like him. He's a fucking child, Nadir. He never grew up. Never will."

"That's not the reason though, is it Gabe?" Nadir pushed the gear stick into first. "Stupid manual shift. That's not why he pisses you off, is it? His emotional maturity?"

"Okay. Alright." Gabriel stared pointedly into the middle distance as Nadir drove off into the busy afternoon traffic. "He reminds me of someone. He reminds me of that bastard who screwed my career in the Company."

"What bastard was that, Gabe, because I'd heard that you screwed your career all on your lonesome." Nadir's accent was slipping, a hint of the mid-west creeping through, seasoned with something more exotic. "I heard that you'd got the bank accounts wrong on a Company fund transfer. I heard that the Feds were told that the money meant to go to some poor, desperate rebels, actually found its way into one of your European savings accounts." She pulled onto the dual carriageway, heading south. "So, who's the bastard who screwed your career up, then?"

"The Company bean counter who found me out. That's who. That's who he reminds me of. That holier-than-thou fucking bean counter."

"I see." Nadir put the radio on as the car approached heavier traffic, red and blue lights ominously flashing in the distance. "I guess you got your own back anyway," she said in a tired tone.

"I didn't lay a hand on the guy," replied Gabriel. Nadir raised an eyebrow.

"Really? Now that's hard to believe, Gabe, what with you being such a balanced and peaceful individual." Gabriel shook his head vehemently.

"Didn't touch a hair on his head, Nadir." He stared angrily through the window at the collection of cars stuck in the traffic.

"Jesus, Gabe." Nadir slipped the car into neutral as it drifted to a stop. "You'd better not let that story get out. You'll ruin your reputation."

"Not really," he replied, still staring through the window, a distant look in his eyes. "He had to resign from the Company anyway to care for his family." He suddenly grinned. "Some idiot drove into his wife, putting her in a wheelchair for the rest of her life. Incontinent. Immobile." Nadir rolled her eyes sadly. Gabriel opened the window and hung his arm out the side of the car, the last vestiges of sunlight catching his sleeve. "Devenish better do exactly what he's told, or he'll have an accident too. And I don't mean another accident with a condom." He chuckled at that, his moods bouncing up and down as before.

"I'm still not sure it's the best way. I still think we should just go direct to the woman," said Nadir.

"No. It's the best way. She's got no reason to go over there, and we don't want to be anywhere near when the shit starts flying. This way, long as Devenish behaves, we're way off in the shadows."

"He'll behave, Gabe." Nadir didn't sound convinced as she threw the car forward into the clearing traffic. "I'll make sure of it."

---oOo---

Chapter three

"May I enquire if you have plans for that biscuit, Master Wolf?" The voice boomed into my daydream.

"Oh... of course." I pushed the little biscuit across the table. "Sorry Bill, I was miles away."

"You were certainly circumnavigating the wilder swells of your internal oceans." In his fifties, Bill Jeremies was larger than life in every way. Obese and proud, he looked like he had been dressed by a blind clown with a grudge against fashion. His lime green shirt was topped by a blue polka dot bowtie, while a wine-red velvet jacket hung over his chair, nicely complimenting his purple corduroy trousers. The final crash of colour came from his ruddy cheeks bouncing happily beneath bright green eyes and a mop of blond hair.

Bill was a historian, respected enough in Oxford for him to sit on various committees, boards and panels throughout the university, making him invaluable when there was a story to dig out from beneath those dreaming spires. He was also my best friend.

"I apologise, Bill. There's a lot on my mind."

I kept getting sucked back into thinking about Gabriel's visit the day before. The shock passed quickly enough, one of the many unreported health benefits of half a bottle of Jameson's whiskey. Now I felt an odd sense of excitement, like the morning before a childhood holiday or the night before Christmas. Somewhere out there was a grown-up son I had never met, and I was confused by embryonic feelings of parental responsibility. Something in my life had changed, and I had a lot of growing up to do if I wanted to deal with it.

"Evidently." Bill unwrapped the biscuit and regarded it curiously. "I know that these gargantuan coffee chains attract negative press, with their nefarious tax arrangements and their soul-sucking omnipresence, but I believe that they have reached deep into the human psyche by giving away these little biscuits with every cup." He snapped it in two and placed half in his mouth. "In Jericho, for example, there's a delightful coffee house offering wonderful snacks, light lunches, and delicious coffee. It's a charming place, run by a local lady and staffed by some of the more industrious and, dare I say it, pretty art students. But it does not give away free biscuits and that, my friend, is why we're sitting here today. This little biscuit speaks to me. It tells me that the monstrous, baby-boiling, oligarchs who make the decisions in this chain of establishments, care enough about our continued custom to give away tasty treats on the side of each cup sold, while our friends in Jericho hope that a homely atmosphere and the alabaster breasts of the waitresses will keep those invaluable bums on their wicker seats." He sadly shook his head.

"Alabaster breasts?" I asked. "I'm missing all the alabaster breasts?" Bill chortled and devoured the rest of the biscuit, flicking crumbs off his hands, one finger at a time.

"Indeed you are, but I daresay you are distracted enough. Now, if you have decided to reengage with this conversation, shall we continue?" I smiled, tapped my notebook, and gestured for Bill to go on.

"Right." I flicked to a page of notes. "So tell me, what are the latest whispers around college about Rodney's resignation."

Sir Michael Rodney had been one of the most respected modern history lecturers in the university until a few weeks ago when he, without warning, tendered his resignation. Although not newsworthy in itself, the few enquiries I'd made carried the unpleasant whiff of sexual misconduct. While I knew that editors loved a sex scandal, and it would help me pay a few bills on time for once, this kind of story made me feel empty inside. They sell because people relish watching the lives of the great and the good fall apart. It was Colosseum justice, the crowds howling with delight as others are torn to pieces before them, and I didn't want to be the one throwing the victims into the ring.

"Oh, the whispers are legion, all concerning where brave Sir Rodney may or may not have been sticking his lance, but what might be of more interest to you are the names of the whisperers."

"Go on..." I said, pen at the ready.

"Rebecca Lowry." My reaction made him smile. "For 'tis she."

"Rebecca Lowry as in 'Chair of the University Finance Committee Rebecca Lowry'? Why should she care about Rodney's resignation?" I knew Lowry, thankfully not in the biblical sense. She was as pleasant as burst piles, and equally desirable.

"My thoughts exactly, but I fear I'm the only one trying to follow the misty strands back from Ms Lowry's little web back to this particular unfortunate fly." Bill fiddled with his napkin, mopping up crumbs from the table.

"Did she ever lecture at Jesus? I don't understand her connection with Rodney, or why she would have any interest in his personal life. She's a chemist, isn't she?" I'd met Ms Lowry a few times before at various functions around the university, and she was one of those bureaucratic types that I instantly disliked. She had spiky features and bouncing eyes, and believed that peppering her sentences with buzzwords made her conversation less banal.

"Oh, I think she may have taught some first-years for a semester or so, but she's not terribly interested in the Pyrex world of Oxford chemistry. It's well known that she seeks power within the college rather than success within academia."

"Interesting. So Lowry is one of the chief whisperers?" Bill nodded. "And what is she whispering?"

"Oh, all very unpleasant things. It must be dreadful for him." He shook his head. "She's suggesting that he was having an affair with a male student. Horrid stuff."

"Isn't that an internal disciplinary matter?" I asked.

"Deep within the bowels of the university there lie policy documents, within which lurk a series of instructions which the powers that be ought to follow should a staff member be interfering with, shall we say, the student body. We blow the dust off these now and then to appease the government inspectors and our internal auditors, but they are rarely used. Remember, our students are adults, and this is a free country. Yes, there are trust issues, along with the nasty ethical dilemma of the power dynamic between master and student, but usually a conversation suffices to sort these issues out." He drained the last of his coffee before continuing.

"True, once in a while one of our academic flock wanders from safe pastures to go and frolic with some bright-eyed lambs, and we have to gently request that they either return to the fold or find another university. If they do neither, the College authorities will convene a most civilised lynch mob, and our erstwhile colleague will receive formal warnings or removal from post. But it is done with subtlety and humanity, as the College has no fear greater than its terror of negative publicity."

"This procedure. Is it evidence-based?" I asked.

"Absolutely. We don't issue career-threatening warnings or P45s based on whimsy and rumour. No evidence? No disciplinary proceedings."

"Are the police ever involved?"

"Oh, good God no!" His cheeks paled at the thought of such an idea. "What a horrendous notion! And why should they? Everyone involved is an adult, and no crimes are committed." He thought for a beat. "Except the occasional crime against taste. Can you imagine some lustrous-haired, twenty-year-old minstrel of the arts hanging onto my arm?" I like Bill, but the image of him with a handsome student made my skin crawl. I pulled a face.

"Precisely. Even I shudder at the thought. Some of my colleagues, however, become seduced by the youth all around them, and begin to think themselves young too."

"And Sir Michael? Was there evidence of misconduct?" Bill raised his hands.

"One would think that the resignation is evidence in itself. The rumours spread and Sir Rodney, being an honourable man, fell upon his sword. But this is not the issue. I am much more interested in why the rumours were spread in the first place, particularly now we know their source. As, indeed, should you." He waggled his finger at me in reproach. "For shame, Wolf. You are meant to be a journalist."

"What do you mean?" I put my pen down.

"Assume, as we are, that these rumours are true." He held his hands together as though in prayer. "Many others have been in Sir Rodney's predicament and weathered the storm. They stop misbehaving, and quietly continue with their work, albeit with the eye of the Master closely upon them, like some grey-haired Sauron. But the college tends to protect their own, including quashing rumours of scandal for the benefit of all concerned. Remember, it is the fear of how others see the establishment that frightens our masters most. On this occasion, however, Ms Lowry seems to have broken this unwritten rule. Without her whispering Sir Rodney would still have his job. So I ask you *why* did she set free these distasteful tales? *Cui male, Cui bene*, as our sandal-wearing forebearers would say. Who is harmed, and who benefits from Sir Rodney leaving Oxford?"

"I don't see how Lowry benefits from Sir Rodney leaving. They didn't even work together," I said. For a moment I forgot my own worries as Bill's mental juggling loosened that part of my brain that loves conspiracies. "It's my guess that she's just a sanctimonious old witch. I've met her, remember, and she certainly seemed like the sort of person who would screw someone's career for fun. Beyond that I don't see any benefit for anyone from this whole affair." He pulled his chubby hands apart as though opening a book.

"When you find out who benefits, Master Wolf, then I think you shall have your story."

"Have you spoken with Rodney since his resignation?" I asked.

"Lord, no! Why would I? Besides, I'm sure there were many professional mourners hovering around his lodgings, seeking favour through their wailing." His nose wrinkled with distaste. "Are you thinking of talking to him?"

"Possibly. Perhaps he'll just tell me what happened."

"And perhaps I'm secretly a professional figure-skater," said Bill. I chuckled.

"You think he won't talk with me?" I asked.

"If you fancy a light chat about the impact of the Marshall plan on modern European power dynamics, I'm sure he'll talk all day," said Bill. "If you ask him why he resigned, I imagine his knowledge of Proto-Germanic swear words will do him proud."

"If it's just Lowry deciding to ruin Sir Rodney's career because he's been buggering a student, then I'm not really interested, Bill. If he got himself into bother and decided to resign rather than face the music, then the poor bastard has been through enough without me splattering it over the papers." Bill nodded in understanding.

"Well, my young adventurer, if you want to find the real story behind this, then I would look to the source of the whispers."

"Lowry."

"Yes. The Dark Queen herself. She has risen to positions of high import within the Colleges, and one does not achieve such a commanding lead in the game of university politics without making every move with caution and not a little guile." He smiled. "Spreading rumours is unbecoming. She will pay a price for it."

"So why do it?" Bill ran his finger around the inside of the biscuit wrapper coating his fingertip with the last of the crumbs.

"Master Wolf," he said, licking his finger. "I think that is your real story."

I considered this as Bill released his flabby frame from his seat and walked to the bar to order more coffee. Although his mismatched clothing did little to conceal the bulges and ripples which wobbled hypnotically as he crossed the room, there was a certain grace to Bill's progress. He returned with two fresh cups.

"Here we are, my young friend. Mind-juice to lubricate the cogs and wheels inside that head of yours."

"Cheers." I passed him my biscuit. "Bill, you meet people from universities around the world during their visits to Oxford, don't you?"

"I have that honour, if one would call it such. There are universities and Universities, you know."

"You old snob, Bill," I chuckled.

"You wound me, Master Wolf! I only mean to say that some visitors are stimulating and others are tiresome. Yet all must be regaled with the appropriate pomp and ceremony, and endless, interminable, speeches, dinners and port passing."

"It must be terrible for you," I said. What a tragedy for the old goat to be forced to enjoy sumptuous dinners washed down with port and wine, day in and day out. His arteries must look like the inside of my shower head by now. "What do you know about the University of New Mexico? Have you ever met faculty from there?"

"Oh, wrong circles, my friend. Wrong circles. UNM, like many establishments in the former colonies, is all about money, missiles and mysteries."

"So you haven't met anyone from there?"

"Oh, quite possibly, but I wouldn't expect UNM to have a stimulating history faculty, and I have little in common with scientists at the best of times. Moreover I dislike American history. It bores me. So short. So derivative. Why do you ask?"

"I'm travelling there next week. Another story I'm working on."

"Ah... how terribly exciting! And what, pray tell, is the nature of this story? Is it going to shine the light of truth into the murky corners of this haunted realm of man?"

"No, no... just a profile piece on a local boy who's working over there. Nothing exciting." *Except if the local boy is your long-lost son.*

"I wish you well on your travels, Wolf. New Mexico sounds romantic and dusty. I've heard that American steakhouses must be seen to be believed. Slabs of succulent, dripping beef, the size of a pampered child, slathered in spicy sauce and loaded with onion rings and French fries. Mmmm. That's where you'd find me, old boy."

"Well, I'll make a point of visiting one and report back." I finished my coffee and gathered my things. "Any idea when I could see Lowry? I don't want to make an appointment. I'd just like to, well, turn up."

"Oh, I can help you there, Master Wolf. Are you free tomorrow evening?" Tomorrow would be my trip to the South Downs. I shook my head. "Alright. What about this weekend?" he asked.

"I should be free then. States on Monday, but I'm free this weekend."

"Outstanding. There's a function at Exeter College on Friday evening, black tie, nice meal, plenty of booze. You can be my plus one, and I wager that Lowry will be there. It's one of those wonderful meet-and-greet evenings. The Master will be welcoming some scholarship winners, two or three important donors, a few politically astute heads of faculty, a clatter of big knobs, and even the odd broomstick. Our Ms Lowry wouldn't miss it for the world."

"Sounds perfect. Shall we meet at the Wheatsheaf around six?"

"Superb! I shall arrive a little earlier and ensure that the ale is properly kept, and the bar staff are suitably saucy." We left the coffee shop and shook hands on the street.

"Cheers, Bill, and thanks for the help." He gave me a little salute, and waddled merrily away, leaving a trail of bewildered admirers in his wake.

---oOo---

Chapter four

It might have been the sunshine, the clear blue sky, the sound of bees bumbling around the hedgerow next to the canal, or the soft nostalgia of a past revisited, but she was stunningly beautiful.

The instructions left by the mysterious Nadir were clear and comprehensive, and I had ignored them completely.

I wasn't going to take some train from Oxford into the heart of the South Downs when I could jump into the Golf and drive there. Besides, the last time I'd been on a train I ended up sitting alone around one of those Formica four-seat tables, which was asking for trouble. For the first few stops everything was great, with plenty of room to spread out the paper, have a cup of coffee from the trolley and put my feet up on the opposite seat. It went downhill at the third stop when two worse for wear guys boarded and took the free seats. Fair enough, they were unbounded in their gratitude, offering me half a tin of some vile-looking economy lager. But it didn't excuse the one who fell asleep for throwing up across the window, his stringy mess splattering over my lap.

Last time I would get on a train. I drove to Loxwood.

I called Zara in advance and explained who I was. It seemed that my name wasn't enough to cause the bell-ringers to run into the tower in Zara's brain, cassocks blowing in the breeze. Nor was my description of how we knew each other, but when I mentioned Big Jake, the guy who hosted the parties back in the day, the penny finally dropped. She seemed delighted at the prospect of catching up, and we arranged to meet and grab a few drinks. So far so good. An afternoon with an old friend, catching up on old times over a few pints in the sunshine, before I throw her life into chaos by telling her I'm the father of her child. Sounds fantastic.

But, God, she was beautiful. I hadn't expected that.

She lived on a brightly painted, antiquated canal boat, with window boxes filled with herbs tacked to its woodwork. As I walked down the tow path, swaddled in the sunshine, she was sitting on the side of the boat reading a paperback novel. She had long, light brown hair which glistened with a reddish tint, and she wore a knee length summer dress which blew in the breeze as she swung her tanned legs back and forth against the hull of the boat.

As she looked at me I felt a buzz of recognition. I remembered her. She looked much younger than her forty years, so perhaps there was something in this 'herbal remedy' thing.

Or perhaps she didn't put away half a bottle of whiskey every other night.

"Hey." Her voice was soft but bright, and her dusky green-brown eyes sparkled as she spoke. "You're not wearing the right colours for today." I stopped and glanced nervously down at my clothing. No. Fully-clothed. Dark jeans and a charcoal grey top, with the sleeves rolled up, and a pair of dusty brown converse on my feet. I even had a decent tan from the good weather, although if I rolled my sleeves up a few inches more it seemed as though I'd been stitched together from spare body parts. Otherwise I looked pretty good today.

"Hi," I responded. "What are the right colours for today, then?"

"Well, not grey, stupid," she laughed. It was a lovely laugh. "It used to be black."

"God! Even worse! On the sunny days, you dress light, keep cool, and reflect the beauty around you."

"Ah. Sorry." I gestured to my clothing. "I'll remember next time." She smiled, put her book down, and cocked her head slightly to one side.

"I know you, don't I?" she asked.

"Yes." I approached her and held my hand out. "I'm Wolf. Wolf Devenish. I called the other day." There was a sudden spark of recognition.

"You." She drew her legs up from the side of the boat, tucking them under her dress. "You're Wolf?" I'm not sure who she was expecting, but it seemed that it wasn't me. "Sorry I didn't recognise you, but most of my old friends, my male friends, seem to have, I dunno, lost weight on top of their head, and gained it down below." She giggled. It sounded like a smurf's ringtone.

"Yeah. I've been lucky." I felt nervous, butterflies flittering around my stomach. "It's been a long time, Zara." Suddenly she sprang off the boat and onto the tow path, beaming at me.

"God, I can't believe you're here!" She leapt over toward me and grabbed me in a hug. "It's been so long! How have you been?" Given time, my relationships with females don't pan out very well. Her delight at seeing me was a pleasant change from sullen silences and terse goodbyes.

"I've been great, Zara... what about you? How have you been?"

"Great! Better than great! But to see you here! God, we need a cup of tea or something... more than a cup of tea, maybe. What you think? There's a great pub just along the towpath."

"Sounds super." I smiled stupidly. Not only did she remember me, but she actually seemed to like me. Which was strange, given the abandoned mother issue squatting in the back of my mind, pulling faces at me and chuckling. "I found you on the internet and thought I'd give you a call. Maybe catch up."

"Of course! We can catch up over a drink. Give me a second and I'll grab my bag." She hopped back onto the deck and went into the cabin. An elderly dog emerged onto the deck. Obviously no stranger to the treat jar, it looked like a balloon animal with fur. Puffing in the heat, it wandered to the side of the boat and regarded me for a moment. Less impressed than its owner, the dog turned away and sat on the deck before dragging its behind across the wood, tail wagging happily.

Zara emerged again with a little cotton shoulder bag, apparently made from the remains of several other bags, and jumped onto the path.

"Right then, alcohol! The Onslow is just in the village. It's great to see you again, Wolf." She glanced at the dog, now unashamedly licking itself in a way that pubescent boys can only dream of. "Stay, Marcellus" she called lightly.

"You call your dog 'Marcellus'?" I asked.

"Yeah. Long story. Old dog."

So I walked, and she skipped, to the pub, Zara happily holding on to my arm every third or fourth step. She smelled of summer, her warm, breezy perfume reflecting my good mood.

---oOo---

As he stepped onto the porch of his thatched Wytham home, Sir Michael Rodney squinted in the sunshine. It did nothing to raise his spirits from the bleakness gnawing at his core.

He pulled the newspaper from the slot in the mailbox, ignoring the collection of bills and double-glazing fliers as the paper tore against the lip of the slot. It was the first time he'd been through his front door in almost a week, choosing to hide away in his study and distract himself from his problems.

It hadn't worked.

He flicked open the *Oxford Times*, relieved that he wasn't the lead story. Scanning quickly through the paper he looked for his name or picture, his heart racing a little each time he turned a page. Colour returned to his pale cheeks when he reached the sports section. The story wasn't there. His public reputation remained intact for another week, but it felt like a temporary reprieve. A stay of execution giving him a few days of peace before the next edition could bring his life crashing down around him.

He threw the paper in the recycling bin and went into the house, pulling the door shut behind him. At the end of the hallway were a few steps leading toward his study, and the bottom stair creaked as he stepped on it.

This whole damned thing started with a creaking staircase, just over a month ago.

Dozens of times a day he walked up and down the old eighteenth-century oak stairs to his office on the second floor of the College building, and every time he did they creaked more and more until, one afternoon, one cracked as he stepped on it, revealing the brittle white wood beneath the layers of ancient varnish.

He filled in the customary work order to the estates maintenance department, submitting it by email. The next day he received a reply, promising to send a joiner round to have a look at it. What confused him was the comment that the entire staircase had been refurbished two years ago at considerable cost.

Sir Rodney couldn't remember anybody working on that part of the building, and he was in and out of it all the time. It was strange.

He sent an email to the finance committee to complain about the work of the contractor, and a few hours later Lowry herself, chair of the committee, replied. She promised to contact the company and have them repair any shortfalls, along with assuring him that she had inspected it herself prior to final payment for the job.

It all sounded fine except the nagging doubt that he couldn't remember the work being done. Surely it would have put the stairway out of action for weeks? It bothered him, but he decided it was someone else's problem.

A few days later the rumours about his relationship with Marcus began and all thoughts about the staircase were pushed to the side, replaced with growing fear and paranoia as he felt his career within the university crumble.

He stepped back onto the creaky step. With a few days of freedom before facing the next edition of the local paper, he decided to dig deeper into the mystery of the Jesus College staircase.

Chapter five

The Onslow Arms was a pleasant 16th century coaching inn, right next to the canal. In keeping with its five centuries of history, it served all the traditional English fayre, scampi, chips, ham and cheese Panini, with Thai stir fry for the adventurous. We sat near the window and I ordered a white wine for Zara and a pint of bitter for myself.

"So, it's been over twenty years," she said. "What brings you down to see me?" This would be a fine time to mention the 'father of your child' issue, but I was concerned that the words 'child', 'father' or, indeed, 'bastard' had not yet appeared in our conversation. Well, the afternoon was young.

"I guess I'm just catching up, Zara." I smiled disarmingly, but probably looked like I was recovering from tetanus. I'm nervous when meeting beautiful women, afraid they'll see through my outward confidence and realise there's a disorganised child hiding within. "Midlife thing, perhaps. I just stumbled across your website, and thought I'd give you a call."

"So you were searching for your *Centre*?" It amazes me that people can pronounce a capital letter that way.

"My what?

"Your *Centre*. The peaceful core of your soul. I work with people offering them spiritual healing. Helping them to find their true self. Their *Centre*." She sipped her wine and smiled. "Sorry, I just thought that was what you were looking for when you found me. You have that look... hey, it's not a bad look, but you do seem to have lots weighing on your heart. There's an aura about you... a mixture of colours. Passion and creativity, but with a shadow around it, clouding your beauty. I see anger too." She put the glass down, reached over and put her hand over mine. "Don't worry... I see too much sometimes."

"It's fine, Zara. I'd forgotten how spiritual you were." While most of us partygoers were content to wear the right clothes, listen to the cool music, and smoke, snort or slurp the right drugs, I'd forgotten that Zara and her pals tended to chill out near the incense sticks, read together, and discuss esoteric mysteries and how much they'd like to have slept with Jim Morrison.

"I understand, but if you want to talk about that kind of thing anytime, just give me a call." She laughed. "I guess you get the first session free..." I was under the impression that my first session with Zara was likely to be very far from free.

"So, Zara... how has life treated you since we saw each other last? How is business going?"

"I'm well, Wolf. Business is good, but I don't like to call it a business. It's more of a calling. Lots of online readings, selling remedies on the 'net, and I still have time for a couple of personal sessions on the boat." I side-stepped the smutty retort.

"Yeah, the boat, that's quite a way to live. How does that work, financially and so on?" I couldn't deny it, but living on a boat was cool.

"Oh, it's great, actually. I live more or less off the grid." I couldn't help thinking about her website with her phone, email, and Skype details emblazoned across it. "And I only pay those taxes that I can't avoid, really. You know, stuff like the national insurance, TV licence, car tax and so on. Just the things you can't avoid paying."

Unlike all those voluntary taxes everyone else loves to pay. I'd forgotten how ditzy Zara and her hippy friends were.

"Oh, I've been trying to think *when* we saw each other last. One of Jake's parties, wasn't it? I remember you were in a band at the time, and you played a little concert in the front room..." I nodded and she continued. "It was the night that John smashed up that miniature guitar and signed all the parts for the girls to keep. I still had my piece until Marcellus decided to eat it a few years ago." A spurt of jealousy flooded my system. John. The guitarist. I remembered battering away on a keyboard as the drummer and bass player worked their ass off too. Yet, at the end of any gig, I ended up in the kitchen with the drummer getting hammered on whatever was available, beer, wine, refrigerator coolant, while John sat in the living room surrounded by beautiful girls fawning over his every word and every chord. Jealousy is a horrible thing.

"Good days. We had some great times then." At least John had, I mused. I recalled biblical hangovers and the girls watching me with curious sadness as I drunk myself to sleep.

"They were fun, a real growing time. I think I found who I was through those parties. I think about them often." Zara looked reflective for a moment before grabbing her wine again.

"I do too." My beer had emptied itself. Must be a dodgy glass. "Would you like another drink, Zara," I asked.

"What?" She seemed lost for a moment, revisiting days long passed. "Oh, wine. Yes please, Wolf. Same type. Fruity." She had a strange look in her eyes, like she was here in body but somewhere else in her mind. I rose to go to the bar. "Hey, Wolf," Zara put her hand on my arm. "Do you still hear from John at all?"

"Actually, Zara, I haven't heard a thing about him since university." Her face fell a little. "Last I heard he had started his third course when I was graduating. He seemed to enjoy being a first year student."

"Sounds like him," she said, and I sensed she had more to add, something else on her mind. "No matter." She released my arm and I went to the bar.

The barman was a gregarious, red-faced chap, keen to bitch about the news of the day at the drop of a hat. Since I wore no hat, he merely grumbled with me about the fact that three foreigners had moved in down the road. He asked his Polish barmaid, a young girl with bright eyes and astounding bosoms, to replace the keg before whispering conspiratorially to me.

"They're Welsh. No idea why they don't stay there, dig coal or join a choir or something." I smiled and paid for the drinks, carrying them back to our seat. Zara was still pensive, rolling her empty glass between her fingers.

"Are you okay?" I asked, placing the drinks on the table. She smiled, sadly, and took a drink of the wine, her lips moistened by the crisp liquid.

"Yeah. Sorry. I was elsewhere." I waited for her to continue. All this talk about parties was leading the conversation into awkward territory. "I think about John a lot."

Zara reached for my hand again, gently resting her fingers on mine. "Can I tell you something important, Wolf?"

"Of course, Zara. You can tell me anything."

"I have a son." I tried to look surprised. "He's twenty-three, a great kid, really, but we haven't gotten on well in the last few years." My heart was beating faster, and I felt like a child about to get told off by his mother. I felt guilty. I should have brought the topic up myself, and I hated myself for my fear of facing consequences.

"A son? Really. I had no idea," I lied. "I haven't stepped on the parenting mine yet." She laughed, much too happily, and I laughed with her. A stupid idea as I was likely to be laughing all the way to the Child Support Agency.

"Not from want of trying, I'd say, Wolf." God knows where she got that idea from. My sex-life had been non-existent recently. She continued, serious again. "Well, I do have a son. That's why I was asking you about those days."

"What's on your mind?" She paused again, thinking for a second before continuing. I felt that my fatherhood was about to become official.

"I lost contact with people after the parties, you know, when everyone buggered off to university and work. It's a real pain in the arse, and you're the first of the guys I've had any contact with for years." She flicked her glass with her long fingers. "Well, you're the first of the *proper* guys I've seen for ages, if you know what I mean? There were loads of people who hung around back then having a laugh and enjoying the parties, and I see some of them around now and then. But they weren't the ones we sat up all night with, or walked round the fields with in the early morning, or met for coffee, or lent books and records to. Not the way we were together. Just acquaintances, not true friends." I nodded. I barely remembered half the people who we used to party with.

"Yeah, I guess it was a hell of a summer, all the parties and the fun times. Then everyone was away. All over the country. All over the world." I smiled and raised my glass to my lips, savouring the smooth ale. She sighed and looked at me in a serious way.

"John is the father of my son. But I never got the chance to tell him. He doesn't know."

I choked on my pint.

Chapter six

Andrew Miller wasn't called Andrew Miller. He was born Andreas Müller, a long time ago.

Andrew / Andreas was born in Berlin in 1953. As with all children he saw many changes as he grew up. One day he learned to walk, and his mother applauded him as he bumped along the walls laughing at how odd the world looked from this strange vantage point. On another day he went to school for the first time, and remembered holding hands with the other kids, their fatty little palms sweating with nerves as they walked through grey corridors from classroom to toilet and back to the classroom again. One day he remembered the men visiting his home, water from the summer rains dripping from their cheap jackets onto the floor. He thought of his father, kneeling on one knee before him, tousling his hair and giving him a kiss. Then the men took his father out of the apartment and out of his life.

Then, another day, he remembered playing with his friends when the soldiers came with their trucks and bulldozers. They shouted at him and told him to go home, as they started to rip the surface from the roads and replace it with long loops of barbed wire. More troops arrived and stood sternly with their faces towards his home, rifles held smartly at their side. Most of the children made faces or played war games with little sticks as rifles, taking imaginary pot-shots at the soldiers as they scrambled back and forth across the road.

Soon enough, gaunt parents emerged to gather their children to the jeers of the young soldiers. A few months later there stood a bleak concrete wall where he used to play.

Andreas was on the wrong side of this wall.

If he listened carefully he could hear modern cars, distinctive because there were no backfires, and people laughing and shouting from the other side. If he focused his attention to his side of the barrier he heard only silent despair.

The sound of the Utopia which was the German Democratic Republic.

Through his school days there were other changes too. As he grew older he noticed that the happy atmosphere before the wall came was slowly replaced with gloominess among the adults. His mother, finding it difficult to make ends meet without his father to help, seemed increasingly withdrawn. Her friends visited less often. She used to have wonderful parties with them when he was younger, Andreas running around the house with his toys as the adults talked and laughed with one another, occasionally tousling his hair or, on the best evenings, slipping him a few Marks to buy sweets with. Those parties had stopped. When people did visit, they talked in hushed tones, and rarely about anything of importance. Everything, even bad weather, seemed to be taboo in conversation. It was as though a disapproving parent was listening, just waiting for the chance to scold their moaning child.

Eventually, it was time for Andreas to finish school and seek work and he was relieved because he knew that an extra income would make a huge difference to his mother. He'd done well at school, being very good at picking up on the little details about subjects that the other children tended to miss, so he anticipated getting a decent job. Not just factory labour, but perhaps a management role organising a group of workers.

One day some men came to the school and told his year group about the opportunities available working for the government. Of course working for the government ultimately meant working for the people, and he was happy to put his name forward.

Before long he was working in the Ministry for State Security, known by most people as the Stasi, in the Administration for the Struggle against Suspicious Persons. His job was to follow and observe foreigners visiting East Berlin, collate information about them, and report to his supervising officers about their activities. It was interesting work. Some of his colleagues spent their lives sorting through citizen's garbage for incriminating materials, but Andreas got to work outside, interacting with real people rather than merely filling in paperwork all day long.

He took Stasi language classes, among the best in the world, and learned excellent English, Russian and Polish, along with a smattering of other European languages. He was good at his job and his superiors pointed to him as a model agent, an example to others in their fight against the creeping decadence just across the wall, and he was viewed with respect by his seniors and with trepidation by his subordinates.

Of course Andreas knew better than most that someone in his position would be observed and followed just as much as any American trade attaché. So he kept his personal feelings deep inside, his relationships with family and friends distant. He couldn't risk giving anybody the slightest hint of how he truly felt.

Andreas hated East Berlin. He hated the Communist Party, he hated the government, he hated the way the people simply sat and accepted this constant bullshit day after day. He hated seeing his mother queue lifelessly for food, only to receive a few paltry vegetables and some grey meat. Most of all he hated the Stasi. They were the stick controlling the people, and the situation had gotten so out of hand that the government no longer even pretended to hold a carrot in the other hand. No, they simply held two sticks and wielded them at will, just as they had with his father.

The last straw had been when Andreas found his father's file. He'd been sent to a re-education camp in Russia because of his strong views about the government. His re-education was finally completed some years later when he died of malnutrition. His father dead, murdered, and his mother living a half-life, he had nothing to lose. Andreas decided that he wanted revenge. He wanted to help bring down the corrupt state from within.

Since he spent his days rubbing shoulders with the enemies of the state, practicing his English and wearing western clothes, it was easy to leak his intentions to people who knew people. Just as he knew that diplomatic attaché were CIA spies, the diplomats knew quite well that Andrew Miller was not an English journalist. That was half the fun of the espionage game, knowing that almost every single word that left your mouth or entered your ears was a lie. His talent lay in seeing the truth behind the lies.

He was good at his craft and was able to make contact with a CIA handler reasonably quickly and without anyone else knowing. He knew enough about his contact from the Stasi files to know that the woman was genuine, a true blue, for God and country, American patriot. Not all the handlers were so clear cut. Patriotism was rarely as powerful a motivator as money or fear, so corruption of one sort or another was rife. The only difference between the sides was that US traitors, if discovered, were usually relocated to a quiet incarceration in an American prison, whereas the East Germans tended to relocate their prodigal sons and daughters in various size pieces to landfill sites surrounding Berlin.

Beverly Richards, a diplomatic secretary and CIA agent, was clever, undemanding, and plainly pretty. After the obligatory courting period where she had Andreas' past pulled apart piece by piece, and gave him tasks to gather small pieces of information to check his worth against information previously known, she informed her section head that she had a mid-level Stasi officer on the books. They gave him the codename 'Cookie-cutter' which, they explained, was well suited to his role. He would be snipping little pieces of key information rather than snatching entire files for his American masters. The CIA paid well, and Cookie-cutter had a bank account set up for him in the US. Of course he would have preferred a Swiss account, but he figured that their choice of bank was another level of security. If he wanted his money someday he'd have to go to America to get it. If he had betrayed America along the way this wasn't an option.

Years passed and Andreas continued to pass snippets of information to Beverley and her bosses. At the same time he sprinkled misinformation through the Stasi files. It was a dangerous game, but one that he played well to the end.

When the end came, even Andreas failed to see it coming. The citizens were noticeably disgruntled, but they were always disgruntled so it was ignored. It was background noise in East Germany, where everyone was miserable and pissed off all of the time. In a world where nobody trusted anybody else the only way rebellion would happen was if everyone became involved and acted together.

In October 1989 they did.

First hundreds, then thousands, then tens of thousands of people took to the streets demanding the end of the state. From top to bottom the security apparatus collapsed. One of his last acts as a double agent was to brave the nervous Berlin alleyways and drop a note to his handlers explaining that there was talk of a tank battalion being prepared to take the streets back and crush the demonstrations. It was never collected. Within hours the border crossings were open, and people were attacking the wall with hammers, axes, vehicles and their bare hands.

The state he hated so much had collapsed. The people, no longer gray and hopeless, had risen up and claimed their city back. And they were hungry for revenge. As Stasi members left the city to avoid retribution, Andreas used his cover documents to pass through the border to the west.

Perhaps the worst thing about spending years living in a world of deception and lies is the inability to trust anyone anymore. When he passed his documents to the US marine at the entrance to the American embassy he didn't know what to expect. After all, what use was he to them now? He'd played his cards, immaculately of course, but he had no more aces left and the Americans had the winning hand.

He shouldn't have worried. Not only did the Americans genuinely seem to believe in Right and Justice and Honour, but they had other uses for him. He was debriefed and given the choice of living in the US or Britain, as a favour from their allies. He chose to go to the UK where he was offered work by the British security services, his skills and experience invaluable to them as they monitored the development of the former Soviet Union into independent, volatile, nations.

Technically retired now, he still did the odd job for his British friends. Simple, safe work such as background checking and surveillance, which took him around his adopted country and kept his mind busy. As he sat in the pleasant canal-side pub, slowly drinking a pint of mild beer, he considered how far he had come from the boy playing at soldiers next to the wall.

And he continued to watch the man and woman drinking wine and ale at the corner table.

---oOo---

Chapter seven

"John is the father of your child?" A week ago the tapestry of my life was a faded, comfortable thing, rich with familiar patterns and well-worn creases. Since Gabriel had appeared I felt like it was starting to tear apart, fraying at the edges, the warp and weft straining to keep it in one piece.

"Yeah. It was a long time ago, though, and we lost touch before I even knew I was pregnant."

Rip.

"Are you certain?" Disgustingly, part of me wanted her to be right and I could get on with my life again. I was a coward.

"You know how nuts those evenings were sometimes, Wolf. But they weren't orgies." She paused for a beat. "There was a night. Not one of the party nights, just a night when John and I round to Jake's. I was visiting his sister, Seraphim..."

"I'd forgotten about Seraphim. Crazy name. What the hell was that about?" I asked.

"Oh, her parents had some religious kick when she was born," Zara replied. "I know they were already strange people, but when I knew them they were part of some weird cult and even more strange. Yeah, Seraphim. I called her Sarah, even if her parents made a big effort to use her full name. It was hilarious in school at roll-call. Cool girl, though." She paused again. "I thought you and Sarah had a thing one time?"

I only vaguely remembered Sarah. She was there, like all the others, attending all the parties. Like most of the other girls she was reinventing hippy chic, mainly by trying to never be impressed by anything that happened around her. If she walked into a room to find the Beatles having a psychedelic reunion in her honour, replete with trumpets and cartoon elephants, she would have given a little wave, sat down in the middle of them, and read a book.

"This might sound a bit bad, Zara, but I don't really remember. I don't think so, anyway." I thought this might be the moment to address the other issue, the 'me being the father' thing. "Actually, Zara, and don't take this in a bad way... but I kind of thought that you and I shared a moment or two during those days?" She smiled, obviously having wondered the same thing.

"Hmm... that's very sweet of you to remember, Wolf, but I'm sure it was just a moment or two of friendly fun." She patted my hand and smiled gently. "We all have our needs, and I remember that we got on well, but, to be honest, you weren't really my type back then." I chewed on that sentence for a spell. Part of me was disappointed that she thought I wasn't her type, because she was a very beautiful woman. But another part of me was reading a lot into the 'back then' phrase. Were they just words, or were they carefully crafted words indicating that I was her type *now*. With a pretty lady sitting opposite me, I was as focused as drizzle.

"So John *was* your type? I don't remember you dating him," I ventured.

"Oh, John was *everyone's* type!" I nodded, wondering if he would have still been everyone's type with his teeth knocked out. He had talent, charm and looks. Most of us had to make up for our shortfalls in these departments by inserting monumental amounts of drugs and drink into our systems to make us *feel* more attractive. "He was wonderful, just *wonderful*," she said, her smile animated.

Okay, Zara. I get it.

"But I never thought you and he," there was a politic way of saying this. "I didn't think that you and he were ever an item..."

"Ah... well, of course we weren't an item! I wasn't his girlfriend." She pulled a face. "But the weekend after I got accepted to university there was a party and we were chatting about the future. I guess it was a mixture of nostalgia, moonlight and some herbs of the field, but John and I shared an amazing night together." I recalled that 'herbs of the field' was how the hippy-chicks referred to dope. It always made me laugh, since most of the dope we ever got hands on was grown in some gaunt fucker's bedroom, with makeshift fluorescent lights, walls plastered with tinfoil, and six budget padlocks on the door.

"So what happened, Zara?" She looked happy, smiling at me in her dreamy way, a sparkle in her eyes. She was reliving the past and the wine was helping.

"We connected," she grinned. "We connected very deeply." She was whispering dreamily, so I felt that I should clarify my question.

"Did you have sex with him, Zara? Because, and I'm no doctor, but I think you need to screw someone for them to be the father of your child." She continued smiling, unfazed, lost in her memories.

"Ahh, Wolf. I've really missed you. I forgot how funny you were." She tapped my lips with her finger. A flirty gesture from a flirty girl. "Of course we had sex that night, but during it our spirits joined as one. It was miraculous. And, the traditional number of months later, my child was born. The moment I looked at the baby, crying and wet in my arms, I knew that all of John's beauty, creativity and love had passed into Stardust's soul. Even if I never saw John again, he would live forever within my son."

I nodded sagely while every fibre in my body was trying to make me giggle. Zara... Queen of the crazy hippies.

"And you weren't with anyone else who could be the father?" Again I felt a guilty relief at her mistake, part of me hoping she was right.

"Sorry, Wolf, but you seem quite determined to call me a whore." Her eyes widened. "Why are you so obsessed with who Stardust's father is?"

"I'm not," I lied again. "It's just that if you were with other guys, then couldn't one of them be the father instead?" I know that women have all manner of obfuscated mathematics they use to determine conception dates, but Zara could easily have chosen alternative methods. Probably something to do with a crystal on a string that does backflips over the right date on a calendar.

"Well, Wolf, if you were a woman you would know." If I was a woman, I thought, I'd be much too busy standing bedroom looking at myself in the mirror to listen to this nonsense. "There was the odd one-night thing. Sometimes I ended up with someone from time to time." She shrugged. "But I'm sure John is Stardust's father."

She was watching the drops of condensation creeping down her glass, her eyes flickering back and forth as she watched them seek the easiest route to the tabletop. Like the memories bubbling to the surface in her mind, they were fighting for her attention. "Yeah, there were a few other guys back then..." She kept staring, lost in thought. Suddenly she flicked her eyes to mine for an instant, catching my gaze. A spark of recognition. A memory unveiled. Then they fell onto the glass again.

"Do you regret having Mar, er, Stardust, Zara?" She paused before answering.

"It depends on how you look at it, Wolf. Everything in life, every joy I've ever known, and every heartache I've experienced, all had their share of peace and regret. It's too simplistic to see life as anything else. When you understand that everything ends sometime you start to develop wisdom. The sad times and the wonderful times, they'll all come to an end, one day or another. Peace and regret are bedfellows." She reached over and held my hand, gently. "It's just part of growing up."

"I guess so. I haven't really thought about it." I hadn't. I didn't think of life as something within which you develop wisdom and knowledge. That seemed to stand in the way of having fun.

"On the other hand, when things are bleak and empty, there is the spark of joy knowing that dark things don't last forever. There's always light just around the corner, even if the corner arrives in a minute, a month or a year. It's comforting." This woman intrigued me. She wasn't all about hugging whales and communing with trees. "Stardust, he changed his name to Martin I'm afraid but he'll always be Stardust to me. Stardust and I had some great times together. Then again we shared some awful moments. Mainly over the last few years, when he decided that his mother was a well-meaning kook. We had terrible rows before he left for America." She looked forlorn. I squeezed her hand gently, and she didn't react or pull her fingers away. "I know he loves me. It's just sometimes I think he really loves who I was when he was a child."

"I'm sorry. Do you hear from him at all?" I was sad that she'd fallen out with her son. It's one thing to hear about it, but quite another seeing the hurt it caused her displayed on her face.

"No. Not really." She smiled awkwardly, a sigh stalling behind her full lips. "He's on his own journey now. It would be selfish of me to ask him to share that journey with him. I just hope he's happy." Zara drained her glass, and stood to go to the bar. "Another?"

I waved my glass, almost empty, and nodded. On such a warm day, in the pleasant bar, the beer was refreshing, relaxing and stimulating, all at the same time. Yes, I'd avoided mentioning that that Martin was *my* son, but I was enjoying myself. We were enjoying each other. There would be time for hard discussions later.

Somewhere inside me I had feelings for this kind, clever woman, whose life I may have turned upside down twenty years ago, and whose life I will likely have to complicate once again. Just not right now.

She went to the bar and I took the opportunity to go to the toilet. I dodged my way round tables and caught the eye of the barman, who pointed me in the right direction before returning his gaze to Zara's bosom.

---oOo---

Chapter eight

I went into the toilet, a modern, clean affair, with real mirrors instead of the shiny metal you find in some pubs, and checked my mobile. Both mobiles. My own had a few messages from friends and such, and one from Bill checking that our arrangements were still on for the weekend. There was nothing else important.

I checked the other phone, the one I'd been given, and there was nothing from Gabriel or Nadir. In fact, it hadn't so much as twitched since their visit, further convincing me it was a weird dream or a strange college prank. However, remembering the threats that Gabriel had made, I assumed that not keeping it with me was asking for trouble. As I popped the phones back in my jacket, a late-middle aged man joined me in the room.

I went to the urinal and got on with business, only to hear the guy walk over to the one next to me, which was terrible form as there are strict rules about male urinal etiquette.

In this case there were five urinals, and I was at the one on the far right. This left four other options for my new companion, and there were three acceptable ones. Far left, although this is obviously avoiding proximity to me, which carries with it the suspicion that he's hiding something embarrassing, like one of those piercing disasters which leave him peeing like a showerhead. A more acceptable place would be second from left, leaving a few empty urinals between us, or even right in the middle would be alright, although it leaves the minimum accepted empty space between you and your companion, but not so much as to make a 'sneak peek' impossible.

Right beside me, with more than half the urinal row empty, is just unacceptable. It was either a definite attempt to size up the competition or – God forbid – it was for conversation's sake.

"Afternoon" said the man who, in fairness, was staring at that imaginary spot on the tiles straight ahead of him which all gentlemen should focus on when using a urinal. Eye contact is best avoided in male toilets, or else you could end up staring at the wrong eye. "It's a beautiful day today." He had a neutral, pleasant accent that I couldn't place.

"Yeah. Lovely." I replied, in a non-committal way. I angled my head that all-important two degrees to the right, sending out the signal to my gregarious companion that the conversation was at an end. Unless he wanted a nostalgic game of 'light sabres', he needed to be quiet now.

"It certainly is." *Shhh...* I thought. *Shhh now.* "So what brings you to the canals on such a beautiful day?" I know I should have ignored him, but I was in a happy mood and I guess two pints of finest were helping me in my decision process. I decided to be a little naughty.

"I'm a journalist. I'm down here on a story about a middle-aged man who's been accosting strangers in toilets." I tutted. "Disturbing stuff."

"That must be interesting work," he said, totally unfazed. "I'm passing through on business too. This is lovely spot for a bite of lunch, so I thought 'why not?' Is that your girlfriend you're with, or does she work with you?" I did the obligatory double shake - one is insufficient, two does the job, and three or more is public masturbation – before continuing.

"A little bit of both I guess. She's a prostitute I met in London. Costs me a fortune, but I'll try and squeeze it onto expenses." I went to the sinks and washed my hands. "We share a *Pretty Woman* fetish," I said, regarding the innocuous figure completing his business in the toilet mirror. He was chuckling quietly to himself.

"Oh, I don't think that's quite true" he said, as he turned toward the sink. "I know Ms Moore," he said 'mizz', "and she's certainly not a prostitute." I paused, letting the tap stop automatically, and watched the man as he did his flies up and turned to face me. From the front he was a completely unremarkable figure. Moderately built, of average height, he had fair hair spotted with flecks of grey. He was clean shaven with even, neutral features, and an amused smile dancing on his lips. He was as memorable as a service station sandwich.

"Who are you?" I asked, hoping to God he wasn't her dad, just popping past to kick the shit out of the guy who knocked his daughter up twenty years ago.

"You took the words right out of my mouth, young man. I was just about to ask you the same thing." He approached and offered his hand, pausing with sudden embarrassment. "Best wash my hands first, I imagine." He quickly rinsed his hands and dried them on a towel, deftly tossing the crumpled paper into the bin. "I once had a conversation with a surgeon in a lavatory, much as we are talking right now, and I noted that he didn't wash his hands after using the urinal. I told him that I didn't think it was very good example to set for a medical man. But *he* told *me* that he washed his willy every day, and didn't pee on his hands. I imagine he had a good point." He offered his hand once again. "I'm Detective Inspector Miller. I work with SOCA, the serious and organised crime agency. And you are?"

"Someone who likes to see ID," I countered, although I felt the hair stand on my neck. I didn't like the police. They had an uncanny ability to ruin my day. He produced a small wallet and held it up to me. Yes. Police warrant card. I loved his picture. He looked slightly surprised in it, as though the cameraman had dropped his trousers as the shutter fell. I had seen a warrant card before, and it hadn't been one of my better days. My nervousness increased.

"Okay, Inspector. Now, as far as I know I haven't committed any crimes recently, so can you explain why you want to talk to me?" He gestured to the door.

"Let's go the beer garden for a quick chat. Two minutes, I promise... Mr...?" He had that expression typical of cops, as though embarrassed about having to do such an unpleasant job. But you just knew that they loved every second of the discomfort they caused others. The power to screw people over, with the full backing of the law, was like a drug to them.

"Devenish. Mr Devenish." I followed him outside. Thankfully there was access to the garden along the toilet corridor, so I didn't have to walk past Zara with Plod by my side. I leaned on a bench and waited for him to start talking.

"Mr Devenish. I'll not trouble you for long. Please understand from the outset that this conversation is confidential."

"Why?" I had problems with the police, I think I'd mentioned it before. Their business was to defend the law and, as a result, defend innocent people from the actions of criminally-minded people. Most of them, however, had figured out that harassing law-abiding people whenever they stepped on cracks in the pavement was safer and easier than trying to catch nasty, criminal folk.

"Because if you divulge what we discuss it could place Ms Moore in harm's way, along with jeopardising my investigation. I'm sure you wouldn't want to do that now, Mr Devenish?"

"Okay. Go ahead," I said. "But be quick, because you're jeopardising my afternoon plans." His eyes flickered on mine, as though counting how many shits he gave about ruining my day. Not a single one, I imagined.

"We believe that Ms Moore, along with several other people engaged in alternative therapies, are under threat from a criminal syndicate based in London. To cut a very long and convoluted story short, we have been investigating some large-scale identity theft perpetrated by a few unpleasant foreign gentlemen. Now that banks, utility companies and mail-order businesses have tightened their security, it seems that small independent businesses, such as Ms Moore's, are being targeted so that the gang can obtain the details of their customer accounts. Since Ms Moore and her competitors tend to have many hundreds of clients over the period of a year, and since they don't usually have sophisticated means to protect client data, they are a good target for this gang."

"So? What's that got to do with me?" The thought of organised criminals rooting through Zara's knicker drawer looking for credit card numbers seemed ridiculous.

"I need you to tell me how you know Ms Moore, and what you want from her. This gang operates by finding a way to get *in* with their target. And that is usually someone the victim knows." He paused. "This brings us to who you are, and why you're showing sudden interest in Ms Moore."

"I would think that's not really any of your business, Inspector. However, if it puts your mind at rest, I'm an old friend catching up. I haven't seen her for over twenty years." I stood to leave, making a show of looking at my watch. It would have been more impressive had I been wearing one. "I'm certainly not interested in stealing her client list, if that's what you're worried about."

"Thank you. How do you know Ms Moore again? Specifically?" I pulled one of my phones out and checked the time.

"I really should get back, Inspector. If there's nothing else." I stepped forward, but he didn't move out of the way.

"How do you know Ms Moore?" he asked again.

"Look. If I'm not a suspect, and if you don't have reason to detain me, can you simply go away? I'm certainly not involved in some foreign fraud operation, and I promise to be a good little boy with Ms Moore." I was actually thinking of being quite the opposite, but I wasn't going to tell Plod that.

"I appreciate your time, Mr Devenish. But answer my question. If you don't, well, I'm going to be in bother with my superiors. You know what bosses are like... every 'i' dotted, and every 't' crossed. You understand my problem? It would be a big help if you could just answer my question." It was the old 'help me out, guvnor', bullshit. Definitely a policeman.

"Okay. When I was younger I used to meet with lots of other younger people."

"Younger than you? What age where you then, Mr Devenish?" Christ, everyone's a paedophile these days.

"What? The same age as me. When I was younger I hung out with friends who were also young. Nineteen... twenty." He nodded and gestured for me to continue. "Okay, we'd all meet up at a particular house, and we'd talk and listen to music together. These people were called friends and we called the meetings, a silly name really, but we called them 'parties'. I knew Zara from our parties. We were friends." He stared at me for a few moments, processing the information. I hoped my sarcasm wasn't about to backfire.

"She would confirm this if asked?"

"Yes. She's sitting having drinks with me, so of course she would. We're friends. Do you mind if I get back to catching up with our friendship now?"

"One moment more," he said. I sighed in response. "And that is it? That is the extent of your current relationship? Nothing else? Just two friends catching up?" I nodded. Since he'd asked four questions, I nodded a few more times. He continued. "And do you plan on developing this relationship further? I was watching you for a time, and you seemed quite intimate."

"That seems to be absolutely none of your business, officer. Whatever I do with Zara is nothing to do with the police or anyone else for that matter. Go screw yourself. In fact, before you do that, can I look at that warrant card again? I'd like to make a record of your police number." He smiled at my outburst and gestured that I could go. I stood firm, staring at him. "Warrant card, please."

He produced his wallet again and held it out for me. As I reached for it he suddenly grabbed my wrist with his other hand, gently pulling me toward him. He was surprising quick and strong for an older bloke.

"Mr Devenish. I am trying to protect Ms Moore. Nothing more. If you don't like my methods, which I think are very informal by the way, then please report me. If you do that, of course, I will have several young officers tear into your background until we find something, anything, that will put your backside into a police cell and in front of a court. Now, if that's clear, you can go. If you speak of this conversation to Ms Moore, I'll be making those calls to my colleagues, and adding interfering with a police investigation to the list of charges. Since there's no-one in the beer garden right now, and the CCTV cameras haven't worked for two months, I can probably take a punt at 'assaulting a police officer' as well. Do you understand me?" I glared back at him. I was slightly bigger than him, younger by a good ten years or so and perhaps capable of putting him through the garden bench. The only thing stopping me was that little warrant card. If he was genuine filth and I visited harm on him, then I was in real trouble. He released my hand.

"Alright, officer. I'm glad I could help you." I stepped away and walked toward the door.

"Thank you, Mr Devenish. Take care, and keep our little chat to yourself." I waved my arm and entered the pub again, a niggling worry forming in the back of my mind. There were too many odd things happening around Zara at the moment.

I wasn't sure I wanted to be there to discover why.

---oOo---

Chapter nine

Andreas sat at the bench, enjoying the sunshine. He thought about returning to the pub and getting a pint, but it was still early in the afternoon and a drink could wait until later. Perhaps Devenish and the girl would leave soon and he could relax, rather than have the man throw dagger-eyes at him across the bar. In the meantime he pulled a little notebook from his pocket and swiftly made notes about his conversation.

His years in espionage had bred habits that were hard to break, so his scribbles meant little to anyone but him. He wrote using a mixture of languages accompanied by some shorthand squiggles, and recorded all the pertinent details about the man, including a detailed description, some observations on his mannerisms and behaviour, and one or two 'tells' that Andreas had detected during the conversation.

Most people in his profession tended to become excellent liars, creating convincing lies so naturally that the truth itself was forgotten to the extent that it took clear-headed effort to unravel it from the web of misdirection and half-truths in which they lived. In comparison the everyday lies of ordinary people were clumsy and easy to detect.

He was fairly sure that Devenish had been mostly truthful about being an old friend of Moore's catching up on old times. But there was something else; something that Devenish was keeping concealed. He'd been careful to bury it deep inside when talking with Andreas, but he was definitely not saying everything about his relationship with the woman. Perhaps they'd been more than friends, or perhaps he merely wanted to be more than friends.

But something was bothering Devenish, and it was something to do with Zara Moore.

Andreas would file a report through to the office that evening and find out if they wanted him to dig a little deeper, but he imagined his job was complete now barring any new developments. He'd found out all he wanted to know; who she associated with, what she was like as a person and if she had any drug problems or significant debts. She seemed to be a genuine, run of the mill civilian, offering no threat to anyone.

Then Devenish turned up, a new development from out of the blue.

A side-effect of working in espionage is an utter disbelief in coincidence. He had been tasked to investigate this woman who lived a quiet life, had few friends, and saw them but rarely. Then, almost at the end of his investigation, along comes an old friend whose name or description matches none of her known associates. A friend who seems to be hiding something.

Stop being so paranoid, Andreas, he thought, smiling to himself in the garden. *You just miss the thrill of the chase. You miss Berlin.*

He took a moment to run through his findings once again, reassuring himself that his job was complete. Zara Moore was clean, and a friend from decades ago turning up to catch up on old times wouldn't change that. Devenish was a mere detail in the story; a footnote in the file. Nothing more.

But the devil lay in the details...

Andreas scribbled a final note, a reminder to request a background check on Devenish, and popped the notebook into his pocket.

---oOo---

Chapter ten

That evening I was still unable to mention Gabriel's visit or what he had told me about Martin. I had other things on my mind.

Firstly, I was thinking about the strange Inspector Miller. In many ways, he seemed a convincing copper. In other ways, it didn't add up. For starters, he didn't have the obligatory be-suited and downtrodden side-kick. No Lewis to his Morse, no Hastings to his Poirot, no Norberg to his Drebin.

For another thing police were usually not very obvious when threatening the general public. With the exception of legal public protests, of course, which had become a sort of police team bonding day, where they could dress in black from head to toe, conceal their identification markings, and kick the shit out of crusties.

No, this is the touch-and-feely twenty-first century, and even hard-nosed rozzers have certain codes to adhere to. True, he was of a suitable age to be part of the old school of coppers, chasing villains across London shouting 'he's had it away on his legs' or 'he's got a shooter.' If so I expected that the closest DI Miller had come to reading a memo about twenty-first century policing was the last time he put his coffee on top of his office computer.

But there was *something* about him that grated on me. And, if a single word Gabriel had said was true, then it wasn't inconceivable that Zara was being watched. To clarify matters I sent a quick text off to a friend who knew people in the Met. Hopefully he could find out if the Inspector was a real copper or yet another weirdo I'd attracted.

Secondly, there was the dog issue. Marcellus, having accepted me as a visitor to the boat, was making every effort to lie on my face. This was irritating because of the final surprise of the day.

My face was currently in very close proximity to that of Zara's, on account of our sudden and urgent kissing.

We had stayed in the pub for another hour or so and shared a bite to eat, Zara choosing the baked potato with cheese and I, in that sad way that men do when they're trying to impress a pretty vegetarian, had a cheese ploughman salad instead of the steak. After the third or fourth drink we were genuinely enjoying ourselves, chatting about our lives and giggling about the past. As Zara delicately dissected the cheesy potato and I chewed on the salad like a drunken cow with no cheeks, she suggested that we head back to the boat for the evening. I made noises about getting a room in the pub and not being an inconvenience to her, but the frequent accidental brushes of her hand on my arm and the look in her eyes told me that, this evening at least, I was definitely her type.

"Ahh..." she sighed, breaking off the kiss, and gently pushing the dog away as we lay on the sofa. "I never thought we'd be doing this tonight." She was incredibly lithe and managed to recline on the sofa, legs tucked beneath her, while leaving plenty of room for me. Her CD player was on, the little speakers filling the cabin with plinky-plonky music counterpointed with synthesised panpipes and the occasional squealing dolphin.

"Maybe it's the wine, Wolf," she continued, almost whispering, "but it feels so natural being close to you." She stroked the back of my neck, kissing my forehead gently.

"I know," I said, and meant it. I was relaxed and happy, excited about how the evening would progress, and acutely conscious of my obvious excitement below my waistband. Of course as a man, brushing against a door frame on the way into the house sometimes felt exciting too. We are simple creatures with simple desires, easily fulfilled. Two minutes in the bathroom with *the Observer* colour supplement usually does the trick.

"You know what, Wolf?" she looked dreamily into my eyes. "I feel like we've been here before. Maybe in another life?"

"Yeah..." I returned her kisses, keen to keep the mood. "It certainly seems that way, doesn't it? So comfortable. So natural." She pulled me closer, breathing a little faster when she felt my excitement, her nipples stretching the fabric of the dress.

My mind was swimming with alcohol and desire, that heady mix that fuels the best romances. Unusually for me I didn't just want her body, I wanted *her*. And that was very odd. I'd long since stopped thinking of love as a realistic thing in my life. It was more of an idealistic concept, like world peace, flying cars, or finding a good pizza in England.

She reached under my shirt and slowly pulled it over my head. In a feat of gymnastics and the kind of multi-tasking men can only achieve when big brain and little brain are both on the job, I unclasped her dress and let it fall from her shoulders. She held her head back on that long neck, her hair flowing across her delicate shoulders, and I brushed my lips along her chest, pulling the dress lower over her tight belly, the hint of white from her underwear slowly revealed next to the goosebumps on her skin.

"Ah..." she bit her lip, cheeks reddening. "You've no idea what that feels like..." This was true, of course, my never having possessed breasts. I alternated gentle kissing with grabbing her nipples delicately with my teeth. Sighs rewarded the right moves, and I seemed to be tuned into her needs. I think that women everywhere would become lesbians if they realised how a bloke making love to them uses the same techniques as playing a computer game. They try to get as many good noises going as possible, preferably in quick succession. It was like naked pinball, albeit with uglier balls, fewer buttons, and a slot you really shouldn't stick fifty pence in.

She leaned around me as I kissed her chest, her slender fingers massaging my back and caressing my shoulder blades. It was my turn to sigh as the pressure built within me. I tried to focus, knowing all too well how long it had been since I had had sex with someone, and how quickly this moment could be over in a teenage splurge of sticky jeans and awkward silence.

She suddenly stiffened, her fingers rubbing a little mole, slightly raised, on my lower back. She leaned her head around to have a look.

"Wolf..." Her tone of voice had changed. "Wolf. I've seen this mole before." She spoke softly, but there was a wary tone which hadn't been there before. "Have we been together before?"

"In another life, perhaps, darling..." I kissed her breasts again, my hand moving down the small of her back to where the downy flesh began to rise.

"No. It's coming back to me." She sat up, pulling away from me, and held my gaze, eyes wide with sudden realisation. "Jake's parties. We had sex then, didn't we? All I remember was the odd snog on the sofa." I stared at her. I didn't want this to end, not now. "Did you know? Did you know and you didn't tell me?" Damn it, I knew our moment was gone.

Unless, of course, I lied.

From below my waist, where the little brain lives, obsessively twisting any situation on the off chance of getting some action, a tiny voice was shouting: '*lie! You know ze women, ze women they like the lies... Ze truth she not so good.*' I never understood why I imagine my little fellow as having a Mexican accent. It was one of life's great mysteries, like Donald Trump's hair, and one of the many things I needed to speak with a therapist about. I was a forty-year old man who thought his penis was Pancho Villa.

I chose to ignore my sombrero-wearing friend, which was simple enough
as his advice was always the same. Feeling low? Have sex with someone. Money troubles? Have sex with someone. It's a Wednesday? Have sex with someone. I decided to tell the truth.

Ish.

"It was a hectic time, Zara, you remember what it was like. But when I saw you today I thought that, yeah, I remembered you, and I had feelings for you from back then."

"Feelings? You had feelings for me for twenty years and never got in touch?" She pulled her dress around her shoulders, sitting further back on the sofa. At least she hadn't put it back on yet.

"Yes. Like the feelings you had for John. Tell me, did you get in touch with him?" I was plainly in the wrong, but I was also a man, so it was natural to try and put the blame onto someone else. Natural and stupid.

"Okay," she spoke softly. "I get your point. You're sure that we were together? Like this? Together back then?"

"Yes. I think so."

"When? When do you thi..." She suddenly put her finger to her lips. "Ah... so this is where all those questions about me being sure that John was the father came from?" She smiled, genuine amusement in her eyes.

"Yes... I guess that's what I was thinking. It just seemed unlike John to... well... you know." She laughed.

"Check out Mr Fertile, here! So you don't think that John could be Stardust's father but *you* could?" She giggled, and the dress fell off her shoulders once more. She didn't pull it back on. "Well, I guess I'd better see what you've got that John didn't have," she teased. I laughed, and began to kiss her neck again.

"Well, Stardust doesn't look like John," I whispered.

I felt her stiffen and pull away from me once more.

"How do you know what Stardust looks like?" she asked, pulling her dress tightly around her.

Damn.

---oOo---

Chapter eleven

The canal glimmered in the moonlight, and there was a sparkle in the air as a warm mist drifted from the water to the fields on either side of the towpath. From the village came the sound of occasional cars passing through, heard above the muffled music from the Onslow Arms. It was still warm, and a number of people sat at benches in front of the pub. Now and then a dog barked in the village.

The canal boat lay securely moored next to the path, its paintwork glinting softly in the moonlight, bobbing gently as the water flowed beneath it. Dim lights shone through neat little curtains and there was a distant 'hoot' as a hunting owl flew by.

Several large houses bordered the canal, some with paths through the hedgerow onto the towpath. Out of the shadows a woman appeared, into the moonlight, walking slowly toward the boat. As she came closer she paused for a few moments, listening intently. Crouching down, she edged close enough to the windows to glance in.

The gentle light from inside the boat illuminated Nadir's dusky features. She was casually dressed, hair loose and flowing, and her quick glance confirmed that Moore and Devenish were both on the boat. She felt the briefest jealousy as she watched them together, but swiftly brushed it aside. It had been a long time since she'd been with someone. Relationships were essentially impossible in her line of work, particularly a lasting relationship. Of course she had brief moments of romance, but they were snatched affairs, immediately forgotten. For her it was feeding a hunger, but not having a full meal. Like having a McMuffin for breakfast, it's technically food, but leaves you feeling even emptier after eating it.

She had found love, a few years ago, but the realities of her work made thoughts of building a relationship with Françoise little more than painful fantasy. It hurt her deeper than she cared to admit.

On occasion, she'd fed her desires with colleagues, both male and female, hungrily achieving some form of satisfaction before going about her business again. Not with Gabriel, though; never with him. Nadir knew that Gabriel was exceptionally gifted in his work, but only because he was an intensely violent, barely controlled, psychopath. She harboured no thoughts of satisfying her occasional loneliness with him. It would be like using a blender as a vibrator.

Still, Nadir and Gabriel worked well together. Light and Dark. Well, a slight darkness and the Pitch Blackness at the end of the universe. It was becoming harder to keep him balanced and focused, and the slightest thing could send him into a manic humour or a sudden rage.

Things like her peeking through the window of the canal boat, threatening to give their presence in the area away. Devenish was meant to be far across the Atlantic by the time he realised Gabriel was keeping tabs on Zara Moore.

Satisfied that he was too preoccupied to notice her peek through the window and that he looked like he would be busy for the evening, she crept away from the boat and walked swiftly down the towpath. It was a beautiful evening and she looked forward to enjoying a cool glass of wine before messaging Gabriel to come and meet her. A half hour of peace to for a change.

She stepped off the towpath and passed by the pub benches, filled with people chatting happily over a cool beer on a warm evening, and entered the noisy bar.

The older man, sitting alone with his pint, watched her as she went inside. He waited until the pub door closed before he pulled a notebook from his pocket and began to scribble a few lines. There was a glint in his eye. Mysteries to unravel.

---oOo---

Chapter twelve

Gabriel hated waiting. He was good at it, but that didn't mean he liked it.

His big rental car was parked in a dark lane, lined with high hedges, pulled into a gap where a dilapidated gate hung before a field. It was a warm, still night, and the only sounds or movements were from the various countryside animals which scuttled around the hedge or flew along the lane.

He sat in the blackness of the car, one window slightly open, the moonlight sparkling off the road surface, making the shadows even darker along the hedgerow. His mind, as always, drifted back to other long, dark, waits.

A huge sky, flecked with distant stars, framed the desolate landscape surrounding the small village of perhaps two dozen houses, scattered haphazardly around a central dusty square. The faint starlight picked out flat roofed buildings, their clay rendering making them appear as though they had grown from the sand itself. A gravelly, poorly surfaced road passed between the watchers and the buildings, beaming away in either direction into the desert.

The younger Gabriel, concealed within a sandy rise a few hundred metres from the road, watched the village carefully.

He was wearing light camouflaged fatigues, and he leaned against a dusty rucksack as he observed the houses beyond. On his head was a floppy cap with some scraps of khaki netting tied through the brim, shielding his face and breaking up his outline. Brown smudges streaked across his jacket, the remnants of the goat crap they'd smeared over themselves to cover their scent from local livestock, although what the hell the animals ate round here baffled Gabriel. Sand, maybe. Rocks, perhaps. A dim green glow leached from the eyepiece of his night vision scope as he raised it to get a better view of the village.

Behind him, scattered around the dune system, were four more soldiers. Two watched the approaches to their little enclave while one lay sleeping in a depression in the sand. The fourth lay close to Gabriel, scanning the area through his rifle scope. Each wore earpieces and neck microphones, and Gabriel half-listened to the terse messages sent from other units in the area as he concentrated on his reconnaissance.

The digital image in the scope flared bright as a vehicle appeared on the road a few miles away, headlights blazing, driving toward their position. His radio crackled.

"Watchman, this is Predator one. Vehicle approaching, over." Gabriel observed the car getting closer, and pressed the switch on his throat microphone.

"Predator one, watchman two. Got it. Wait for actual. Over." Gabriel sensed his boss, Lieutenant Elliot, creep up behind him, sweeping his rifle to point it down the road. He spoke quietly.

"Predator one, watchman actual. Eyes on, awaiting identification. Over."

"Watchman actual, this is Predator one. Copy your last. Contact Angel four for package delivery. Out."

Gabriel watched the car grow closer and slow as it pulled into the village, turning off the road between two squat houses. Elliot brought his rifle to bear on the car, peering through the magnified sight, and whispered to Gabriel.

"Can you make out the driver yet, Gabe?" Gabriel shook his head.

"Not yet."

"Watch and wait... the drone's glassing it too. Keep your eyes open." He went on comms again. "Angel four, this is watchman actual. Sit rep, over." There was a pause before the communications crackled again, the new voice hard to make out against the noise of the jet engines in the background. The voice had that irritating assurance of fighter pilots, as if the troops on the ground were toddlers that needed mommy to wipe their arse for them.

"Watchman actual, Angel four. In position. You boys alright down there? Over."

"Roger, Angel four. Fine here. Join us sometime. Get some dirt on those shiny boots of yours. Out." Gabriel grinned in the dark, and whispered to Elliot once again.

"Bit of financial overkill, don't you think? Couple of dollars for a 7.62 round, or a cool half million for a smart bomb. Hope this guy's worth it. Hell, for twenty large I'd crawl over there and bite the guy to death."

"No doubt, but stick to the plan. Here we go." The car stopped and there was stillness for a second except for a dog scuttling between the houses, yapping as it went.

"Two rags in the car," murmured Gabriel.

"Got them. You're right, sergeant," said Elliot, adjusting his rifle sights. "If it's our guy, I could slot him from here."

"Course," drawled Gabriel, "course you could, sir. But then we'll have us a chase through the desert, our asses hanging in the breeze when the hadjis come running. Let the fly boys sort it. They like pressing buttons." The radio hissed.

"Watchman actual, Predator one. Do we have positive ID on subject?"

"Predator one, this is watchman actual. Wait one. Over."

The car doors opened and two men emerged from the vehicle. One stretched as though the journey had been long, then reached into the footwell and pulled out a rifle and a bag. The other looked around, disturbingly staring straight at Gabriel for a moment. He recognised the face. Farrokh Hamidi, the Iranian explosives specialist, currently working with Iraqi insurgents, training them in guerrilla warfare techniques and improvised bomb making. Although no Iranians were officially involved in the increasing attacks on the occupying forces after the recent war, Gabriel was looking right at one. He cursed the politicians. If they would just say what was really going on here, there would be embarrassed faces across the Middle East, and governments would do anything to make sure they didn't find several US armoured divisions deciding to vacation in their country. For once, though, after a twenty-four hour covert observation, the intelligence was correct. The poster boy of Baghdad bomb-making was straight in front of him. Gabriel tapped the lieutenant on the shoulder.

"Positive, boss. That's him. It's the target." Elliot immediately sent a message.

"Predator one, watchman actual. Target confirmed. Repeat, target positively identified. Waiting for go." There was an immediate response.

"Watchman actual, predator one. Copy your last. What's your confidence on ID? Over." Elliot looked through his scope at the figure for a second.

"Predator one, watchman actual. Confidence is high. Awaiting instructions. Over." There was a slight pause.

"Watchman actual, we copy. Wait one, over." Elliot set his weapon down and reached over for the laser unit he would need to target the building.

"This is it, Pete. Watch the building." He turned behind him and whispered instructions to the rest of the team. "Be advised, target acquired. Get your shit together for evac." Gabriel continued to scan the buildings as the figures from the car entered through a side door. He moved from window to window, looking for movement. The radio crackled.

"Watchman actual, this is predator one. Light it up. Over."

"Predator one, roger. Targeting now." Elliot switched on the invisible laser, and took aim at the top of the house. Gabriel could see the laser hit the building through his night vision scope, bright reflections scraping over the building, sparkling into the night. Without the scope the scene was quiet and still. Gabriel knew that, high above, the jet will pick up the reflections and send a bomb to fly straight into it. Like an invisible, silent banshee, the laser marked everyone in the house for death.

"Watchman actual, this is Angel four. Weapon away. Time to target, ninety seconds. Enjoy the fireworks and keep your heads down. Over."

"Angel four, Watchman actual, roger that. Keep the coffee warm for us. Out" said Elliot. "We're hot," he whispered. Gabriel continued to scan the building and the street. He could see the two men in the front room of the house, shadows against the light inside. They had no idea that their world would end in just over a minute. On reflection Gabriel thought it wasn't the worst way to go. The slow, lingering death in a sterile hospital room must be more terrible. For these guys, one of whom made it his business to kill and maim people through deviously hidden bombs, the end would come instantly. It would be like switching off a light.

He scanned away from the house and around the adjacent ones. They would probably be untouched... possibly. Whoever lived in them might end up with sore ears, but as long as they stayed inside they'd be fine. The house on the right had seemed empty all evening, and the one on the left was abandoned, its door secured shut with two planks. There shouldn't be collateral damage.

Sometimes Gabriel wasn't sure about this life he'd chosen. A recon marine was rarely more than a pair of eyes which brings death to people. Although he was an expert marksman, he rarely had to use his weapon. His job was to creep in, observe, report, wait for the attack, and slink off again. While he knew that it was far from cowardly, recon marines being among the bravest men he knew, something didn't sit right with him. It seemed unsporting. He smiled at the thought of war ever being sporting. When it came down to it, the Marine Corps weren't big on giving the other guy a fighting chance.

"Fuck. Check right, Pete," said Elliot, urgently. Gabriel scanned beyond the target house. A door was open and a child was standing outside the house, a tiny dog in his arms. He let the dog down using a string as a lead and began walking toward the road, right past the target house. "Shit. A fucking kid." Elliot went straight onto the comm net. "Angel four, watchman actual. Time to target? Over."

"Watchman actual, target in fifty-five seconds. All alright down there? Over."

"Fuck," said Elliot, but Gabriel was already moving. Without thinking he jumped out of their position and ran as fast as he could toward the boy. In thirty seconds flat he was on the road, and the boy turned at the sound of the big American running at him. "Get down, marine!" shouted Elliot, but Gabriel ignored him. "Get down!" In his ear, Gabriel heard the crackle of communications.

"Angel four, watchman actual, abort weapon! Abort weapon!"

"Watchman actual, that's a negative. Hot and acquired. Ten seconds. Over."

"Watchman actual, Predator one. What is happening? Over." The comms crackled as the drone pilot watched Gabriel's heat signature run to the buildings.

"Get down!" Gabriel shouted in rough Arabic as he kept running, a few paces from the boy. He careered straight into him, his mass and muscle flattening the kid against the wall. The little dog, his string dropped, ran back into the house, tail between its legs. In an instant Gabriel grabbed the boy by the arm and pulled him to the right hand side of the house. *Just a few steps more*. He opened his mouth wide, both from screaming at the boy and to withstand the imminent blast pressure. Communications were buzzing through his headset, but he ignored them and kept running.

Then they were lifted into the air like sand on a breeze.

A shuddering blackness surrounded him. He could feel his consciousness being crushed into nothing, his vision narrowing to a pinpoint of fiery light on the sand before him. He pulled the boy close to him, the body armour and his own flesh between the kid and the explosion. The air left his lungs with a hiss as the pressure wave hit him, and he felt the 'ping ping ping' of objects smashing into his back. Then he gave in and surrendered to the blackness, barely aware of slamming into the soft ground as a wave of heat surrounded him.

Lifetimes seemed to pass as he lay on the ground, but it was mere moments before he awoke. Someone was shaking him.

"You okay? You okay, you crazy fuck?" It was Sanchez, one of his squad. Gabriel slowly opened his eyes. The glimmer of light from the flames made the walls of the houses flicker like brimstone, and he felt like he had awoken in Hell. The boy squirmed beneath him, vital and alive, and Gabriel tried to move his weight off him. The effort hurt, his muscles stiff and numb when he moved them. He rolled to the side, releasing the boy. The kid was covered in dust, evidently in shock, but he was bright eyed and wailing. Gabriel got to his knees and stood up slowly. He breathed through a wave of nausea and dizziness as he straightened his back.

"We gotta get the fuck out of here, Gabe. Now. We're in a world of shit. Everyone in the village is awake. There are some pissed off hajis out here. We gotta go. Now. El Tee's trying to get an airlift, but it's ten clicks out. Boots all the way, man. Get going."

Gabriel felt something wet and sticky dripping down his side against his body armour, but there was no pain, his adrenaline levels were too high. His left leg was not as responsive as usual and moving it was difficult, but he was still breathing. Most people that close to a *Paveway* blast weren't so lucky. He looked around, taking in the pile of rubble that was the target house. He'd misjudged the impact, the adjacent houses having lost parts of their adjoining walls too. The kid looked up at him.

"Now, Gabe! Get fucking going," said Sanchez.

Gabriel noticed an assortment of people, wearing all kinds of clothing from nightwear to full Arab dress, although the difference between the two was negligible. They stood outside their homes or by the road, staring in shock at the devastated house. Some men shouted. Women cried. He saw the rest of the squad in defensive positions next to the road, and realised his earpiece had fallen out. He tried putting it back in, but his ear was full of blood. Giving up, he let it dangle on its cord. Elliot approached him and tossed him his rifle, which Gabriel caught as though in a daze.

Roughly, the lieutenant grabbed him by the shoulder and walked him a few paces away from Sanchez.

"Listen to me, Sergeant. Listen well. As a human fucking being, I know what you just did. I admire you for it. If we get out of this, you're getting a medal for it." He stared hard at Gabriel. "As your squad commander. As your fucking lieutenant, I am really, really pissed at you, Sergeant. We're in it so deep we can't see the sky for shit. Get yourself together, and let's get out of here."

"Sorry, boss," said Gabriel. "Couldn't let the kid get zapped. Not his fault. Sorry."

"I told you, I understand, but this is a shitty job in a shitty place, and people will die. Kids will die. This isn't the time or place for this conversation. Look, I got through to support.

We've got three birds coming in with a RRT to secure the LZ. Ten minutes out. It wasn't in the plan. If this works out badly we're screwed. Now let's get going and secure our position before the locals get all Alabama on our ass."

"I'm from Alabama, sir."

"Then you know what I mean. Move it sergeant." Gabriel looked back at the kid, quietly moaning on the ground. In the dim light of the flames, Gabriel noticed a dark shadow around the boy's neck as he lay on the sand.

"Shit," said Gabriel. "The kid's hit." Elliot glanced down.

"I see that. What we meant to do about it?"

"He needs help. He needs medevac. Give me a hand." The officer looked at him for a beat, defiance in his eyes. Then they softened and he helped Gabriel lift the boy to his feet.

"Right. Fuck. Let's get back to the berm, but they'll not take him on a chopper. He'll have to take his chances with the locals."

"Just ask, el tee. Just ask."

"Right." A pause. "You owe me, Sergeant."

The two men hurried across the road to the lay-up position in the sand. Gabriel pulled a field dressing from his kit, dressing the boy's wound. There was a small cut, a tear across his neck, which bled in a constant, seeping flow. Not arterial blood. Good, but not great. Gabriel used his hand to apply pressure, using his water canteen to wash dust and dirt from the kid's face. The child, pale from shock and loss of blood, licked at the water as dirty rivulets poured over his mouth, murmuring words that Gabriel didn't understand. The rest of the squad took up covering positions, weapons pointed toward the village.

The crowd, though small, were noisy in their shock and grief. Now and then there were gunshots as some people with rifles fired them into the air in defiance. Even so, they knew well enough not to fire at the marines. The noise of helicopters drifted across the desert behind Gabriel as he checked the wound again, pleased that the bleeding seemed reduced. The kid had his eyes closed, but his breathing was stable and his heart strong. Gabriel wished there was a corpsman there to help. His own battlefield first aid didn't seem enough.

"Choppers on our six, boss," said Sanchez. Black shadows scudded against the night sky, growing larger. The crowd, numbering twenty or thirty people, milled around next to the ruined house, their outlines scratched in the darkness by the fires flickering in the wreckage. The noise of helicopters increased and the sand began to swirl, flying into their eyes, mouths and noses, as they landed. Elliot, crouched, ran towards the first chopper, as gray figures jumped to the ground and moved towards the road, weapons at the ready. The chopper loadmaster talked urgently to Elliot.

"We've got word of heavy resistance in this area, lieutenant. We've got to get on the way soon as. Do you have any casualties?"

"Yes. One marine wounded, and one civilian."

"Can't take civilians, sir. We got to go."

"No... no. We're going to take this one."

"No can do, lieutenant. There's no room on the chopper. We'll give you fire support to bring the casualty back to the village, but then we've got to get going. Like right now. This is a hot area. Intel reckons at least two RPG teams in the area alone. We gotta go." Elliot paused for a beat. Thought. Decided.

"Roger that. Let's do it." He shouted to Gabriel and Sanchez. "Pull some dressings, meds and shit, and get that kid back to his family. Leave the medical stuff with them. Now. Then we're out of here. There's no room at the inn. We have to go."

The loadmaster nodded, and the rapid response squad sprinted towards the road taking up positions on the near side, away from the village. One of them spoke some Arabic and began shouting and gesturing for the crowd to move back. Sanchez lifted the boy and the collection of bandages and walked out towards the road. Gabriel tried to sit up, but felt weak. His legs had lost their strength, and he felt blood chilling against his skin. Pulling himself to the edge of the sand he watched Sanchez carry the boy to the road, flanked by marines waving their rifles to force the crowd back.

As he watched a woman emerged from the boy's house, dressed head to toe in black. Sobbing, she raised her arms and walked through the crowd to the side of the road, straight towards Sanchez. With his free hand he motioned for her to stay back, shouting at the woman.

"Is this your kid?" She kept walking slowly, arms wide, crying softly. "This boy yours?" She didn't respond. The Arabic speaker translated and she stopped, nodding and simpering. Sanchez set the boy gently on the ground and left the small bag of medical supplies next to him. He gestured for her to come and collect him.

Gabriel felt tired. But somewhere in the sluggish thoughts crawling through his head alarm bells were ringing. He raised his weapon, which felt unusually heavy in his weak hands, and peered through the sight. The marines and rapid reaction force were focused on the crowd, weapons raised. Nobody was watching the buildings.

He willed his arm to raise his rifle and scan the houses, just as the first flashes appeared from a rooftop behind the crowd.

The ground around Sanchez and the others began spitting sand and rock as rounds from the old Soviet PK machine gun struck home. The marines tried to scatter and grab cover, but two men fell almost straight away with multiple wounds. Gabriel depressed his trigger, trying to put fire onto the rooftop, but his numb arm couldn't hold the rifle steady. His tracers flew harmlessly high above the roof.

Operating on instinct the remaining troops started unloading toward the muzzle-flashes, the snare-drum sound of their own machine gun adding to the cacophony. In an instant it was over, villagers sheltering behind walls and within the burning rubble, the gunfire echoing across the desert. The firing from the rooftop had stopped, the insurgents smashed to pieces by incoming rounds, and the surviving marines grabbed the wounded, including the Iraqi boy, and ran for the helicopters. Two figures tried to help Gabriel to his feet, but loss of blood made the world spin before him.

As Gabriel passed out, he vowed to learn his lesson. Kindness was for fools. His attempt to save the boy had only succeeded in hurting his own men, and he wouldn't make the same mistake again. Blackness in his head and heart consumed him, and he fell into it willingly.

As he sat in the cooling car, Gabriel was jarred from his waking dream by the brightness of headlights coming up the road behind him. He adjusted the rear view mirror to watch the car drive past, aware of the dull pain in his side that came and went whenever he had the thoughts about that desert evening.

The headlights flicked to full beam in the mirror, flooding Gabriel's hire car with light. The approaching car was slowing down.

"Oh, you are kidding me," said Gabriel, out loud. "Just drive the fuck past."

The car pulled to the side of the lane, about ten metres behind Gabriel, and came to a halt. Nothing happened for a few seconds, then a row of flashing blue lights appeared above the roof, a few embedded in the radiator grille for good measure.

"Fuck." Gabriel moved his arms smoothly in front of his body, trying not to move his shoulders which could be seen from behind. He pulled the body of his automatic swiftly back, releasing it with a satisfying 'snap' as the round was chambered. He slipped the weapon back into his shoulder holster, checking the safety was on, and straightened his jacket to conceal the gun.

He watched the policeman emerge from the car behind, pausing to put his cap on, then walk slowly towards Gabriel, his flashlight scanning the car as he approached.

---oOo---

Chapter thirteen

Dirty Harry, CS fucking I, Miami Vice, Ashes to Ashes, Hill Street Blues, and Dixon of Dock Green.

Wankers, every last one of them.

PC Karl Jacobsen hated cop shows, and held them personally responsible for everything that was wrong with his life. He'd been a policeman for ten years now, one of Surrey Constabulary's finest, and every single day was a disappointment.

There were few serial killers for one thing, and his chances of going maverick and tracking down his own plastic-faced, cackling Scorpio were slim. As were the odds of delivering his own brutal justice to the scumbag, while the applause of *Daily Mail* readers drowned out the weasel-mouthed moaning of his superiors and their civilian lawyer masters.

The television shows had also taught him to expect a sense of teamwork, the 'nobody left behind' attitude he'd seen in the buddy-cop movies and police soaps. In reality he may as well work as a shelf-stacker in Asda for all the team spirit there was on the force. He didn't even have a cynical, spirit-swilling, hard-boiled boss who, when push came to shove, would take a bullet to protect his young protégé. No. His sergeant was the captain of the local golf club and was concerned with filled rotas, polished boots, and avoiding contact with the public as far as possible. He also thought that Jacobsen was called Paul, which would have really ruined the last-words, bleeding-on-the-pavement, 'I'm proud of you, rookie' speech.

He'd also expected to be armed and dangerous as a member of Her Majesty's 21st century constabulary, but all they'd issued him with was an extendable metal stick and, occasionally, a bright yellow Taser, which looked like a toy gun made from Lego. Yes, there were firearm courses he could apply for, but his sergeant reckoned he didn't have 'the right stuff' to be an armed officer, and wouldn't forward his name to the right people.

But worst of all were the stripper jokes. Every bloody time he had to turn up to a pub or a nightclub to sort out some disturbance there would be the stripper jokes. 'Hey hey, who ordered the entertainment?' was the most popular one, usually coupled with winking and the odd arm-squeeze. Time was he would laugh it off and get on with his business, but the jokes kept coming. One night, in a student bar, he heard the same joke forty-seven times.

'Dirty' Harry Callahan wouldn't stand for that shit. Christ, even Inspector bloody Morse wouldn't have stood for it.

No, Karl had been deceived by every television cop show he'd ever watched, and he blamed all of them for him having an evening shift roaming the lanes of Surrey, keeping the farmers happy, and making sure the quiet spots were clear of perverts out dogging and seventeen-year-olds hoping to score large with their girlfriend in the backseat of daddy's Mondeo.

Mondeos like the one in front of him.

He flashed the light array and watched to see if shadowy forms leapt off the backseat. Watching them wipe the rear window and peer through the windscreen, all flustered from their fumbling and pale with sudden fright that the filth had turned up was the only fun part of this particular job.

Nothing happened.

He thought he could see someone in the front seat, but it was hard to tell from inside the patrol car. Otherwise there was no response to the lights. He briefly thought about sending a location report in on the radio, but they'd laugh at him back at the station. Hell, the guy was probably just on the phone, or dead of a heart attack or something.

Karl climbed out of the car, and it *binged* to warn him that his keys were still in the ignition and the lights were on. He grabbed his hat, carefully straightened it on his head, and walked toward the big Ford, shining his torch around the vehicle. The front windows were free of condensation, as though the heater had been running, and a single figure sat in the driving seat. Karl stopped beside the door and smartly rapped the window. There was a momentary pause and the window spun down halfway. Karl shone his torch directly at the driver. It never failed to piss them off.

"Can I help you, officer?" The man squinted a little at the torchlight.

A bloody Yank.

"Is there a problem with your vehicle, sir?" The bloke was better looking than most of the sweating, overweight scum who usually lurked the country lanes. You have to give it to the dogging fraternity, but they're nothing if not classy.

"No, officer. Everything's just A-ok here." The American smiled broadly, shiny teeth catching the moonlight. "How are you this evening?"

"May I ask why you're parked on this lane, sir?" The one thing Karl had perfected in this job was the impassive face. He could be seething inside, but his facial expression wouldn't change. The man shrugged slightly.

"Well, now, officer, I don't seem to be causing anyone any harm, so I don't rightly see why what I'm doing here is your business, with all due respect." Karl stared at him.

"I asked you a question, sir, and I would like an answer." He continued to stare at the driver without letting the shadow of an emotion creep upon his features. It was something he'd learned from watching David Cameron on TV. That man could take a dump on a homeless person's dog without so much as twitching an eyebrow.

"Why, I'm just waiting for some local chicks out looking for a good time." Karl's face dropped. He lowered his torch slightly.

"Wha?"

"Well, boy, what the fuck do you think I'm doing sitting out here all on my lonesome?" Something about the man's expression had changed. There was iciness in his eyes, a sudden tautness to his skin.

"Can I see some form of identification please, sir?" The man merely shrugged.

"No." Karl paused a beat, wondering if his ears were working properly.

"What?" The American smiled.

"You asked me for some form of identification, buddy, and I'm not minded to show you any, so I said 'no'." Karl's mind raced to process what he was hearing. It wasn't part of the usual script. And the guy looked so relaxed, like he was talking to a *Big Issue* seller rather than a cop.

"Get out of the car, sir." Karl stepped back a few paces. A knot had formed in his stomach and the hair on the back of his head was standing up. This had never happened to him before.

He wasn't sure what to do.

"I'm fine right here, boy. Why don't you just run along now and catch some nice safe criminals rather than bothering me." Karl didn't know what to do, so he improvised.

He reached behind his belt and pulled out his Taser.

"Get out of the car now, sir!" He stepped back again and raised the weapon, silently cursing the stupid bright yellow casing. It should have *Tommee Tippee* written on the side.

"Oh, that dog's not going to hunt, boy." The door cracked open and the man climbed out of the car. He was taller than Karl had hoped. "You best put that toy away before I stick it up your ass."

"Stand still, sir." The American smiled again.

"Don't you want me to put my hands where you can see them?" Karl swore under his breath. He wasn't thinking.

"Hands up, sir." The words sounded stupid in his mouth. Crockett and Tubbs wouldn't say "sir"... they'd say 'Hands up, motherfucker.' But then Crockett and Tubbs didn't have the Independent Police Complaints Commission to answer to. The American brought his hands smoothly forward where Karl could see them.

His stomach heaved when he noticed the gun being raised towards him.

Karl's jaw dropped, and he snatched at the Taser trigger. *Do you feel lucky, punk?* The American slipped sideways just as the Taser made its pathetic little 'ping" and the electrodes spat forward.

Straight into the side of the car, scraping the paint as they sparked and fell onto the tarmac.

"Oh, you are kidding me." Gabriel lunged forward and smacked Karl on the side of the head with the pistol. It felt like being hit with a brick. He dropped the Taser and fell to his knees, clutching his head. "That's a fucking rental car, asshole." The American rubbed the scrapes on the paintwork with his thumb, keeping his pistol pointing at Karl.

"I'm arresting you on suspicion of..." Karl tried to get to his feet and got another slap on the side of the head for his troubles.

"Yeah, yeah, fuck that." Gabriel stepped back and contemplated the policeman as he clutched his head again. "Why didn't you just drive on by?" He waved his pistol, pointing down the road. "Now what are we going to do?"

"Are you going to kill me?" The reality of the situation was squeezing into Karl's mind, yet another reason to hate his job. God, he knew there were elements of danger in what he did, but the worst he'd expected on his beat was a thrown glass at a nightclub or a thrown fist from a drunk. Not a tall American pointing a semiautomatic in his face.

"Well now, we're certainly in the shit, aren't we?" He pursed his lips in thought as he considered Karl kneeling on the ground before him. "I guess that popping you would be the easiest way of dealing with our little problem, don't you agree?" He took aim at Karl's head. The colour drained from the policeman's face.

"No... no, please! Don't shoot! I'll not tell anyone about you..." The American smiled.

"Well isn't that decent of you, boy? I'm much obliged." He tapped his forehead with the barrel of the pistol in salute. "Fact is, if you were nice and quiet for a day or so, then there'd be no need for any unpleasantness." He thought for a few more moments. "Toss me those cuffs." Karl pulled his handcuffs from the pouch on his belt, hand brushing against his extendible baton. His fingers paused next to the patterned hand grip and his eyes flickered up to the big American. The man was scanning the lane, not looking at Karl. He had half a second to decide if he wanted to be a hero. His fingers curled around the grip.

"Don't," said Gabriel.

Christ, he wasn't even looking at Karl, but his pistol was pointing directly at his face again, unwavering. Finger on the trigger. Those sparkling eyes flashed back onto the policeman.

"I said don't."

Karl released the baton, brought his hands round and threw the handcuffs onto the lane.

"Good decision, buddy. Up you get." Karl got to his feet. "Drop the batman belt, boy, and toss the comms on the deck." Karl unclipped his belt, then stood, confusion on his face.

"Comms?" he asked.

"Radio and cellphone." The man reached over and pulled Karl's radio and mobile from his stab vest, dropping them on the lane. Useful things, stab vests. Particularly when facing a pistol at point blank range. "Alright, now pop the hood on the patrol car." Karl just stared at him. "Jesus, boy. Let me at the engine." The policeman nodded, and they walked back to his car.

Karl reached in and pulled the bonnet lever. "Good man." The American approached him. "Hands behind your back, buddy." Karl did as he was told, and the man slipped the cuffs on him. "You chill out right there, boy," he said as he leaned over the bonnet, shining the torch around the engine.

"Ah, there we go." He produced a Leatherman from his pocket and reached into the compartment. *Snip.* He pulled out a small device, a ribbon connector hanging from it. The vehicle video feed hard-drive.

"Hop in." The American dropped the bonnet, opened the passenger door, and Karl slid into his car. Gabriel grabbed the bits and pieces from the road, jumped into the driver's seat and drove the car a few dozen yards down the lane to the old, overgrown field gateway. He hopped out and pulled the gate open, the rusty iron protesting as he dragged it through the dry, uncut grass..

The American drove into the field, pulling the gate shut again afterwards. Instead of hinges, the rusty metal pivoted on an ancient piece of half-rotted rope and a torn strip of fertiliser sack. He jumped in and drove the patrol car further along the grass towards a clump of trees a few dozen yards wide, tucked away in the corner of the field. A little stream passed through the copse, separating it from the neighbouring field. The muddy ground was a minefield of animal tracks and cow shit.

"What are you doing?" Karl didn't like the look of this.

"You need to keep out of my hair for a day or so, officer, so I've got to find somewhere cosy for you to stay." He slowly drove into the trees, bumping down into a small depression bordered on one side by a scrubby hedge. It would be hard to see into the copse from the road, and the branches stretching above would make it hard to see the car from the air. It was a good spot to hide the police vehicle, at least for a few hours.

"'Scuse me, my friend." The American used his pistol butt to smash the touchscreen computer on the dashboard, and tore away the radio handset. He reached across Karl and locked the car door, before snapping out the unlocking assembly with the Leatherman. Taking a pack of plasti-cuffs from the glovebox, he used a couple to attach the handcuffs to the seatbelt, trapping the policeman in the vehicle. It would allow Karl to move about a little, but not much.

"Right, now you're going to stay here for a spell while I get on about my business. I'm sure they'll start looking for you soon enough, but I'll make a little anonymous call tomorrow afternoon just in case. That gives you plenty of time to make up a pretty story about what went on here this evening." He smiled. "If, of course, I could star in this story as a five foot four black dude, that would be great."

"Right... yes... whatever you want." Karl nodded, just wanting the guy to go away. Outside the light was fading further. It would be pitch black in the copse soon.

"One more thing my man." He reached beneath the chair and removed the small first aid kit. Taking a wound dressing from the box, he tore open the packet and put the pad over Karl's mouth. "Say ahhh." Karl opened his mouth a fraction. Gabriel pushed the wound dressing gently into his mouth, tying the straps tightly behind his head. Karl could taste disinfectant on the bandage, the metallic iodine flavour numbing his mouth.

"Nice one." Gabriel slipped his pistol into a holster beneath his coat, and hopped out. He cocked his finger and thumb, pointed them at Karl and let the thumb drop. "See ya, buddy." Gloom filled the car when the door slammed shut, and Karl heard the big man slip away across the field. A few minutes later he heard a car starting and driving off, leaving only the sound of leaves and branches shifting in the breeze.

Fucking cop shows, thought Karl as he sat back in the seat trying to get comfortable.

---oOo---

Chapter fourteen

Andreas placed his pint on the counter and watched in the mirror as the door opened and a tall man entered the bar, pausing to scan the room, taking in the people drinking, talking and laughing. He held his breath as the man's eyes paused on his reflection for a fraction of a second longer than necessary, then slide away.

He'd been observing the Indian woman for close to an hour now, trying to figure her out. When she ordered another wine he picked up on her American accent, but she wasn't behaving like a tourist, and she looked increasingly uncomfortable sitting alone in the corner of the bar. It was possible she'd been stood up on a date, but the way she was constantly checking the room rather than her mobile wasn't the behaviour of someone pissed off about their boyfriend. She was behaving exactly as an agent in the field should behave, watching her arcs and observing everything around her, just as Andreas had decades before. Of course, if Andreas had noticed her, perhaps she had noticed Andreas in return?

And now there were two, he thought.

They exchanged a perfunctory kiss, like friends or bored lovers, and nothing more. But as his lips brushed her cheek, his eyes flicked back to the mirror, and straight on to Andreas. It was a challenge. He was saying 'I've seen you, and you've seen me. Now see how few shits I give about it.'

Andreas chuckled quietly. They were probably here to keep an eye on him, part of the paranoid games and internal auditing that security agencies were so obsessed with playing. He'd be sure to ask the office about it tomorrow. Or else it was a simple case of double-booking, where the Americans had asked for help in doing the background clearance only for another department to go ahead and order their own staff to do it. The right hand not knowing what the left hand was doing. Christ, in the Stasi there had been so much internal surveillance he often thought they spent their days just watching one another.

Or was it something different? They might be off duty on another job, just taking a bit of time out somewhere quiet. They could even be having an affair, hiding away in the countryside to avoid awkward questions from colleagues. Everything was possible.

But they were definitely in the same business as Andreas.

The barmaid returned with another pint of the heavy beer. He had developed a taste for ale since moving to England, and it reminded him of *Dunkelbier*, a favourite of his in Berlin after the wall came down. A hell of a bit better than that fizzy piss the Americans drink.

The man may have noticed him, but there's more to being a professional than avoiding the notice of others. Quiet misdirection, just a muddying of the waters, can be enough to slip down the list of 'people to watch' in the mind of others. He needed to do something which would confirm to the stranger that he was right to mark Andreas as being different to the other people in the pub, but not because of what he suspected. In this case the solution was obvious.

He spoke to the barmaid in Polish.

"Thank you," he said, his Polish fluent and fast. "Your English is very good." The barmaid seemed delighted, and answered in her native tongue.

"Oh, you speak Polish? Very few people speak Polish in England." Andreas nodded and asked her a little about herself, how long she'd been over, what her plans were and so on. In turn, she asked him about himself, and he told her he was a travelling European businessman, which explained the Polish for one thing. As they spoke, the tall man arrived at the bar with an empty wine glass, waving it in the direction of the Polish girl with a big smile. Good teeth, decent tan and bright, sharp eyes, noted Andreas. A handsome bloke. The waitress seemed to notice too, quickly leaving Andreas and visibly brightening as she welcomed the sexy newcomer.

"Dry white wine, honey. And please tell me you have Coors on tap" said Gabriel, all smiles and charm.

"I sorry sir, but we have not Coors today. We have Miller in bottle, if that okay?" Andreas stifled a sigh as he realised how much she liked the look of the tall man. His trained ear picked out the American accent, and he tried to place it. Southern states... Tennessee, Louisiana, Alabama... somewhere where the family trees had more circles than straight lines. *Coors, for God's sake. Coors. Processed, tasteless, decadent poison in a glass.* Gabriel turned to him with an amused coolness in his eyes. Like frost on a pearl.

"Hey, buddy. How's it going?" Andreas felt a threat that only another spy would notice. To a regular guy, this American was merely being friendly and open.

To Andreas, he was as friendly and open as a bear-trap.

He was sizing Andreas up. If, after this mundane bar chat, the American was still interested in him there might be a problem.

"I'm fine, thank you. I trust you're enjoying your visit old boy?" Andreas used his best, cut glass, English accent. As British as rain and bad food.

"Indeed we are, friend. Great part of the world. Got a folksy feel to it. Kinda quaint." His beer and wine arrived, and he pulled a note from his wallet, handing it to the Polish girl. Gabriel swivelled his head back to regard him, raising his beer in salute and taking a deep, deep draft from it, his eyes burning into Andreas' own. "Cheers, buddy."

"Cheers, old chap. We don't get too many of our colonial friends so far south." Alarm bells were ringing in Andreas' head. He should have gone to the hotel, but the curiosity about the Indian woman was too much for him. Now he was building lies upon lies, and it would only take a single mistake for them to collapse, leaving him stranded naked before the frightening American. Worse still, if that Devenish man returned and said something to him, even glanced at him the wrong way, Andreas' story dissolved like Russian jeans in a washing machine.

"So you speak Polack, then? Where d'ya pick that up?"

"On business, actually. Multinational company. Quite dull really, but I had a penchant for the old linguistic arts in college. So the bods in the leather chairs thought I was the man for the job." He turned away to return to his conversation with the

Pole, but she'd gone out front to collect glasses. He tried staring into mid-space as a signal that the conversation was over.

"What business, friend? What you guys do?" Gabriel put his near empty bottle onto the bar, and waited for the answer.

"Oh, now... it's terribly dull work actually. Frightful. Just selling point of sale equipment... cash registers, if you will. Pays the bills, though." Gabriel stared and waited. "I have a card, actually, if you fancy buying some cash registers... what is it you do for a crust back across the pond?"

"Lots of things, my friend. I do lots of things." Gabriel held his hand out expectantly. "Let's see this card buddy." Andreas reached into his jacket for the wallet and noted the tiniest risk assessment run across Gabriel's expression. Weighing things up. Wallet or weapon? The tension lifted slightly as he produced his wallet. The fat leather fold contained many things that would be hard to explain if he was hit by a car one day, although he'd replaced the fake warrant card with a normal driving licence after his conversation with Devenish. He carefully extracted the correct business card and offered it to Gabriel. 'Andrew Miller', of course. It was much easier to stick with the same name.

"Here you go, although I'm not terribly sure it'll be of service to you unless you plan to open a shop in the near future." He passed the card over, and Gabriel took it between his fingers, turning it around without looking at it. "Andrew Miller, by the way. Pleased to meet you." Gabriel paused for a second.

"Pete Gabriel, out of Fort Payne, Alabama... the U S of A." He put the card in his pocket, and Andreas started sliding his wallet back into his jacket. Gabriel stopped him with a gentle touch on his arm. "Hey, buddy... I ain't never seen a British driving license. Can I have a look? Ours are real cool these days. Biometric this, biofucktric that..." Andreas paused a moment, trying to maintain his smile, before answering.

"Certainly. Here you go." At the last moment he remembered to wince slightly at the bad language, just as Andrew Miller the polite salesman would. Then he extracted his British driving licence, one of four current licences he had at the moment. He handed the licence over as Gabriel gestured for the girl, who was ducking behind the bar with two armfuls of stacked pint glasses, to get him another beer.

"Cool." Gabriel held the licence, tapping the plastic, but staring at Andreas. He didn't once glance at the picture, but he had a quick scan of the driver number which he would no doubt remember. A few phone calls to the right people and he would have Andrew Miller's whole fake life story.

"Looks like a toy licence, man. Something a kid would throw together on his mom's computer to buy liquor." He looked Andreas in the eye. "Something fake about it." He held the glance for an instant, then smiled and placed the licence on the bar surface. He seemed suddenly distracted, as though a forgotten anger had reappeared in his mind and he had to make an effort to silence it within him. "I don't get you British sometimes." His beer arrived. He stood and offered his hand to Andreas. "Nice to meet ya, bud. Have a good one." They shook hands and Gabriel grabbed his drinks and returned to his colleague.

Andreas noticed dampness at the small of his back. This Gabriel person was a serious, unsettling man. Pulling at the layers which were rapidly forming around naive Ms Moore may be more dangerous than he'd imagined. Of course, Andreas had dealt with scarier things in his day. He'd participated in toppling one of the most unforgiving, brutal, paranoid regimes in human history. And he had survived, too cunning and too careful to make mistakes. People tended to underestimate him, and just because he was older now it didn't follow that he was less good at his job.

He sat back on the bar stool, keeping an eye out for the barmaid on slimmest of slim chances she fancied taking the Polish conversation that bit further.

Gabriel scribbled down the driving licence number after setting the drinks down next to Nadir. *Fucking amateur*, he thought. Nadir was watching him with tight lips, and he knew she was cross at his ebullient behaviour with the salesman. *Christ*, thought Gabriel, *she's going to have a fit when I tell her about the cop.*

Andreas ran through a few scenarios in his head and decided both that Devenish wasn't coming back to the pub or he would have been there already, and that Gabriel was now more interested in his pint than anything else. Leaving suddenly would reignite suspicions, so he would sit tight, enjoy his drinks, and enjoy the company of the barmaid, however far that company would go. As she returned with another drink he remembered his licence sitting on the bar. There were some smears on the plastic surface, and one of them bore the unmistakeable mark of a thumbprint. His heart started to beat a little faster as he carefully wrapped the licence in a napkin and put it in his pocket.

He watched the American and his partner in the mirror for another while, curt glances out of the corner of his eye, and was amazed when their quiet conversation became more animated. They were evidently having an argument, although keeping their voices clipped and low. At one point the woman pointedly drained her glass, all the while glaring at her companion who simply sat back in his chair and smiled, slowly sipping his beer. After a few minutes his own expression darkened and he leaned toward her, whispering something in her ear. Slamming the bottle onto the table to the surprise of the neighbouring tables, he stood suddenly and left the bar. The woman set some coins next to the bottle and followed him outside, her face like tropical thunder. Andreas, his eyes wide, watched her leave, more interested than ever in this strange couple.

Fucking amateurs he thought as the door swung shut behind her.

---oOo---

PC Karl Ericsson woke suddenly. It was dark, but his eyes were adapted to the night and he could make out hundreds of different shades of grey outside the car, bleak splashes between the black shadows of tree branches swaying overhead against the charcoal sky. Occasional pinpricks of light appeared and disappeared as the leaves caught the breeze and allowed specks of starlight through.

There was a tapping sound on the driver side window, metal on glass, and Ericsson twisted towards the noise. Two figures stood next to the car, one slim and medium height, and the other unpleasantly familiar, even in silhouette.

The American had left the side window open a crack to let some air in, and it was quiet inside the car except for a repetitive *tick tick* of some electronic thing-me-bob near where the radio assembly had been smashed. Karl heard the voice clearly.

"Well, buddy," he said, quietly. Gently. "I'm afraid there's been a change of plan." There was a shift in the shape of the shadow, and a splash of light through the trees caught the edge of something metallic and shiny next to the glass. Karl tried to shout, but only a muffled groan could get past the gag in his mouth. He tried to squeeze his body as close to the passenger door as possible, willing himself to disappear into the gap between the seat and the chassis, and he felt warmth envelope his behind as he lost control of his bladder.

"Sorry, boy," said the American.

There was a sudden crash as the pistol smashed the window, and Ericsson shut his eyes against the little crumbs of safety glass which showered the inside of the car. Gabriel reached through the broken window and popped the door open from the inside. *Of course... he didn't have the key.*

"Spooked ya, kid," beamed the American, as he reached across and opened the handcuffs. "Shimmy on out through this door, buddy." He shifted across on his wet behind, stiff legs protesting, and got out of the car. The American directed him gently around to the bonnet of the car, while his colleague, a slim girl, ducked into the driver's side.

Nadir pulled a torch from her bag and shone it around the vehicle, and used a microfiber cloth to quickly wipe down the steering wheel and door handles.

"Right, kid. We're letting you go on a little adventure." Gabriel beamed at him and patted him on the shoulder. "Bet you're sorry you didn't just drive on, boy?" Ericsson looked at him with deep wariness and the slightest touch of hope.

"Yes. You could say that." He tried to control his voice, conscious of the piss down his legs and his racing heart. "Are you letting me go?"

"Yeah, buddy... we're setting you free." Gabriel turned to his colleague. "You wanna do this, or will I?" She looked out from the car and thought for a second, before standing up and removing a small case from her bag.

"I'll do it." She made a turning motion with her fingers, and Gabriel gently, but firmly, pushed Ericsson around so he leaned over the bonnet. "Just a little prick, officer," she said.

"How'd she know that, son?" whispered Gabriel as she plunged the syringe into Ericsson's buttocks. "You been getting carried away with your stop and search?"

"Jesus!" exclaimed the policeman, as the needle drove deep into his muscle. "What are you doing?"

"Not shooting you, buddy. Don't tell me you're one of these 'glass half empty' people?"

"What's in that injection?" Ericsson was beginning to feel very odd indeed, strange feelings bubbling through his system almost as soon as the woman pulled the hypodermic from his behind.

"Oh, liquid party juice, my friend. Like a frat party in your ass. You're in for quite an adventure, Poindexter." Ericsson could feel his heart kicking against his ribcage, his senses sharpening, his nostrils filling with the countryside scents overwhelming the sharp cologne of the American. He looked around him, the indistinct shadows of his surroundings becoming edged in sparkling pixels of primary colours.

"Drugs?" His tongue felt fat in his mouth, but his body felt light as air. Like he would float away if he didn't start running around. The muscles in his legs twitched with a desire to start moving. He was finding concentration difficult. He had to keep looking around at the American and his friend, as though he forgot they were standing behind him. The woman smiled at him, and her bright teeth elongated as he watched, dripping like milk down her chin.

"Well done, Sherlock." The American spoke to his friend. "Think it's time we let our young friend go, eh?"

"Will he remember?" The woman looked unaware of the way her hair crawled across her head, like a million brunette eels trying to throttle her.

"Well, in this state I doubt it, but a little sudden shock might help things along the way." Ericsson flicked the aerial on the car, fascinated at the fan-like patterns it made in the starlight. He turned to the couple again, momentarily surprised to see them. A massive grin cut across his face, and he flapped his arms like a bird.

The American produced his pistol from his pocket, aimed it slightly above Ericsson's head, and fired twice.

The policeman's face went suddenly red, his eyes darting around, blinded by the flash, his ears burning from the sound which echoed and echoed within his head. He grasped the side of his skull and squeezed hard, eyes clenched shut, but the sound wouldn't leave.

Suddenly he turned and dashed off across the field, arms flailing at his side as he ran. Gabriel watched him scuttle off into the distance.

"That should do the trick."

"Have we finished with this stupid charade, then?" Nadir shone the torch on the grass for Gabriel to collect his spent shell cases. Gabriel glared up at her.

"What charade? Letting the kid go? He's just a stupid kid. I figured maybe I'd let him go. Alright? I thought that maybe, just this once, I'd let the fucking kid go."

They both slipped over the gate, Gabriel taking a moment to plump the grass up to remove most of the traces of car tracks and footprints, while Nadir used the cloth to wipe some mud around the areas they had touched. Job done, they quickly walked up the lane to Gabriel's Mondeo.

"They'd have every cop in the land looking for us if I'd shot the poor bastard. It would screw everything."

"Well, it's done now, Pete. Let's get on." She rarely called him by his first name, and only when she was annoyed.

"Yeah." Gabriel stopped at the junction with a larger road, and waited for several cars to go past. He turned on the stereo and searched the stations before finding a song he liked. R.E.M.'s *Nightswimming.* "Enjoy the ride, kid." He pulled onto the road and drove towards Guildford. Nadir glanced at her boss.

Perhaps it was the strange light as headlights caught his features along the way, but he looked almost content, the shadow of a smile on his lips.

Chapter fifteen

The morning came too soon for me. The last time I had been with Zara we were both half our age, and I envied those younger than me. They could drink for longer and stay up partying, screwing or talking till the dawn scraped over the horizon. And they didn't think twice about it.

Then again, kids these days drank cheap cider or alcopops, their parties were inane and dull, their sex was about as exciting and innovate as sweeping a chimney, and they talked about nothing except post-pubescent, angst-ridden shit.

Much as we had done. Every successive generation of teenagers feels special and unique, clearly different to those that had come before them; those who now set boundaries and rules around their own children's lives. But each generation recycles the same clichés, acting just as their parents had done, while convincing themselves that they are the first human beings to feel and experience these emotions, trials and adventures. There is little new under the sun.

The bedroom of the little barge grew steadily brighter, and I could make out the edges of things rather than just shapes in the gloom. Colours sparkled as the sunlight sprinkled around the room through the loose curtains. I felt her warmth before I could see her outline beneath the sheet, and I put my arm around her and held her as she slept.

I'd been left with no option but to tell Zara about Gabriel and Nadir, including their obsession with me being Martin's father. Sorry. Stardust's father. Strangely, given the weirdness of the tale, she had taken everything at face value, making repeated references to her son's 'vitally important' work.

She was initially angry that I hadn't told her earlier in the evening, and I sensed that something had changed between us. The sorry truth about deceit between two people is that, even when forgiven, distant clouds of mistrust remain, quietly threatening to rain down on future happiness.

Finally, after we discussed my going to New Mexico to meet with Martin, and Zara asked me to pass on her best wishes, the evening had fallen back on track.

Some crusts covering my personality had crumbled away during it, and I awoke feeling warm and relaxed, comfortable and peaceful. My normal desire to get up, showered, dressed and on the road as soon as possible was replaced with a strong urge to simply *remain*. To stay right there, in that place at that moment, with her. I intended to put off the drive back to Oxford for as long as possible in order to do just that.

Ideas of trying to make Zara breakfast in bed circled my mind for a second but swiftly vanished as she moved closer to me in her sleep. Casually, she reached across me and drew me close. Her eyes, with fading remnants of mascara dotting the corners, flickered open. She paused, smiled softly, and kissed my lips.

Marcellus looked on, his hot chocolate eyes calmly watching as we slipped into each other once again.

"What are we going to do, Wolf?" breathed Zara. She moved her leg behind mine and instantly I was inside her again, thanking all the gods that I didn't know how to make scrambled eggs.

"About what?" If last night had been vigorous and exciting, this morning was gentle and carefree. My whole world-view collapsed into this single feeling, sharing this one moment with this one woman. "About us? About Mar... Stardust? Or about Gabriel?"

"About it all, Wolf..." she half-smiled and took my lip between her teeth, kissing me gently. "But mostly about us. I hadn't thought of you and I in this way before. I like it." Her belly twitched beneath me for a moment and she threw her head back with a gasp. It was either an orgasm or a fit and, judging by my performance in preceding years, more likely the latter. I kissed her forehead.

"You okay," I whispered. She exhaled gently, and a smile began to form.

"Oh... more than okay, Wolf." She lay still, holding me inside her for a few beats, then her face became more serious.

"Would you like to try this? Would you like to try being proper lovers together?"

"What so you mean?" I asked, softly. She looked into my eyes, her skin glistening.

"I think you know what I mean. I think you feel it too."

By one of those damnable coincidences, just as she spoke my own body shook as I achieved release inside her. Waves of pleasure swept over me.

My first *Mills and Boon* moment.

I think fast sometimes, but I could feel anxiety from Zara as she waited for a response. I had to roll the dice. We'd only really met, but I knew I was feeling something more than childish lust or adolescent desire. I had to make a decision. I had to do it now.

"I think we can," I said. "I think I might be falling for you."

And then the music started.

From next to the bed, something was singing. A children's song, something that I remembered from my university days. A bizarre tune, all bells and whistles, plinking pianos, and a laughing baby. Moving into some sort of marching music... then vocals... '*over the hills and far away, tellytubbies come to play...*'

What the fuck? Zara, her expression changed, eyes wide, looked at me questioningly.

"What the hell is that?" I stared bemused, wondering what was in the muffin she shared with me last night. Then I understood. A phone ringtone. Not *my* phone... the other phone. Gabriel's phone. He had used the theme from *Tellytubbies* as a ringtone.

The twisted bastard.

I reached for my coat near the bed and pulled out the mobile. *Incoming call, unknown caller.* I pushed the receive button.

"What?" I was certainly much tougher when on the other end of a phone, far out of dismembering range.

"You having fun, Devenish?" said Gabriel. I sighed but didn't answer. "Where are you?" I didn't answer. "Vagina got your tongue, Devenish? Let me ask you again. Y'all having fun?"

"Yes, Mr Gabriel, I was having fun until you called. What's the story with the ringtone on this phone? *Tellytubbies?*"

"Psychological warfare, Devenish. Psychological warfare. Glad y'all havin' a good time. Where are you?"

"I'm in the hotel," I lied.

"Right. The pub hotel? The one that hasn't got you down as a guest?"

"I used a false name."

"You'll need a false leg if you keep talking shit to me, son. I know where you are and what you're doing. Fuck, but you're not very imaginative. Not content with having one kid you didn't know about, you're trying to have another with the same girl twenty years later. Jesus H Christ, boy, but you should be gelded." A pause and then a chuckle. "Hell, no reason for me to get all upset and gnarly about where you stick your Johnston, just as long as it's not within three feet of me, Devenish."

"That's kind of you. And where are you, Mr Gabriel?"

"I'm hovering three feet above you like a 250 pound sword of Damocles buddy."

"Fair enough." To my shame my eyes flicked to the ceiling of the cabin, but thankfully there was no Gabriel-shaped indentation in the wood.

"Tell me about yesterday. Did you speak to someone other than the poor bitch you've been ploughing away at all night? Think hard before you answer." Zara was sitting up now, listening intently to Gabriel's tinny voice.

"Only the bar staff," I lied. There was no answer, but I could hear him breathing. Thinking. Considering.

"You sure?" he asked, his voice calm but quiet.

"Yes, I'm sure."

"What about the girl? Did you tell her about us and what we told you?" I paused, trying to remember if I was allowed to tell her or not. I couldn't remember. "I told her a little. It explained how I knew about Martin." Zara raised her eyebrows slightly. There was a sigh from the other end of the line, then Gabriel spoke again.

"Doesn't matter, I guess. So long as she knows that you need to meet this kid. Say, it probably won't hurt for him to know that you're fucking his mom again. Like a family reunion, yeah? A family reunion in West Virginia, where they unchain cousin Zeb so he can join in too."

"What makes you so certain that Zara and I are together?"

"What else you doing with her at this time in the morning? Fixing her bilge pump?" he chuckled. "What did she say about you being the father?"

"She's not sure I am. She thinks someone else could be the father."

"Oh. God, really? Shit. I'm sorry, son. We must have made a mistake." Gabriel sounded genuinely remorseful.

"What?"

"Hey, I'm sorry Mr Devenish. Must have been our mistake. I'm sorry to have troubled you. Tell you what, why don't you just apologise to the nice lady, head on home, and forget all about it?"

"Really?" I asked, and for an instant I hoped he was serious.

"In a pig's ass. We've got the DNA. You tell her that, with the deepest regret and all of our sympathy, you are Martin Moore's father."

"Okay."

"I hope you are," whispered Zara, pulling closer to me.

"As I say, don't matter to me. Just be on that plane next week. And Devenish?"

"What?"

"You tell another soul about me or my colleague, and our dealings with you, the next thing you'll be kissing will be the soil at the bottom of a damp, shallow grave. We clear? Particularly not the people at Los Alamos. We're a strictly private organisation, just passing you a message and helping you get done what you need to do." He stopped.

"But surely they sent you to see me?"

"Listen boy, cause I think you have a problem with listening, and I'm real big on helping out people with learning difficulties. Don't mention us to anyone else unless I tell you to, Wolfie-boy. Period."

"What?" Click. The phone went dead. Zara looked at me, puzzled.

"Did you mean what you said?" she asked.

"About what?"

"About thinking you're falling for me?" I gathered my thoughts, wondering how a woman could remain so focused after her lover just got threatened by a nutcase.

"Yes," I said and, shockingly, I meant it. "I can see myself falling in love with you." In a moment her face brightened, and she held me close in an embrace, warm against the cooling sweat on my chest. I was surprised, given my mealy-mouthed, twisty-turny expression of love, with more caveats than an insurance document.

"I think so too, Wolf." Her eyes glistened with happiness. "Shall we give it a try?"

"Yes." I kissed her, conscious of my morning, beery breath. "I would like that."

"Now who was that wanker?" she said.

"I fear it may be wankers, Zara. With the soft 'z'. Plural." She kissed me gently on the lips.

"Well, I'm sure the wankers can wait another half hour before we work out what to do," she said, as she pulled me back onto the bed.

---oOo---

The brown Labrador careered into the lounge, skidding across the polished wooden floor as usual, before piling into the leather sofa.

"Max! Calm down!" The woman sat on the sofa, and reached down to ruffle the fur of the dog's head as it looked up at her, all floppy tongue and wide, coffee-coloured eyes. Although it was still early, the woman was dressed in a smart woollen skirt and a beige blouse, with a patterned scarf tied loosely around the neck. She was of slender build and in her early fifties, but carried her years with an elegance and fluidity that spoke of years of taking care of herself, outdoor walks, and otherwise soft living. The dog barked twice.

"What is it, Max? You silly thing!" Max flicked his gaze between his owner's eyes, and she couldn't help but smile at him. She'd read that dogs used this trick to detect the moods of their owners. Dogs and people had a long history together, longer even than that of her family.

Lady Barbara Ingrams could trace her family history until just after the Norman invasion, and for almost a millennium her ancestors had ridden the ebbs and flow of political fortune as bit players in the British aristocracy.

Then came the Great War.

Most of the males of the family had died in the trenches. If nobility had any traditional function, it was to lead the commoners into battle. In the past this had brought her family honour, favour and wealth, except for that unfortunate incident in the 1600s when a certain Mr Cromwell tried to burn their family home to the ground for picking the wrong side.

Of course success in battle was much easier when supported by the power of the crown, protected with the best plate armour money could buy, and surrounded by hundreds of unkempt peasants who could be relied upon to throw their unfortunate bodies into the paths of the various knights and lords determined to kill you.

Unfortunately this strategy didn't work so well with machine guns, and her family was decimated during the First World War, leaving only a handful of women, the elderly baron, and a sickly teenager.

The financial crises of the late twenties had an impact too, and suddenly the Ingrams could no longer afford to run their stately home or keep so many staff. Breaking the cardinal rule of the wealthy classes her grandfather, a sickly teenager no longer, had dipped into the capital to keep the family afloat. His shrewd investments seemed set to bring wealth and favour back to the family, allowing them to support the lifestyle they were accustomed to, while still setting aside a considerable inheritance for Barbara's father. Particularly important to this plan were their extensive textile interests in Czechoslovakia, which were already bringing in a good return and looked set to mature favourably in the future.

Hitler and Stalin both took turns at reducing these investments to worthless sheets of expensive paper, and the family capital dwindled rapidly. The final nail in their coffin came with an outbreak of woodworm in the Big House, followed swiftly by a fire in the servants' wing.

Left with no option but to sell the property to pay off creditors, the Ingrams, hereditary heirs to the barony of *Darcy de Knayth*, moved into a more conventional home, and started to work for a living.

They may have lost their lands, the family seat, their servants and a great deal of their prestige, but they could never part with their Labradors, and Max was one of a long line of faithful and pampered hounds.

A noble dog, currently chewing on an interesting bit of fur around his noble arsehole.

Task completed, he leapt to his feet and dashed into the hallway, crumpling the expensive Afghan rug before running into the kitchen and barking in earnest.

"Oh Max..." Lady Ingrams stood and slipped her feet into sensible leather loafers, before primly walking into the kitchen to see what all the fuss was about. At the far end of the dining area were two huge oak picture windows, on either side of the back door.

Outside the right window, pressing his cheek onto the glass, was a young man in a police uniform.

His sweater and shirt were pulled up, and he was rubbing his nipple against the window, eyes wide with pleasure as his tongue darted in and out of his mouth in delight.

Barbara screamed while the dog barked and wagged his tail at this great game.

The policeman didn't seem to notice either the barking or the scream, and carried on with his rubbing, his nipple red and angry against the cool of the glass.

Lady Ingrams, however, was made of stern stuff. After her brief loss of control, thirty generations of stiff upper lips and keeping the peasantry in their place kicked in. She took a deep breath, lifted the kitchen phone, and keyed in a number.

"Yes. I require the Police, thank you." She kept a wary eye on the figure on the patio. "Yes, that's correct. I'm dreadfully sorry to bother you, but one of your chaps seems to have rather lost his marbles, and is currently rubbing his chest against my picture window." There was a pause. "No officer. That wasn't a euphemism. I would be delighted if you could have someone drop by and collect him."

It would be three days before PC Ericsson was discharged from the psychiatric wing of Guildford hospital, and two weeks before his disciplinary review was completed and he was allowed to return to duty.

It would be six long months before he awoke with a start one morning after the strangest dream, one filled with visions of a smiling American and a country lane.

It was a story he chose to keep to himself.

---oOo---

Chapter sixteen

Laura Berne tapped the mouse, and the dead man appeared on-screen.

He was a striking-looking man, certainly, but not dissimilar to the many hundreds of other idealistic young men who had met their demise in the oil and blood-soaked sands of Iraq and Afghanistan in the last ten years. Just another statistic in a war that seemed endless. One thing, however, marked this man from the other ranks of the Glorious Dead.

They hadn't been buying drinks from village pubs in the English countryside just the evening before.

Andreas left the licence to the office that morning before returning to Loxwood, and it was the start of a puzzle indeed. This wasn't a bad thing necessarily, as Laura loved puzzles – she always had – and puzzle solving was, essentially, her job. Since quitting work as an IT manager and taking up employment with the no-longer-shadowy organisation called MI6, 'The Security Service', because even spies had mission statements and straplines in this media-conscious century, Laura had been charged with sifting through puzzles to find out which were important to solve, and which were merely anomalies in a complex world.

A dead American marine knocking back pints in the South Downs was certainly a puzzle, but she was not yet sure if it was a puzzle of importance or merely something very straightforward and innocuous. Sometimes people just wanted to be dead. There were many reasons for it, and a glance at Sergeant Gabriel's file showed several damned good reasons why he would prefer to be dead and start his life over again.

However, there were alarm bells ringing as she scrolled down the page. Firstly there was little or no detail about the event that supposedly led to this man's death in theatre. He was merely listed as 'KIA – enemy fire'. Normally there would be more information than that.

Secondly, it was *where* in England he had appeared. Faking your death so you can go travelling and start a new life was one thing. Faking your death so you can go travelling to places where MI6 were conducting covert background checks on individuals at the behest of their American colleagues was something different. Initially that smacked to Laura of CIA involvement, and that worried her.

The CIA regularly recruited talented individuals from many fields, including the military, to conduct some of their more shadowy operations around the globe. In most cases, particularly in this era of reasonably open communication between the western security services, recruitment to the Central Intelligence Agency would be noted on the file. There was no mention of this on Gabriel's file.

If he *had* been recruited, this meant that the Agency didn't want anyone to know about it, and that, invariably, meant that he was meant to do things both unsavoury and politically deniable. Almost always it meant that they were recruited to do very bad things to one or more 'persons of interest'.

As she clicked away, opening other parts of the document, she thought of her best friend Gillian, working in the old IT firm. About now, it being lunchtime on a Friday, Gillian would inevitably be clawing her way around Facebook, leaving notes for her friends and comments about this relationship or that picture, happy in the knowledge that her little computer was reaching across the internet and cheering her friends up.

Laura, however, was clicking through bland, uninformative, text and pictures about someone who, quite probably, was a government assassin.

She had arranged to meet Gillian at seven that evening in a local wine bar, a relic of the eighties which was considered cool again in a quaint, post-modern way, and she would definitely need more than one glass of wine tonight. Even the hint, even the slightest sniff of an off-reservation assassin roaming the countryside, meant that she had to go and speak to her boss.

And she hated speaking to her boss.

If her branch of the Service, intelligence processing, could be visualised as one of a set of ladders all tied together, then Laura would be on the middle rung of one of these ladders. Parkinson, her boss, stood at the top of them all like a skeletal puppet master. He answered to god above, the director of MI6, and to no-one else. One would expect Parkinson to be a shadowy, powerful figure, surrounded by intrigue and bathed in geo-politics. One would imagine that he drank the finest brandy from crystal glasses as he sat in a dusty gentlemen's club beside other shadowy figures, discussing the fate of countries and their citizens as they played gin rummy. Laura reckoned that she could cope with that image: Parkinson, the super-powerful intelligence magnate who could destroy lives with a signature or alter the borders of nations with a stroke of his pen.

She hated speaking to him because he was none of these things.

Parkinson could be best described as a cross between Nosferatu the vampire and an accountant for a drainage company.

He never drank alcohol. He was slender and tall, but not muscled in any way. When he grew his body he evidently decided that muscle would be a waste of the few nutrients he consumed, and instead forced each and every molecule of his being into the production of skin and bone.

He was essentially personality-less. Parkinson merely *was*. He never exhibited mood swings and never varied his weekly routine, including his eating habits. Monday was a roast beef sandwich with butter on plain bread. Tuesday was an egg sandwich. Wednesday was a miniscule salad roll. *Etc*. It was always the same. He had coffee at eleven precisely. Lunch at two. He left the office at eight pm. He was driven home by one of the junior agents, where he had dinner with his wife, read *the Telegraph* for an hour, and then painted his model soldiers for the rest of the evening. He was trying to recreate a scale model of the D-day invasion, focusing on 'Gold beach' where his great-uncle had died. If there was an emergency he would put the soldiers back in their glass case and use his secure communications to speak to the office and deal with the crisis. At eleven each night he retired to bed in his carefully ironed pyjamas, ready to emerge, once again, at precisely six am, like a determined spider with OCD.

Now Laura had to make an appointment and report to him. Which raised another issue to ruin her day.

Parkinson's diary and office was guarded not only by scary large men with weapons concealed in their jackets, but by Mrs Gordon, a shrieking harridan of a secretary, for whom Parkinson was a minor deity and all other human beings were scum before him. It was said that one of the reasons Parkinson would never make the top position in the Service was simply because no-one could imagine Prime Ministers and Secretaries of State getting past Mrs Gordon without her fiery glares reducing them to depressed shells of their former selves. Resigned, Laura dialled the extension.

"Mr Parkinson's office. Who's calling please?" warbled Mrs Gordon.

"Laura Berne, Mrs Gordon. I'm wondering if I can see Mr Parkinson this afternoon, please." Laura heard typing over the sigh.

"Are you wondering if you can see Mr Parkinson, or do you wish to make an appointment with him Ms Berne?"

"I'd like to make an appointment, please."

"What does it concern?"

"I think it might be eyes only, Mrs Gordon." Another sigh.

"You think it 'might be'. I for one am not impressed that the safety and security of this great country depends on what 'might be'." Sigh. "Mr Parkinson is very busy this afternoon. I can fit you in for five minutes on Monday."

"Sorry, but I think it might be more urgent than that. Can I see him this afternoon?"

"Again, you 'think'. Don't you know? Will a memo not suffice?"

"I'm afraid it's regarding unprocessed intelligence, and I need to discuss how to proceed." More typing, and a pause.

"So you haven't processed your information, and you wish for Mr Parkinson to do that for you? Mr Parkinson does not deal with raw intelligence, Ms Berne, as I'm sure you know. That is what you are paid to do."

"I understand that, Mrs Gordon, but I need to know the depth of processing he requires. I believe there may be a threat involved."

"I would suggest a memo would suffice rather than waste Mr Parkinson's valuable time. In the meantime I also suggest that you should process your information further to clarify the situation," said the secretary.

"Mrs Gordon, I'm sorry I can't go into more details, but I need Mr Parkinson's authority to process the information further. It involves a cousin agency, and I don't have clearance to dig any deeper." More typing. Another pause.

"Mr Parkinson is available from five thirty pm for five minutes. I will expect you here at five twenty-five pm. Do not be late, and bring all your information with you. Good day."

"Thank y..." Click. Printing off all the necessary background information, she looked at the picture of the dead marine, smiling as he emerged from her laser printer. "Thanks for that, Sergeant," she muttered to no-one in particular.

---oOo---

Chapter seventeen

"You've met someone!" Bill stood back against the bar, regarding me above his pint. "You old bounder!" It had taken him less than the time it took for the barman to pull me a glass of Churchill Pale for him to unravel my body language and come to his conclusion. "You absolute hound," he beamed, his cheeks bright as a guardsman's jacket. "Who's the lucky fellow?"

"I met *her* on Thursday, Bill, so it's much too early for you to be so excited." My smile betrayed me.

"But you like her, Master Wolf." He raised his glass. "Well, I must say I'm glad. I've been growing tired of watching you drift around Oxford like an unloved orphan who spilled the last of his gruel. I think it's high time somebody made an honest woman out of you, young man." Clink.

"Cheers, Bill." God, I'd been with Zara for only a few hours, barely worth the toast, but I *was* happy. "Bit of a surprise to me too."

"Indeed! Of course, when speaking to a writer of your calibre, I must ask you 'who, what, when, where, why, how?'" I wasn't sure how much about Zara I wanted to tell Bill. He was far too clever for his own good, and it would take a single slip to give away too much and leave the full story open for Bill's annoying criticism.

"Her name is Zara Moore, and we had few drinks and a meal in a delightful pub in the South Downs. When? Well, Thursday, but you knew that already. Where? See above. Why? I would have to say soft moonlight, romantic, canal-side surroundings, several pints of ale and three bottles of wine. How? Bill, I would prefer to keep that to myself."

"I trust you slept on the sofa, young man, and preserved this fine lady's dignity," asked Bill, pretending to frown.

"Yes, Bill, we slept on the sofa." *And in the bed. And on the towels in the bathroom.*

"Sounds fabulous, Master Wolf. I am, of course, delighted for you. Have you made plans to bring the beautiful Ms Moore to Oxford to meet yours truly?"

"Oh for God's sake, Bill. I've only met the woman." My pint was delicious and sneaking down my neck rapidly. I signalled to the barman to get us two more. "Should we cancel this evening and go find us an old-fashioned bible-believing preacher and a shotgun licence?"

"I fear such clergy are few and far between in our beloved Oxford, young Wolf. But I would like to meet this siren who has brought your youthful wanderings to an end."

"Okay. I'll ask her if she wants to visit when I'm back from America. Is that acceptable?" The pints arrived, and I paid the barman.

"Perfectly acceptable. Now we must complete our quaffing, lest we be late for the Master's sherry reception." We both attacked our fresh pints whilst chatting about love, life and the evening ahead.

As we left the pub and wandered along the street to the College entrance, I found myself hoping that it would work out with Zara. I hadn't been in a relationship for a long time and I missed having *someone* to care for. Moreover I missed having someone to care for me.

Zara was funny, attractive, and independent. She lived far enough away not to get annoying, and was possibly the mother of my child. Trying to make a relationship out of it was the right thing to do.

I almost sounded grown-up.

---oOo---

Chapter eighteen

"What can I do for you, Ms Berne?" Parkinson sat behind his oak desk, the blinds on the large window behind him shuttered against the afternoon sunshine. As always, Laura was shocked at his appearance. Gaunter than she remembered, he sat in a wide, high backed leather office chair, and his long frame was lost within it. His charcoal suit jacket hung loosely from his shoulders which were, at a glance, mere bumps on either side of his long, turkey neck. In front of him was a pad of yellow A4 paper, beside which a selection of identical pencils was neatly arranged. He took one and made a few marks on the top of a fresh page.

Parkinson documented everything. *Everything.* One of the more junior employees in Laura's team once joked over a glass of beer that he probably made notes during sex with his wife. Nobody laughed, though. It wasn't the kind of organisation where you laughed at the bosses.

And nobody wanted to imagine that stick insect of a man naked.

What amazed Laura most, though, was that he had *had* sex at all. But he was the father of four healthy children, all having grown up and left the crypt far behind, so it seemed that at some point Parkinson had inserted tab A into slot B. Rumour had it that they were all normal, balanced, fun-loving people. Two were in medicine, both surgeons and one working towards a consultancy. One was an entrepreneur, running a selection of successful leisure businesses and making considerable sums of money. The final, and youngest, daughter was an outdoor pursuits instructor in Cornwall. The word round the water cooler was that she was also something of a looker, and collected male conquests as her father collected pencils and cryptic meeting notes.

"Well?" Parkinson's mouth barely moved when he spoke, his voice echoing from somewhere behind his face like the death rattle of a ventriloquist's dummy.

"We have an operative doing background checks on a woman in the South Downs for our American cousins, sir. Andrew Miller, in fact." Parkinson scribbled away, and made the slightest incline of his head as he acknowledged Miller's name. "Yesterday evening he encountered this gentleman who was accompanied by a woman as yet unidentified." She passed some files to Parkinson, with the Gabriel file at the top. He deftly flicked through the document and she watched his eyes darting across the content, taking things in. Every few seconds he made another note. She noticed him add a large question mark after one of his notations.

"And?" He closed the files and regarded Laura again, his eyes flickering to the clock on the wall behind her. Perhaps he was as much in fear of Mrs Gordon as the rest of the department, and he didn't want to overrun his allotted time.

"Well, he's dead, sir, as you can see from his file."

Parkinson looked at her for a beat, before quickly scratching a few notes on his pad and motioning for her to continue.

"This leads me to believe that he is involved in something for the Company, but that it is something they are not telling us about. I thought you would want to know if the Americans had an agent roaming the countryside which they had neglected to tell us about."

"Thank you. Your judgement is sound and, of course, I do like to know such things. I shall make some calls to my opposite number and see if they have any information to offer. In my experience files such as these usually indicate that the subject is involved in, shall we say, unpleasant work. I'm afraid, however, that this information is likely to end up being processed at a higher clearance level. I'm sure you understand."

"Yes, sir. Would you like me to ask Miller to pursue the matter further?"

"Not immediately. I must make my calls first," said Parkinson, scratching another sentence onto his pad. The lead broke as he wrote. He stared at it for a moment as though it had committed an act of treason against him, before discarding it and picking up a fresh pencil.

"What should I tell him to do? He was after all, the one who identified this man and obtained his fingerprint for us." Parkinson flicked through the file once again, lingering for a moment on the picture of Gabriel.

"I should tell him to keep well away from this man and his partner, Ms Berne. Whatever his appearance here means, I am sure that he is most ably equipped to deal with any obstructions placed in his way. I advise you to tell Miller to complete his own clearance task, make his report to us, and return home. However, if he has further contact he should keep you appraised. And, of course, you will keep me fully briefed of any developments."

"Absolutely, sir. Thank you for your time." Laura stood to leave.

"Hold." This was a peculiarity of Parkinson. It was a strange word that he enjoyed using. He never asked people to 'wait a moment'. People had to 'Hold' for him.

"Yes, sir?"

"Who is this Devenish individual?" Parkinson pointed to one of the bottom files. "Do you believe him to be involved in this? I see that Miller has requested a full background on him."

"I have run a preliminary check on him, sir, but he appears to be just a regular civilian. Miller was concerned, though, that he has made contact largely out of the blue with the subject," she looked at her own notes. "Ms Zara Moore, thirty-nine years old, unmarried with one son who lives and works in America. She has few friends, or at least few who visit her on a regular basis. Much of her life and work is carried out online, and Miller has been looking into these records as a matter of course, but has found nothing of a sinister nature so far. However, Mr Wolf Devenish, born nineteen seventy-two, listed as a freelance journalist and writer, did not appear on any of the earlier lists of known associates."

"What does he write? Anything I may have read?" Parkinson gestured to the groaning bookshelf lining the wall of his office. He was a keen reader, well-versed in both modern and classical literature, and he was an accomplished Latin and Greek scholar, having translated several pieces during his university days. He may have had the personality of an empty Tesco bag, but nobody doubted his intelligence.

"He seems to make his living through regular news articles in local and national papers, and from an inheritance left to him by his parents who died of cancer some time ago, the mother two years after the father." Parkinson shook his head slightly as though sympathetic to the tragedy. "As a writer, he's largely unpublished, sir. He has had a few articles in small journals, but they're on unconnected subjects," she flicked down her notes, "one piece on forgotten cinema buildings in the south-east of England, and a small article about," she checked again, reading from her page, "the role of the alpaca as a fox deterrent in chicken small-holdings." She smiled nervously.

"All laudable works, I imagine," said Parkinson. "However what are your theories about him appearing for drinks with our subject right in the middle of an investigation?" Laura took a deep breath.

"Miller thinks, with fairly high confidence, that he merely is an old friend of Ms Moore, and that he was simply catching up with her after many years of no contact."

"But..."

"Miller also reports that the man seemed to be hiding something. Now this could be anything. Miller was using his police cover when he spoke with Devenish and, as you imagine, many people are nervous and withdrawn when talking with the police. As you see in the notes, Devenish has had occasional run-ins with the law in the past. Perhaps he was just nervous." Parkinson stared at her for a moment, then sighed.

"I'm afraid you're not thinking clearly, Ms Berne. You are putting too much faith in Mr Miller's hunch. I am sure that he has a very accomplished record of being right about gut reactions, but we deal in facts, not hunches." He paused, making a few more notes. "I believe both you and Mr Miller have heard hooves and are imagining zebras in this instance."

"I see, sir."

"Indeed. Please have Mr Miller finish his checks on Ms Moore and return his report. At the same time, run a more thorough check on Mr Devenish, just to be sure there are no connections or patterns linking him with the American. Finally, I shall pursue my own channels to see if we can unravel what Mr Gabriel is doing in the home counties."

"Yes sir."

"Of course, you will report directly to me should any further information connecting Moore or Devenish to this mysterious American. In fact, pass anything you see regarding Mr Gabriel directly to me. We will call this investigation 'Operation Onslow', and you will refer to that when making appointments with Mrs Gordon. I am aware she jealously protects my time."

"Of course, sir." Laura rose to leave, as Parkinson scribbled a few more sentences on his pad.

"Hold." Laura sat back down.

"Sir?"

"This background check we are doing on Ms Moore. What it is regarding?" Laura flicked through her notes once again.

"It is a deep background check on her son, sir. One Mr Martin Moore. original name Mr Stardust Moore..."

"Sorry. Could you repeat that?"

"He was registered for birth under the name 'Stardust Moore', sir." Parkinson made a note, but his face remained impassive.

"Carry on."

"Mr Moore is working with the Americans, in a capacity not fully known but, given the background check request, I would guess that it is a defence project. He is an accomplished and gifted young physicist."

"So he, or his work, is of sufficient value to the Americans to warrant an extensive background check?"

"Yes sir. Although, in fairness, our cousins are very paranoid at the moment." Laura risked levity. "When they buy a burger these days they run background checks on the cow the meat came from." She smiled. Parkinson didn't.

"There *are* some coincidences here, Ms Berne. I shall make some enquiries at my level, but I would like you to find out what you can about Mr Moore junior. In particular what work he is involved in. You may have to develop alternative channels here, as our American friends may not be forthcoming."

"I will sir. However, I don't see why they would be reluctant to cooperate with us. Shared intelligence, and all that."

"Ms Berne. You have been with us for several years, now. Tell me, do you know your Anglo-American history? In particular, from 1939 onwards?"

"Not really, sir, other than our cooperation and dependence on them during the Second World War."

"Yes. That. Allow me to enlighten you about that particular episode, Ms Berne. During the Second World War, prior to the Americans becoming actively involved following the attack on Pearl Harbour, we British depended on our American cousins for supplies, food, and weaponry to fight our enemy. This much is true. However, the Americans did not do this for free. In return for every tank, every rifle, and every bullet they sent us, they wanted something in return. Radar technology. Our prototype jet engines. Countless other pieces of British ingenuity were the price we paid for our corned beef, our spam and our Sherman tanks."

"I read that, sir. However, I understand that as our cooperation grew, we became more as friends than partners..."

"Ms Berne. Believe me. Our American cousins think primarily of themselves. It is their way. It is their policy. It is their lifestyle. This is why they had nuclear weapons at the end of World War Two, and we had not. We were useful to them as a foothold in Europe, so they built a 'special relationship' with us, but it was merely to benefit them in their struggle with the Soviets. As time goes on our use lessens. If Mr Moore is working on something novel for the American military, the only thing we shall learn about it is when he retires and writes his memoirs. If he is allowed to retire."

"I understand, sir." The buzzer on Parkinson's phone softly hummed.

"Our time is at an end this afternoon, Ms Berne. Operation Onslow will remain strictly between you and me. Report directly to me about your findings, and I want your staff working as independent cells on discrete parts of the investigation. You and I will be the only ones assembling the overall intelligence. This is a mysterious story, and I would like to discover the implications of it for Her Majesty's Government before acting further on it. You have done well to highlight the matter."

"Thank you, sir." Laura gathered her things.

"Good day, Ms Berne."

With that the door opened and the dragon-secretary ushered Laura out, as an anxious parent shoos the bad children away from their own child before any nasty habits can spread.

---oOo---

Chapter nineteen

"Another brandy, dear boy?" After five wonderful courses, several glasses of wine, sherry and port, and the third or fourth brandy, Bill's cheeks were, by now, practically luminous, clashing terribly with his choice of dark purple velvet dinner jacket.

"A small one only, please Bill. I really ought to, well, you know."

"Naturally, Master Wolf, but it is true that good brandy lubricates the tongue and the brain." He grasped the ancient, crystal decanter, and poured me several fingers of the amber spirit.

"It's not *my* tongue that needs lubricated, Bill." He beamed and splashed a healthy dose in his own glass. "Are you having a good time?" I asked.

"I am having a delightful time, as always my friend. One of the joys of being a historian is developing a deep understanding of the brevity of life and the potential for misery within it. The lesson one learns from such salient contemplation is that one must always, *always*, enjoy the company of Bacchus, Pan and, as you know only too well from your recent antics, dance the dark dance with Venus at each and every opportunity." He toasted the room.

"And what does your doctor think of this philosophy?" I asked, already knowing the answer. Bill despised his doctor with a passion almost as strong as his doctor's trepidation of suggesting lifestyle changes to Bill.

"Bah, the miserable old charlatan of course disagrees with many of my lifestyle choices. It appears to me that medical professionals often confuse prolonging life with merely prolonging a heartbeat. Surviving to a ripe old age on a regime of early nights, exercise and moderation does not, for me, equate with having *lived*." He swirled the brandy in his glass and took a delicate sip. "Enough, Master Wolf. I see that the scintillating Ms Lowry is currently available. It is time, my young friend, to start poking your nose where it is most definitely not wanted.

Paul Cartmell. *Gabriel*

Come." He topped his glass up once again, poured a modest fresh one, and carried both across the hall to where Rebecca Lowry was studying a painting hanging on the panelled walls.

After a brief and not altogether comfortable bout of introductions and some small talk regarding the choice of menu this evening, Bill feigned spotting a colleague down the hall.

"My apologies, my dears, but I simply have to speak with the esteemed Watson before he scuttles back off to his dusty old books. I shall leave you, Rebecca, in the charming and chivalrous hands of young Master Wolf." With that he was off, careering across the hall in a cloud of purple velvet and wild fair hair.

There was a short silence as we watched Bill catch Professor Watson before he could gather his jacket from his seat.

"What a wonderful character Doctor Jeremies is. Oxford would be a dreary place without such, er, eccentric people." Lowry gave me what she imagined was a coquettish, girly smile, but looked more like a bulldog caught on a fishhook. "Of course the modern world is catching up, with its demand for results, endless rounds of cost-efficiencies, and constant competition with other universities, and I fear the era of the eccentric academics is coming to a close." She shook her head sadly, her spiky features slicing through the air like fleshy, blunt scythes.

"Oh I don't know about that, Ms Lowry..." I countered.

"Please, call me Rebecca." Perhaps it was the brandy, but she didn't seem to mind talking with me tonight. Our previous meetings had been cursory and, to be frank, borderline rude on her part.

Perhaps she had developed a little crush on me. My spine chilled at the thought.

"Rebecca... Where was I?" I asked.

"You didn't know about something," she said.

"Yes. I don't know about the world no longer needing eccentric academics. What would be left? Efficient, consistent ranks of lecturers and faculty heads, lacking in imagination and focused on the bottom line." *People like you.*

- 120 -

"Oh, I disagree, Mr Devenish. Efficiency and consistency are the hallmarks of a great university. It is on these criteria that reputations are made. They are the standards which raise the name of an institution across the world." She sipped her brandy, barely wetting her lips. She likely absorbed liquid through her skin, like an amphibian in a Laura Ashley dress.

"But what of brilliance, genius and inspiration? Aren't these the things that separate great universities from the rest?" I'd been in the conversation for less than a minute, and she was already annoying me.

"Of course these things are to be valued," she laughed shortly. "But they are fickle and unreliable. Sometimes our top staff and students will have moments of brilliance, or flashes of inspiration, but they cannot be predicted. They are impossible to plan for. As such, they have little monetary value to the university or to our sponsors." She pursed her lips and shook her head.

"That strikes me as quite a cynical viewpoint, and I think the university would be poorer without eccentrics like Bill. He's a wonderful academic." *And he's my friend, bitch.*

"In what sense poorer, Mr Devenish? If you mean in terms of background colour, you may have a point. But we will certainly not be poorer financially, and background colour does not pay the bills." I raised my glass, determined to get to business and away from this depressing woman.

"Well, for the meantime, here's to the eccentrics. Long may they freak out the rest of us." She smiled and we touched glasses. I savoured the brandy for a moment before continuing.

"I was hoping to see Sir Michael here this evening. I'm working on an article about the declining popularity of history in the university, and I thought he might be able to give me his perspective on the story." Her eyes flickered a little between mine when I mentioned his name, but her smile remained fixed. She kept my gaze for a moment before answering.

"I'm afraid he won't be along this evening, Mr Devenish."

"Oh, that's a shame. I always find people are more relaxed after a few brandies and a nice meal. Perhaps I'll make an appointment and visit him next week." She continued to look at me, thoughts darting behind her eyes. Assessing. Weighing up my words. Calculating her response. Bill was right, there was something going on here.

"Well, I imagine you'll find out soon enough, but Sir Michael has left the College I'm afraid. I'm sure his replacement would be happy to talk with you once he or she is appointed." I feigned surprise. I was good at feigning surprise, largely because I was usually surprised by everything around me.

"Really? That was very sudden. I hope he's not unwell." Again she paused, searching my expression for guile. Suddenly she reached a decision, and a hint of delight appeared in her eyes. I knew that I'd sneaked in under her radar. She was going to try and spread her rumour to me.

I had her.

"No, he's well I understand. He just decided that he, hmm. Well, he decided that it was time to move on." There was the slightest hesitation in what she said, just enough to add a seasoning of scandal to her words.

"Oh, that's a shame. Bill tells me he was a lovely man." I decided to throw her a hook and see if she bit down on it. "Very popular with the students," I said, and her eyes lit up.

Something which amazes me about narcissistic, borderline sociopathic people, is how easy it is to fool them. They are so convinced of their superiority to everyone else that it is shockingly willing to believe that their attempts to manipulate people have been successful. It's a huge chink in their armour, but only useful when one finally sees them for what they are.

Sadly they are too often successful in their games, particularly within organisations and the workplace. Their self-absorption is seen as focus; their occasional callous treatment of co-workers is seen as strong management, their narcissistic characteristics are confused with ambition, and they stomp their way through the broken corpses of the competition and into positions of power.

They disgust me. The office-sociopath's usual refrain of 'it's business, not personal' doesn't excuse the shattered dreams and personalities they leave in their wake. Given a different role of life's dice, some sharp blades, and a subscription to *Cross Stitch Monthly*, they would be making coats from human skin in a basement somewhere, laughing as they licked the condensation off the walls. It's pure chance that they end up in management, where they merely psychologically flay their victims instead.

"Oh yes, he was *very* popular with the students." She inclined her head slightly, inviting me to join her conspiracy. "Some might say friendly, almost. At least in some cases." She waited for me to take her bait, but I wasn't in the mood.

"Why did he resign, Rebecca? Do you know?" She seemed disappointed and suddenly less interested in the conversation. Lowry would have little patience for those who wouldn't let her little drama play out according to the script.

People like me.

"Hmmm. I must be careful, as you are a journalist," she said, starting to spin her web. "I shall simply tell you what I heard. Sir Michael decided that moving on would be best for the College and best for his students." She strummed another thread to try and trap me in the nasty, sticky threads of scandal she was weaving. "One student in particular." She nodded her head in that horrible way which patronising people do when pretending to be sad about something they secretly delight in.

"Are you saying he was involved with a student?" I asked.

"I'm merely saying what I heard, Mr Devenish. I am deeply sorry for Sir Michael. Sorry for what he is going through. But I think he has done the right thing."

"Who was the student?" She stopped in mid-nod and grinned.

"Why, it would be completely inappropriate for me to comment on that. Student confidentiality."

"They're adults, Rebecca. If they make allegations against your staff, then they stand in the light of slander and libel laws. And they have no right to confidentiality." She adjusted her stance slightly. My God, she was squaring up to me. Freaky lady.

"Did I say that a student had made a complaint, Mr Devenish? I believe I..."

"Please, call me Wolf," I said, and she stumbled mid-sentence. "You were saying?"

"I believe I said nothing about a student making a complaint."

"So who's behind these rumours? Where did they start?" There was the slightest reddish tinge creeping up her neck. I hoped it was the precursor of an embolism, but it seemed, disappointingly, merely to be anger. I was pissing her off.

What a fantastic evening.

"You're a journalist, Mr Devenish, you know..."

"Please. Wolf," I said, breaking her stride once again. Being interrupted must feel like having a hot needle in the eye to someone like Lowry.

"Wolf. You know how these things spread." She smiled, but it was a forced smile. She was going to run off in minutes. Hopefully off a cliff.

"That's true, actually. Rebecca. I hear a lot of rumours when working on stories. And do you know what the strange thing is about rumours?" She shrugged.

"They always start with someone deciding to spread a rumour. They tell someone, who tells someone, who tells someone else. But they always start with a single person deciding to whisper something about another person." I paused. Stared at her. She returned my gaze, calmly, although with a flintiness and coolness in her eyes.

"What are you suggesting, Mr Devenish?" she asked, coldly. I think I had just been erased from the Christmas card list.

"I'm suggesting nothing, Rebecca. I'm asking who passed this rumour on to you."

"I'm not at liberty to say." Her lips were tight as she spoke.

"Did you start the rumour?" The red tide edged higher, reaching her cheeks.

"Why on earth would I start a rumour about Sir Michael? Her voice was level, but she was obviously annoyed.

"I think I'll try and find out why, if that's okay with you, Ms Lowry." Her face fell into what must be her default pose. Pale lips, slightly turned down, but rigid-tight with tension. Eyes darting to and fro, with sharp little wrinkles beneath them and prickly flashes of rage glinting against her flecked irises. Her voice was clipped as she answered.

"You do what you think you have to, Mr Devenish." She stood back slightly, physically indicating that she had delivered the last word.

Had she my arse.

"I think you're trying to get me to spread your story, and I won't play that game. Particularly not when it involves some indistinct rumours of undisclosed indiscretions between a well-loved and respected member of faculty and unknown others. That's not a story, Rebecca. That's a badly written episode of *Eastenders*." She silently fumed while forcing a smile across her maw.

"Well, it's a shame, Wolf. I thought that you would enjoy a good story." She maintained her smile, but her features were rigid with anger.

"You were offering me scandal, Rebecca. You were offering me unsubstantiated slurs against one of your colleagues."

"Former colleague." I could hear her teeth grind together. Or perhaps her fangs. Whatever it was that the bitch had.

"Do you have a card, Rebecca, so I could catch up again should I decide to pursue this tale further?" I held my hand out with a smile.

"Yes, here." She delved into her purse and produced a card. Good, heavy stock, with the University of Oxford logo prominently displayed. "My secretary and PA's details are on the card, and you can make an appointment with either should you wish to talk with me." She looked over my shoulder, spotting a group of people chatting on the other side of the room. Raising her hand to catch their attention, one of them half-heartedly waved back while his companions glared at him. "My apologies, Mr Devenish, but there's someone I simply must see."

"No problem. Have a good evening, and I'll be in touch." She paused for a moment, as though to say something else, then nodded her head and walked off.

I watched her insert herself into the cluster of unfortunates, all smiles and arm-touching, and I checked the details on her card more closely. The PA was a bloke called Terence Summers MA(Oxon), and the secretary was called Emma Jones. After the States, I think a little chat with Mr Summers MA and Ms Jones would be in order. While it was likely that they knew what connected Lowry to Sir Michael, it was even more likely that they knew not to tell a passing journalist what that was. Of course, if their version of events seemed to place their employer in some potential trouble, they'd be rushing over themselves to tell me what really happened...

Particularly if I lied about what Lowry had told me.

---oOo---

Gabriel was having a quiet evening, relaxing outside the little Inn he was staying at. He liked pubs with rooms, as they were usually lax about taking information from guests, and therefore quite handy for staying under the radar. British pubs also reminded him of his days in Hereford, with their heavy, warm beer, and long evenings with Rachael. They were happy days, on secondment to the UK's Special Air Service.

He sipped at his ruby-red ale, thinking about the past and trying not to catch the eye of the two pretty girls sitting at the table near the car park. He wasn't that interested in sex these days. Try as he might he always found emotions bubbling to the surface when he made love. It made him feel vulnerable and less able to do the things he had to do.

Things like the phone call he had to make.

He took the throwaway pay-as-you-go phone from his pocket and dialled the number from memory. It was answered almost immediately.

"Yes." A man's voice, flat and neutral.

"We should be able to meet in five days, midnight, at the agreed location," said Gabriel.

"Good. And you will bring a gift with you?"

"Yeah, sure. A new toy for you to play with."

"Excellent. I see that the money paid to you was money well spent, Mr Gabriel." The voice remained steady, although Gabriel picked up an overtone of excitement in it. The response to good news.

"You wouldn't have contacted me otherwise."

"Of course. My superiors will be most pleased."

"Good. Shall I be meeting with them too?" asked Gabriel, lightly.

"Perhaps. I will see you next week, *inshallah*."

"No problem." He finished the call and opened the back of the phone, removing the SIM and the battery, before breaking the little circuit board between his finger and thumb and tossing it onto the grass, stepping it into the ground with his shoe.

Inshallah my ass, thought Gabriel. 'If God wills it.' Gabriel was fairly convinced that there was no God of any shade or description, and not because of some trite notion about the things he'd seen during his life. It just made no logical sense, and he had yet to see a single scrap of evidence to suggest that the various gods, religions and sects that people kept inventing were anything other than just that: inventions made up by people to try and explain things they couldn't understand.

Besides, if there was a God or Allah or whatever, floating out there in the ether, the last person on the planet that It would associate with would be Abdul-Khaliq Hassan. Well, Gabriel's dealings with the Saudi scumbag would soon be at an end.

He smiled as he took another sip of the beer, his mood lightening. Everything was going to plan, and he figured he could enjoy a little downtime before the next phase, perhaps even take a little emotional hit along the way. He stood and brought his pint across to the table next to the car park, smiling broadly as the girls watched him approach.

"My name is Gabriel. You mind if I join you?"

They both smiled in return.

---oOo---

Chapter twenty

Arnold Schwarzenegger stared at me down the corridor. He sat there, ten feet tall, with his creased tan, white teeth, beautiful partner and two glasses of wine on the table. The slogan "California - when can you start?" straddled the bottom of the poster.

I wondered if they had these posters in Tijuana.

The International departure terminal was hectic, as it always seemed to be. I don't recall ever seeing Heathrow quiet. I used to find it interesting to see so many people from so many different parts of the world, each with their unique clothing, looks and language as they navigated their way to the right gate, right coffee shop, or the right spot to pickpocket fellow travellers.

Luckily, Gabriel seemed to have thought of everything, although I imagined that it was Nadir who had made my flight arrangements. With an online check-in for my flight to Albuquerque, I was already in possession of a shiny boarding pass, and found myself with a few hours to kill until I had to make my way through security and into the airside part of the terminal. If Gabriel had made the arrangements I'm sure I would have been buying my own ticket – probably using pennies in bags – and there would have been a number of amusing errors on my visa just to give the security staff the opportunity to add my colon to their 'interesting things I stuck my fist in today' list.

I sat stirring my coffee and trying to outstare the chicken baguette I had bought, which seemed to be largely stuffed with more baguette. I had received a number of texts from Zara already today and, provided I was reading the right tone into them, we seemed to be getting on great so far. There were lots of 'x's at the end of each text, which could only be a good thing, but she may equally have been censoring her rants of piratical swearing against me.

I'd been replying with much the same, although I thought her latest 'miss you already' was going a little too far. A few days before we wouldn't have recognised each other had we ended up nailed together in a botched crucifixion.

But I did miss her. It was another thought to work out at a later date.

Tinky winky, la la... Gabriel's phone rang.

"What?" I demanded, feeling buoyed and confident after my time with Zara and my success annoying Lowry the previous evening.

"Just checking that you got to the airport safely, Mr Devenish." It was Nadir, her voice calm and smooth.

"Oh... hi. How are you?" It disgusted me how easily I become pleasant and endearing when talking to a pretty woman.

"I'm fine, Mr Devenish. Thank you for asking," she said. "I see you have checked in successfully. Please be sure to go through security soon, though, as one can never tell how long it takes with intercontinental flights. Particularly in the current climate."

"Longer, wetter summers?"

"Terrorism, Mr Devenish."

"I know. I'm just grabbing a bite to eat then I'll go through."

"Good. It's not likely that we'll be in touch much after you meet with Mr Moore, but we'll be keeping track on how things go."

"So what happens then? After I meet with Martin?" Nadir paused for a beat.

"That's it, Mr Devenish. You've done what we asked of you. Mr Moore will, no doubt, have his curiosity assuaged, and you can get on with your life. It's largely up to you, Mr Moore and, of course, Ms Moore if you wish to remain part of each other's world. The important thing is that you have done what we asked you to, and that Mr Moore has achieved his aim of meeting with his natural father." She paused again. "This is, er, unusual work for Mr Gabriel and me, as I'm sure that you understand. It's not our usual kind of project. We are not family counsellors, Mr Devenish. On this occasion we are merely messengers. However, keeping Mr Moore happy is our client's number one priority."

"I understand. But it isn't the kind of work I'd associate with secret agents. Not very James Bond, really." I noticed a small child sitting a few seats away eating yoghurt, now staring at me in awe as he eavesdropped on my conversation.

"We're not secret agents, Mr Devenish, but if it makes this easier to understand then please, by all means, think of us as such. We are occasionally asked to solve problems that would be difficult, or awkward, to solve without our help. Your case is fairly unusual. Not what we normally do. I would advise that you remember that should you wish to renege on our arrangement." I wouldn't forget it. Gabriel's image was emblazoned in my mind, his combination of intelligence, power and violence, all bubbling beneath a thin crust of control.

"Do you enjoy your work, Nadir?" I asked, expected her to hang up. I heard her sigh quietly.

"Very few people enjoy their work completely, Mr Devenish. Sadly, this is one of the few job opportunities left for me to do. It's just work."

"Hurting people is work? Killing people is work?" The child was looking at me in awe. I needed to lower my voice.

"We're not killing you, Mr Devenish. In fact a lot of what we do doesn't involve violence. We find things, discover information, move items around from place to place. Every day is different. And when we are asked to eliminate people from a situation, the people we remove are very bad people and it is very important that they are removed. For the benefit of others." Another sigh. "I know you will never understand what I mean, because you live in a different world. You think that there is an order and a structure to your life. You believe that there are bright people at the top of society who keep things flowing. People in control of all the variables which impact your life. Sometimes their influence is more positive than other times. We have years of relative peace and prosperity, and you have money in your pocket and a smile on your face. Other times you have less money and life is a bit more frightening. But in general you think that economies, countries, factions, families and people merely continue from year to year. Some years good. Some years bad. It's not like that, Mr Devenish."

"So tell me how it is?" Nadir seemed keen to talk, as though there was something on her mind.

"Take the blinkers off your eyes and look around, Wolf" she used my name. Such a sexy voice as well. Suddenly an image of Nadir and I embracing, me pulling her blouse off to reveal perfect breasts and a hidden nine millimetre pistol flashed across my mind. Instantly the thought of Zara and me together just two days before deflated the image in a pinprick of guilt. "How the real world works is all around you. Watch some news. Read a book."

"I want you to tell me," I said.

"Alright. The world is grey, Mr Devenish. It is grey because it is perched on the edge of chaos. There is no black and white, just a mixture of colours, passions, drives and ambitions... all mixed together as a child will mix vibrant paints and produce only grey sludge. People like me. People like Gabriel. We manage this balance, never allowing things to become too black nor, for that matter, too white."

"You sound like it's a religious thing."

"Definitely not religious, Mr Devenish. It's reality. Heaven and hell, they're right here, and you're living in them. The trick is to walk a path between the two. There's no happiness without experiencing sadness too. No joy without sorrow. No good without having tasted evil." She sounded like a violent version of Zara.

"And you. You kill people. Does that make you evil?" I spoke more quietly, but the child's mouth gaped open, his yoghurt now dripping on the floor as he held the tub on its side, intently focused on my words.

"No. It makes me sad. But it is necessary." She paused. "Let me tell you a story, Mr Devenish. About six months ago there was a gas explosion in a flat near Hamburg, Germany. When the emergency services arrived they found one man, a Mr Abdur Rahman, dead at the scene."

"And?" I asked.

"Abdur Rahman, Mr Devenish, was in the middle of planning a terrorist attack on several major European cities. It was, perhaps, fortunate for many people that he met with an accident before he could finish his plans and send his co-conspirators on their way to complete the attack." She paused. "It would interest you to know that Mr Gabriel was in Hamburg the evening before the explosion."

"Gabriel killed this guy?"

"Oh no. Of course not. That would be crass. It seems, however, that Mr Gabriel is not a very good gas engineer." She chuckled, although it sounded empty.

"If people knew this guy was a terrorist, why didn't they simply arrest him? There are laws, you know."

"There are, of course, but laws require proof. The burden of evidence to arrest someone and know that you can convict them is often too much to obtain in these cases. Additionally, we knew about Mr Rahman's activities, but no-one could identify the activists he was communicating with. All the security services knew was that he was up to something, that this *something* was imminent, and that his role was to make the plans, arrange the funding, and give the go ahead. But there was little evidence to that effect. Therefore another option was sought."

"Killing him." The child dropped his yoghurt with a splat on the tiles.

"Yes. Removing him from the equation. With Rahman gone the activists would be unable to complete their mission and would dissipate into the population until some other radical got their hands on them."

"Why are you telling me this?"

"I'm explaining to you, Mr Devenish, why we do what we do. It was estimated afterwards that the attack he was planning was going to involve at least three explosions in three separate European cities, all planned to happen simultaneously in tourist areas, which would cause the greatest loss of life to the most nationalities. Our gas explosion probably saved around one hundred lives. Maybe more."

"And arresting him wouldn't have stopped it?"

"That is doubtful. He would have been prepared for arrest and left some method of carrying out his orders even while in custody. Probably through a lawyer. However, once dead, that became impossible unless he also employed a good medium. The world is not black and white, Mr Devenish. It might be a million shades of colour, but it's never black and white."

"Don't you wish you were part of the world I live in, Nadir?" She paused before answering.

"Your world? Your make-believe, happily-ever-after world? You cannot understand how impossible it would be for me to return to my old life or, for that matter, what my current life is like."

"Of course I can't. No-one can know another person's life." I'd touched a nerve. "I'm only suggesting that you can surely back down from that line of work and give yourself some peace doing something more, er, constructive." She laughed.

"Are you a career advisor now, Mr Devenish? So what would you suggest the next step on the career ladder is for a *secret agent,* or whatever it is you think I am?" She continued to chuckle on the other end of the line.

"Something where you can be who you really are, perhaps. Something where you find some happiness." There was a pause. .

"You're good, Wolf. A pain in the ass, but good." She almost giggled. "Tell you what, you get to the States on time, see Mr Moore, answer his questions and get his mind back on the game, and I'll be a happy girl. Hell, I'll even bake some cookies. But I'll leave you with this..." There was another pause. A long one, but I sensed she was still on the line.

"I do what I have to do. Sometimes I get it wrong, but that's part of the game. But I admit it, there is a price I pay for what I do. You can only do what I do by shutting off feelings. Boxing them away, and never looking too closely at them. Emotions are too painful. Too hard to handle." Her tone was suddenly serious. "You ask me to leave this work and do something that makes me happy? I'll tell you what, Mr Devenish, what I would love to do... crave to do... is to simply feel something, anything, once more, just as other people do. To experience emotion, surprise, happiness and joy again, without the fear of them being corrupted by my work..."

"So quit. Find somewhere peaceful and happy. Meet someone. Get drunk. Laugh. Fuck. Why can't you rejoin normal life?" Nadir laughed again. Not a bitter laugh this time, but one with genuine mirth.

"And be like you people? Wandering your way through life while powers you don't even know exist control your every move and influence your every desire? I might not be happy, Mr Devenish, but at least I'm not blind. At least I know what life is actually like, and I have the power to control and change it. Enjoy your flight, Mr Devenish, and good luck with Mr Moore. I hope he doesn't punch you in the head. Goodbye."

And she was gone.

I left my empty cup and half-eaten baguette on the table, slipped the mobile into my jacket, and picked up my bag. The small child watched me intently, unaware of the yoghurt trickling down his jeans. It was time to enter the shoeless and beltless world of airport security check in. After talking with Nadir I found myself looking around at the cameras, both the subtle ones and the more obvious, the guards, the armed police, the suit-wearing customs and Special Branch staff, the posters splattered everywhere, and the rows of people emptying bags, raising their arms, and putting their shoes on trays. I thought about what Nadir had said. What if all of this is just the public face of shadowy cogs and terrible wheels, spinning beneath the surface of our world, driving our destinies along in some dreadful, heartless game where the only rule we understood was that we would ultimately lose?

And I wondered if I'd somehow become caught in one of those cogs.

Chapter twenty-one

Rebecca Lowry was worried.

Her PA had called her earlier that evening, wondering why a journalist wanted to speak with him and not her boss. From Lowry's point of view Devenish was certainly not playing the game the way she'd expected. Why wouldn't the little bugger just do what any other self-respecting gutter hack would do and deal the dirt on that bloody nuisance Rodney once and for all, ruining his reputation and getting him out of her life?

But, no. Devenish had to go fishing, and of all the places he decided to cast his hook he plopped it straight into her particular pond.

When her secretary called to tell her that Devenish had contacted her as well she began to get properly worried.

The little bastard. And she was fairly certain that that irritating, fat waste of space Bill Jeffries was involved somehow too. Like an old queen in a bathhouse, all he did day in and day out was gossip. But he was smart, too smart for his own good, and she desperately wanted to know what he'd been feeding Devenish to get him so interested in her.

She couldn't think of any possible way that he knew about what had been going on with Sir Rodney, but her guilty conscience was making her paranoid.

Making her scared.

On her third glass of wine already, and it not even 8pm, she decided that she couldn't sit back and wait to see what Devenish would uncover. Just the hint of the truth getting into a newspaper would be enough to give the great Sir Rodney enough balls to come forward and spill everything, whether he'd been fucking that Asian kid or not. And if the whole truth came out it would be more than her reputation and career at risk.

It would be her freedom.

She finished her wine and poured another, before scanning through her phone contacts for the number she wanted. It was one she hoped that she would never have to use again, but this situation was becoming too frightening not to act, and act decisively. She dialled the number. A voice answered after the third ring.

"Yes?" A man's voice, with a soft Scottish accent.

"It's Lowry. I need to meet." Her voice trembled slightly as she spoke.

"Okay. Are you free tomorrow morning?"

"Yes."

"Good. Eight am, next to the boathouse. Don't feed the ducks, I read that bread is bad for them," he said, perfectly seriously.

"Alright. I'll see you then."

The man hung up and she scrolled through her phone to delete the traces of the call... just in case. If things got to a point where somebody looked at her phone records it would be too late to worry anyway.

Her eyes shone as she finished her wine. Yes, Devenish and the whole damned thing was a problem. But she was smarter than any of them.

And prepared to fight dirty.

---oOo---

Chapter twenty-two

"He's a fucking intelligence agent" said Gabriel to Nadir as he flipped his laptop shut. They were sitting in a coffee shop, one of those 'honest, we're not a chain' chains, which have popped up all over the UK in the last ten years. The coffee was adequate though Gabriel was close to causing a scene when they asked him to pay for his refill.

He was in a bad mood anyway. His night with the two ladies from the Inn had gone to plan, but he was feeling horrible bursts of feelings this morning, and he missed Rachael. He'd missed her for fifteen years.

"The guy from the pub? The one you were speaking to?" Nadir couldn't quite pronounce 'pub' correctly. Her American twang switched to *faux* cockney each time she said the word.

"Yep. Andrew fucking Miller. He's an ex-red, working freelance gigs for the Brits since the Wall fell. Cassiel got the file in moments. He's a player alright, but not very high level otherwise we'd have to do more digging. Seems that he's been doing background work for Brit and US employees. Bit of private work too for the odd blue chip company."

"An information man?" asked Nadir, and Gabriel nodded.

"Observe and record. Nothing more."

"So. He observed you. Likely recorded you, too. But I wonder if he reported you. Should we be worried?" Gabriel drained the last of his second cup, then stopped himself as he raised it to indicate he wanted a refill.

"Stupid fucking coffee house. Can you believe the size of these cups?" He fumbled in his pocket for a few more pound coins.

"Should we be worried, Gabe?" asked Nadir, wanting him to focus.

"No. Miller should be worried." He gestured to the barista for another large Americano, and tossed the coins onto the table.

"You told him your name, Gabe," said Nadir as she sipped her latte. "Why did you tell him your name?"

"Why not? What does it matter? By the time Miller reports about us, and by the time the Brit intelligence have had their afternoon tea and decided to cross-reference descriptions, the job will be finished. Besides, there are plenty of Mr Gabriels running around the countryside I'm sure."

"Not too many American ones, though. And not too many dead ones with a DoD file on record."

"Seriously. Relax. If Herr Miller causes the slightest problem, then Herr Miller is in a world of shit." The barista arrived with a fresh cup, and Gabriel began the laborious process of tearing open sugar packets and pouring them into the black liquid. Nadir took the coins and paid the guy, who looked anxiously at the big American glowering as he threw torn wrapper after torn wrapper into his empty cup. Gabriel stopped and turned to the barista.

"You want a fucking tip, boy?" The young man shook his head quickly and returned to the safety of the other side of the bar.

"What about the cop?" Gabriel tore open another sugar packet with a sudden snap, and the sugar spilled across table.

"You know what, Nadir? I really don't know about the fucking cop. Maybe sometime someone will compare records and find a link, but in the meantime I think it just looks like a cop went feral with a pile of party drugs. They'll probably think he got them as a pay off from some gangster for looking the other way."

"In Surrey, Gabe?" Nadir opened her palms to indicate her surroundings. "You see many gangsters here?" Gabriel raised a finger, pointing over Nadir's left shoulder. She casually undid her scrunchie and slowly shook her head, releasing her black hair, and taking the opportunity to glance behind her. An old lady with purple-rinsed hair sat wrestling with a cupcake the size of a fist. Nadir scowled at Gabriel who smiled in return.

"Did you find out where Devenish is now?" asked Nadir.

"Yep. He should be making his final connection to Albuquerque in an hour, so he'll be at the hotel this evening." Gabriel stirred the coffee, the liquid thick and sticky with the sugar he'd added.

"Good. So what's next?" Gabriel took a deep draft, half emptying the cup in one go.

"You got a few days before we find out how he got on. I suggest you do some sightseeing, lie low, and I'll contact him when he meets Moore."

"Sightseeing? What's there to see?"

"Oh I'm sure you'll find something. If Miller reported us then it's probably wise to separate for a few days. They'll be looking for the two of us, not one guy and one girl on their own. You take the car, I'll hire another one, and I'll text you when we're ready to go with Devenish."

"Fair enough. Though I haven't a clue what I'm going to do for three days."

"Oh do something, Nadir. Act natural. Hit the tourist spots. Go see Stonehenge. Go get pissed. Enjoy yourself for Christ's sake." He finished his cup, set it on the table, and gave Nadir the hire car keys. "You have a good time now. I'll text you when I need you."

"What are you going to do?"

"I was stationed near here for a few months in the nineties. Secondment with the Brits. Think I'm gonna revisit a few old haunts. Look up a few folk I haven't seen in a ways."

"But you're dead, Gabriel. Isn't that going to be a bit awkward?"

"Nah. They don't know I'm dead, Nadir. Just a few drinks and swapping a few war stories with old friends. Nothing more." There was a look in his eye that Nadir found unsettling.

"Old friends or old scores, Gabe?" He caught her eye. Held her gaze for a beat.

"Just some buddies putting away a few cold ones, Nadir. I promise," he said, all teeth and hidden agendas. "Give you my word."

As she said goodbye and left the coffee house, Nadir thought about Gabriel's word. How it meant jack-shit to her, and even less to Gabriel. Still, there wasn't much of anything she could do about it. Like a force of nature, Gabriel did what Gabriel did. Most of the time it was what he was paid to do, but sometimes it wasn't. Usually things worked out. Usually people got hurt.

But, days away from one of the most ambitious projects she'd been involved in, worth millions of dollars to her personally, she couldn't fully quell the worries inside. She set the sat-nav on the car for Gatwick airport, having made a split second decision about what to do, and it wasn't going to be sitting around here worrying about Gabriel.

Paris would be her place of calm for a few days, before the storm began. With luck it would be the place she'd start her new life when the waves had settled.

---oOo---

Chapter twenty-three

Gabriel thought about medals as he drove.

Two heavy, shiny things on pretty ribbons. One ribbon red, white and blue, and the other a deep purple, both pinned to his pillow as he lay in the ward.

His entire body felt stiff and sore now, some weeks after his evacuation, and it was an effort to turn his head to view his Silver Star and Purple Heart. He felt he should have had three of the damned medals given how sore he was, but one would have to do.

His Colonel and several other officers, including Lieutenant Elliot who sported some paper stitches over a shrapnel wound on his cheek from a richochet, stood at the end of his bed. The Colonel read out the citations and congratulated Gabriel on his bravery before saluting him solemnly. Gabriel managed to sit up a little and return the salute, almost pulling his drip out as he snapped his hand to his forehead. A marine photographer told the officers to gather beside Gabriel, before shooting off a few pictures for posterity. Everyone shook hands, and the senior officers walked off up the ward.

"How you feeling, Sergeant?" asked Elliot.

"Fine, sir. A little stiff. How you doing?" Gabriel motioned to the nasty cut on his lieutenant's face.

"It's nothing. Doc says won't even leave a scar." That was hard to believe, thought Gabriel as he looked along the jagged outline of the wound. "So... congratulations on the star, Pete."

"Guess that's down to you, sir. Thanks for the recommendation," he said.

"You risked your life to save a kid, sergeant. It was a no-brainer." Elliot's expression, however, was troubled and guarded. He seemed in conflict with himself. There was something on his mind, and he was reluctant to speak about it.

"Guess anyone would have tried to save the kid, lieutenant. Was the humane thing to do." His superior nodded.

"Well, the Marine Corps are proud of what you did. You protected the innocent, and that's good PR in anyone's book," said the lieutenant, distracted.

"But..." Gabriel let it hang.

"But what?" The reply came a little too fast, and carried an edge to it.

"Let me make it easy for you, boss" said Gabriel. "I guess you've been getting it in the neck since the evac. These medals and all, well now, they're kinda a necessary evil for the powers that be. Keep morale up. Get a story and find a hero to hold up to the troops. One for the hearts and minds. Yeah?" The officer was silent. "But, back in HQ where the bullshit flows, the top men are pissed. They're pissed at me, and pissed at you. No-one gives a fuck about a rescued hadji rugrat. But they give one helluva fuck about three dead marines. Specially if they didn't need to be dead 'cept for what I did. I am right, aren't I?"

"Yes. I'm sorry." Elliot looked pained as Gabriel spoke, and it wasn't because of his wound.

"So what's next? Guess they're gonna want payback for those marines. Don't reckon a good press story is worth three body bags." The lieutenant raised his hand to stop him and.

"Four."

"Four? What you mean? Last I heard there were three KIA and four walking wounded, you and me included. Who's the four?"

"Sorry, Pete." Again Elliot looked crestfallen. He was in his early twenties, but his eyes betrayed a sadness and knowledge about life more common in the elderly. "The kid died. Infection from the wound. Didn't respond to antibiotics and died in the hospital." The news hit Gabriel like a blow. He stared at the lieutenant, willing him to laugh and tell him it was a poorly judged joke.

Elliot returned the stare.

"Ah fuck," said Gabriel quietly, as though praying.

"Yeah. I'm sorry, man." The lieutenant paused as Gabriel unpinned the Silver Star from his pillow and gently rubbed his thumb along the shiny metal. "Come on. It wasn't your fault. It was an infection. Nothing you could have done."

"When did he die?" asked Gabriel, his eyes bleak.

"Two days ago. The docs say he was comfortable."

"How the fuck was he comfortable, lieutenant? How? Morphine? He wasn't fucking comfortable, he was stoned off his skull. He spent the last weeks of his life in a field hospital surrounded by strangers, dying of an infection, doped to his eyeballs. I don't call that fucking comfortable."

"Calm down, sergeant. Just calm down. You did your best, and so did the doctors, but there was nothing they could do." Elliot framed his words... "It was his time."

"His time?" screamed Gabriel. "No it fucking wasn't! It was his time when the bomb hit. He would have been gone... vaporised. He wouldn't have even noticed. But, no... I have to be a hero and rescue him. For what? So he spends weeks in agony and dies anyway? So three marines get blown to hell because of me? What the fuck was it for?" Along the ward a few other patients regarded the commotion, as did an uncomfortable looking nurse. But anger and shouting were not uncommon here.

Most of the people in this ward had good reason to be angry.

"That's enough, sergeant. Get your shit together, and that's an order." Elliot didn't need to shout. The word 'order' carried weight with marines. They hear it and obey. It was like breathing to them.

"Yes sir" said Gabriel, and he forced himself to calm down. His head was spinning and he wanted to strike out against something or someone to release the anger inside, but he obeyed, forced his breathing to steady, and pushed his rage deep inside where it froze hard and cold for another day.

"You've been round the block, Pete... more than most in recon. You've seen shit happen. Hell, you've caused shit to happen. You gotta get a handle on this. It's just shit. Not your fault, not the docs' fault, it's nobody's fault. It's. Just. Shit. You got that?"

"Yes sir." Gabriel was stony faced, but calm. Inside him the ball of rage was almost physically present. He could feel it chill his heart, a heavy bleakness threatening to fill his body with violence and revenge.

"You want to blame someone then blame the hadjis. If they hadn't got that asshole to plant IEDs all over the place we'd never have been at that village in the first place, and the kid would still be dreaming of his first camel." Gabriel nodded, but he felt like he was in another world. He heard the words and saw Elliot say them, but it was like he was watching it all on a distant television screen. He was detached from the moment. His wounded body lay on the bed, and his mouth made the right noises, but his essence – his soul – was elsewhere, embracing his anger and helplessness. Learning from it. Making plans to set his anger loose and to be helpless no more.

"There's other news, Sergeant. Maybe equally bad. You calm?" Gabriel nodded, gaze fixed on his lieutenant. "Surgeon reckons that hole in your leg means you won't pass fitness for the recon anymore. It's looking like desk or support work from now on, but I should be able to put requests in to get you on the training staff if that's what you want." Gabriel didn't flinch. "I'm sorry, Pete."

"No more action then, boss?" he asked, deflated.

"You've seen enough, Pete. Time to stop waving your ass in the grass. It's been shot off too often." Elliot tried to smile.

"Those the only options? Support or training?" Elliot's smile dropped again, the troubled look flashing across his features. His wound glistened as he frowned.

"There was a third, of course. Honourable discharge on medical grounds. Full pension, all that kind of thing. I didn't think you'd want that."

"Discharge?" It was Gabriel's turn to grin, albeit wryly. Like the grin of a shark when it spots a surfer. "This is the payback for the body bags? Nothing to do with medical reasons, is it?"

"I'm afraid so," said the lieutenant, grimly. "I had to put my ass on the line with the old man to pull the training or support role." His 'old man' was an admiral in the US Navy. Elliot came from navy stock, but his father was not impressed that he chose sand and mud under his boots instead of the steel and paint of a warship deck. "The Colonel wasn't impressed writing those letters to the families of the KIAs. Told me he wanted to tell them that their kids would be alive if you had stayed on mission."

"And the other kid? The hadji?"

"Fuck the hadji. We've been over this. OC lost three good recon marines in the blast, and at least two, including you, look like being invalided out. That's the unit blown in half. That's around ten million US dollars invested in each of you marines gone in an instant. The deal is you get off the line, wear your medal, and don't mention it again. But the OC wanted you to take the medal and fuck off."

"Well now, that would be a waste of Uncle Sam's dollars then wouldn't it? It's just another inch of the green dildo," said Gabriel.

"Yeah, just another inch. Doesn't matter, there's nothing more I can do. He reckons you've had enough. That was the only reason you left that berm and went for the kid. OC doesn't like that. It worries him." Elliot raised his palms in supplication. "You see where he's coming from, what with the hornets' nest you kicked off." Gabriel said nothing. "So what do you want? Training, support or just get out?"

"I want to stay in action. That's all. You can make that happen. Your dad can find a way. That's all I want. Please." The younger man was silent. "Just ask, boss. See if there's another way."

"I'll ask, but I tell you Pete. It'll not be with the Corps. If you see action again, it'll be with someone else." Gabriel looked around the ward. Some of the families of the injured marines had brought pennants and posters to hang near the beds of the wounded. One poster was simply the Marine Corps coat of arms with the motto *Semper fi* proudly displayed. Thinking about leaving the Corps almost brought a tear to Gabriel's eye, but he pushed it back and stayed impassive. All he could think about was the well of anger and hatred inside him. The overwhelming urge to hit back. The need to get back into the middle of the war – this fucked up, random devastator of lives and dreams – that had chewed him up, stole his humanity, destroyed what good remained within him, and laughed in his face through the death of a young boy.

"*Semper fi*, boss" was all he said. Elliot nodded and shook his hand.

"*Semper fi*," whispered Elliot, before leaving Gabriel to his black thoughts.

Chapter twenty-four

America is huge. On my connecting flight to Albuquerque, New Mexico, I passed over a great deal of it, and it whatever else it might turn out to be, it was certainly enormous.

I flew over vast expanses of emptiness, criss-crossed by linear freeways and interstates passing through tiny towns and huge settlements, the typical American grid pattern clearly visible from seventeen thousand feet.

You could almost see the golden arches on every corner.

Americans, also, are huge. Actually, that's not entirely fair. *Many* Americans are huge. There seems to be a dichotomy within human beings in America. It's a world where there are no in-betweens. It looked like a world where people had evolved separately, as H.G. Wells' morlocks and eloi had split from a common humanity to form their own subspecies.

On one hand, sitting two seats in front of me, there was *Homo americanus hugeicus.* This guy had a throat the width of my waist. His head perched precariously somewhere in the middle of his massive neck, then haphazardly welded to his bovine torso. The rest of his construction was, thankfully, concealed by the aircraft seat, although I could make out through the thin spaces between the backrests that parts of him had settled firmly onto either seat beside him.

I'm sure that he was a lovely bloke underneath it all. A man of passion, ambition, loves and lusts, like all other men. I just couldn't understand how he came to be that *big*, or how so many of the people on the plane had ended up being the size of small cars.

There must have been a point in time, perhaps a collection of moments, when each of these people had looked in the mirror and thought 'Jeez... I'm putting on a few pounds. Maybe I should cut back a bit.' Sadly, for many these moments of clarity seemed to have passed them by, ignored and unheeded.

On the other hand there is the second subspecies: *Homo americanus perfectus.* This sub-species are the way human beings would be if God was a great artist.

And something of a perv.

They are perfect in the extreme. Their bodies are toned, smooth and flawless, inside and out. Their eyes are clear, bright and shiny. They have teeth which gleam like navigation beacons, their hair glows with inner health and lustre, and their idea of a vice is spending an hour in the gym each day rather than an hour and a half. They have names like 'Candy' and 'Chet', and I was sitting right next to one on the connecting flight.

Her name was Kristal, and she was from Albuquerque. She had two brothers who lived in New Hampshire, and both were orthodontists by day and extreme sports fanatics on the weekends. She was on her way back home from a family party as the elder brother, Josh, had recently announced that his wife and he were pregnant.

Both he and his wife. That's one for the newspapers and science journals.

Kristal was a realtor, which seemed to be the American version of an estate agent. She knew several important people in Albuquerque, including the mayor, the sister of a Senator, several congressmen's wives, the main TV anchor for the local station, and she played tennis on Wednesday afternoons with one of the weather girls on CNN. She was single at the moment but dating a number of guys. Her favourite colour was scarlet, and she drove a Prius because she believed in saving the planet for her brother's shiny new prospective child.

I found out all of this within two minutes of her sitting beside me. In return she learned that I was from Great Britain, and was called Wolf.

She chatted away to me, unnervingly holding eye contact the whole time, even when the flight attendant came round with drinks. She had iced water with 'medium' gas, which she sipped at like a humming bird, between recounting further episodes of her life story. I ordered a bourbon and branch water, not because I like bourbon and branch water, but because I'd never had one before.

It wasn't very nice. The bourbon was like a harsher and more complex form of whisky, and I'm fairly sure that the branch water was *Evian*. But at least it gave me something to do with my mouth, as speaking definitely wasn't going to be an option with Kristal. She simply wouldn't stop talking, like a children's TV presenter on speed, gazing into my eyes the entire time.

I've had less eye-contact at the opticians. Honestly.

Kristal had been a cheerleader, an actress, a singer and an athlete before she started her own business four years ago. Since she looked in her mid-twenties, I doubted that she was particularly successful at any of the above, but the sincerity with which she poured out her story showed me that she, at least, believed in her own success.

And that's the thing with *Homo americanus perfectus.* They genuinely believe that they are the real deal. They put a hell of a lot of effort into looking wonderful, staying healthy, and overflowing with exuberance at all times. They put a lot of money towards it too, if Kristal's sculpted nose and perfect bosoms were to go by. On the plus side they have become a class of people which transcend class boundaries. Whatever the background, economic status or profession, if you put in the effort and look the part you are accepted into the Beautiful People set, and you can spend your days and nights admiring how wonderful everyone is.

Still, it was better than sitting next to the many larger folk, who would wrestle me for a salted peanut.

Staring resolutely at Kristal's angelic face I allowed my mind to run over more important matters. After a brief moment or two wondering if Kristal had sweat glands, or if they had been bred out of her, I thought about what awaited me in the US.

I was booked into a hotel near the airport in Albuquerque for the night, and in the morning a car would pick me up and drive me to the town of White Rock, which was the nearest place to Los Alamos and, I presume, the nearest place to young Mr Devenish-Moore. There, in a local restaurant, my son would arrive and we'd both see what happened.

The driver, incidentally, would introduce himself as Mr Cassiel and, yes, I'd put the name through Google. Another angel-name, just like Gabriel and Nadir. This one is the angel of temperance, one of many laudable virtues I intended to disregard during my trip.

"Hey, Wolf... are you in there? Did you hear me?" tinkled Kristal.

"Sorry, Kristal... just jetlag. You were saying?" She just wouldn't stop beaming that perfect smile. I felt like a hunted rabbit caught in benign, perfectly made-up, headlights.

"I know a great cure for jetlag!" she leered, and I sensed that the conversation was taking a more primal turn. "But, hey! I was saying, before you went all Eng-a-lish on me and zoned out, but d'ya fancy a drink when we land? I've got nothing on tonight and I know a great bar. It's an authentic Irish pub, just like you have in Eng-a-land."

"Oh, I don't know, Kristal... it's been a long, long day." This was British reserve and exhaustion versus American openness and effervescence.

"Go on, Wolf... live a little! I think that a nice drink at the end of a long day is, how d'ya guys say it, you know, like that girl Ross married on *Friends*, what was her name? Emma. You know who I mean, the British chick he said the wrong name to at the wedding..."

"Helen Beckinsdale. She was in *Cold Feet* too." I was a secret *Friends* aficionado. One of many horrible secrets I keep hidden.

"That's the one... what did she say? Yeah, that would be 'just the ticket'..." Kristal laughed at her attempt at a British accent. Meanwhile, an ocean away, the remaining Pearly Kings and Queens jumped to their deaths off the steeple of St Mary le Bow church. "I think a nice drink with some fun company," she threw her hands out to indicate herself, almost pushing a passing flight attendant across the plane. "I think that would be," she pulled a face which I only imagine was meant to be an attempt at a British expression, "...just the ticket!"

I laughed. Really. Tiredness and anxiety had crumbled in the face of her exuberance. She was genuinely endearing and funny. The actress in Kristal beamed at my laughter, and she repeated her line again. 'Just the ticket!' I kept laughing, finally holding a straight face long enough to speak.

"Okay... one drink? Fair enough?" Delighted, she squeezed my hands, grinning like a deranged supermodel. "You're sure that you're not too busy," I asked, hoping there might still be a chance to hit the hotel and sleep for Eng-a-land.

"Oh... I'll make sure that I've got nothing on," she winked, a double-entendre which Sid James would be proud of. "It's no problem, really! We're going to have such fun! None of my friends are British, so this is great! Oh, you'll have to meet Stacey... and Walt! Walt loves the British!" She practically applauded with happiness. I would love to feel that good about anything just once. Even for a second. "Or maybe I'll just keep you all for my lonesome! My own eccentric British writer..." She threw me a naughty schoolgirl look. I smiled, but had no idea if I could keep up with this girl tonight. I felt like my internal organs had been replaced with heavy sods of damp clay, and my brain had crystallised into butter. Slow thinking as I was, I knew what was coming next.

"Oh Wolf, tonight is going to be 'just the ticket'!" She pulled her eyelid down in an exaggerated wink, and I suspected it was a pastiche of Dick Van Dyke's chimney sweep in *Mary Poppins*. She grabbed my arm with excitement. Cue hysterical giggling to camera, then fade to credits.

I will grant Gabriel and his kin the following: life certainly became more interesting since they visited.

---oOo---

Chapter twenty-five

Parkinson felt the hint of a scowl cross his impassive features for a fraction of a second, then, as though the bones and skin which served him for a face realised he lacked sufficient muscle to hold the expression, it slipped away like a breeze through a graveyard.

"Benjamin," he said, as he held the phone a few inches from his desiccated ear. " I'm merely asking for co-operation from you. I'm not asking for blood. I have some evidence which indicates that an ex-marine of yours, who is listed as deceased, is currently visiting or living in Britain."

"Richard, my man," said the voice across the Atlantic. "Richard, do you not think that your boys have made a mistake? It happens, y'know. Now and then."

"There is no mistake, Benjamin. I have a fingerprint less than a week old which matches your files. The owner of the fingerprint is apparently dead. However, in death he appears to have developed a thirst for English ale." There was a pause.

"What you want me to do, Richard? Really. What you want me to say?"

"I would like you to tell me, as a personal favour, if you know anything more about this deceased Sergeant Gabriel. I don't want details, but I want to know that somebody is at least aware of his existence, and that I can read my paper this evening in peace without the nagging fear that you have a rogue assassin wandering around my Home Counties. As you can imagine Her Majesty's Government gets rather upset about foreign assassins, friendly or otherwise, arriving in the UK without our knowledge."

"Of course, Richard. Hey, would I leave you swinging in the breeze? D'you think I'd let you take a bullet if I could stop it?" Benjamin Cornfeld, Parkinson's opposite number in the Central Intelligence Agency, did his best to sound sincere.

"I would hope not, Benjamin. It depends, of course, from whence that bullet came and, indeed, whether the vested

interests of the USA were the reason for its discharge."
Benjamin paused before replying.

"What?" Parkinson sighed. *Illiterate colonials.*

"Benjamin," he continued, "we have known each other for
many years. We have worked together. When you visit here, I
consider you my friend."

"Me too, buddy. But what do you mean about bullets and
discharge and whence it came? You been reading that
Shakespeare again?"

"Of course I have, and you would do well to read him too.
Shakespeare has managed to distil the sum of human emotion,
triumph and tragedy, and elucidate the lot in a modest canon of
verse and narrative. However, in layman's terms, what I mean
is that our friendship notwithstanding, if US interests were at
stake you would not only fail to warn me of impending disaster
to my career or life, but you would also endeavour to expedite
said disaster upon me."

"What? Can you translate for me, Richard, because I don't
have a fucking clue what you're telling me?"

"I don't trust you, Benjamin. And I trust your government
even less." There was a laugh on the other end of the line.

"Well, that's just swell, Richard. Least we know where we
stand." He chuckled again. "Hell, I wouldn't trust you Brits to
carry a glass of water for me from one side of the room to the
other."

"Good. So we understand each other. Now, as a friend, and
under these terms of engagement, please indicate to me in some
way whether or not I should be worried about this man on our
soil. As your countrymen are fond of saying, 'throw me a bone'
please, Benjamin." There was another chuckle, a pause, and
then the sound of a keyboard being tapped.

"Alright, Richard. But understand, this conversation never
happened. Hell, I'm playing golf right now. Leastways I will
have been when I get to my appointment book. I'll throw you a
bone. I'll even give you some advice."

"Go on." Parkinson lifted a fresh pencil from his collection.

"He used to be one of ours. After his 'death' he became
very useful to the Company. But we had to let him go. There

was a very, very quiet scandal. There was the whiff of fraud. There was a hidden investigation. He was asked to leave. There was talk of ending his contract in a more permanent way, but the bastard had left a web of information in various places. He had information about our actions in a variety of theatres which would prove very difficult to justify if they became public. So we had to let him walk. He had more on us than we had on him. He vanished off the grid."

"And that's it? So could this man be simply enjoying his retirement?"

"Heh. Enjoying his retirement? I met him once. He enjoyed one thing, and one thing only. And I'll give you a clue, it wasn't fucking gardening."

"So, what is the latest you have on him?" asked Parkinson.

"We've got a word. More a phrase. But pretty much nothing else solid. Let's just say that he seems to be practicing his skills, only this time it's for money."

"What is this phrase or word you mentioned?" The line fell silent for a moment.

"This goes no further, right?"

"Of course."

"Archangel." Parkinson scribbled a note and circled it.

"And what is this Archangel?"

"I'm not certain. But it's not anything good."

"Speculate, please." There was an intercontinental sigh.

"I think that Gabriel missed the Company. Leastways he missed aspects of the Company. I think he's started his own version. A private version. Available for hire. Archangel."

"I see, however, that seems impossible. How can one man accumulate the resources of an intelligence agency? Surely, at worst he is just a gun for hire and, at best, he is an expensive private detective?"

"You'd think so, eh? Even though I know that there's more than just Gabriel involved. Other agents. From other organisations. But the rumour is that if you want something done, and you're not too fussy about international law or human decency, Gabriel and Archangel will sort it out for you."

"I must say, I'm slightly relieved. So this man and his associates are not sanctioned by you? Therefore, should we need to, we can have him detained and placed in a secure location with one of those interminable but terribly useful anti-terrorist custody orders."

"I didn't say he wasn't sanctioned, Richard. Frankly, I'm a bit off my jurisdiction on this one, because getting facts about Gabriel at the moment out of this computer is like catching a breeze with your fingers. However, and this is more speculation, I think he is sanctioned to be there. Just not through any official channels."

"Please clarify, Benjamin. Is he working for the US government, or is he not?"

"Okay. This is just my theory, Richard. So understand that. But I think Gabriel and his little project work for anyone who pays them. Us included. The question you need to ask is who he working for at the moment. And what is he up to."

"I believe I just asked you that question, Benjamin." Parkinson tapped his pencil against his pad in frustration.

"And I believe, *Richard*, that I just told you that I don't know who he's working for. But he's working for someone. Always is."

"You are saying that he's not sightseeing, then?" asked Parkinson, still concerned.

"Gabriel doesn't do sightseeing, Richard. Gabriel doesn't do human. He doesn't do reading a good book by the beach. If he's there, he's up to something. Just hope that it isn't something against you or yours."

"I would think, Benjamin, that our respective parties should be keen to isolate and restrict this person and his private organisation. Don't you?"

"Not when he's useful to us, Richard. Yes, we can investigate him and see what he's up to but, when the shit hits the fan, some word from high, high above will quietly shut the investigation down. He has his uses, Richard. Now and then."

"You tolerate a private operative, a rogue, to have connections within your network?" The idea of the Americans using some form of freelance intelligence agency grated on

Parkinson's nerves. It simply wasn't how the game was played. It was bad enough that most things, from bookkeeping to cleaning contracts were outsourced these days, but to contract out actual intelligence activities was the lemon on a particularly bitter cake.

"Hey, Richard. If you're so good, you try to find them. All I know, at least all I imagine, is that he has holds over many, many people. As do his other colleagues. And you can bet your ass these aren't pleasant holds over them. Not like a hidden debt or a touch of playing away from home with the neighbour's wife. Whoever these contacts are, they are shitting themselves that they don't piss Gabriel or his pals off." Benjamin chucked shortly.

"This is a scandal. You expect me to believe that you know all of this and aren't worried? This is an enormous breach of national security."

"National security? You gotta be bullshitting me, Richard. National security? Yeah, so Gabriel and the boys have a bit of pull on our information. Yeah, they can find shit out. Yeah, they could be considered to be handling moles within our little corridors of secrets. But, when it comes down to it, while we pee our pants every six months about this threat or that threat, when the metal needs to hit the meat our lords and masters can make a call, and Gabriel will be there to sort out the problem. Maybe one day he'll come up short. Maybe one day the metal will hit his meat. Maybe then the leaks will be plugged, and we'll be back to issuing stern warnings to the bad guys. In the meantime, if someone is fucking with us, we can pay Gabriel and Archangel to fuck with them right back."

"So he's loyal? He's loyal at least."

"Gabriel is loyal to one thing, and one thing only. And that thing is green and has a picture of a dead president on it." Parkinson winced. A thug working only for money was, in his eyes, the lowest of the low.

"I see. You were going to offer me advice," said Parkinson.

"Yes. I offer you advice, and I offer you my sympathy. When you called me and mentioned Gabriel I honestly hoped that your boys had made a mistake. You want Gabriel in your jurisdiction the way you want cancer in your bowel."

"So what is your advice?"

"Watch him. From a very, very far ways off. But watch him. And pray that he is on a plane someplace else as soon as possible. You want him gone, and you want to be left dealing with minor threats like global thermonuclear war and mass terrorism..."

"Really, Benjamin. He is just a man," laughed Parkinson, aware of the American love of drama and hyperbole.

"And Satan's just a guy with goat feet. I'm telling you. You want this man, and any of his friends, far away from you."

"What if I could sanction my organisation to eliminate him?"

"Two problems. First, you don't do that kinda thing. It's unsporting. Secondly, even if you did, Gabriel wouldn't take kindly to your attentions. If you failed, and by fail I mean fail to remove him, all his associates including the ones we don't know about, plus all these dead information drops he has set up to embarrass various governments around the world, then it would go poorly for you."

"Define poorly."

"Oh... dirty bomb or nuclear device detonated in London poorly? Or perhaps assassination of your Queen poorly? Or, if Gabriel was feeling just a little ornery about your attempt to remove him, he might just settle for the rape, torture and murder of your family and friends."

"Really?"

"Really. Richard. Listen to me. Watch, but don't touch. And pray that he's working for a friendly. If he isn't, we both could be in a lot of trouble."

"Thank you. I owe you dinner."

"You do. Try to make sure that London's still in one piece by the time I get over again. I hate eating in radioactive rubble."

"I will. Goodbye." Parkinson hung up. He looked at his notes. At the bottom of his set of scribbles he had written the word 'damn'.

And underlined it several times.

He resolved to send more information to Benjamin in the morning. Perhaps, as his American counterpart had hoped, the problem, and the mysterious Gabriel, would simply fade away and disappear.

Parkinson had been at this game long enough to know that this problem wasn't going to just disappear. Something unpleasant was going to happen here...

... he could feel it in his bones.

---oOo---

Chapter twenty-six

She was still beautiful, after all of these years. If anything she looked more stunning than before. Age had softened her looks, but not in a bad way. She was still trim and, as she walked along, he recognised her lithe stride and agile movements. They were just as he remembered. The girl beside her had inherited some of her posture and looks.

It was a sunny evening, and perhaps that added a veneer of warmth to the scene. When he thought of this place, this life, he usually remembered the incessant rain. Herefordshire rain didn't fall like other rain. It descended like an act of God, soaking you from the inside out. He had spent weeks soaked to the skin in the nearby hills, soaked and freezing. But he'd been younger then. Younger and harder. He didn't mind the rain, or the squelch his boots made each time he moved, or the frigid droplets seeping down the back of his battle dress. But he remembered the times when he was warm. The times when he had been happy.

Happy and warm beside Rachael.

She reached her car, unlocked it, and the teenager jumped into the back. A striking young girl with naturally blonde hair, she was already a good inch taller than her mother. He watched the kid as she fastened her seatbelt and put her mp3 player earphones on. Then he shifted his attention once again to the woman, as she jumped gently into the front seat of the car. He leaned back slightly in his seat as she checked behind her and started the engine, before pulling her car onto the road and driving slowly to the junction of the road. There was a brief pause, a burst of acceleration, and Rachael was gone.

Gabriel started his own car and drove off in the opposite direction. He felt moisture on his cheek, and instinctively reached up to wipe it off. A single fat tear.

As sudden and relentless as Herefordshire rain.

---oOo---

Sir Michael Rodney looked terrible.

He hadn't shaved for three days, and his patchy grey stubble gave his skin a deathly, unwholesome appearance. He inspected himself in the bathroom mirror, half-heartedly trying to freshen up with a few splashes of warm water before giving up and drying his face on an old, rough towel.

In the kitchen he cleared some scattered papers to the edge of table and prepared a strong cup of tea. Still wearing his pyjamas and dressing gown, damp patches visible beneath his armpits from another night of worried sleep, he sat down heavily before pulling across his battered laptop and switching the machine on. He took a sip of the hot tea, but it tasted like bitter ash in his mouth, and he held back the urge to retch.

Once the computer had finished its interminable boot sequence, Rodney opened the spreadsheet program and scanned through the data entered so far, pinching his grey lips as he thought about the numbers on the screen. He cross-checked the data with some of the printed sheets his remaining friends had been kind enough to send him, although they were becoming fewer and fewer now as the rumours about him spread. As though scandal was infectious, people were keeping their distance from Sir Rodney.

Apart from the staircase, he'd found at least a dozen more capital expenditure maintenance projects in the university which appeared to have never taken place. The invoices and costs for these works, when added together, were well into the six figure range, but he could find little actual evidence of the work having been completed. Some of his former colleagues remember an occasional workman turning up from time to time, but certainly no concerted large-scale works being carried out.

Quite the opposite, in fact, as several of the sites where maintenance had supposedly taken place were in worse condition than before the work orders were submitted.

His mysterious creaky stairway was now joined by a set of blocked drains next to one of the college cloisters, some potentially dangerous electrical work in one of the college canteens, and a hugely expensive re-leading of a stained glass window in one of the refectories, but which still let water seep through when it rained. And these were only the larger jobs, as he had found half a dozen or more minor works which were equally poorly completed.

It was as though the workmen never turned up in the first place.

Yet each of these building repairs had been subject to sub-contracts involving various companies with addresses across Oxford and the home counties, and each of them showed that the work had been inspected, signed-off, and all invoices for the work subsequently paid.

Rodney took a fresh sheet from the printer and stared at the details. It was another work order, completed and paid for in full, for replacement cisterns in a large male toilet next to one of the lecture theatres. Yet old Wetherby, the caretaker in that building, had told him on the phone just the previous evening that the 'bloody things leak like my granny's knickers', which Rodney took to mean that they hadn't been replaced. Another mystery to join his spreadsheet of shoddy building work.

As he finished typing the details he put the completed work order to the side and noted the signature on the authorisation section.

Rebecca Lowry.

He saved the document and poured his tea into the sink in disgust.

---oOo---

Zara Moore awoke early, refreshed after a peaceful night of sleep and good dreams. Outside the sun was shining, and it suited her mood as the light streamed into the barge. She hadn't changed the bedsheets since Thursday night, and she could still smell Wolf as she curled beneath them. Marcellus, as always, snored peacefully at the foot of the bed.

She checked her phone, but there were no messages from Wolf. She felt the briefest pang, then realised that the time difference and the journey had probably left him exhausted. Nevertheless, she keyed in a quick message, her mood reflected in the keystrokes.

```
Hey, you.  I hope everything's going well over
there, and that you're not too jetlagged.  I
dreamed of you again last night, and I wish you
were here with me this morning.  Good luck with
SD.  Please keep in touch.  I'm missing you.  Z x
```

She rose from the bed and leant over to the window, peeking through the curtains at the sunshine. A mild breeze in the nearby trees caused splashes of colour to drift across her bare skin as the sun shone through the sycamore leaves. She smiled and dropped back on the bed, pulling the sheets across her body.

She was, by nature, a positive person. But today, well today, things just seemed more positive than usual. Marcellus shuffled onto the bed, turned around several times, and flopped down beside her. In an instant he was snoring again, his chest rising and falling as he dreamed his doggie dreams.

---oOo---

Laura Berne woke reluctantly, clinging to sleep as a child clings to their security blanket.

She'd had enjoyed a dreamless, motionless rest but, as her body began to report in for the day, she remembered why. Her head began to throb. She recalled the night before. Gillian had been there, along with some Italian bloke called Ivo who was visiting Gillian's company on business. Several bottles of wine had been there too, at least for a while. In the dim light of the bedroom she realised that she had fallen into bed naked. Normally she wore a set of jogging bottoms and a tee shirt at least. There was a sudden noise beside her, a low grunt, and she felt the bed move slightly.

"Jesus!" She flicked on the bedside light.

The Italian was lying beside her, resting on his side with his back towards her.

"Is things alright?" Even through her hangover his accent sounded smooth and attractive. Her head thumped in time to her heartbeat.

"I'm fine, thanks. Sorry. Just a bad dream." He turned around, resting on one elbow, and smiled at her. His chest was well muscled and tanned, his smile broad and open. She couldn't believe that she'd jumped into the sack with a total stranger on the first date. She was meant to be a professional intelligence agent, wary of others and full of self-control at all times. Instead, she had become the female Roger Moore. *God, she thought, I hate Gillian.*

"I hope she not about me," said Ivo.

"No... no... not at all. Gosh, that was quite a night." He smiled broadly, like the Cheshire cat in a cream factory.

"It was *bellissimo*," he said. "And the night, I think, she still young." She found herself smiling back at him.

"Oh, I think it's probably old enough by now... Ivo, isn't it?"

"*Si, sono Ivo.* Sorry, my English not so good with sleeps." He gently slapped his head and pulled a face. "No... the night, she still young. This is for us, what, medicine ordered by the doctor? *Come il cacio sui maccheroni...* maybe this is, what you say, *amore a prima vista*? The love she knows herself on first seeing?"

"Oh I really don't think so, Ivo." She stifled a laugh. She pitied Italian women, even corny lines sound so sincere in that language, pouring from his full lips like music. "But I've got to go to work anyway, so I guess we'd best get dressed."

"Work? No work the Saturday," he said. Laura ran through the days of the week in her head. Damn, it was 'the Saturday'. Of course, she *could* go to work if she wanted. Overtime was well respected, albeit unpaid, in her profession. Ivo shifted higher on his elbow, and the sheet slipped further from his waist. His abdomen was toned and tanned too.

"Of course. Saturday. Silly me." Laura ignored the pain in her head and lay back on the bed.

"*Bene, tesorina mia,*" said Ivo, as he reached for her.

"Screw it," she said aloud. "Eat, drink and be merry, for tomorrow we die."

---oOo---

```
Today is not a good day to die, Andreas. x
```

Andreas read the end of the email again, and he couldn't agree more.

Berne, his MI6 contact for the current case, had confirmed his suspicions about the impulsive American, but was reluctant to tell him more. Perhaps she didn't know anything further, or perhaps she was keeping him out of the loop.

Andreas, however, still had a network of contacts from his former life who could be pressed to deliver a favour on occasions. With the unspoken understanding, of course, that the favour would be recalled in the future.

He called in several of these favours the night before and, as he logged into his secure email, he was reaping the rewards.

The email was from his old CIA handler, Beverly, with whom he occasionally kept in touch with. She was officially retired now, although retirement was rarely complete in their world. Like repentant smokers, intelligent operatives often craved the occasional buzz. It was a short, terse message.

```
Keep away from this man, Andreas. Everything I
have seen, and much of what I cannot get access
to, tells me that you need to keep away from him.
Stick to what you know. Put your curiosity to
bed. Keep safe.
```

She signed off with a stark warning.

```
I mean it, Andreas. I love you as a brother, and
respect you as a friend. This man could be the
end of you. Today is not a good day to die,
Andreas. x
```

In many ways Andreas agreed with his former handler. He had a good life, one that he enjoyed, and he felt freer than he had for decades. He could decide if he wanted to work or if he wanted to take time off and relax. It was up to him.

Of course, the problem with relaxing lay with his overactive mind. The deceased Sergeant Gabriel was a puzzle that Andreas wanted to solve, and he would continue to pick at the pieces until he had satisfied his curiosity.

He reached into his small suitcase and removed a small package wrapped in brown paper, tucked inside the case lining. Carefully unwrapping it, he eventually revealed a squat pistol, with two short magazines pre-charged with rounds. It was a simple P38 pistol, similar to those he had used with during his days in the Stasi. Old but effective, worn but well-maintained. *Today is a good day to die*, he thought.

He hoped that Gabriel felt the same, should he cross his path again.

---oOo---

Parkinson had not had a good night's sleep. He had risen several times during the night to use the toilet. On occasion, his visits had become painful, and he felt worn out and tired. Rising early, he was already halfway through the paper when he turned his attention to yesterday's mail, unopened after yet another long day at work. Amidst the bills was a letter sealed in a smart, textured envelope. He took a deep breath and opened it. He scanned through the contents and picked out the keywords, as he did every hour of every working day.

Malignant, significant spread, inoperable, prognosis poor, immediate treatment may only improve short-term prospects.

He wasn't used to reading documents about himself, and he knew the contents anyway after his consultation the previous week. The letter confirmed what he already knew, although the child in him hoped that the doctor had made a mistake and had written to apologise. In any case, he felt as removed from this piece of paper as he did from the reports and intelligent briefings he read each and every day. A creak on the stairwell alerted him to his wife coming downstairs, and he crumpled the letter up and tossed it into the little fire he had burning in the kitchen grate against the morning chill. The sun was shining outside, but he could not keep heat inside him these days. He felt as weak and drawn as the greying ash of the letter in the fire.

"Richard? Is everything alright?" His wife, plump and concerned, stood in the kitchen doorway. He felt a sudden urge to cry; to tell her everything, to fall into her arms. To be a child once more. To be told that he would be fine.

But he did not.

"Everything is fine, darling." Her look of concern didn't fade. "I just have some work things on my mind. Everything is alright."

"Do you mind if I go back to bed, Richard? It's terribly early," she asked, watching him curiously. She knew he was keeping something from her, but it was normal in their relationship given the nature of his work.

"Of course not, darling. I'll bring you some tea in a few hours." She shuffled over in her slippers and held his head in her hands, kissing him gently on the forehead.

"Thank you. That would be lovely." Parkinson noticed a tear in the corner of her eye. A tear born of tiredness and worry. "I love you, Richard."

"I love you too, my dear," said Parkinson as she left and ambled up the stairs again. "I really do" he whispered, as his own tears appeared.

---oOo---

Nadir awoke to the smell of fresh baked bread.

The thin linen curtains blew in the breeze through the old sash windows, bringing with it the smells and sounds of the market below. She hopped out of bed, wearing a faded tee shirt with a washed out 'ATF' seal on the front, and a pair of cotton shorts. Her skin, more dusky than tanned, gleamed in the Parisian sunlight streaming through the window as she took a few minutes to observe the traders below.

Men and women were unfurling canvas roofs for their stalls. Here and there people carried large trays of goods, hundreds of little rounds of cheese and loose sausages and smoked meats. A fish counter at least six metres long groaned under the weight of all shapes and sizes of fish and shellfish. At the corners of the rows of stalls, people operated steaming boilers in tiny boxcarts, preparing fresh coffee and hot chocolate which the traders fell upon thirstily as the shoppers began to arrive. A butcher was dressing a dozen rabbits, caught the evening before, while several bakeries, their tiny ovens sending whiffs of woodsmoke into the morning air, operated in overdrive, the bakers bringing fresh rolls and croissants out of the ovens and onto the wooden boards just faster than hungry shoppers were purchasing them. Some prepared pastries and delicacies, while the croissant-makers continued to knead and fold their dough, their hands twisting and turning like lightning as they talked, laughed, and cajoled one another.

It was a riot of activity, sights and smells. The market seemed to balance somewhere just over the line between order and anarchy, and verbal altercations over the price of a piece of cheese or the freshness of a piece of halibut erupted every few minutes. Fiery disputes, bitter for a moment, were forgotten seconds later. Nadir found the entire spectacle relaxing and refreshing.

She was home, even if just for a day.

Nadir had grown up in Paris, and her heart had remained part of the city ever since. Although she had spent most of her working life travelling from country to country, and the closest she had come to laying roots in the States was a six month lease on an apartment during her tenure with the Alcohol, Tobacco and Firearms bureau, she was not without property.

This small and somewhat rickety apartment on the top floor of the grand terraces on *Boulevard St-Germain*, on the edge of the Latin Quarter, had been hers for over a decade. Each month, even when on a government salary, she put most of her money aside towards the repayments on the place and for servicing the management company who cared for it when she was away. Now that money was less of an issue she owned the place outright, and employed a maid who tended to the apartment on a weekly basis, occasionally bringing in various tradesmen to repair leaky pipes, cracked plaster, or to repaint the ancient woodwork.

In return she had a place to call home. Even if it was mainly a memory for much of the year, it remained an anchor in her otherwise fluid life. And there were other anchors for her heart in this great, vibrant city.

Even if they caused her more pain than joy for much of the year.

She lifted the phone, a refurbished antique affair with a dial to spin and a rack of modern electronics inside to complete the call. It was the only fake thing in her apartment, and that only because the modern French telecoms system would no longer marry with the old fashioned technology. She spun in the number from memory.

"Hallo, Françoise?" she said.

"Denise? Is that you?" answered the woman in French.

"Of course. How are you? How have you been?"

"I've been fine. Things are good. Where are you? I haven't heard from you for months."

"Been busy, Françoise. Sorry." Nadir bit her lip anxiously. "I'm home, just for a day or two, but I'm home." There was a pause. "I want to see you, if I can." Another pause.

"Of course. It's been a long time. What about this evening, at the cafe on the corner of *Basilique Ste-Clotique*, say seven?"

"What about here. In an hour?" Nadir heard Françoise sigh.

"Oh, Denise." There was a sadness in her tone, but desire too. "We need to talk. I don't think meeting at your place is a great idea. It hurts too much."

"We'll talk. I promise," said Nadir.

"Will we? Will we talk? Will we talk about us? The future? Where you go off to for months at a time? Denise, it just won't do. You know how I feel about you, but you're like a stranger to me. It hurts too much." Nadir could hear the hurt in her lover's voice.

"I promise, we'll talk," she lied.

"You'll tell me things, then? We'll talk about our lives?" asked Françoise, suspicion in her voice. Nadir thought for a moment. She was deeply tired, but Paris energized her; made her reckless.

"Okay. Give me an hour to shut the shop, and I'll be along." Nadir smiled and her eyes gleamed. "Denise?" asked Françoise, softly.

"Yes?"

"Please. I mean it. Talk to me. Talk to me about us."

"I will."

"Good. An hour then. See you then."

Nadir hung the phone back on the elaborate cradle.

Quickly she dressed, grabbed her purse and headed to the market for some supplies. If the day stayed shiny and magical she doubted if either she or Françoise would be leaving the apartment for some time.

---oOo---

It wasn't so much a feeling of guilt, but a feeling of deep sadness which filled me as I lay with Kristal. The opposite emotion one normally felt in this situation.

Kristal had been true to her word. There was an Irish bar in Albuquerque, one of many as it turned out, and it was full of her various friends. I listed at least two Brads, one CJ, one Savannah, a few variations on Ched, Chuck and Chet, and several other names that I couldn't remember.

With the aid of some excellent Jamesons I was enjoying myself. True, it was hard not to realise that it was as authentically Irish as a tepee. For one thing, there was no peat-encrusted old bloke perched on a barstool, leering at the girls and grabbing at passers-by with black-nailed claws. Secondly, the toilet facilities were pristine, rather than partly shattered ceramic tiles held together by dried phlegm and super glue, with a sawn off hose dripping down the wall for washing your hands.

The final difference I recognised from my last trip to Ireland, and hence to a genuine Irish pub, was that there was no need to arrange a second mortgage in order to afford a pint.

When the time came to go to the hotel Kristal offered to walk me to it, and we laughed our way along the sidewalk until we reached the place. To make sure I was in safely, she accompanied me through check-in, and then upstairs to my room.

When we tumbled in and raided the mini-bar for two cold beers, she found a music channel on the plasma TV which was playing laid-back soul, and we chatted together for a while. I confess to even dancing with her for the best part of thirty seconds. This was more dancing than I'd done in thirty years, by the way. Then she kissed me, and the nightmare began.

I should have stopped right there, kissed her goodnight, and gone to bed with a good book.

Instead I went to bed with her.

She was perfect, and her kiss was perfect, as though it had been honed over many years in some lab by kissing professionals. Her hair smelled like an orchard in high summer, and her skin was immaculately soft and smooth.

With economy and skill, maintaining her kisses and nuzzles on my neck, she removed my shirt to reveal that most British of things, the short sleeved tan. My chest, although in reasonable shape for me, must have seemed like an anaemic slab of lard to Kristal compared to what she was used to. After some minutes she pulled her own top off and, for good measure, removed her bra. As expected, her breasts were sculpted and proud, and not a blemish marred her tanned torso. If the surgeon had been at work, his work was as invisible as that of the finest seamstress. It was certainly an erotic moment, but something inside me was holding me back. Exhaustion, guilt or plain old self-disgust.

Zara's image kept appearing in my mind.

I thought of calling the whole thing off, and just holding her for a spell, but she had a script and was determined to follow it.

Like every single thing in Kristal's life, there was a Right Way and a Wrong Way to do everything, from choosing clothes to getting a hairstyle, from dental hygiene to the correct choice of car. It seems that there was an established and accepted way of doing sex too.

As she undid my belt the sadness started to develop. It seemed so fake; so manufactured, so clinical. It was like having a car serviced, or being smiled at in some form of fucked-up church group. We were playing out a popular story rather than trying to conjure passion. We had but a fledgling friendship, and little in common beyond that, and it showed.

The final act began and I did the best I could, but waves of self-loathing swept over me the entire time. I felt empty and alone, while Kristal had fake orgasm after fake orgasm. It was all part of the game.

But I had had enough. There was no sense of abandon and no desire or lust. It was as if we were two people impersonating lovers on a stage.

It was as fake as that Irish bar.

On position number five or six – I honestly don't remember, as I was counting ceiling tiles by then – I found myself behind her as she lay on the bed. In defiance of every single rule of maleness, where back massages are strictly a prelude to trying your luck with a girl, I slowed down and began to gently rub her back with my fingers. There were a few moments when she tried to stick to the plot, but soon the relaxation of the massage soothed her. As she relaxed, I relaxed, and my sadness began to leave.

After ten minutes or so she sleepily turned to me, as beautiful as before, and embraced me with her head on my chest. We shared a few more kisses, tender friendly affairs, before falling asleep in each other's arms. Just two new friends who needed some comfort and some company.

I felt a calmness that wouldn't last.

---oOo---

Book Two. Bad Parent

Chapter twenty-seven

"You can call me Mr Gabriel" said the figure sitting on the edge of the bed. He flicked on the bedside light just as the woman, in sudden shock, dropped her small, brightly coloured fabric bag on the floor. "We have a mutual acquaintance."

Marcellus, returned from his walk, merely looked at the stranger, torn between getting his evening meal and greeting this new addition to the family. It had been a busy week for Marcellus, with many new faces to lick and sniff, but things had calmed down now the man-who-smelled-of-beer had gone away for a few days. He was an old dog, however, and he took it in his stride. Gabriel stood, his right hand outstretched. Zara's gaze focused on the pistol he was pointing at her midriff. Her colour drained.

"Oh my God," she said. "What do you want? I don't have anything of value." Then the name hit her. *Gabriel.* The Gabriel that Wolf had spoken of. Her mind twisted and her stomach turned, her guts suddenly full of cold, heavy stone.

"I'm here to talk to you about your son, Ms Moore," said Gabriel. "Please come inside and close the door." She did as she was told. The dog, too old to worry about things like stressed humans, merely decided that the new stranger wasn't much fun and ambled off to his dog bed, pausing briefly to slurp a drink from the dog bowl.

"You're the one Wolf spoke about, aren't you?" asked Zara.

"Yes. My old buddy Wolf." He grinned lewdly. "Of course, I hear that he's more than just an old friend to y'all, though. That right?" She stood silently, some colour slowly returning to her features. "You two been getting along like a house on fire, I hear." He beamed. "Well, a New Orleans cathouse on fire anyway."

"What do you want?" she asked.

"Good. I like getting to the point. Your special new friend Wolf is a pain in the ass when it comes to getting to the point. He needs everything spelled out for him. Glad you're straight down to business." He gestured to a chair opposite the bed. "Come and sit. Just a moment."

"I'd rather stand, thank you." Gabriel smiled, and looked at his pistol. He stood and, with the embarrassed look of someone merely doing an unpleasant job, put the weapon away under his jacket. He approached Zara, his smile wide, his hand outstretched for a handshake. When he was mere feet away, Zara flung her hand out across the galley worktop, grabbed a dish of leftover veggie pasta bake, and threw it hard at Gabriel's face.

Before the heavy ceramic dish had left the work surface, Gabriel slapped her arm to the side and it toppled harmlessly to the floor. Marcellus observed first the food, then the distress of his human, and decided to stay put for a moment. The food would be his anyway, since his stupid human thought floor-food was bad-food.

"I am," said Gabriel, still smiling, "getting really fucking sick of you people throwing dishes at me." He regarded his jacket sleeve, which had a gob of brown mozzarella hanging off it. With great care he flicked the cheese strand into the sink before, suddenly, he punched Zara hard in the belly, right in the solar plexus. Though he used a fraction of his speed, she didn't see the blow coming.

Her eyes widened as the wind left her, and a dull, awful pain spread through her abdomen. She doubled up, reaching for the floor with one hand, the other gripping her belly. An explosion of pain blossomed slowly through her body.

She wretched a few times, trying to get air back into her, but didn't vomit. As the pain continued to grow she slipped further onto the floor, ending up lying in a foetal position. She was too shocked for tears, but there was something bleak about Gabriel's harsh and precise attack that swamped her senses. He was so casual, and the pain was so great.

She'd never felt so scared.

"Sorry 'bout that, hon," said Gabriel. He easily lifted her to her feet by the arm and dragged her onto the bed, where she lay pale and gasping. "You and I are going on a little trip. You throw something at me again, or you try to run away, or you try to cook me eggs but you make them sunny side up instead of over-easy, and Mr Fist here will be saying hello to your ovaries again." Gabriel stroked her hair casually. "Course, if you do just what I say when I say it, then we're gonna get on just like Frankie and Jonny, and we'll have a whale of a time. Any luck and you'll be back to your ol' herbal cures and fucking Devenish in two, maybe three days." He gripped her chin, forcing her to look at him. "What you say, baby?"

"Okay. Whatever. Just don't hit me again." He smiled. Zara couldn't believe how sore she was. In the movies people whack each other all day long, and still get up for more. One punch and she was down. "Are you kidnapping me?"

"Yes, honey, I'm kidnapping your hippy ass. That okay with you?"

"What do you want? I don't have any money..."

"Really? I've got loads... you want some?" he asked, seeming perfectly sincere.

"What?" Zara's head was in a whirl, and she could barely think.

"Really. Knock yourself out, babe. I've got tonnes of the stuff. More than I know what to do with. Pain in the ass, really." Gabriel looked momentarily forlorn.

"So why are you kidnapping me if it's not for money?" He regarded Zara's confused face for a moment, before beaming at her and pointing.

"Christ... that's it! You are like Devenish. Peas in a goddamn pod." He snapped his finger and thumb. "Half of the fucking Marx brothers. I'm kidnapping you, honey, to get something else. And I don't mean your grilled pasta." He smiled and put his finger on his lips.

"All will be revealed later... but we got to do some revealing of our own first." Gabriel stood. "So, hon, you're gonna get out of these clothes of yours, and you're gonna sit right there in your tighty whiteys." he pointed to the chair he had indicated earlier, "and I'm gonna start this tub up and get on the road."

"My clothes? Why? God, what do you want? I'll cooperate. You don't have to do anything else to me. I'll cooperate." Zara pulled her arms around her dress protectively.

"Oh, I know you'll cooperate, Ms Moore. Now get out of those clothes and sit on the fucking chair." She looked terrified. Suddenly Gabriel smiled. "Ahhh... I see. Well, pretty lady, let me tell you this. First I'm too damned busy for some sport-fucking. Second, well, honey, you just aren't my type. Third, and most important, when people are half-naked they're just that little bit easier to control. Less likely to be heroes or to make a run for it. So get out of those clothes. Now." He picked up her bag and rifled through it before emerging with the keys for the barge cabin. Zara sat still. He stopped and considered her for an instant.

"Oh for fuck's sake," he said, dropping the keys next to the sink.

Gabriel stepped across the room and she recoiled back from him. In a single fluid motion, he grabbed the front of her dress and ripped it from her shoulders. It was her favourite dress, bought in a market in Camden Town two summers ago. She wore it only when she was very happy. The dress made her feel like she glowed. The bright fabric resisted for a moment, then tore clean down the middle. Zara wore no bra, and he pulled the torn fabric from around her until she was left covering her breasts with her arms, wearing just a pair of plain panties.

"That'll do. Now sit in the chair and don't move. I'll be back down in an hour or so, but first we gotta move this hunk of floating shit someplace different." She did as she was told, noticing a red bruise on her belly where he had punched her. "You just cost yourself a pretty dress. You sure you don't need any money?" She stared at him, still shocked. "Fair enough, but do what I say next time. Alright?"

Pale, vulnerable and half naked, Zara curled her legs up beneath her and started to cry.

"Ah hell," said Gabriel. "We haven't even reached the crying part yet." He pointed at her with sudden venom in his expression. "Just you pray that we don't reach that part, honey." Then he was gone, turning the key in the lock on the living quarters as he left.

The engine of the old boat began to throb, and she felt slow movement as the barge set off. The 'chug chug chug' of the motor and the onboard pump throbbed in time with her sudden, unstoppable sobs. Marcellus, suddenly aware of her distress, hid in the corner of her half-open wardrobe.

Her dress lay torn on the floor along with her hopes for a happier life.

---oOo---

Chapter twenty-eight

Mr Cassiel was quite the conversationalist, and I feared that I wouldn't be able to get a word in edgeways past all the ominous, heavy silence.

He drove a plain black car with a powerful engine, and wore an expensive suit of a deep, dark fabric. He called me "Mr Devenish" outside the hotel, and helped me to load my bag into the car, then we sped off. That was the extent of our conversation, and any further attempts to engage with him prompted the reply "fuck I know" and nothing else.

Kristal and I had parted on good terms, and I realised that I liked her. It was impossible not to love her enthusiasm for life or her bubbly nature. But I think that even she realised that the most we could expect between us was casual friendship and little more. We exchanged numbers and I made a tentative arrangement to meet with her before my flight back.

In an outstanding example of how complex and pathetic the male mind can be, the moment I left her with our return meeting arranged I had thoughts of being naked with her once again. It's not true to say that men are simple creatures who think about one thing, and one thing only. We think about lots of things, many of them laudable and moral, and we consider dozens of future paths of consequence during our Zen-like calculations about our actions.

But, yeah, most of these deep and contemplative thoughts end up being to do with getting laid.

The landscape we drove through was stunning and dramatic. Wide deserts stretched forever on either side of the freeway, and there were few specks of human civilisation to mar the view. But it was the sky – this enormous, endless sky – that stole my attention. For a while. After an hour, though, it was too big, too infinite, and the landscape seemed too flat and empty by comparison. It was overkill, and I wished I could curl up under a nice, well-defined, blanket.

Eventually we arrived in a small, spread out town called White Rock. It was sunny and warm, and Cassiel pulled up outside a diner called the *Bandolier Grill*.

"We're here," he said, turning off the engine.

"What now?" I asked.

"We're early. I were you, I'd go in and wait. Grab a coffee and use the john."

"Is the coffee good here," I asked pleasantly.

"Fuck I know." Cassiel pulled a card from the breast pocket of his jacket. "When you're done, call this number. I'll pick you up." The card was a triumph of graphic design. It was a plain white affair printed on heavy stock, with a single phone number in *Courier* font. No name. No strapline.

"Okay. Can you open the boot for my bag?" I asked, pleasantly.

"It's a trunk. Won't need your bag," said Cassiel. "You got your passport with you?" I nodded. "Good. Your boy Moore he gonna have some people with him. If I was them, I'd come in to see you first. Get some *bona fides* before letting you chew the fat with our star player. Passport show them you're who you say you are." He shrugged. "Mightn't believe that, though. Might wanna check for themselves. That's up to them. You just do as they say and sit tight. Drink your coffee."

"What do you mean by 'check for themselves'?" I asked.

"Fuck I know. Just that they might. Know I would." He started the big engine again.

With that, I left Cassiel and headed for the diner. No kiss, no 'good luck'. I walked into the place, which was fairly empty and looked like any other diner I'd seen on countless US TV shows, and I took a seat in a booth beside a window. A waitress materialised and I ordered coffee.

I checked my phone. Reception was strong here and I had an obscure text message from Bill, a rarity given how much he loathed texting.

```
Brave Sir Knight, the gallant Sir Rodney seems to
have pulled up his banners and gone on Crusade to
unknown lands. He answers neither telegram nor
knocks upon his castle door. I shall dispatch
missives when I learn more. B
```

So, our Sir Rodney had gone missing. If I was him I would have headed south to weather the storm too, and put as much distance between myself and the Oxford rumour mills as possible. I resolved to call Bill in the morning.

And so I sat in the strange diner in the middle of nowhere, feeling vulnerable and tired, and I waited to meet my son for the first time.

---oOo---

Chapter twenty-nine

Nadir cried, and couldn't stop.

She knelt on her bed, legs tucked beneath her, with her back straight and her head buried on the shoulder of her friend, Françoise's long wavy locks tumbling across Nadir's own midnight black hair. The two women wore simple tee shirts, Françoise's hand resting on Nadir's, holding her protectively. Outside the street had grown quiet, and the Parisian twilight drifted duskily through the drapes, flickers of light from the century-old street lamps adding shape and pattern to the two figures as they embraced.

"I want out of this, Françoise," said Nadir, between sobs. "I can't keep doing this. I want *this* life. This life right here. I don't want to be that other person anymore."

"So leave, Denise. Just leave it. Stay here. Don't go back." She was shocked that, after several years of knowing and loving this woman, she had had no idea about what she was... about what she did.

They had been together all day, in the little room above the market. As always, once they saw each other, they were in each other's arms immediately. Hours passed that morning as they lay together, smiling and kissing, exploring each other like it was the first time. As always Françoise expected to meet only silence when the time came to talk. And so it was. For much of the afternoon, as they shared some wine and ate the delightful breads and cheeses from the market, Nadir would evade and distract Françoise from her questions.

She had expected it, and wasn't surprised. Nadir's gentle kisses, which grew so quickly in passion and depth, soon distracted her from her growing upset. They had something so real and pure when they were together, even Nadir's evasiveness and reluctance to talk about anything outside of this room, anything beyond this city, couldn't ruin the moments they shared.

In the afternoon they showered together, and Nadir loaned Françoise one of her many tee shirts as they sat together on the bed sharing more of the deliciously dark red wine. They kissed and laughed and toasted their love, as though the day would never end.

But Nadir wouldn't open up about her own life. It was the elephant in the room, sitting fat and ugly in the corner, snorting at them derisively whenever they spoke of a future together.

Then Françoise fell silent, a sad expression on her face. Nadir tried everything, all her tricks, to get her to smile and kiss again, but Françoise refused. With a tear in her eye, she thanked Nadir for a wonderful day and began to get dressed. Nadir wouldn't let her leave the bed, and showered her with kisses and embraces, telling Françoise that she loved her and asking her not to leave.

"Anything, my love... I'll do anything... just don't go! Please stay with me!" cried Nadir. Françoise, wearing just the teeshirt, her long legs slightly parted, her hair drifting across her face and framing her sad eyes, stood facing her.

"Just tell me, Denise. Just tell me about your life when you're not here. I love you, but I don't know you. And I need to know." They both remained still, locked in each other's gaze, Françoise waiting for Nadir to look away and as she always did.

She waited for Nadir to lie to her again.

Instead she began to cry. From a few sobs it escalated into full blown hysteria, and Françoise held her tightly, deeply shocked at her lover's upset, and between the tears Nadir told her everything. Frightening things. Her lover, the woman she loved more than life and who she couldn't get out of her head, lived in a parallel world to her own. She did things that shocked Françoise to her core.

And, most importantly, her beloved Denise Nadir wanted out of it.

"Why don't you just walk away, Denise? Tell this Monsieur Gabriel that you're leaving... moving on with your life. Surely you can just tell him that and walk away?" Françoise held her hand tightly, imploring her to listen and take her advice.

"Do you think I can just *leave*? Tell Gabriel and the others that I'm quitting? Have you been listening to me about what these people are like, Françoise? Have you?" Her anger mixed with distress made her face twist in an unnatural, ugly way. "He *kills* people, Françoise. He enjoys killing people the way other people enjoy wine and a good meal. If there is the slightest threat to him or the others, even the whisper of a threat, he will start to kill people. And it doesn't matter who they are. Friends, partners, strangers, politicians, priests, children, wives... fuck. It doesn't even faze him." She fiercely wiped her face, and drank deeply from her glass. "But there's something wrong with him now. He's operating loose. Dangerously loose, like he doesn't care anymore. It makes him even more unpredictable." She bit her lower lip. "He's been leaving me totally exposed, and I've got no option but to do what he says."

"Can't you go back to... what was it, the FBI?"

"ATF... it's similar," said Nadir quietly.

"Can't you go back to them and tell them about Gabriel... tell them he's blackmailing you or threatening you or something. Won't they be able to protect you?" Nadir snorted.

"Against him, maybe, but Gabriel has dozens of people working for him, and I don't know more than two or three of them. If I turn him in he'll simply disappear and I'll be looking over my shoulder for the rest of my life. Hell, it would be even worse if they catch him. The things he could tell them about me. Horrible things that I can't deny."

"Surely they'll understand? Tell them you had no option," said Françoise.

"That's the thing. That's the problem." Nadir smiled, sadly. "I had every choice, and I chose to work with him."

"Why?"

"I would love to say it was for the benefit of others, that it was to protect people from things that the law can't save them from. Perhaps it was to an extent. But, ultimately, I did it for the thrill, and I did it for the money. Christ. If my bosses knew... if they knew for a second about my work with Gabriel. Shit, Françoise, do you know what 'treason' is? Do you know what my own government would do to me for that?" She shook her head, shuddering at the thought.

"But they're not your government. Your country, your place is right here. Right here with me." Françoise stroked her lover's hair gently.

"I know... but how can I get out, Françoise. If Gabriel pulls off this next job, and if it goes wrong, then they'll know. *They'll know* that it was me who was the mole. That it was me on the inside."

"You have to stop Gabriel, then. Can't you just go to the Americans and just *tell* them? Surely they'll understand!" Nadir laughed, a coarse harsh laugh.

"Françoise, my love. You are so innocent. You can trust *no-one* in this job. For one thing, the Americans, understanding or not, will still call me traitor. I might, just might, get extradited back to France, leaving me to live my life. Just as likely, I'll end up in an American gaol or dead in a ditch."

"I love you, Denise. I'm on your side. And I want you, I want you and me, here, like this, for life." Françoise kissed her on the forehead, stroking her hair as the sobbing stopped. "I'll do anything for you, my love. I mean it." Nadir held her tightly, and raised her head to gaze into Françoise's eyes. Her expression was a flickering mixture of flinty hardness, unrestrained love, and the merest spark of hope.

"Anything, Françoise? Would you do anything?" Françoise held her gaze and nodded, a tear forming in her own eye. *Yes,* she thought. *I would do anything for this woman.*

"Help me kill him," whispered Nadir. The room stilled, both women paused in their breathing, her question hanging in the air between them. "If I kill him before this job is over then maybe, just maybe, it'll be over. I can resign from government work and never have to worry about him again. But nobody must ever suspect that I was behind his death. His associates, if they see any reason to think I was behind it, will come after me." She wiped her face and held her jaw firm. "Maybe come after you, too. And nothing will stop all of them."

Calmer now, she lifted her glass and took a sip of wine, brushing her hair away from her wet eyes with her fingertips. "I can't pull it off alone. I need you to help me."

"Show me how," said Françoise, and the fleck of hope in Nadir's eyes burst into flame.

"You mean it?" Nadir put her glass down and gripped Françoise's arms, gazing into her eyes. "You would help me kill someone?"

"I'll do it myself, if it gives me you."

They fell into each other's arms, crying and kissing. One wineglass overturned, forgotten, and its contents turned the wooden floor black in the half-light from the street outside.

It looked like blood.

---oOo---

Chapter thirty

Benjamin sat in his office, flicking through files. His afternoons were usually like this, catching up on different reports from the various subordinate departments beneath him. Reading swiftly, he set each report onto different piles depending on importance and whether further action was needed. Occasionally he scrawled notes in his cramped handwriting in the margins of reports before stacking them.

The next file was a slender one, sent from his MI6 opposite number. The first page was a printout of the military record overview of the mysterious Sergeant Gabriel, culminating of course in the brief and entirely false KIA report, a few supplementary notes making up the rest of the report.

"Damn," he said aloud. He'd almost forgotten about Gabriel or, at least, he hoped that Parkinson would have. Some scabs don't respond well to being picked. He flicked through the details, the photograph of the young marine challenging him from the paper. "So, you're in England now," Benjamin whispered. "What are you up to there I wonder?"

He reread the last few pages, one of them a short summary from the British agent who'd bumped into the esteemed Sgt Gabriel. Something caught his eye, and he went over the sentence again.

Operative conducting background check on UK Citizen (details attached) as per request US NSA.

Benjamin knew that there could be a hundred reasons why the NSA wanted a background check on a Brit, and most of the reasons were inane and of little value. Still, the sentence gave him pause to think. He looked up the attached details of the woman, a seemingly everyday citizen, living her life out in the UK. The son was listed as working in the States, and this was probably the reason for the check. Work visas were becoming harder to get, even for allied countries, and more and more jobs were listed on the Homeland Security list of security sensitive professions. Almost certainly the whole thing was routine and innocuous. Nothing to work a sweat up over.

Until Gabriel appeared right in the middle of it.

Benjamin made a note on the file, requesting full information about the son and what he was doing in the US. Still hoping that Gabriel was there for an entirely coincidental reason, he put the file at the top of the 'urgent' pile, and began working through the last of the dozen or so reports about olive skinned men with wild eyes and dreams of martyrdom which he had to assess by the morning.

Not one of them looked as scary as Gabriel.

---oOo---

Andreas put his phone away and continued to pick at the cheese salad. It was good cheese, different to the German stuff, hard yet creamy and with a tangy aftertaste. He thought about what he had learned so far.

So, this Gabriel was to be left well alone. He was known to MI6, although they had very little information about him. Normally that would mean he was a bit player, but Berne had intimated that they suspected he was something different. Something dangerous. Perhaps he should finish his work today, get on the road to London, and hope he didn't cross paths with Gabriel again.

It was the sensible thing to do.

He finished his lunch, paid the barman who said he'd call him if he wanted to upgrade his cash registers with the latest touch screen versions, and went for a walk by the canal. Outside the pub he lit a cigarette. It was a rare vice for Andreas, who would smoke perhaps one or two a day, and then only after good food. With the taste of the tobacco complimenting the aftertaste of his cheese and wine, he turned onto the canal.

The barge was gone.

He stopped and quickly ran through what he had discovered so far. Zara Moore came here every summer, from late spring through to early autumn. She had done for seven years, with no variations. She was known and liked in the area. She had friends here. She had work here. He had read her appointment book just the other day, while her fat guard dog munched on a treat he had handed it as he crept onboard. She had appointments here until at least two weeks from now. But now she was gone.

Andreas didn't believe in coincidences, and he didn't believe in sending in a report half-finished. Yes, it might not be the sensible thing to do, but he was becoming bored with the sensible life.

Gabriel or not, Andreas wanted to find that barge, and find it quickly.

---oOo---

Chapter thirty-one

My, what large necks you have, I thought as the two men entered the diner.

I was on coffee number three, and 'john' visit number two, although I had yet to bump into someone called John in the toilet. I'd met a Chuck earlier, but that was it. Beyond that the restaurant had been quiet. The occasional local had been in, ordered food, looked at the stranger in the crumpled jacket with the floppy hair, ate their meal, flirted with the waitress, and left again. That was pretty much the height of the excitement so far.

These two were coming to meet me, though. The moment they entered they scanned the room, picked up on me straightaway, and then scanned the room some more. They approached my booth, the larger of the two speaking first.

"Mr Devenish, sir?" I nodded and he extended his hand. As I shook it, I noticed that they both had carefully cropped, neat haircuts, bright blue eyes and perfectly clean-shaven jaws. Lean muscle rippled under identical, cleanly pressed, jackets.

They looked like Mormon bouncers.

"I'm Agent Sharpe, sir, and this is Agent Mary." Sharpe sat opposite me and, with the smallest of gestures for me to move over, his colleague with the girl's name sat next to me. Just like old friends, but old friends who can see every corner of the diner and every person in it.

"Hello. I'm Wolf Devenish. How can I help you?"

"We work for the United States Government, sir. We understand that you have an appointment to meet Mr Martin Moore here today. Is that correct?"

"Yes. That is correct." I smiled, albeit a tired smile. Sharpe regarded me intently, not a flicker of recognition or emotion crossing his face. Mary continued to stare around the room, while the waitress arrived and asked for our order.

"Two coffees, large and black please ma'am." Sharpe looked at me, an eyebrow raised. I pointed at my cup. "And a refill for our friend." The waitress trundled off, and Sharpe continued talking.

"What is the nature of your appointment with Mr Moore today, sir?"

"It's private family business, I'm afraid Mr Sharpe." The man barely blinked. He just held eye contact with his sapphire-blue eyes.

"Special Agent Sharpe, sir. It's our job to protect Mr Moore, and we need to know the nature of your business with him, sir."

"I'm his father," I said.

"I see, sir. And have you and Mr Moore ever met?"

"No. I only recently found out that he was my son." Sharpe considered me a moment before continuing.

"How did you find this out, sir?" His gaze continued, unflinching and unnerving.

"One of your people told me."

"How, sir? By letter, or did they meet with you?"

"She came to my house. Her name was Ms Nadir. She told me that my name had come up on some vetting process about Martin, and that he wanted to meet with me." I shrugged. "So here I am." He nodded when I mentioned Nadir.

"Do you have any identification, sir?" I gave him my passport, watching his eyes track my hands as I delved into my jacket pocket.

He took the passport and looked at it, comparing my face with it, and checking all the other details including the visa stamp. Apparently satisfied, he returned it to me.

"Thank you, sir." Mary, beside me, pulled a small tablet computer, like an iPhone but larger, out of his jacket pocket.

"Can I have your hand please, sir?" Mary spoke with the same, generic American accent, but with a deeper voice. I held my hand out and he placed it onto the screen of the device. There was a brief flash and the imprint of my palm and fingerprints were left on the screen, fading rapidly. "And the other one, please, sir." The process was repeated with the left hand. Then Mary put the device back in his pocket. "I'll be right back," he said to Sharpe, and he rose and left the diner just as the coffee arrived.

Sharpe and I sat in silence for a few moments. He seemed comfortable with that, but I'm English and I wasn't.

"So... you work for the government?" I ventured.

"Yes, sir."

"Must be interesting work."

"It is, sir."

"You can call me Wolf if you want..."

"Thank you, sir." And we drank more coffee, and sat in silence.

"Mind if I check my phone?" I asked.

"Go right ahead, sir" said Sharpe.

I checked the mobile, and there was another message from Bill. But none from Zara, and she was really the only message I was looking forward to getting. I put my phone away, and saw Sharpe regarding me again. The slightest expression of puzzlement on his face.

"Must be a big day for you, sir," he said.

"In what way, Agent Sharpe?"

"First day meeting your son. Must be a big day for you."

"Yes... I guess it is. I haven't really had much time to think about it. Do you have kids?"

"Yes, that I do sir. I've got a boy and a girl. They're my whole life. They're the reason I get up each morning."

"That and your government work, I suppose," I said.

"Well, sir, for me they're one and the same thing. My family are everything to me, and everything we are is tied up in this country, so this country and my family are all one and the same to me, sir. I keep my country safe, I keep my family safe. Two ends of the same hotdog, sir."

I had a sudden urge to salute him, a patriotic tear in my eye.

"How come you didn't know you had a son, sir?" He seemed genuinely curious.

"I just never knew. The mother didn't tell me." He considered this.

"See, sir, and I don't mean to be rude. Just forthright if you will. But, if I had been with some lady one night, then I would have made an effort to make sure that she was okay, sir. Or so it seems to me." He was huge, probably armed, but I was tired. I didn't want to be insulted by more Americans.

"Well, not everyone's like you Agent Sharpe. I guess you've stayed with your high school sweetheart all these years and live happily ever after in a beautiful house with beautiful kids, a flag flying on the front yard, and a fresh apple pie in the oven. Isn't that the way it is?"

"Not really, sir. My high school sweetheart and I were planning to get married, but it didn't work out. I met my wife five years ago."

"I'm sorry. I didn't mean to be rude. I guess love runs as smoothly here as it does in the UK."

"I don't know about that, sir, because Courtney and I were engaged to be married. We'd been happy together since we were sixteen years of age."

"So what happened?" I asked. He looked uncomfortable, as though revisiting painful memories.

"Nine eleven happened, sir. My fiancée was in the second tower. I joined the service right after that. I wanted to fight back"

"Shit. I really am sorry." Christ. Even I would want to fight back after something like that. These people with their curt tones of voice, immaculate suits, obsession with flag and country, really weren't that different to anyone else I'd ever met. I resolved to sit silently and wait for Agent Mary, but Sharpe wasn't finished.

"She died because of a combination of high achievement and bad luck, sir. She was top of her class, and got an internship with one of the financial institutions. If she'd been dumb, she'd never have been there. If she had been stupid," he pronounced it 'stoopid', "she'd have been working as a waitress in some Manhattan cafe instead of as an intern up the tower. Dumb bad luck," ne said, sadly.

I was warming to Sharpe. He had an inner conversation going on where he thinks issues through. I couldn't tell if it made him a good agent or a bad one, but it made him more human.

"Well, I'm sorry anyway," I said, meaning it.

"Don't be, sir. Shit happens."

"Anyway, thank you for the conversation. My driver wasn't very talkative."

"Who was that, sir?" he asked.

"Mr Cassiel. He picked me up from the hotel this morning."

"Don't know him. Must be a different department, sir."

"Well, thanks for the chat anyway."

"It's okay, sir. I enjoy discussing the tragedies of my life with total strangers. It's healthy to relive painful memories that I've tried for years to forget." His face was impassive, and I couldn't tell if he was being serious, sarcastic or just plain angry.

We sat in silence, waiting for Agent Mary.

After a few more minutes he returned and sat next to me again, nodding at Sharpe.

"Checks out," was all he said.

"Okay, sir," said Sharpe, suddenly all business-like again. "Sorry for the cloak and dagger stuff, but your son is an important person and it's our job to protect him. I'm sure that you understand."

"National security?" I volunteered.

"Exactly, sir." Sharpe and Mary stood to leave, each offering me their hand in turn. "We'll confirm with UNM that you're here, and that Mr Moore is free to visit. I imagine he'll be along in an hour or so, if you don't mind waiting." I shook my head.

"Guess I've waited over twenty years. I can wait another hour or so."

"Of course, sir." Mary walked to the exit and Sharpe, momentarily undecided, turned to me again. "Good luck, sir. I hope that you and Mr Moore get along."

"Me too," I said, and he was gone leaving me to wait some more.

---oOo---

In a driveway across from the diner, Cassiel put down his scratched and worn Nintendo DS and watched Sharpe and Mary get into their Lexus and drive off. He punched the speed-dial number on his phone. Across the Atlantic, Gabriel answered.

"Go."

"He's clear. The kid should be along anytime now."

"Good. Let me know when Moore arrives and I'll call Devenish. I'll give him twenty-four hours to get his shit sorted, so you'll need to keep on top of him till it's done. Don't underestimate him, Tony. He's got a mind like two wildcats fighting in a bag. He'll try something to fuck things up. Make sure he doesn't."

"Will do." Cassiel paused for a moment. "And after the exchange?"

"Haven't thought that far ahead yet. Depends how things play out. I'm thinking about forcing Devenish to make the delivery."

"The Brit? Why would you do that? You've just said he's trouble."

"I know that, but I'd love to see his face when he has to hand it over to me."

"I think the postal route's the way to go, if it were up to me. Ten minutes after exchange, both players out of the game, and the item is on its way along with a hundred million other packages. They'll never find the fucking thing. You get Devenish involved, and you push the timescales. Leave a window for someone to get wise and stop him." Cassiel had worked with Gabriel for a long time, and was used to him changing plans at the last moment. It was what made the work so interesting. In this case, though, his judgement seemed rash.

"I know that too. I'm just thinking of the poetry of it. Devenish is about to face up to a kid he never knew he had. He'll feel like shit as it is. I love the idea of forcing him to betray that kid too. You know what I mean?"

"Fuck I know," said Cassiel.

"Let me know when Moore turns up."

"Roger that, boss." Gabriel hung up, and Cassiel returned to his game.

Gabriel put the phone back into his pocket and looked at the woman sleeping under the sheets. It was very late in the UK, but he didn't need sleep. Not for a day or two at least. Moore, however, when the adrenaline and fear had worn off, asked him if she could go to bed. She lay with the blankets pulled protectively around her.

He took a drink from the sticky cola he'd bought earlier , some energy drink which made his tongue feel furry and his vision jumpy. But he was used to stimulants. Back in the day he'd stayed more or less awake for four days just on caffeine and adrenaline, and it was one skill that hadn't changed with age. From his bag he took a small tablet computer, a little web cam built in to the screen, and set it up on a stand so it had a clear view of the bed and the woman sleeping in it.

"Show time, honey," said Gabriel, as he shook the woman awake. For an instant she looked peaceful, as one does when lost in a dream. When she focused on Gabriel her eyes widened in alarm then resignation.

"What do you want?" she asked. "Can't you let me sleep?"

"Nope. We're going to make a little video for your lover and your son."

"What? Why?"

"Hey... relax. You want this over, don't you?" She nodded. "Well this is something you gotta do to get this over."

"What do you want me to do?" asked Zara, the sheets pulled around her for comfort.

"Well, honey. You just gotta sit there on the bed beside me and look nervous."

"I am nervous."

"Then it'll be easy." He pulled the sheets off her, and she covered her chest with her arms again, visibly shaking.

Gabriel checked the small computer, making sure that the sound and picture were right. He put his bag, a small black rucksack, next to the bed.

"Let's get this done," he said, and sat beside her on the bed as she trembled, her face red from sudden tears.

"Howdy, Mr Devenish," said Gabriel. "And, I suppose, a big hello to your newly discovered son..."

---oOo---

Chapter thirty-two

Benjamin threw the file across his office and grabbed the phone, stabbing at numbers until he got a dialling tone.

"Word is 'Anchorage'. Counterword please," said the voice on the line.

"Counterword is 'meadow'... hurry up, son."

"Yes sir." Benjamin waited to be connected to his contact in Fort Meade, Maryland. Headquarters of the NSA.

"Benjamin... how you doing?"

"Hi Paul. I'm doing fine. How's the family?" Benjamin could never decide if it was more appropriate to consider Paul Weisner as 'very high up' in the Intelligence game, or 'very deep down'. He guessed it depended on whether you looked at it from the outside or inside. Either way, he was considerably more senior than the 'Systems Manager' his wife thought he was.

"Great, thanks. You gotta come round for some suds next time you're over this way. Anyway, what can I do for you today?"

"Right. A few names crossed my desk the other day from the Brits. I'm trying to join the dots, but I've hit a brick wall."

"This a favour for the British?"

"I guess so. But it might involve us too."

"How so?" asked Weisner.

"One of the names was Gabriel."

"Shit. He still around? I'd hoped he'd retired, or died, or been recalled to whatever fucking mothership he came from."

"Nope. He's in Britain. I'm trying to find out why," said Benjamin.

"Okay. Shoot. What's the brick wall?"

Benjamin ran through the details he knew so far, giving his NSA contact a short but precise summary.

"The brick wall, Paul, seems to be at your end. The son, the one who kicked off the background check, is working for us in New Mexico. Physics genius. Usual sort of thing. However, files won't give me any information about what he's working on. Just a name. 'Project Phoenix', and the rest of it is so classified God Himself wouldn't be allowed to read it."

"What you want me to do? If it's classified that much, it's for a reason. You know that." Weisner tutted down the phone. "Best just leave it, Benjamin."

"Of course I know that, but it's the missing piece of the puzzle. If Gabriel appeared in the same sleepy British village as the mother of someone working for us on a classified project, then what would you think?"

"Coincidence?"

"Bullshit. And you know it," said Benjamin, angrily.

"Still, doesn't get past your problem, though. Bullshit or not, I'm not able to give you more information. But thanks for the heads up about Gabriel. I'll get someone on it."

"Paul. I don't want a teeshirt, a tour or the mother-fucking blueprints. I just need to know if Project Phoenix is something that Gabriel could be trying to get near. That's all. I just need to know that it's not some asshole theoretical project to see if we can make troops shit bullets or fart lightning. I need to know if it's real or not." There was a pause, which was good because if Paul was going to lie to him it would come as naturally to him as breathing. The pause meant that he was thinking. Considering.

"It's real, Benjamin. It's a real project, with real results. That's why it's classified so highly," said Weisner, shortly.

"Right. So Gabriel could be a threat?"

"No. Not a chance. It's tight as a duck's asshole. No-one can get near Phoenix or anyone working on it, without a background check right back to Adam and Eve. Gabriel's out of luck."

"Alright. So nothing to worry about?"

"Not from where I'm sitting. Relax. I'd say Gabriel's in Britain for another reason. Stealing the crown jewels, goosing the Brit Prime minister, burning down London. Something easy, anyway," said Weisner, a little too smoothly for Benjamin's liking.

"Okay. Thanks Paul," he said.

"No problem. Get in touch about those beers, my man."

"Will do. Thanks."

"Cool. Oh, one thing. Forget the words Project Phoenix, will you? You don't want that kind of thing bouncing around your head. Alright?"

"Already forgotten."

"That's my boy. See ya down the line." And Paul was gone. Benjamin considered the conversaion. If he believed Weisner then there was probably no problem. Definitely not *his* problem anyway. He'd done the Right Thing, followed up his hunch, and passed the information along to the right people.

In a private, unrecorded conversation.

He walked across the office and retrieved his file. Yes, there were his requests for information about the son, all sent from his office and authorised with his signature. And, even if his conversation with Weisner was deniable and unrecorded, his refused request about Martin Moore's work for the government was certainly not. His name would have been flagged, as it always is when access to a classified file is made, regardless of if the request is denied or not.

He tapped the file against his leg as he thought, standing in the middle of the office and staring into the middle distance as he processed scenarios and outcomes in his head. Best case, it was all a coincidence and nothing would happen. Worst case, Gabriel was up to something and it concerned Project Phoenix. Regardless of how secure Weisner believed it was, Benjamin had done this job for too long to believe that anything was perfectly secret. He'd seen too many careers hit the wall because of undue faith in systems and procedures. Every layer of security they depended on was, ultimately, designed by fallible human beings.

And people make mistakes.

If Project Phoenix, whatever the hell that was, became threatened or compromised, and only he knew about the threat in advance, then it would be a demotion at best, a pink slip and no career at worst. He had to protect himself, protect his job, and protect his future. Benjamin decided to pull in a few markers. He needed to find out what Phoenix was all about and, more importantly, see if it was vulnerable. Once he'd worked that out he might be able to relax. What concerned him most was that if he found a vulnerability ,he was sure Gabriel would have found it too.

And probably a long time ago, leaving Benjamin far behind the game.

He made a few calls and organised a car to be brought round for him. It was time to leave the office, and get back into the field. Time to get some answers.

---oOo---

Chapter thirty-three

I had not expected this.

In the last week I'd been imagining what Martin Moore, okay, *my son*, would be like. I wondered how tall he would be, or whether he would be slim or heavy. I'd been curious to know if his eyes or nose resembled mine, or if he had kept an English accent or developed that peculiar mid-Atlantic bastard-accent like Madonna or Lloyd Grosman. Would he be a funny person, with a humorous glint in his eye, or was he a shy creature more comfortable with mathematical equations than human contact. These questions bubbled around the back of my mind, and I left them to simmer away without paying them too much heed.

But I had never, not once, imagined that the little bugger would be more grown-up than me.

"Are you okay, Mr Devenish? I know that it's been a bit of a shock to you too, and I hope I haven't caused you distress, but it's something that's been on my mind for many years. A mystery which I wanted to solve. You were a question that I wanted an answer to," said Martin.

He was taller than me and had dark brown hair, slightly unruly, but it looked like the locks which hung carelessly over his forehead and over his eyes were deliberate. A style statement which he had chosen and maintained. Clean-shaved, with a firm jaw and sharp features, he had sparkling eyes like Zara. He dressed casually but well, in a dark polo-neck top which complimented his long neck and, beneath the soft fabric, I could see that he was well toned. Dark, expensive jeans, a pair of black half-boots, and a leather jacket completed the look.

"Of course, Martin. I'm fine. I totally understand that you would want to know about your past... about your father. Who wouldn't?"

"Actually, I wasn't that interested about who my father was for many years. It didn't really matter to me. I'm sorry if that upsets you." His expression was confident yet concerned for my welfare. I felt somehow proud of how mature he was, but wasn't totally sure if I liked him.

He reminded me too much of what I should be like; of how I should behave, and he was twenty-odd years my junior.

"It doesn't upset me, Martin, and please call me Wolf. I think our situation is too strange to use the word 'dad'." I smiled rakishly, and he returned the smile, albeit in that slightly awkward way people smile at the drunken uncle who thinks they can dance at wedding discos. "Was it not odd for you, growing up without a father?"

"Not really. It was just how things were. Lots of people at my school came from single parents. You're aware that over a third of marriages in the UK break up?" I nodded. "So I had plenty of friends who lived alone with their mother. I was just in a similar boat. Literally, of course. It wasn't a problem, you know. I grew up in the nineteen-nineties, not the eighteen-nineties."

"And it didn't cause you any distress? Any feelings of disconnection to your roots?" He laughed shortly.

"Really Mr Devenish... okay, Wolf... What exactly was your role in my life before today?" He paused and I held my hands up in submission. "Precisely. Your role in my life was merely to supply my mother with some DNA, from which I emerged. Your role in that worked out perfectly, and fairly early on I realised I had to get on with living my life rather than worrying about some theoretical nuclear family I may have had."

"I find that hard to believe... you must have had questions..." I felt hurt. Surely I meant more to him than that?

"I did, and I asked them. However, what's the point of asking questions if you don't accept the answers. It's just a waste of everyone's time. So, when my mother told me that she wasn't sure who my father was... when she started to cry about it, and apologise again and again to me, I simply accepted that answer. I didn't want to see her suffer by repeating the question. There was no point."

"Why did she cry?" I could visualise Zara in distress, and the part of me that had feelings for her twisted inside me. Recent events, and my recent behaviour, tumbled across my mind and I felt alternately angry with myself and sorry for those who knew me. I made a snap decision to see what would happen between Zara and me before I moved on with my life. When your son reminds you of what you could be like if you weren't such a selfish idiot, it's high time to make these kinds of decision.

"She cried because *she* wanted that family. She wanted it more than I did. She knew what a family could be. Of course, having never experienced that, I was in no position to know if I wanted one or not."

"*She* wanted us to be a family?" I asked, amazed.

"More than anything. It didn't have to be you, I guess, but my mother is a very honest woman. Very true to herself. If she was going to play happy families, she wanted it to be with her true family. My father would have to be my father. And he would have to *want* to be with us." A brief moment of sadness flashed across his features. "But she had some form of mental block. There was something which stopped her from figuring out who the father was. So she tried the second best option, and dated a few guys over the years. That was fine by me, I didn't really care, and it was nice to have a man about the place to talk to, particularly in my early teens when I had all these ideas and I found that guys were more interested in what I liked. Science fiction programmes, fantasy novels, technology, computers... My mum didn't really enjoy those things, but she encouraged me anyway."

"So, if you were never concerned with finding me or getting to know me, why did you ask to meet me now?" He paused for a moment... constructing and tasting his words before he spoke.

"Personally, because I could. You are the answer to a question I asked when I was very young, and I wanted to meet you and put the matter to rest."

"So I'm a question you wanted answering? Is that it?" I felt cross, but I was just reacting to my feelings of self-importance being attacked. I understood exactly what he was saying.

"See? You think I'm dispassionate. But you're confusing common sense with emotions. Ask yourself, what else were you to me? You certainly weren't a father, and I can't have emotions toward a man I only met ten minutes ago." I held his gaze and nodded. "We may develop a relationship in the future,

Wolf, but, at the moment you're just a living, breathing answer to a question I've had since I could first speak."

"That's it, then, is it? Are you happy with the answer?"

"I am, actually. It makes sense to me. I see some of my characteristics in you. Particularly in your emotional confusion about things." I raised an eyebrow in puzzlement. "Oh, don't think I don't have emotions, Wolf. It's the damned emotions that made me decide to meet you. I've known about you for almost a year now, but only recently made up my mind about contacting you."

"Go on."

"There are two other reasons for getting you back into my life..." He sighed for a moment, again framing his words with precision. "The main one is my mother. We fell out a year ago, and it's been hard on both of us. But I couldn't carry on the way we were. As a kid it was difficult enough accepting her ideas and ways when I was convinced she was deluding herself every day. When it ended up in flaming rows more often than not, I stopped engaging with her. My moving to the States was the last straw, and we've barely spoken since."

"How do I help with that?" I asked.

"She needs a family of her own, Wolf, more than she needed a son. She deserves the chance, finally, to try and make one."

"Hold on... so you contacted me to get me to get back with her... is that it?"

"Of course not. I'm far from stupid, Wolf, and I'm not disassociated from the real world. But I do ask you to give her the chance... just one chance to confront her demons and find out for herself if there was ever the chance of building the family she believed I deserved. Just meet with her, please? Talk through things." I didn't say that we'd talked through things already... at length... several times... in multiple positions.

"And that brings me to the second thing. I've met someone, Wolf. Met her in university. Her name is Cassandra, and we are getting married." Again his features flickered between emotions as he put together the next sentence. "I would be very proud if you, as my father..." the word seemed strange to him. Hard to pronounce through lack of use. "... if you and my mother would attend my wedding together." He seemed embarrassed. "It might seem artificial but I would love one day where my whole family can be together, and I can say a proper goodbye to that family and begin my own." He put his palms onto the table suddenly, like a dealer about to turn over the winning hand. "Would you do that for me, Wolf?"

"Of course I will. Whether we know each other well by then or not, it would make me very proud. You already make me very proud. And I'm sorry I missed out on your life." I reached over to him and offered a quick embrace, which he responded to. It was brief and slightly uncomfortable, but satisfying nonetheless. "When is the wedding?"

"We're planning for early spring next year. Say six months or so. It depends on my work." At the mention of his work I sensed anxiety.

"Well, congratulations Martin. I mean it. Tell me about Cassandra..."

"She's a wonderful person, Wolf. A little kooky perhaps, but wonderful."

"A bit like your mother then?" I smiled.

"Hey, hold on..." he laughed. "She wears funky clothes, likes strange music, and studies human evolution. But she singularly *does not* believe in faeries, crystal energies and that Barak Obama is actually a reptilian space alien."

We both laughed, and then my phone rang.

The other phone.

Tinky winky... La la...

Martin raised his eyebrows as I answered.

"Yes." It was Gabriel.

"So how's the family reunion, lover boy?" Gabriel asked. "Going well? Have you told him you were fucking his mom again last week?"

"Things are great here, Mr Gabriel. Thanks for asking. Shouldn't it be about time for you to leave me alone? I've done what you asked."

"Oh, that's not very nice thing to say, now is it? Well, Mr Devenish, I'm 'fraid you haven't done everything I need just yet."

"What do you mean?" I asked, anxiety in my voice.

"Well, son, I need to talk to you both, I'm afraid. To save us both time, and to stop you making your stupid interruptions and attempts to be all comical, I've recorded you a video message." The phone made a bleeping noise, a warning that a message was incoming.

"So, what stupid threats are you going to make now?"

"Oh, Mr Devenish. You and I gotta work on our relationship if we're gonna stay friends. Tell you what, I'm going now and I'll leave you two boys to listen to my message. Anyhow, do what it says, and exactly what it says or, well, you'll figure out the rest, smart boy like you."

"What the fuck do you mean?" I almost shouted. Martin looked shocked at my outburst.

"See ya'll later, boys..." There was a short laugh and he hung up.

On the screen was a flashing icon telling me a video message had arrived.

"Is everything alright?" said Martin. I gestured to the phone and held it between us so we could both see the screen, before opening the message.

There, on the tiny screen, was Gabriel and, sitting scared, sobbing and half-naked on the bed beside him, was Zara.

"Jesus," I said. "I think things are far from alright."

---oOo---

Chapter thirty-four

"I hope you're enjoying your family reunion. I wanted to bring the final piece of the Moore-Devenish love fest to the party," said the tiny Gabriel on the LCD screen. He indicated Zara before continuing.

"Now, remember how I told you all about how reuniting families wasn't really what I do? You remember that, don't you?" I nodded at the screen and Martin touched my arm.

"Recorded message," he said, pointing at the screen.

"Oh. Of course." I was losing it.

"Good. Long as we understand each other," the tiny Gabriel continued.

"Can you pause this?" asked Martin. I stopped the playback and we looked at each other. He was noticeably pale and I was sure that I looked pretty much the same. "Wolf..." he still tasted the word as he spoke my name. Chewing on it as though it was an unusual dish that he couldn't decide if he liked or not. "Who the hell is this and what is he doing with my mum?" There were no shortcuts to answer that, so I quickly ran through my encounter with Gabriel and Nadir. He stopped me when I mentioned the Indian woman.

"But I've met Nadir. She was the one who told me about you. She works for the government. FBI or someone, I think. But I've never heard of this Gabriel before."

"I think, Martin, that she maybe works for someone else as well."

He nodded and I pressed play again. The video Gabriel sprung into life once more, his tinny voice dripping with menace.

"Now Martin, our boy here, little Professor Poindexter, well he's quite the little inventor. Now I'm sure that he won't tell you jack shit about what he's been inventing the last year, but I know all about it. Thing is, y'see, I really want to get hold of his latest little discovery, but I've been all chasing my tail like a hound with ticks trying to work out a way of getting it from him."

"Then we found out about you, Mr Devenish, thanks to my top girl, and I got to thinking. I kinda figured that even the US government, with its hard-on for national security, wouldn't deny our boy here the chance to meet up with his long lost pappy. After all, America is big on family values, isn't it?"

"Turns out I was right." He chuckled. "So, here's the deal. A ways ago, the good old US government was getting a shit load of flak from the media about this war and that war, and this dead civilian and that dead civilian. I didn't understand it myself, what with war being war and all, but it seems to me that the government didn't like all this negative attention. They didn't like the bad press they got when they blew up a village full of people to get to one bad guy, or when a riot broke out in some Iraqi shithole or other and the grunts in the grass ended up taking a pile of civilians out to shut the place down. Far as I'm concerned, it's all eggs and omelettes."

"But it wasn't up to me," he added, sadly.

"So some bright spark with a PhD and more pens in his pocket than hairs on his ballsack came up with the notion of 'less than lethal' ammunition. Ways of putting a population down without killing them. We dug out the old plastic rounds, but they were no good when one hits you in the face 'cause you're dead anyways. We had shotguns full of pepper and cartridges that fired bean bags. Hell, we even had a speaker system that made people shit themselves, and there weren't too many ragheads who wanted to cause trouble to the troops when their crap was trickling down their legs. It was a growth industry. Still is, far as I know."

"Then there were the microwaves. Now, Mr Moore, this one you'll know about just fine but, for Devenish here, who lives in fucking Smurfland, I'll give an explanation."

"You got a load of people who're causing trouble, right? And among them you got maybe a suicide bomber, or some radicalised fucking moon-man with an AK. And their plan is to get the troops into the middle of the trouble, then either pop a few from a distance knowing that they'll be too damned terrified of going to jail for them to fire back or, if you're feeling really pissed off that day, you pop off a suicide bomb and take the whole village square out."

"Nothing much your sticky guns could do then, I reckon. So the boys in Los Alamos came up with this idea. If you bring a truck onto the field with a fuck-off emitter on the top, and you blast the rioters with low level radiation, then their skin starts to feel like it's on fire. It's not, but it sure feels that way. It's like being stung by a million invisible wasps, and you'll just do anything to get your hands on some camomile lotion. You forget about your cunning little suicide plan and you run for it. If you're one of those unlucky fuckers where the belt is tied onto you, and your trigger goes off when you drop it... well, I guess before you can say 'allahu akbar' you're nothing more than bits of human pebble-dash splattered over the walls, wondering when all the fucking virgins you were promised are arriving."

"Bottom line is the troops are safe. The trouble ends. And no-one, except maybe the weak fisted suicide bomber, gets hurt."

"Great idea, isn't it? But it had its problems from the start. Too expensive. Too unwieldy. You had to get too close for it to work."

"Now, along comes Mr Moore here, with his big brain and his big university bursary, and he gets to thinking about resonance. What if, he figures, we could increase the focus of the radiation only using certain wavelengths which will make only certain objects heat up? Since the radiation is focused into a narrow band, you don't need so much power. If we could do that, he thinks, then we can cut down the size of the device and have the same effect." He laughed.

"Neat idea, in my book. Even neater, though, was the way you developed a man-portable version. By making it lower energy, you don't need big batteries or generators. So you can have all the fun on a smaller scale." Gabriel stopped talking for a moment, and pulled something out of the bag next to the bed. It was a black device, about the same size as a 1980s mobile phone.

"Here's one. So, you see they're not *that* much of a secret anymore Mr Moore." He fiddled with the device for a moment and turned to Zara. "Works like this..." He pointed it at Zara's side, beneath her arm which was still curled around her breasts. Suddenly the picture became fuzzy and distorted, but the sound was clear.

The sound of Zara screaming.

In a moment, the picture cleared, and we could see Zara, her face twisted in pain, frantically brushing at the skin beneath her breast. Although the picture was low resolution, I could see an angry redness to the skin where the device had burned her. Gabriel hopped out of view, and I heard water running. He returned with a damp cloth and gave it to Zara.

"Here. Put that on it. And stop crying! Didn't you hear me say 'less than lethal'? Christ. You'll be fine." She stopped sobbing, and breathed deeply as the cloth took the pain away. Gabriel returned his attention to the camera.

"Now this is a lovely little device. I like it. Wonderful for those times when you gotta cause somebody a bad day, but want to avoid getting onto those nasty little Amnesty International shitlists."

I paused the video.

"Is that what you designed? You designed an instrument to torture people?" I was close to shouting again, surprised that I had reacted so strongly to this. The idea of torture disgusted me on a visceral level. Martin held my gaze defiantly.

"What I designed was not for use in this way. It was a non-lethal riot control device. Like a taser but less dangerous. You're getting attacked, you point, you fire, and the attacker suddenly has other things on their mind."

"It's still a bloody weapon," I said, my lips tight.

"Yes, it is. Because there'll always be conflict and there'll always be war. But I thought, and I still think, that dispersing conflict using non-lethal means is a hell of bit more humane than shooting someone in the head. Don't you?" He had a point.

"Okay. So you've been designing these things that make people believe they're burning. Right."

"Not quite 'believe they're burning'. They are burning, but only in a sense. It causes temperature changes round the receptor nerves, triggering the pain but without causing the damage you normally get with burns. It's not permanent, and the devices have limiters built in to stop anyone over using them and causing actual damage." I held his gaze for a beat and considered this.

"Bullshit, Martin. A limiter? Like the US Army isn't going to find a way to bypass the limiter and kill people with these things."

"They can't. It's totally self limiting. The part of the device that generates the waves burns out long before it would cause real harm." He held his hands up. "Honestly. That's been the biggest problem designing them, and it's one that no-one seems to be able to overcome."

"Well that's good then, eh?" He nodded, but he was concealing something from me. I looked at him for a second before starting the video again.

"Now then, Mr Moore. To business." Gabriel tossed the device back into his bag. "Two months ago the fruit of your loins was running his usual day to day experiments, tweaking this thing and that thing, and testing his little toys to see their effects on different stuff. Then something happened. Something that no-one, especially our Mr Moore here, didn't expect."

"He set up his little target, a leg of meat or something, and he switched the machine on, then boom!" Gabriel grinned broadly.

"The meat went from being nice, pink and rare, to being very well done in a few moments. Then it went a bit further and burst into flames. Then it exploded. My eyes and ears on the ground tell me that the whole barbeque lasted no more than twenty seconds."

"By the time the jerky hit the floor and the ventilators switched on, our boy here was suddenly the subject of a lot of attention from a lot of very serious people with medals on their chests and stars in their caps. Like kids in a toy store the week before Christmas, these guys had all these great pictures in their heads. Pictures of Moore's device mounted on humvees, tanks, drones, even attached to the side of an old M16 or two. Just think of it... Point it, click the button, and set fire to the whole place and everyone in it."

"And so, Project Phoenix was born." Gabriel looked gleeful on the screen. "Project Phoenix..." said Gabriel expansively. "A wet dream for the good old green machine." He paused for a moment, regarding Zara who was listening intently. "Now, this is the bit you need to listen carefully to, I want to make you a deal. And, cliché or not, it's one you can't refuse."

"Somewhere in your lab, on a little computer, is a hard drive with all the information about your experiment. All the original data. It's also got information about the schematics and settings you used for your pork roast. Now, I happen to know people who know people who know things, and I know that that hard drive is the only one in existence with all the information on it. In case the data went missing your paranoid masters copied bits of it onto separate drives, and they encrypted the ass out of it. But the original is still there, safe in your little laboratory."

"What you're going to do for me is remove that harddrive and get it out of the lab. I know you can't copy from the machine, and I know you can't communicate the data electronically. It's a sealed system. The only way I can take a peek at it is if you bring the harddrive out of the lab and give it to me."

"Now. A deal has two sides and a deadline. So, here's the deadline. I want the drive in my hands in forty-eight hours. If I have it in two days, then you've fulfilled the terms of the deal. I know you can't leave the country or anything like that, but your good ol' pops can, and he's gonna bring that drive with him back to the UK, where he'll give it to me. Follow me so far?"

"In return for the hard drive you will receive your mother, safe and well, and free from any unpleasant scars or other misfortune. Unless, of course, you choose to see her new relationship with Mr Devenish as a misfortune. I'd call it a catastrophe for humanity, but I'm kinda cynical that way."

"Now, terms and conditions. If I don't get the hard-drive in two days your mother dies. Then I'll find Devenish, and he dies. Then I'll find you, and you will die too. Look in my eyes." On the little screen, Gabriel held the camera right up to his eye, sparkling and blue, and up-close you could see flecks of grey in his iris. His voice was muffled slightly with his face so close to the camera. "I mean what I say." He withdrew from the camera and winked.

"Now, this is what you're going to do. You're allowed to bring your laptop to work, right? Tomorrow, bright and early as normal, you go to work with your laptop. At some point in the morning there will be a distraction. You'll know it when it happens. You'll be left alone for a few minutes. You take the hard drive from the computer, and you put it inside the shell of your laptop. I've checked sizes and stuff, and it will fit, although you'll not be downloading much porn anymore on your laptop once you've torn the innards out of it.

Now, a wonderful little Mexican lady who cleans your room in the University also works for me, and she has left a substitute hard drive in your desk drawer. It should have the same serial numbers and such, but I'm afraid it doesn't seem to be working very well, and has just enough recoverable data to convince the men in suits that it was the original component. So you should be free and clear."

"You leave as normal, they search you, find only your laptop and that condom you hope to use someday in the future when all women have become blind and stupid, and they let you go. You come back here for your dinner date with daddy, pass over the laptop, and he's on his way."

"Mr Devenish. I think your role is clear enough. However, I want you to send me a text now to say that you have read the message and you understand what to do. If I don't receive a text within an hour of sending this message, I'll hurt Ms Moore again, so I hope you boys haven't been chewing the fat instead of getting on with the business at hand."

And with a smile and a wave he was gone. I checked the time the video was sent – only twenty minutes ago – and I looked at Martin.

"Well," I asked. I could sense his mind racing through options... looking for a way out of this.

"I think we're in trouble, Wolf," he said. "But you'd best send that text."

Chapter thirty-five

Nadir and Françoise walked together through the modern emptiness of the Gatwick arrivals hall. Nadir's summons had arrived the evening before, a simple message from Gabriel. N. Sherlock Holmes, book four. Page 48. G

Gabriel didn't care for tradecraft anymore, something which chagrined Nadir more often than not. She was still angry, for example, about his bludgeoning manner in the Onslow Arms, practically blowing both of their covers during his conversation with the man Miller. She was furious, and terrified, about his treatment of the policeman. However, when it mattered, or when there was real risk, he resorted to tradecraft and oblique references which would be hard for an eavesdropper to untangle. 'Sherlock Holmes' was a prearranged signal, meaning 'the game's afoot'. 'Book four' told Nadir where he was holed up, one of the seven prearranged places that he would take the woman to once the plan was underway. As they'd discussed during planning, it also meant that there were forty-eight hours until the end of the operation. Just thirty-seven hours remaining.

Nadir had even less time if she wanted to be free from Gabriel for good.

The two sat in the luggage collection hall, close together but not touching. London wasn't Paris, as Françoise was at pains to point out. Occasionally she would glance about the terminal at people coming to and fro, and you could see the disdain in her eyes at the lack of care some of these people took of their appearance. Although Nadir had her belongings neatly packed in a small carry-on bag, Françoise had insisted on bringing a larger case. Nadir laughed when Françoise told her that any idiot can travel, but only the beautiful can travel in style.

She had spent most of the previous day with Françoise, talking about their lives, their future, and how the world would look if Nadir retired from her government work, and if Gabriel was to retire from breathing. In truth Nadir was surprised at the calm way her lover was able to discuss their plan to murder him.

She remembered the first time she had to use her weapon on another human being, and how shocked she was by her own reaction.

Karl Bennett was a white separatist, one of many of his breed tucked away in the mountains and wide prairies of the US. In his self-imposed isolation from the rest of the world his mind had become twisted and delusional. His contact with the outside world was either through rare visits to the local town for supplies, or through interacting online with nasty web pages.

When he was still interacting with other humans, he would occasionally meet his friends, who were few and becoming fewer, for beers in the local bar. Inevitably he would steer the conversation to his extreme theories about the world. He would tell them that he believed nothing he read and nothing he heard on TV. After a few more cold ones he would expand and tell them about the military-industrial complex; Zionist conspiracies, government collusion in 9/11 and how politicians were all illuminati who worshiped an owl god. All the usual nonsense that nutcases find on the internet. His friends would nod and grunt as he ranted, and then make excuses to leave before the crazy infected them.

Of course, if Bennett had applied his maxim of not believing anything he read or saw on TV, he wouldn't have believed the conspiracy merchants whose every word he hung on in the low-volume *Truth Behind* books he studied voraciously, or the seething vitriol he read in the dark corners of the Internet where the strange folk lived. If he had refused to believe this garbage as well, he would never have ended up the subject of a federal investigation.

He came to the ATF's attention after a row in the local gun store. Although he had amassed quite an arsenal under the liberal gun laws of his state, he continued to want more ammunition and more powerful weaponry. On this occasion, though, the manager of the shop refused to run his application for yet another assault rifle.

"I need it for hunting," lamented Bennett.

"Well now Karl," the manager had said, "I figure them critters near your place ain't got much of a chance as it is, without you swinging another AR in their direction."

He told him he could only process his application if he decommissioned some of his existing hardware.

"How many rifles can one man fire at the same time, Karl? And what about all your handguns?" the manager asked.

"Sel' defence," said Karl.

"Well, Karl, I'm thinking that you're all self-defended up right now, and you need to hand a few pieces in if you want to buy a new one. Hell, you got enough hardware up there to storm Omaha beach, never mind take down a few squirrels." The manager chuckled.

He stopped laughing when Bennett produced a revolver and shot him in the face, the bullet blasting away half his cheek and jaw, before tearing through the base of his brain and stopping his heart.

By the time the Sheriff's office had checked the CCTV, talked to eyewitnesses, and made a note of the additional weaponry Bennett had stolen, they knew that they had to inform the federal authorities. Nadir, as a rookie agent, found herself part of the team around the besieged farm.

A few days passed with no contact from Bennett, except the occasional pot shot from the upper windows whenever he fancied he spotted a sniper in the woods behind his home. He wouldn't answer his phone, or respond to the negotiator who tried to reassure him and calm the situation down through a bullhorn. It was a stalemate and, if previous sieges were to go by, stalemates rarely worked out well.

As it turned out, it was Bennett's wife who tilted the balance toward a successful resolution. On the evening of the third day, Arlene Bennett lowered her son from the window of the kitchen whilst Bennett was prowling upstairs, firing off the odd round at shadows in the trees. The kid ran towards the cordon as his mother climbed out the window behind him.

She ran almost ten yards before her husband saw her and unloaded an M16 magazine in her direction. It turned out, for all his machismo and his groaning weapon racks, Bennett was a terrible shot. He fired twenty rounds on full automatic, and the weapon immediately tracked high and right of his initial aim point. When the action clicked on empty and the discharge gases cleared, he saw his wife arrive unharmed into the ranks of waiting agents. From the point of view of the watching authorities, the dynamic had changed. He was no longer a lunatic with a gun and two hostages. He was now just a lunatic with a gun. They waited for a few hours in case he either surrendered to the federal agents or turned his weapon on himself and surrendered to the reality of the situation. But the house stayed silent.

The order was given to assault the place that night.

It was a three team assault, and Nadir was in the team that would break in through the kitchen. A mixed bunch of agents and a SWAT team which carried out the assault. FBI and ATF agents, wearing their bulletproof vests emblazoned with their respective acronyms, were accompanied by stern ex-military types with full body armour and concealed faces. The orders were simple: get in, find Bennett, and eliminate his involvement in the scenario either by disarming and restraining him or by removing him from the human race.

Nadir followed the SWAT team through the kitchen into the living area, and toward the stairwell to the bedrooms upstairs. Like many old farmhouses, this one had an array of little storage rooms and rickety doors leading to the basement or garage, and each one needed carefully cleared and checked before moving on. She picked a door that led down dilapidated wooden stairs to a dark, dusty basement.

As she stepped on the first stair, her automatic pistol held in front of her and a torch in the other hand, she realised she wasn't alone.

"Armed Federal Agent! Step where I can see you, with your hands on your head." She was proud that she'd kept her voice commanding and level, just like in the training. But there was no response.

She panned the beam of the torch over the banister and into the basement. It was a disorganised room packed with tools, old boxes and chests, and shelves filled with tinned goods and half empty paint cans. Piping for the heating system spread from the centre of the room, twisting and coiling across the walls and ceiling in a confused web of metal and torn glass wool insulation. Next to the boiler, which was an ancient affair that sat in a pool of leaked water and oil, she saw a movement. Bennett moved from the shadows beside the rusty iron monster and rose to his feet, sweeping his assault rifle toward Nadir.

"No," said Nadir, her weapon aimed directly at the man. "Stop." There was a hint of pleading in her tone, but the muzzle kept rising.

She fired three times. The first round clattered into the boiler, and steam shot out almost hitting Bennett square in the face. The next two rounds landed true in his body mass, one glancing off the rifle on the way into his chest.

Bennett stood still, staring at Nadir as his hands dropped uselessly to his sides, the M16 sliding out of his grip and slipping onto the floor with a metallic clatter. All colour drained from his face, seeming to condense into the dark tumble of blood emerging beneath his shirt, but still he stood and stared.

Nadir willed him to fall, but she stood transfixed as the man stared at her with his wide eyes, the skin surrounding them developing an unnatural blue colour. She considered firing again, putting him out of his misery, but she stood firm, allowing this man his last view of the land of the living. It felt as though he was pulling her own living essence from her. As if he could suck sufficient life through his gaze to prolong his own.

In moments, which stretched in Nadir's mind into minutes and hours, Bennett finally crumpled. His head tilted forward and his legs gave way, his body collapsing under him as he landed in a kneeling position. His head hit the concrete in front of him with a dull, empty thud.

He looked like he was at prayer.

Other officers poured down the stairs, and two SWAT personnel ran to the body, shouting at Bennett to raise his hands. Nadir lowered her weapon and placed it on safe. Part of her was already engaged in deep debate, telling her that she had no choice, that it was her or Bennett, and that she'd done the right thing. Another part was running through the scenario again, offering up outlandish and heroic alternatives that would have resulted in Bennett being captured alive. She could have jumped off the stairs at him. She could have shot at the boiler again to blind him with steam. She could have talked him down. She could have thrown the torch and knocked him out. But the deepest voice, the one that occasionally talked sense after a sleepless night, quietly reassured her that she had no choice. She had done what needed to be done, and there had been no other option.

In her core, though, deep within her heart where her joy and love lived, she felt as though something had burned out. What remained was as grey and cold as Bennett's eyes. Rightly or wrongly, she'd crossed a line and broken a taboo, and that she would never be the same again.

"Darling," said Françoise, jerking Nadir back to the present. "Where are you?" Nadir smiled and refocused, as usual surprised that someone so beautiful could love her.

"It's okay. I was just thinking."

"Good things?" Françoise smiled softly but suggestively.

"Not really." Nadir reached to Françoise's cheek, and stroked one finger delicately down ending with the slightest touch to her pale neck. "I can't let you do this, Françoise. We'll have to think of something else."

"But I'm ready and it's all organised. I know what I have to do. Once it's done you are free. We are free, Denise. We can be together." Nadir shook her head, her expression sad and worried. "Don't you want that? Don't you think I'll carry it through?"

"I know you will, Françoise. I know that, and it means everything to me." She thought for a moment. "But, once it's done, we will not be together. Not really."

"Why not? Why won't we be together?" Françoise couldn't keep anger from her voice.

Nadir framed her words, although she knew that it was impossible to explain to someone who'd never killed another person. It was like trying to describe nothingness.

"Because you won't be I anymore. If you do this, Françoise, you will no longer be the Françoise I love. You'll become someone else."

"But he's a bastard, Denise. Working with him is torturing you. Why should I feel anything about getting rid of him?" Françoise was slow to anger but, once angered, her Gallic blood made her difficult to calm. "I would feel less about getting rid of this one than I would standing on a cockroach."

Nadir closed her eyes and thought of Bennett, staring at her as his rifle fell and his blood poured. The man was a lunatic. He was also a murderer, coldly eliminating the gun shop manager without a second thought. He deserved what he'd got.

But, in his last moments on earth, he took something of Nadir with him into the abyss.

"No. It doesn't work like that, Françoise. It doesn't. A man is not a cockroach." She smiled and touched her lover's shoulder. "I will work something out, but you will not do this. I love you. I adore your joy, your excitement about life, your passion and your dreams. I won't have Gabriel steal those from you." Françoise thought for a moment, then smiled gently.

"Okay, Denise. We'll work something out." She touched Nadir's arm. "Thank you. I think I understand."

Nadir smiled back, but thought again of her own emptiness inside, the hole left by Bennett's death. One more death, she thought. I can cope with death's gaze one more time.

And then she'd be free to start living once again.

---oOo---

Chapter thirty-six

Both Martin and I slipped into shock when Gabriel's message finally sunk in. I think it's fair to say that we both felt helpless. We both felt trapped.

Somewhere deep inside me, though, an emotional valve had opened, and it was pouring an unfamiliar set of feelings through me. I am not a person who has ever hated anybody. Perhaps I don't feel emotions that strongly, or perhaps I haven't been in a situation that engendered hatred before. When my parents died, one after the other, I felt no overwhelming grief. Rather I had a perpetual feeling of impending loss, as though every day was the end of a wonderful holiday. The feeling stays with me even now when I remember them.

But these cold, coppery feelings that I felt within me were strange and disturbing. I think I understood then how a cornered rat must feel, and how strongly the blood can boil as it leaps at the throat of its attacker.

I had read that a cornered rat does not leap at the throat of a person, it merely seems that way as the angry ball of fur and claws leaps toward you. The scientists and the tree-huggers had determined that the rat merely sees the patch of light behind the figure that is cornering it, and tries to leap towards it in order to escape.

Perhaps I was like the rat. I felt like I wanted to tear Gabriel apart, but equally I might be bubbling with adrenaline and cold emotion merely to get ready to jump to safety and away from this situation. The bravery of the coward.

I just couldn't see the patch of light marking the exit. Gabriel had cornered me, and cornered me well.

Martin and I spent a good half hour discussing Gabriel's message, and trying to work out a plan. Even putting our brains together on the problem, i.e. Martin running through all the permutations and possibilities in a clear, realistic way, and my contributing to the brainstorming session by muttering the word 'fuck' now and then, left us in no doubt that we were stuck. Martin and I had to do what he asked.

"This whole thing is ridiculous, Wolf," said Martin, as we prepared to leave. "Really. How can this guy benefit from the data on that drive? I mean I barely understand it, and I'm fairly sure that the whole thing was a complete fluke. Not repeatable. Not a viable weapon system. But he seems just as damned stubborn as my bosses from the Pentagon. I tell them and I tell them that I don't think this could be repeated in an organised way and, even if I could repeat it, it would never be stable enough to build a weapon. But they simply refuse to listen. They just tell me to keep working on it." He pulled his jacket on, still pale from the shock, and raised his hands in submission. "Last week a two-star general called me 'champ'." He dropped his hands.

"This guy Gabriel will be just as stuck as I am, and probably more so. The data is useless at the moment. Maybe forever. I don't know what he stands to gain. Although if he could build a weapon from the data it would be a horrific device. Truly horrible."

"We have to take that chance. He's got your mother, Martin, and he's threatening to kill her," I said. "And kill us afterwards. We have to do what he says. There's no option."

"Alright. We'll do what he said. Call me if anything comes up? Just remember, my phone is likely monitored. I'll see you here again tomorrow at six." His face fell briefly. "It's been good to meet you at last, Wolf, even if the whole thing has turned to shit thanks to your friend Gabriel."

"Yes." I shook his hand. "We'll make it right, and I'll see you tomorrow. Good luck with all the espionage and stealing state secrets, Martin." I tried to smile. "Don't get caught, will you?"

"I'll try not to. See you around, Wolf." With that he left, leaving me with the bill, some empty cups, and a feeling of dread in my stomach.

---oOo---

Chapter thirty-seven

It wasn't finding a barge that was the problem for Andreas. It was finding the right barge, since the little web of canals, rivers, tributaries and streams extending from Loxwood seemed packed with the things. Most of them looked just like the one belonging to Zara Moore.

The evening wasn't helping either. In the fading light most of the barges he walked past looked similar in colour. He cursed himself again for not making a record of the name of the barge Moore lived on. The name of it flittered around his mind, but wouldn't settle so he could see it clearly. Such a stupid mistake. Perhaps he was getting too old for this. 'Rivers End' kept popping up, as did something to do with bells... 'Wizards Bell' or 'River Belle'.

He couldn't remember.

There was even worse news when he consulted the Ordinance Survey map of the area. The network of water courses here was complex, with most of them accessible only on foot. Within a few miles of the spot Moore had been moored, dozens of branches and tributaries opened up to allow travel in almost any direction. He'd been looking now for almost eight hours, and had still only covered a fraction of the possible routes available to her. He had decided to follow the downstream tributaries purely because that was the direction the barge had been facing, however he was starting to doubt himself on that point too. He was a spy, not a boat builder, and barges look pretty much similar at either end.

If she had travelled west instead of east Andreas was in completely the wrong place. He was also worried about the time factor. He hadn't seen the barge for over a day now so, if she had cast off twenty four hours ago, even at the sedate pace of the houseboat she could be sixty or seventy miles away.

He had to call it in. He was tired, hungry, and far from his hotel, and he hated the thought of driving back in the dark through the tiny country lanes. It would be for others to decide what to do and how to do it. His initial plan to unravel the

mystery of the missing barge himself had failed, so he dialled
the number he should have called seven and a half hours earlier.

"Unified Payment Solutions, out of hours support. How
may I help you?" The voice was unfamiliar.

"Hi. This is Andrew Miller. I have a problem with a client.
Is your manager there?"

"I'm sorry sir, but she's not here at the moment. Can I take
a message?"

"No, it's important. Can you put me through to her mobile
number?"

"Of course, sir. Please hold the line."

---oOo---

Laura was enjoying both dinner and the time of her life.

Ivo, as it turned out, was more than just an Italian looking
for a touch of English *amore* during his time in the UK. He was
good company, amusing and intelligent, and he seemed to
genuinely like her. It was his suggestion that they go out for
dinner that evening, and Laura barely gave it a second thought
before agreeing. It had been some time since she'd had a date,
and a very long time since she'd had a reason to look forward to
a Sunday evening.

He had chosen a small place called *Savoir faire*, not far from
the Strand. She'd asked Ivo why he chose French food and not
Italian, to which he sneered slightly and told her that Italian food
is not Italian food unless it is eaten in Italy. But it was a
romantic spot and she was enjoying the delicious food and the
company of this attractive man. Of course the candles, the
smiles, and the tranquillity faded a little when the phone rang. It
was one of those annoying numbers that she had to answer.

She apologised to Ivo and slipped away to find a quiet spot
to answer.

"Unified Payment Solutions," she said. "Laura speaking."

"It's Andrew Miller, Laura. I have a problem with Moore."

"Sorry to hear that, Mr Miller. What type of problem?"

"Her boat is gone." Laura thought for an instant. The
trouble with her job is that she had to be available most times of

the day or night. There was a hot Italian guy waiting for her in the restaurant, and she was forced to talk to a middle-aged East German.

But she was worried. Her mood darkened a little. A problem with an agent in the field could spell the end of her evening.

"Oh dear. Do you think something has happened?"

"I don't know. She wasn't due to move on," said Miller.

"Does she do this regularly, to the best of your knowledge?"

"No. She was due to stay near Loxwood for another few weeks at least." Laura thought furiously.

"Do you think she had business elsewhere?" she asked. There was a pause on the line, and she could swear she heard Andreas sigh.

"Not that I know of."

"Okay. I'll contact the office and see if they can send some people to have a look tomorrow." She knew as she spoke that it was an unsatisfactory response. She felt unprofessional, but desperately wanted to have her night free to spend with Ivo.

"There's no time for that, Laura," said Andreas. "She's gone. The boat's gone. I've no idea where she is, and I'm worried. You need to do something right away." Laura's mood darkened even more. Miller was genuinely concerned.

Andreas walked along yet another stretch of canal, the dusk around him becoming night, and the dim lights from the various moored craft sparkled brighter in the darkness. Around the corner he saw another barge moored in a secluded bend beneath some overhanging trees.

"I'm sorry, Andreas. It's a free country, and Ms Moore is entitled to go where she wishes. Why are you so worried?"

"Our American friend, Laura. He worries me. And now Ms Moore is missing," said Andreas, approaching the canal boat.

"We're quite sure that the gentleman you met yesterday was there by coincidence," said Laura, a hint of impatience in her voice. *Surely this can wait?*

"Maybe," said Andreas. "Hold on a moment." He walked a little further, and took the phone from his ear to listen. Yes. He thought he heard a dog barking on the barge. An old dog with an old bark.

"Mr Miller. What do you need?" asked Laura.

"Wait a minute." Andreas moved away from the river, closer to the undergrowth and shrubs at the side of the path. His voice was quieter. "I think I've found her."

"Oh good." Laura tried to think quickly. "So everything's okay?"

"I'm not sure. Can you triangulate my phone signal? I think you should get a fix on her. I'll leave the phone on."

"Andreas," Laura whispered. "I'm on a date... I'm in a restaurant, and I don't think the *maitre'd* can triangulate mobile phones for me."

"Then get to the other office. I'm not sure where I am. About eight miles from Loxwood, I think. A tributary."

"Have found the boat?" Laura crossed her fingers. She loved her job, and had a strong sense of duty, but there were marinated duck breasts on the way and a wonderful Italian waiting for her. Surely work could wait? "If you've found her again, just retrace your steps and work out where you are on the map."

"Perhaps you're right, perhaps I'm overreacting." He knew he wasn't. He had that annoying little fluttering feeling in his gut which told him that something was wrong. "Give me a second to confirm."

"Well, Andreas, at least you found her. If you're happy that everything's okay, then I think your little job is at an end for now." *Duck breasts getting cold.*

"Is that what you want me to do? Is that an order?" Andreas hated the ideas of orders in his work. Often situations became too fluid to stick with straightforward orders. They were a hangover from the past, like army officers wearing red jackets to dinner, or David Hasslehoff's hair.

"There could be many reasons she moved the boat, Mr Miller. If everything's okay now, then I think it's time to come back to head office for a chat." Andreas walked a little closer to the barge, passing one of the many little overgrown tracks that emerged onto the river. From where he stood, he had to admit that everything looked fine. Perhaps he'd misread her appointment book, or not understood her little scribbles properly.

"Okay. I'll check things are okay and let you know if there's another problem." After the anxiety of losing Moore he felt deflated. He wanted to check a bit more closely, then find his car and get to his bed. Hiding in hedgerows in the middle of the night was a young man's game.

"Alright, Mr Miller. I'll hear from you soon."

"Thank you," said Andreas. "I look forward..." He felt a movement of air behind him and heard a woman's voice.

"Now this is handy," said Nadir, as she swung the pistol butt onto the base of Andreas' neck.

Andreas collapsed into the hedge, Nadir catching him as he fell. His phone smashed open as it hit the gravel, little pieces of glass and plastic scattering across the path.

Laura looked at her own mobile phone. Her signal was strong, but Andreas had gone. In a moment the operator from the office came on the line.

"Sorry, ma'am, but I lost the connection," said the agent.

"I see that, Jeremy. Thanks." Laura thought quickly about what she had just heard. Andreas stopping mid-sentence, then a muffled voice, a dull thud and then the connection ended. She thought of Italians and good food. She wondered how stupid she would look if Andreas had merely tripped and dropped his phone. She thought about the muffled female voice. She thought about Sergeant Gabriel.

She knew that her date was over.

---oOo---

Chapter thirty-eight

Cassiel was his usual gregarious self on the way from the diner to my hotel for the evening. This time, of course, I knew what Gabriel was up to, and knew that Cassiel knew what Gabriel was up to too. His grin suggested that he was enjoying watching me squirm.

He discussed this at length by smiling at me in the rear view mirror. It wasn't a pleasant smile. It was a combination of smug satisfaction, coupled with ridicule at how pathetic I looked in his world of shadows and bullshit.

I wanted to hit him, but my getting beaten to death in the back of his car wouldn't help resolve matters.

We pulled into the Hampton Inn, a stylish-enough establishment, and Cassiel parked the car and switched off the ignition.

"Okay. You're booked into this joint for the evening, yeah? When are you meeting Moore tomorrow?"

"We're meeting for dinner. Sixish."

"Right. I'll collect you here, fifteen before six."

"I'll be hanging on the edge of my seat till then," I said.

"You being funny?"

"Do you find me funny?" I asked, smiling ingratiatingly.

"Fuck I know..." He considered me for a moment. "Fuck you too."

Our endless conversation sadly exhausted, I left the car, collected my bag, and went into the hotel lobby to check in. As I approached the reception desk my phone chirped and vibrated. For a moment I thought it was a text from Zara, that somehow this was all a bizarre joke, but it was from Bill. To receive two texts in 24 hours from a man who despises modern technology as much as Bill, meant that something was up back home.

Wolf, my boy. Terrible news. It seems Sir Rodney
has killed himself. He was found in his garage,
sitting in his car. He poisoned himself with the
car fumes. What is most peculiar is that he sent
me an email a few hours before he died. A very

short message, but with some damned attachment
thing along with it. Of course I don't have the
first idea how to view it, so I shall ask a
postgrad to help me send it to you tomorrow. I
liked the curmudgeonly old Queen immensely, and
I'm horribly sad to hear of such a tragic end.
More tomorrow. I shall raise a glass to the
beknighted old letch later. Your humble servant,
Bill.

My head was so full with worries about Zara, Gabriel and all the craziness surrounding me at the moment that I had forgotten about all about Rodney, and I was too exhausted to give the news much thought. I piled it on top of my other concerns to deal with another time.

As I checked in I smiled wryly to myself. How had my life become so fucked-up in seven days? I went to my room, the door barely having time to close behind me before I opened the first beer from the mini bar.

---oOo---

Chapter thirty-nine

"So, Mr Miller... Or is it Detective Inspector Miller? Or Herr Müller?" Nadir smiled as she leaned around the passenger seat, regarding Andreas as he rubbed his neck, eyes bleary and bloodshot as he slowly came to. His hands were bound with a plastic self-locking tag, but he wasn't in any mood to try any heroics. Nadir was flicking through his wallet, each different ID making her smile broaden.

"Miller will do." His head ached, but he recognised the professionalism of Nadir's blow. Any softer, and he wouldn't have gone down. A little harder, and he wouldn't have gotten up again. Still, he had a few professional skills of his own.

Skills like resisting interrogation.

"My name is Nadir, and I have to say that this is a nice little weapon, Mr Miller," she said, inspecting his little semi-automatic. "A bit industrial, perhaps, but I'm sure it does the job. Eastern German, right? A pretty little DDR relic. Something of a collector's item I imagine." She removed the magazine and moved the action back and forth, seemingly impressed at the smoothness.

Miller said nothing. He decided it was time to shut down and let this woman fish for answers which he wasn't going to give. Whatever her questions, or whatever she did, he would die before giving her the answers she wanted. It was all part of the game, and he was a good player.

"Have you been to a range recently, Mr Miller? Been keeping your eye in?" Nadir asked.

Miller said nothing, trying to descend deeper into himself, although so far it didn't seem much like any interrogation he'd ever witnessed. Perhaps the woman in the driver's seat, the one who looked like a model, was going to play the bad cop. Regardless, it was worth paying a little attention, as the more that Nadir smiled and leaned over the passenger seat, the further down her top he could see.

Every cloud has a silver lining, thought Andreas.

"I keep my eye in," he said, making sure he was keeping his eye firmly on her bosom.

"That's good, Mr Miller." Nadir leaned over more, and the interrogation was starting to look more like the prelude to a porn film than some bleak Q and A in the bowels of a Berlin basement. "Because we need to you to kill someone for us."

"What?" Andreas' eyes flicked up and held Nadir's gaze. "You need me to do what?"

"We need you to kill someone for us, Mr Miller." She put the magazine back into the P38 and pulled back the action to chamber a round, bringing the little weapon up to point directly at Andreas' temple.

"Otherwise we are going to kill you." A chill passed through Andreas as he looked in her eyes.

She wasn't bluffing.

"Now, let me tell you a story, and then we'll discuss how that story will end..." Nadir lowered the weapon and began her tale. Piece by piece, she filled in the blanks that Andreas had been puzzling over, and slowly he began to understand what he had to do.

---oOo---

Chapter forty

Rebecca Lowry put her phone down and held her head in her hands. In the space of a single phone call her mood had changed from elation at the news of Rodney's death to horror when her contact finished the story. Her heart was beating rapidly, and she was pale and frightened. The man had been certain about what he found, which chilled her to the core.

"I checked several times, Ms Lowry, but Sir Rodney definitely sent an email a few hours before I got there to b.jeffries@oxford.ac.uk. The email didn't say much, but the attachment was interesting. It's a csv file, made up of numbers, dates, and what seem to be purchase order codes. The dates are scattered over the last few years, and the numbers, if they're currency, add up to six figure sums." The man paused for a beat. "I imagine this is to do with why you needed my help."

"Shit." Fear flooded her system, a whirlwind of possible futures filling her mind, none of them good. She felt panic rising, and it was a horrid feeling. She was so used to being in control that the sensation that of events spinning away from her fingertips terrified her deeply. The voice on the phone was perhaps her only hope to grasp hold of her future again, whatever it would take to achieve that.

"Ms Lowry? Are you there?" the man asked.

"Yes. Sorry. I need your help again, as soon as possible." She tried to sound business-like, but her tone was pleading.

"Of course. Just one thing, though. If these numbers are what I think they are, then I'm going to need a larger payment to resolve your current problems."

"Anything. Whatever you want." She paled further, a taste of bile in her throat.

"Good. When shall we meet?" he asked.

"There's no time. I need you to act now."

"Okay. What do you need?"

"Jeffries. He cannot be allowed to spread what's in that email. You must stop him."

"I can do that, but what about the email? It'll be on the servers, not just on his computer."

"If Jeffries is gone, and you delete the email, then nobody will ever look for it."

"Alright. I'll get right on it. But I expect one hundred thousand for this." Lowry's jaw dropped, but she had no option but to agree.

"Fine. I'll send you it as normal when it's done."

"Good."

"There must be no suspicion. He just has to go away, okay?"

"I understand. That might take a little time. How long do you think you have?"

"Jeffries is off tomorrow, and the old fool probably doesn't know how to use email. But when he's back, he'll likely get one of his students to help him. We have, perhaps, thirty-six hours."

"Fine. I shall deal with Jeffries, and call you tomorrow." The call disconnected, and Lowry leaned back in her chair telling herself that everything would be okay. She found her eyes drifting towards the drinks cabinet, her hands already reaching for the brandy decanter and a crystal glass. *It will all be okay*, she thought.

But her heart would not stop pounding.

---oOo---

Chapter forty-one

"I'm genuinely concerned, sir. He hasn't made contact for more than 12 hours." Laura regarded Parkinson across his desk, as he made notes on his pad. "He has never lost contact before."

"Hold." Parkinson raised his hand as he finished his scribbling. "And you think that this loss of contact is linked to our mystery American?"

"There are too many coincidences here. I think we should send some people to find Miller. He was working for us, and deserves at least that."

"Agreed." Parkinson made a few more notes and Laura half-thought she saw his hand shake a little as he wrote. "I need to make some calls, Ms Berne, but I shall contact you later with an update."

"Thank you, sir." Laura rose and left the room, ignoring the steely eye of the secretary on her way out.

---oOo---

Benjamin was having a terrible day, and his head was throbbing.

He sat in an austere outer office, watching the marine sergeant type away on his computer, his immaculate dress uniform flexing as he worked.

"Sergeant, I'm not accustomed to having to wait so long for a meeting. I'm a busy man, and I have urgent business with the General."

"Yes, sir. I understand. The General will be with you as soon as possible." He returned to his typing. Benjamin reached across the desk and pulled the phone across.

"Mind if I use the phone?" The sergeant, initially surprised, nodded his head and gestured for Benjamin to continue. Benjamin bashed in a few numbers and held the phone to his ear.

"Situation room, please. Yes, it's Benjamin Cornfeld, CIA. 49731 slash A2." The sergeant's eyes widened. "I'd like to speak with the Chief of Staff, please." The marine's mouth began to open.

"Sir, are you on the phone to the Joint Chiefs? Do you know the Admiral?" Benjamin held his hand up.

"I helped him with a parking ticket once." He paused for a moment, before a voice answered on the other end of the line. "Good day, Admiral. I have a young marine here who seems to think that National Security is best served by having me wait in General Manning's outside office, rather than speaking with the General myself." He paused. "Indeed I will, Admiral. Thank you." He held the phone out to the marine, who gulped and held it to his ear.

"Master Sergeant P. Channing speaking, sir." There was a terse exchange, and Benjamin heard the word 'Alaska' mentioned. "Right away, sir." The marine, visibly shaken, put the phone down and stood. "One second Mr Cornfeld." He walked into the inner office, closing the door behind him.

A few moments later he returned with the General, who smiled gregariously and shook Benjamin's hand.

"Sorry for keeping you, Mr Cornfeld. Come on in."

---oOo---

Everything seems different when you're scared, thought Martin, as he waved good morning to Big John and walked through the new security doors and into the lab complex, laptop bag over his shoulder. Even John's smile looked different, as though he could see right through Martin and recognise that he was up to no good.

He felt a chill of fear run through his spine, and a bead of sweat under his arm. For a moment he thought that there would be no chance he'd get away with this... not one chance in a million. When he entered the lab Bradley spun around on his chair and looked at him with concern.

"Well, bud... how'd it go yesterday?" Brad's look was one of sympathy. Martin paled for a moment, wondering how Bradley could know what had happened the previous afternoon. Then the penny dropped.

Of course. If he looked anxious or if his thoughts were wandering, everyone would simply think it was because of meeting his father for the first time. Hell, they'd all known about it for days. It was the perfect cover. Gabriel had thought of everything.

He might just get away with this.

---oOo---

Cassiel just loved the crazies. Nothing made his various jobs easier than being able to blame everything on the hordes of nutjobs that America was so good at producing. They provided the perfect cover for all his dark dealings, throwing law enforcement far off his tail and deep into the boonies where the lunatics howled at the moon.

But he loved explosions even more. When you just have to mess up somebody's day, a few ounces of C4 is guaranteed to do the trick.

He switched off the engine of the battered pick-up, parked up a few hundred yards away from the UNM physical sciences building, and pulled down his cap in case there were CCTV cameras about. He checked that he'd left all the necessary 'evidence' scattered around the vehicle, with some bits and bobs in the glovebox in the hope they might survive the blast, and reached beneath the seat to arm the charges.

Hopping out, he put his head down and walked swiftly out of the car park toward the small service bay where he'd left his motorbike. After a cursory check to make sure no-one was watching him, he swapped cap for helmet, kicked the bike into life, and drove down the access road onto the nearest highway. Another mindless attack on the American military-industrial complex was ready to go.

"Thank fuck for the crazies," he laughed, as he accelerated away from the campus.

---oOo---

Benjamin's headache was getting steadily worse.

"General, I understand that you won't tell me anything about Phoenix without higher authorisation. That's fine. But can you please, for heaven's sake, ensure that you raise the security on the project? At least check that everything is secure?"

"Mr Cornfeld. Firstly, regardless of your friends in high places, Project Phoenix is classified above your security rating. In fact, you shouldn't even know that it exists, and I shall be informing the Director of this visit."

"Yes, fine. Do whatever you need to do, General. But I know things that are outside of your security rating, and I think our mutual bags of secrets are starting to get mixed up." Benjamin was used to dealing with this nonsense when dealing with the Pentagon, where internal politics and ambitious officers meant that each visit he paid to the place ended in an inter-agency pissing match. But his gut was throbbing almost as much as his head. Something was going on, and it involved Gabriel and Project Phoenix.

"Be that as it may, Mr Cornfeld, I can assure you that the Phoenix project is exceptionally secure, even for a codeword operation. Everyone involved is highly vetted and constantly monitored. All information regarding the project is kept separately and encrypted. The project is too complex for any of the principle researchers to carry all the necessary information to replicate it from memory alone, and no sensitive elements are permitted to leave the research facilities. To reiterate once more, Mr Cornfeld, the project is utterly, belt and braces, secure. I have staked my third star on this."

"Alright, General." He placed his card on the desk. "As a courtesy, if anything untoward should happen involving Phoenix, can you give my office a call? The agency has an interest in you getting that third star."

"Thank you, Mr Cornfeld, but I'm sure that there will be no reason to call you. The project is secure," said the General, rising and offering Benjamin his hand.

Benjamin regarded the officer, taking note of his absolute confidence in what he said, and wished he could be so sure.

Chapter forty-two

Burritos will be the end of me, thought John, as he leaned on the little fence outside the security hut, a fat chicken, chilli, cheese and tomato burrito in his hand, the juices dripping onto the warm asphalt.

In high school Big John had been an athlete, spending most afternoons on the grid iron as the first choice quarterback for the Braves. Back then he could do the flat hundred in under 12 seconds, remarkable given his size and build. Success on the field, however, didn't equate to good grades, but he wasn't worried as the College teams were already sniffing around him offering football scholarships. Until, of course, he smashed his knee in an awkward take-down on the field, and his future career prospects evaporated in an instant of agony.

Then he discovered burritos.

He knew that the other security guards, particularly the new ones who arrived after the accident in the lab a few months ago, thought he was a laughing stock. Close to three hundred pounds now, Big John was eating his way further into the bad parts of the BMI chart, but he had strong arms, good eyes, and got on with the staff a hell of a bit better than the new guys, all tight lips and tight muscles, not at all like the rest of the security team.

Ah, fuck them, he thought. *I might be fat, but I'm way happier than those losers.*

He took a hefty bite from the burrito, savouring the way the sauces mixed in his mouth, seeming to taste even better in the crisp warmth of the sun.

A sudden flash in the periphery of his vision caught his eye.

At the far end of the parking lot, like something out of a film, a battered old pick-up truck had jumped several feet into the air, plumes of bright orange flame encapsulating it as the panels popped and the glass shattered. John kept his cool, and kept hold of the burrito.

An instant later the ground shook, and the windows of the security hut rattled and cracked. The sound of the blast surrounded him, followed moments later by the chirping of dozens of car alarms. He could see debris flying through the air, and he jumped behind the hut as glass and bits of metal clattered onto the asphalt around him. He threw his arms up to protect his face, dropping his beloved burrito in the process.

From the main entrance other guards, particularly the skinny new guys, came running onto the forecourt, many with weapons drawn. One of them, that miserable bastard Kennedy, was shouting into his wrist.

Jeez, John didn't even know the firm had wrist mikes. Why hadn't he been given one? *Typical America*, he thought, *they don't give the good stuff to the fat kid.*

Scattering around the lot and rushing to close exits and check for any casualties, he had to admit that the new boys were pretty good at the job. Hell, one of them had an MP5 machine gun... where the hell did he get that from?

As the debris stopped falling, and the only sounds left were the car alarms and the guards shouting to one another, Big John continued to crouch behind the security hut. He looked around for his lunch, a tear forming as he spotted the squashed burrito covered in tiny fragments of glass and gravel.

The new guy, Kennedy, appeared around the side of the hut, and kneeled beside Big John.

"You okay, buddy? Are you hurt?" He put his free hand on John's shoulder.

"Nah, dun' thing so," said John, still staring at the squashed burrito. "Anyone get killed?"

"No. No reports of casualties so far. Best get inside now, lots of work to do." Kennedy stood and ran back onto the parking lot, pointing here and there for his men to check and secure the area.

John slowly got to his feet, casting a final glance at his ruined lunch.

No casualties my ass.

---oOo---

Even deep inside the laboratory complex, the blast shook the walls and rattled the apparatus. After the initial shock had passed, it dawned on Martin that the diversion was underway, and the moment he'd been dreading all morning had arrived.

"What the hell!" Bradley was furiously mopping one of the benches where his coffee had spilled.

"I told you not to bring the damned drink into the lab, Bradley. If Manning or one of his goons came in now you'd be suspended." Bradley waved a hand by way of apology, and finished wiping down the formica surface.

"Fine, I'm sorry. But what the hell was that?"

"I don't know. Do you get earthquakes here?" Martin went to the bench with the old computer on it, turning the monitor off and on again to test that it was working properly. One of the security guards, part of the new team with the distant stares, rushed into the lab.

"Sirs, there has been an incident in the parking lot, and we need you to stay where you are for a moment until it's resolved." He waited for a response and both Bradley and Martin nodded their heads. "Thank you. We'll have more information shortly."

With a nod the guard left, leaving the two scientists staring at each other.

"Brad, can you run to the lockers and get my cell phone from my jacket? I need to make a call." *And I need to get you out of the lab for two minutes*, thought Martin.

"But security said to wait here..." Bradley looked puzzled.

"I'm sure he meant to stay indoors, not in this particular room." *Oh, get the fuck out, Bradley...*

"Why don't you use the phones in here, or grab it yourself?"

"Because I have to check that the damned computers are okay, and because I haven't got the bloody number, Brad! Can you just go and get the damned cell for me?"

Brad stood and stared, unaccustomed to Martin being angry. It was out of character and took him by surprise.

"Please, Brad... get my phone?" Martin's voice almost broke halfway through the words, a whirlwind of nerves building within him.

"Alright, Marty. No problem... I'll be back in a minute." He looked back at Marty as he left, his face puzzled and concerned.

"Cheers, Brad." Martin felt guilty. He liked Brad, and didn't like shouting at him. "I appreciate it." Brad nodded and left the room.

As soon as the door closed, Martin ran straight to the computer. Pulling the cables out of the back, he disconnected the power and started to open the case, acutely aware of the steel cable attaching it to the wall along with the little alarm wire linking it to the desk.

The security measures on the box made taking it apart tricky, but he managed to get the case open enough to reach inside.

"Fucking thing," said Martin, surprised at how much the stress was making him swear. A tangle of ribbon cables wove through the innards of the machine and pulling the harddrive out was harder than he'd anticipated. He got the main ribbon loose, but couldn't reach the little plastic tag locking the power cable into the unit. "Fuck, fuck, fuck..."

He kept working at the lead, the edges of the motherboard ports cutting at his fingers, his eyes flicking from the computer to the door. Brad must have been away for two minutes already.

Suddenly the lead popped loose, but the tiny sound of a piece of plastic falling into the box told Martin that something had gone wrong. He pulled the drive out of its slot and inspected it.

The locking tab for the power supply had broken off.

"Oh, for God's sake give me a break," he whispered. With finger and thumb he started to feel around the inside of the case, feeling for the tiny plastic tab and praying there was some superglue in the lab.

"What are you doing?" Martin pulled his hand out of the case and spun towards the voice, his face pale and eyes wide.

Bradley stood watching him from the doorway, looking more puzzled than before.

---oOo---

Three thousand miles away, the taxi stopped outside Bill's modest detached house, and he emerged from it like a conquering hero, cheeks bright red from the brandy he'd enjoyed with his dinner.

"There you go, dear boy," he said as he passed a crumpled note through the window to the driver. "Always a pleasure to ride upon your wonderful chariot." The driver, an Armenian, smiled happily and drove off.

He'd understood perhaps four words of Bill's constant commentary during the twenty minute journey to his home.

Bill fumbled with the gate and ambled up the short path through his little cottage garden, pausing briefly to uproot a dandelion which had the audacity to poke its head up beside his little *Pittosporum* bush. Tossing the weed away, he fumbled for his keys and opened the door, tutting quietly at the scratched paint around the lock. He headed through the hallway into the lounge, and straight over to his drinks cabinet.

Pouring himself another brandy, he noticed a low whirring noise in the room. Flicking on a few lights, he looked around the lounge, trying to find the source of the sound. There was a faint blue light coming from his desk in the corner and, as he approached it, the sound became louder.

His laptop was on, which was odd given that he hated the damned thing and barely ever used it.

"Bloody thing has a mind of its own," muttered Bill, as he pulled the screen open. His email program was open, but he was sure he'd shut it down that morning after texting Devenish. He moved the cursor around a bit with his fat finger, before deciding better of trying to navigate the computer and looking for the off switch instead. Something trickled into his brandy-infused brain as he finally found the button, and he held his finger hovering above it while he followed his thoughts.

The email from Sir Rodney was gone.

"Now isn't that very strange indeed..." Worried about doing something stupid to the mysterious device, he carefully closed the screen and resolved to bring it in to one of his post-grad students in the morning to see if they could find the email again and forward it to Devenish. He lifted his glass and toasted the computer. "I'll deal with you in the morning, my micro-chipped nemesis."

The blow came from behind, the soft carpet hiding the sound of the man's approach. A wisp of movement in the air behind Bill was his only warning as the crowbar smacked him hard on the side of his head, fracturing his skull instantly.

He dropped to the floor with a crash, the spilled brandy mixing with the steady flow of blood from his wound. With no pithy jokes, no amusing word play, and no grandiose gestures, Bill Jeffries made his final exit from this life like a bag of mail tossed from a truck.

---oOo---

Chapter forty-three

"What are you doing with the computer, Marty? You realise how important that machine is?" Bradley entered the lab and walked over to where Martin crouched next to the open case, confusion still evident on his face. Martin scrabbled for something to say.

"Whatever that damned shaking was, it shook something loose in the machine and it wouldn't switch on. I'm just trying to find the connection." Martin ventured a smile.

"Jesus, Marty, we've got an entire IT department for that kind of stuff. If you think I would be in trouble for bringing coffee into the lab, have you any idea what Manning would do to you if he found you fucking around with the machine? Particularly *that* machine."

"It's just a loose cable, Brad. We don't need IT to come down and stick a cable in now, do we?" Bradley didn't look convinced. "Did you get my cell?" His assistant pondered the open case for a moment before answering.

"No... that's why I'm back. You forgot to give me your locker key." He knelt next to Martin, looking at the computer, a worried expression on his face.

"Oh, damn." Martin rose and put his arm around Bradley, leading him away from the machine. He found his locker key on the main desk and held it out to Bradley. "Here you go."

"You sure you don't want IT down? Or d'you want me to help you?"

"No, no... I found the lead, just trying to put it back in now." Martin tried to change the subject. "What's all the fuss about anyway? Did you get to speak with anyone?" Bradley absently took the key, his lips pursed.

"Yeah, they're talking about an explosion. They think it might have been an accident," said Bradley, his brow still furrowed with worry.

"Jesus. We might be here for hours then. I really need that cell phone, or I'll miss my next meeting with Wolf. Can you grab it for me?" pleaded Martin.

"What? Oh, yeah, I'll go now." He looked once more at the computer. "Are you sure you can put that damn thing back together?"

"Yeah," said Martin. He smiled and shrugged, trying to appear calmer than he felt. "I think a first class honours from Cambridge should provide me with the skills needed to plug a loose wire in." At last Bradley laughed.

"Cool. But seriously, Marty, don't scare me like that." He put the key in his pocket and left the lab again.

"Jesus," whispered Martin, before returning to work on the computer.

---oOo---

Benjamin's phone rang when he was still on the beltway.

"Cornfeld," he answered.

"Mr Cornfeld, this is General Manning." It was certainly not the call he expected.

"What can I do for you, General?"

"I need you to come back to the Pentagon, Mr Cornfeld. There's been an unsettling development regarding Phoenix." Now there's a surprise, thought Benjamin, his gut tightening.

"What exactly?" he asked, an edge of sarcasm in his voice.

"An explosion. A car bomb near the research facility. It's too coincidental for my liking. It exploded so soon after, er, our conversation." Too damn coincidental by far.

"I'll be there in twenty minutes." Benjamin hung up and gave his instructions to his driver. "What is Gabriel up to," he murmured, as the car took the next exit from the beltway.

Martin put in the last recessed screw, and tightened it gently. He reattached the power supplies and monitor leads, took a deep breath and turned the computer on. For a moment nothing happened, and he could feel his heart beating faster.

Then the fans started around the processor, and he breathed again.

He stood and popped open his laptop, tucking away the stolen hard drive into the space where he'd removed the innards of the machine. Stuffing some crumpled tissue paper around it to keep it secure, he popped the keyboard back onto the laptop and put it back in its case. Forcing himself to look at the screen of the tampered computer he was amazed to see the same UNM screensaver and log-in field had appeared, and for an instant he thought he'd mixed up the drives. But that was impossible, even with his frazzled nerves affecting his performance.

Once again he was impressed at how clever Gabriel had been.

For a moment he allowed himself to relax. The hard part was over, and all he had to do was get out of the lab and meet Wolf. Whatever happened after his mother was released didn't matter right now. He'd deal with that another day.

---oOo---

Chapter forty-four

I guess I could have done some sight-seeing, but it seemed to be impossible to do anything in America on foot. I wandered out of the hotel to the main road just to have a look around, and it would have taken me several years to walk from there to the nearest fast food outlet. Besides, most of the sights that I could see around me were all the same: desert, scrub and huge, huge skies.

I decided to spend the afternoon around the hotel instead. The swimming pool, although inviting, was out of bounds to me on account of the tee-shirt tan and the dozen or so beautiful people using it, their flawless bronzed skin glistening in the sunshine. The gym was also out of bounds for similar reasons. It was too early and I had too much to do later that day to head to the bar. I resolved to spend an hour or two roaming the internet on one of the access computer points around the hotel.

My email was a little thin on the ground, a disturbing reminder of how little work I had on these days. The expected email from Bill hadn't arrived but, on the plus side, the spam folder was full of useful information telling me how to urgently reset the Barclay's account which I didn't have, and seven different ways to satisfy a woman.

I flicked around various news sites for a while but, unhelpfully for a journalist, I found news fairly boring. The Oxfordshire BBC site was also a little depressing, with a litany of nasty little stories about Council Tax increases, a fight between rival rowing teams in the city centre, and a breaking report of a man murdered in his home as part of a burglary gone wrong.

The place was going to the dogs.

I couldn't concentrate on anything much anyway, and I was feeling lonely and frightened about everything that was happening around me. Drawn out and running on adrenaline, I just wanted to get home, see Zara safely released, and get Gabriel and his cronies far away from my life.

I went for a late lunch, just willing something to happen so I could get on the plane out of here.

Halfway through picking at a chicken salad my phone rang. It was Martin.

"Wolf, I'm just checking that everything is still good for tonight." I remembered that Martin's phone might be monitored, so I watched my words.

"Yeah, Martin. Everything's good here and I'll see you at six. Is everything still okay at your end?"

"Of course, everything's fine here. I look forward to seeing you again." I breathed a sigh of relief. He must have stolen the drive. "I've got a present for you to take to mother, if you could do that for me?" That's what I wanted to hear.

"Definitely. Well, thanks for calling, and I'll see you in a few hours." We disconnected, and I sat back in my chair suddenly hungry.

This would all be over soon.

---oOo---

General Manning had been under fire many times before, and he knew the mind-numbing fear of hearing rounds smash down around him as he scrabbled into the sand with his fingers to try and find somewhere to hide. As they used to say in the 'Nam, he'd seen the elephant and he had survived, and he was stronger as a result.

He wished he could find somewhere to hide now, as this damned CIA man stared at him with disdain.

"So, if I understand you correctly, the bulk of research for Phoenix is performed in a civilian university, by civilian researchers, with the majority of security provided by the university's own security team." Benjamin could barely believe his own words. "You're hiding it in plain sight."

"That's not quite true, Mr Cornfeld. We're not naive. We have increased security on all the laboratory facilities, including full vetting for everyone involved in the work, and we have supplemented the university security with an undercover SEAL team led by Colonel Kennedy. The team also keep full inventories on every piece of equipment and information in the place, along with several of your NSA colleagues who work undercover in the IT department. It's not simply hiding in plain sight."

"I suppose the SEAL team are helping to bump the New Mexico Lobos up the league as well?" asked Benjamin with disgust.

"Don't be disingenuous Mr Cornfeld. The security around that lab is equivalent to that around your own place of work. It's simply more covert. By keeping it low key, we detract unwanted attention from the project."

"Was allowing a car bomb into the parking lot part of your deception plan too?" In fairness, Benjamin knew the logic of the 'hiding in plain sight' strategy, although it wasn't something that his agency approved. The more top secret a project needed to be, the deeper in the Langley basement it belonged.

"I've spoken to the FBI on the scene, and they have found some initial evidence that the bombing was carried out by a separatist extremist. There is nothing to suggest that it is in any way linked to project Phoenix." In spite of the General's flinty gaze, Benjamin could see he was holding something back. After all, it was his job to discover the things that people tried to conceal. Back in the day he was very good at it.

"Yet?" The General paused a beat before answering.

"I don't like coincidences either, and this seems a bit too coincidental for comfort." Benjamin nodded. "If you were sitting here with two stars on your lapel, and another possibly on the way, what would you do Agent Cornfeld?"

"I'd lock the place down. I'd question everyone, and check everything is as it should be. And I wouldn't take another step before you know for certain the entire project is secure." Benjamin smiled. "And then I'd move the whole shebang into the deepest, most secure, hole you can find."

"Right. I'll make it happen. Can your agency dig a bit further into this Gabriel thing?" asked the General. "Just in case."

"Already on it, although we know, or think, our boy is in the UK. With any luck he has no more idea about this affair than I did last week." The General nodded, and Benjamin watched him for a moment as he gathered his thoughts. "Tick, tock, General," he said, gesturing to the phone.

"Of course." The General dialled a number and spoke commandingly. "This is Manning, get me Colonel Kennedy right away." There was a pause. "Colonel, this is General Manning. Lock it down, right away. Nobody in or out until they've been questioned and searched, and I want a full functioning inventory check. If you're missing a single post-it note, nobody leaves until it's found. And check all the logs, I want everyone's movements accounted for." He hung up, looking at Benjamin.

"That should do the trick, General." He rose to leave. "I'll put my feelers out with my sources and get back to you." He paused at the door. "Make sure Kennedy checks *everything*... I still have a bad feeling about this." He left through the corridors quickly, a list of urgent things to do forming in his mind.

---oOo---

Martin was itching to get out of the lab and away from the campus, but the more he looked at the clock, the slower the second hand seemed to move. It was like being back in school on a Friday afternoon, with triple-Latin standing between him and a weekend of playing next to the river.

He was racking his brain for some reason to slope off early but was acutely conscious that another display of unusual behaviour in front of Bradley might give the entire game away.

Still, the more he worried about it, the slower the time seemed to pass. He could not remember a day of such emotional highs and lows, and he was already exhausted by mid-afternoon. If this day didn't end soon he wasn't sure how much more he could take.

Then the scary security guard, Kennedy, arrived at the lab, followed by several of his team, clipboards in their hands and pistols on their belts.

"Sirs, as a result of the incident outside, we have been instructed to secure the facility and conduct a full check of all equipment and inventory." Martin's jaw visibly dropped, and Bradley sighed.

"How long will this take?" Bradley asked. "I've got a date this evening."

"I apologise for any inconvenience, sirs, but with your co-operation we will be done as soon as possible." Kennedy regarded Bradley calmly, but it was plain to read on his face how little he cared about Bradley being inconvenienced. Martin felt his heart fall through his bowels for the third time that day. He could sense the hairs on his arms rising and the blood flowing into his core to hide. He wished he could join it and disappear into himself.

Step by step, bit by bit, the team moved through the laboratory checking items off against their inventory list while Martin sat next to his desk, slowly calming down as he realised that there should be nothing missing from their list... at least, nothing that they would notice. Kennedy, the leader, was checking the serial numbers on one of the work laptops before making a short tick on his list. He set the machine down and moved along the bench. Martin felt relief pour through him once again.

Then Kennedy stopped what he was doing, returned to the laptop, and pressed the 'on' button, watching the screen carefully as it booted up.

Oh holy Jesus, thought Martin, as his heart turned into a leaden block of fear in his chest. He glanced across his desk where his own useless laptop lay inside its case. In his mind the damned thing looked like it was highlighted by beacons, sitting there on the formica, his mother's safety hanging on the slim chance that Kennedy's men overlooked it...

...sitting right next to another cup of coffee that Bradley had sneaked into the lab, giving Martin one last chance to turn this around.

He stood and stretched, pretending to rub his neck. As he turned he sat down on the edge of the desk, knocking the cup over, the tepid coffee pouring all over his laptop case.

"Shit!" Bradley saw the spill and went straight to the paper dispenser on the opposite wall while Kennedy and his men turned to see what the commotion was about. Martin noticed that at least one of them had lowered their hand to their holster, as though by pure instinct. *Campus security my arse*, he thought. These were scary men, unlike Big John, who's only threat was to the take-away food industry.

Grabbing the paper from Bradley he removed the laptop, acutely conscious that his laptop bag was waterproof. He made sure the sticky liquid poured onto the computer as he withdrew it.

"Oh bloody hell, Brad," he muttered, as he dabbed the paper onto the machine, making as big a deal of it as possible. A sudden worry hit him as he wiped the plastic case. If the coffee got inside would it screw the hard-drive up? If so the game was over anyway, and he, his mother and Devenish were done for. He wiped harder, determined to stop coffee from leaching through the casing.

"What's that computer?" asked Kennedy, looking at his list.

"It's my personal one, but it's signed in at the desk each day." Kennedy nodded and approached him.

"Can you turn it on for me, sir? I'll need to check it against the signed in items and check what's on the drive."

"Bloody Bradley has just covered it in coffee! Is that such a good idea?" asked Martin, perhaps a bit too quickly.

"Can you just do as you are asked, sir? It is important that everything in this campus is checked." Trying to look deflated and subdued, Martin plugged the machine in and pressed the start-up button.

Nothing happened, which was hardly a surprise given that the innards of the machine were in a drawer in his flat.

"Oh, for heaven's sake Bradley!" Martin gave him an angry stare and, biting his lip, he moved down the lab to tidy away some items checked off by Kennedy's team.

"Let me try, sir," said Kennedy. He expertly checked the connections, rubbed more paper around the keyboard and screen, and tried to start it up again. He stared at the machine for a moment, before trying again. Martin felt his hair rising once again.

This was it.

"Sir, I think the power supply has blown from the moisture. You should bring it directly to the IT team for data recovery, particularly if the information is important to you. I'm afraid I'll have to report this incident to my superiors as you both know that drinks are not to be taken into the laboratory." *Report away, my son,* thought Martin. *Report away.*

With a final glare at Bradley, he thanked Kennedy and left the lab, following the corridor to IT. Halfway along he took a side door back to reception, stopping at the locker for his car keys along the way. Big John sat at his desk half-heartedly watching a few monitors.

"Af'noon, Doctor. Wassup?" John beamed at Martin.

"I have to sign out, John. Bloody Brad spilled coffee on my laptop and I need to take it to town for a new power supply. The IT boys gave me the address to go to."

"Thas a shame, Doctor. See, tha new bo Kennedy, he don't want no-one leavin' till he says so. Not no-one. Not afer tha explosion this a'noon."

"This is urgent, John. Some of my research is on this machine."

"No 'ceptions, Doctor. Sorro."

"John, you've been here longer than Kennedy, right? You know more about how this place works than he does, yeah? You know me, Martin Moore, and you know I don't break any of the rules, right?" Big John paused for a moment, thinking.

"Lemme make a call, Doctor." He lifted the phone and dialled a number, considerably longer than an internal extension, and had a brief, quiet conversation. When he hung up he smiled broadly. "You's right, Doctor. Screw Kennedy. He a new boy. Sign out right here." He pushed his signing-in book across and Martin scribbled his signature, before thanking John and turning to leave.

"Doctor..." said John, quietly. Martin turned to him.

"Mr Gabriel says 'hi'." He smiled as Martin dashed through the door, his eyes wide with surprise.

Big John chuckled as he checked his watch. Almost four o'clock. He reached for the delivery menu for the Mexican joint down the road.

Chapter forty-five

Benjamin threw himself into his office chair and hit the phones.

The traffic had been horrendous, and it was half five already. There was a reassuring message from the General telling him that lock-down had been lifted, and everything checked out. The FBI had found some papers in the exploded truck which pointed to it belonging to a nutjob out east who thought UNM was working on alien technology to establish mind-control over the population using DNA experiments. The usual crock of shit.

But his gut feeling that something was wrong wouldn't go away.

He put a call into to his contact in NSA, and from there through to the undercover team leader in the university IT department. Again he was told that all seemed to be well, but he wasn't convinced.

"What about the incoming logs to the systems. Have you seen any odd traffic over the last few months?" The guy placed him on hold for a spell, and returned to the call.

"Not really, sir. Nothing significant on the incoming logs, and certainly no hacking footprints."

"What about insignificant oddness? Is there anything weird on the logs at all?" he asked. Benjamin was certain that something was up, but he just couldn't pin it down.

"Well, there was something slightly unusual a few weeks ago, sir. An incoming set of requests from a registered user which were a little weird, but only because of what they were viewing."

"How so? What were they looking at?" Benjamin felt his hunter instinct step forward. He smelled the prey at the end of the chase.

"Well, there were different requests going to all sorts of different d-bases, sir. Inventory details for campus equipment... some service history records... software licence confirmations... a few bits and pieces of front end data. Pretty much the sort of thing you could find just wandering around the place looking at the machines. Nothing sinister."

"What equipment inventories exactly?" asked Benjamin, reaching for a pad of paper.

"Computers, sir. Most of the labs have half a dozen or more machines in them, and the user was looking at some of the technical specs for the computers. They mostly build their own here, you see, so all the components are listed, as are the operating systems, software builds, all that kind of thing."

"And what were the front-end things this guy looked at?"

"Oh, they were nothing. Just university screen saver files, wallpapers and such. All open source for students and staff."

The pieces of the puzzle were right there, staring Benjamin in the face. He was racking his brain to put them together.

"Check the details for the user for me, please, and call me back on this number." It was right there... and he was inches away from putting it together.

"No problem, sir. Be right back at you in twenty."

Benjamin hung up and thought hard, pushing the information around in his head. He glanced at his in-tray hoping that it hadn't filled too much since he was out of the office. On top was the file from Parkinson, the picture of the British woman sitting next to the photocopy of Gabriel's army resume. He picked it up and read it again.

Zara Moore is being checked out as a favour by MI6 as part of a background check on her son, who works in UNM for Project Phoenix. That wasn't unusual... standard practice these days. Then, quite by chance, Gabriel turns up in the same village as Moore, totally out of the blue. He knows from the grapevine that Gabriel is something of a spy for hire, and doesn't do things on a whim, so that raises suspicion. Beyond that suspicion, nothing else raises flags. It could easily be pure coincidence.

Then, today, again apparently randomly, a conspiracy loon launches a car bomb attack on the same campus as the Phoenix project. It could still be just chance. The phone rang again, the NSA plant in UNM calling back. He sounded anxious.

"Sir, we checked that user out, but it was an old account. The original owner died in a car crash last year, and the IT department forgot to clear the log." Benjamin held his breath.

"Where were the requests sent from?" he asked, knowing full well that IP addresses are easily masked.

"They were made from a WiFi hotspot in the UK, sir, as best we can tell."

"Where in England?"

"Some town called Crawley, sir. They were made from a cafe there." Benjamin looked up the town on his computer, then checked the details Parkinson had sent about the encounter with Gabriel. The two locations were less than twenty miles apart. Shit.

"Tell me, and think fast, this information that was downloaded from the university server. What possible use could it be to anyone? Why does the university even keep it?" The NSA guy paused for a second before answering.

"Well, the university keep it for auditing mainly. If a drive fails or a machine dies, they can write the unit off against the recorded serial number. Otherwise it's just a way of keeping up..."

"What did you say? About components failing?"

"If a drive or board fails, they can use the serial number to write it off. It makes managing the budget easier."

"Fuck." The pieces fell into place with a clatter.

"Sorry, sir. What did you say?"

"It's the fucking drive. Gabriel's stealing data from Project Phoenix, and you won't even know it's gone. Don't you see, he got all the information to make a duplicate of any bit of equipment in the lab he feels like duplicating. And you guys won't know a damned thing about it until it's too late."

"Who's Gabriel, sir?" but Benjamin had hung up.

---oOo---

Rebecca Lowry still had one outstanding piece of her particular problem to solve and she would be home free, but she couldn't control her worry. She felt like a child on Christmas

Eve, albeit one waiting to see if Santa brought her favourite toys or a life sentence in prison for fraud, false-accounting, and accessory to murder.

"I told you, Ms Lowry, there was no sign that Jeffries had forwarded that email to anyone. I don't think he knew how to. You ought to have seen him trying to shut the computer down!" said the man.

"Still, you have to check. You must. I need you to check Devenish's place, check his computer, check his files. Make sure there's nothing at all about me there." Lowry couldn't keep the fear from her voice.

"Alright, but I assure you it's clean. I'm telling you that the trail ended with Jeffries. The journalist can poke about all he wants, but he won't find anything. It's gone cold." Lowry waited before answering, her words catching in her throat.

"Fine, but I n... need you to check. And soon." She was losing composure, and felt tears starting to flow. She couldn't let this man, particularly not *this* man, sense her weakness.

"I'll check, okay? Just calm down. Try to forget all about this. It will help your deniability if you ever need to deny anything." It was the wrong thing to say.

"What do you mean? Who's going to investigate me that I need to deny things to? What do you know? What have you done?"

"Nothing! No-one! Jesus, Ms Lowry. Pull yourself together. It's a figure of speech. Now go a pour yourself a glass of wine and I'll check out Devenish's place tomorrow night." *Bloody civilians*, he thought.

"Tomorrow? Can't you do it tonight? Or right away?"

"No, I can't. I need to prepare, check the place out, get the right gear to break in. All the sort of things you need to know nothing about. Besides, I'm off to gym tonight and then I'm on a date."

"But this is important!"

"So is my date. I've been flirting with this bird for weeks. Good day, Ms Lowry. I shall call you tomorrow night. I assure you that everything will be fine." He hung up, leaving her staring at the phone. She went to the kitchen and opened the fridge, regarding the bottle of white in the door tray. Having second thoughts, she returned to her living room and poured a glass of Scotch from the drinks cabinet. Downing it in a single gulp, she poured another and sat on the sofa, staring at her phone.

Suddenly she began to cry, her mascara trickling down her cheeks onto her blouse, her back arched forward as she convulsed with the sobs.

---oOo---

Chapter forty-six

My son looked like he'd aged years when he entered the diner, and he flopped down opposite me, pale and exhausted. Beneath the table he passed me a laptop bag.

"This is it. Christ, Wolf... you would not believe the trouble I had getting this." He ordered a beer from the waitress, and I indicated she might as well bring two.

Or twenty. Martin looked like he could use them.

"So, what's next?" he asked, raising the bottle to his lips.

"Cassiel, the driver, is taking me straight to the airport after this, then it's what they call a "red-eye" back to Heathrow. He says that Gabriel will phone me when I arrive to give me the arrangements, after which time he can shove his phone right up his arse for all I care." Talk of Cassiel reminded me that I was being driven around today, so I gulped most of the beer down in a single go, and indicated for the waitress to bring another couple. "What happened to you, then? I thought everything went well this morning."

Martin told me about the explosion and the subsequent lock-down, and I could see the strain in his eyes as he related the story.

"I don't know, but if they look at the files on that computer before you're in England, we could still be screwed. That security guy, Kennedy... he seems on the ball, and there's no way he works for campus security. Not a chance in hell." He looked at his watch, considering if he could risk another bottle. "God, I haven't even eaten yet." He asked the waitress for a bowl of chilli, and I asked for another beer.

She raised an eyebrow as she took the empties away, three bottles, and we'd been there for five minutes. I always knew the Yanks were puritans at heart.

"Have you had any word from Gabriel?" asked Martin, as he waited for his food.

"Nothing. I've heard from nobody. I've been hiding in the hotel all day while you've been doing your James Bond thing." We both laughed at that and, for a moment, I felt a connection between us. Well, they do say that relationships blossom in crises.

The food arrived and Martin ate, while I savoured my third beer. The conversation fell into small talk, little bits and pieces about our lives, which seemed easier to cope with in the middle of all the stress. I told him about my work and mentioned my friends whom, he said, he'd love to meet. As I'd not heard from Bill for a while, talking about my life back in Oxford made me feel deflated. There was a sense of an adventure coming to an end, and normality getting ready to slap me in the face afterwards like returning home after an exotic holiday. It made me gloomy, and I mentioned it to Martin.

"It's not over yet, Wolf. We've still to get mum back." He paused. "And there's still every chance that Gabriel will want to, er, tie up loose ends. Do you believe he owns one of the security guards working at my lab?"

"You're kidding me! Why didn't he just get him to steal the damned computer?" Martin put his hand on my arm to calm me down.

"He wouldn't know where to start. But I was shocked about it too. The man has people everywhere." He contemplated his beer, glancing at his watch. "What about the other thing?" he asked, looked me in the eye. "The tying up loose ends?"

"I've got no choice but to do what he says regardless. I'll have to take the chance. Besides, I don't think the guy gives a shit if we're still running around afterwards. In fact, getting rid of us would give his game away." I didn't believe a word of it, but I let the optimist within drive me forward to whatever conclusion lay ahead. "Besides, who would believe us? It's crazy stuff. They'd Section us before listening to this story."

Martin nodded and finished his beer before rising to his feet.

"Wolf, I have to go." He looked me in the eye and I glimpsed familiarity in his gaze, like looking into a broken mirror. "Please get my mum back." He shook my hand, and left the booth pausing before he left the diner. He turned back to me. "And keep in touch. I think you're a good man, and I would be proud to call you father."

"I will." I said, and I would.

I finished up and left the booth, grabbing the laptop on the way, and jumped back into Cassiel's car.

"You get it?" he asked.

"Yeah, I got it. So what happens when I get back to England?"

"Fuck I know." And off we drove.

---oOo---

Martin pulled into the accommodation parking, glad he hadn't fallen foul of the over-zealous highway patrol on the way home. He didn't drink often, and wasn't sure if two bottles of beer were too much to drive, but he felt a slight buzz and, given the breaks he'd enjoyed so far today, he thought he was eating too far into his overdraft of good luck to survive an encounter with New Mexico's finest.

He lived in the post-grad accommodation near the university, which was a pleasant array of small mini-apartments surrounded by some welcome greenery and trees, all irrigated every evening by automatic sprinklers. As he passed along the path, exhausted, the sprinklers switched on and he felt refreshed as the spray gently fell around him, turning the gravel black with moisture.

He used his card to get into the reception lounge and took the stairs two at a time to his flat where another beer and a comfortable bed awaited. He passed a couple of other grad students from his block on the way up, and they looked at him with strange, guarded looks on their faces. Perhaps he was just tired and paranoid. God, he wished this day was over.

He entered his flat, threw his jacket on the hook by the door, and went into the little kitchen-living room area. There were four men sitting around his coffee table, and they rose when he entered.

"Mr Moore?" said the one in the crumpled suit who he hadn't seen before. The others he recognised from around campus as the new security team, Kennedy standing in their middle.

The three of them were still armed.

"Yes?" Martin croaked, his throat suddenly dry.

"I'm Agent Cornfeld from the CIA, and we need to ask you some questions. Please sit down."

"What do you want to ask me about?" asked Martin, his heart racing.

"Please, sit down." Martin sat, two of the security team joining him on either side of the futon. Kennedy and Cornfeld sat down opposite them. "Well, doctor, we need to talk to you about your father."

---oOo---

Chapter forty-seven

Leaving this damned country was as hard as getting into it, I thought as I waited in the international departures security line. Eventually it was my turn, and I gave my boarding pass and passport to the elephantine gent in the crisp uniform.

"Keys?" he said, so I tossed my keys and other metallic items into his tray, and he passed them through the x-ray machine before pointing to my bag and Martin's laptop case.

"Laptop?" I nodded, wondering if we were playing some game of eye-spy that I wasn't party to.

"Tray," he said, pointing to another grey plastic tray. I laid the laptop on it, and he slid it through the flaps on the conveyor belt.

"I spy with my little eye, something beginning with 'x'," I offered. He regarded me curiously, before pointing to my jacket.

"Jacket," he said, pointing to yet another tray.

"Nope, the answer was 'x-ray machine'," I smiled as I folded the jacket up and he passed it through.

"Yeah." The guy watching the monitors nodded, and he waved me through to the departure lounge.

I love meeting new people and having conversations with them.

My plane left on time, and soon I was sleeping somewhere high over the Atlantic Ocean, the starlight casting strangely beautiful reflections around the cabin.

---oOo---

"We need that fucking hard-drive, pal, am I clear about that?" Parkinson held the phone away from his ear and took a drink of his tea.

"Benjamin, I would appreciate some civility during this exchange, and I believe that our actions will be better served if

we remain calm." He took another sip of the warm liquid, it
seemed to take away some of the pain inside him, pain which
grew stronger every day.

"Fine. Could you please get us our hard-drive back, please,
Mr Parkinson, sir? Devenish is due in Heathrow in a few hours.
Just stop him, take the case, and bring it to our embassy. That's
all I'm asking." Benjamin's voice faded as he put his hand over
the receiver, far away in New Mexico. "Stuck-up English
prick..."

"Well, Benjamin, I'm sure that Her Majesty's Government
will be able to retrieve the missing item on your behalf, but we
would like to be able to do the same on our own terms."
Parkinson smiled. There were few fun things in his job, but
winding up his American colleagues was one of them. He could
hear Benjamin hyperventilating on the end of the line.

"What terms? What do you mean?" Parkinson thought he
heard teeth grinding.

"It is not the policy of Her Majesty's Government to
sacrifice her citizens in order to help the United States retrieve
lost toys, I'm afraid. Therefore I propose that we allow Mr
Devenish through Heathrow, whereupon we will tail him to his
destination. At that time we shall endeavour to recover your
missing hard drive, secure the safe release of Ms Moore, and
take action against your sadly deceased Sergeant Gabriel which
will result in him spending the rest of his afterlife at Her
Majesty's pleasure." Benjamin was silent for a time before
answering.

"Look, Parkinson, I don't think you get how dangerous this
guy is," he said, coldly.

"The Security Services of the United Kingdom are more than
sufficient to handle one rogue agent, Benjamin. Surely you've
seen James Bond?" Parkinson was almost chuckling now.

"Don't take the piss," hissed Benjamin. "What if he gets
away? What if he figures he's being watched and breaks off the
deal? What if he just slots the girl and Devenish anyway, just
for fun? What then? You'll be the one with egg on their face,
not us."

"I rather think that if we don't supply Mr Gabriel with what he's after, he will, as you so humanely put it, 'slot' the lady anyway. No, I suspect we shall do this our way. I have a fine agent already on the case, and will assign every resource to ensure a successful conclusion to the operation."

"So that's a no, then? You won't pick up Devenish at Heathrow?"

"No, Benjamin. We shall not."

"Right. Well, the United States of America will have something to say about that." Benjamin tried to sound threatening, but in reality he couldn't see any other option short of turning the plane around. As it was a British Airways flight, they'd probably just tell him to fuck off. Politely, of course. *Fuck off, please.*

"Say all you want, Benjamin, but it shall be done our way, and you shall have your little hard-drive within the week. Oh, and please ensure that no accidents happen to Mr Devenish, a British citizen, on arrival in the UK. I am fully aware of some of your tactics." There was silence.

"Okay. Look, I'm going to fly over. Keep me in the loop until I arrive, right? As a favour to me."

"Of course, Benjamin. It is late there, you should try and sleep."

"I'll not be sleeping until that box is in my hands. Try not to fuck this up, Parkinson. Please. It's important."

"Her Majesty's Government is not in the habit of 'fucking things up', Benjamin, as you well know."

"Tell that to King George, you old romantic. All the best to James and Moneypenny." With an exasperated laugh, Benjamin hung up. Parkinson dialled a number.

"Send Ms Berne to me, as a matter of urgency."

---oOo---

It felt good to be home, and I took full advantage of the delicacies of my homeland by eating a tepid sausage roll on the way out of Heathrow arrivals. Smothered in HP sauce, a sachet of which had cost me fifty pence, it reminded me of all the things I didn't miss about living in England.

There were no messages on my phones when I switched them back on but, as I finished the sausage roll, a familiar figure approached me across the concourse.

"Good afternoon, Mr Devenish," said Nadir, smiling broadly. She moved closer and I thought she was going to kiss me but, at the last moment, she flicked her fingers across my lips and dislodged some pastry which had stuck to my cheek. "I trust your trip was profitable."

"Yes, thank you." I scrumpled the empty paper wrapper up and tossed it in a waste bin, before taking the laptop case from my shoulder and offering it to her. "This is what you want, I think." She smiled and gestured for me to keep it.

"It's what Mr Gabriel wants, and you will have to bring it to him. I shall give you a lift to meet him. You'll be pleased to hear that your girlfriend is also there. I'm sure she'll be delighted to see you again."

"She's okay?" I asked, with genuine concern.

"Of course. Come along now, we don't want to be late." She regarded me for a moment, a kindness in her eyes. "Let's get this over with, eh?" I nodded and followed her to the car park before we drove off in her black rental, pausing to let a woman returning from holiday wheel her luggage past us as we left, nattering on her mobile as she walked.

I didn't hear her repeat our registration number into the phone as we descended the ramp and on to the Heathrow circular road.

Chapter forty-eight

Jimmy Coulhoun was a hood. He always had been, even when he was in the army. He was up to his eyeballs in every scam, every fight in the NAAFI, and every bit of sloping off work he could get away with. But he was a good soldier.

Hard as nails.

He reached full corporal three times, having been busted back twice after his schemes became too much for his superiors to ignore, and was finally discharged on medical grounds after the second Iraq war. The rumour on the barracks was that he'd let himself get carried away one afternoon after a bunch of insurgents ambushed his squad, killing two of his mates. The remaining squaddies had captured three insurgents for questioning, and Jimmy was in the back of one of the Warriors taking the frightened kids back to Camp Bastion.

The problem was, only one made it back alive. The others were beaten to death on the way.

The surviving insurgent was too scared to speak, and soon handed over to the Americans who shipped him off to God knows where. The rest of the Warrior crew seemed to have had collective amnesia as well, but Jimmy claimed that the two guys set on him, trying to get his weapon.

Of course, they were tied up and hooded, and Jimmy wasn't carrying his rifle as it would have been dumb to have a loaded gun so close to the suspects.

The senior medic in the unit consulted with the Colonel, and it was decided that Jimmy was no longer stable enough to function in the unit. For the sake of regimental PR he would muster out of the army, and the incident would be forgotten. With his skills and experience, he would find an excellent job in the private sector, which he did.

Although not the kind of job they had expected.

Jimmy became muscle for hire, living quietly most of the time until called upon to visit harm on people for money. The police were vaguely aware of him, but there was never enough evidence to pursue an arrest never mind a prosecution. He moved around the country occasionally leaving his name with people in the underworld, and half a dozen jobs a year kept him in all the money he needed. Sometimes he was asked to get rid of people permanently, and he was happy to oblige if the price was right. He was surprised how many people there were in Britain who needed rid of someone and were willing to pay for it.

Suited him fine.

He built a persona as an ex-SAS man, adopting the clipped and precise conversational style of the few genuine special forces gents he'd met in Iraq. The customers loved it. They believed that their interests were safe in the hands of such a professional, not realising for a second he was a mere wash-out from a rifle regiment.

Lately he'd been doing other stuff, the odd bit of industrial espionage such as stealing passwords and the like from the homes of business rivals, or some bodyguard work for shady businessmen. It was good work, well paid, and he'd learned a lot along the way. It just wasn't as much fun as beating the tar out of someone, so Lowry's job had been ideal, even more so since the work and pay had spiralled since he'd begun.

It was almost full dusk when he arrived at the Devenish house, and he checked that there were no signs of life inside before shimmying up the back wall and opening the bathroom window. He was fairly sure that there'd be no need to visit damage on the boy if he came home which, disappointing as it was, might be a good thing given that three deaths in a row around Oxford might finally arouse suspicion among the local constabulary.

Silently he crept around the landing, checking rooms for computers or occupants, and then sneaked down the stairs. The lounge was still quite bright from the fading light shining through the large French windows, and he noticed the wooden flooring with a sigh. It was hard to walk quietly on a wooden floor, and if anyone was in the house they'd hear him before he saw them. He waited for a moment before continuing.

No signs of life.

He entered the lounge and looked around for the computer. The guy was a writer, so where the hell was the machine? He considered telling Lowry that he'd checked it anyway and it was clean, as he was certain Jeffries hadn't forwarded the email. In fact, thinking about it, he could have done that from the pub instead of breaking and entering Devenish's house. But he was there now, so in for a penny, in for a pound.

He tiptoed into the kitchen-diner and, there on the little table, was a laptop. Just in time too, as the light was fading fast and he didn't want to get his torch out in case it was spotted from the road. He flicked on the power and waited for the machine to warm up, rubbing his hands together as he waited, his smooth black gloves stretching across his long fingers.

Once in the system he found the email program and brought up the inbox. Nothing. Not a single message from Jeffries. He did a quick search of the mail history, but nothing came back. It seemed that fat boy just didn't know his technology. He shut the program down, pausing to remove the browsing history for the last few minutes, turned off the computer and flicked the switch at the wall.

He wiped the machine down and made sure it was in the same position he'd found it, before standing up, carefully pushing the chair beneath the table, and walking into the lounge.

There was a tall figure standing in the room, between Jimmy, the stairs, and a clean exit. Much too tall to be Devenish.

"My name is Mr Gabriel," said the figure, "and it looks like you're in for a shitty night."

Jimmy reached into his jacket, pulling out a vicious-looking knife. Slowly, keeping his legs wide and his centre of gravity low, he began moving toward Gabriel, sidling around with the tip of the blade held far in front, his fingers flicking the knife back and forth towards the American. Just as he'd seen on TV.

"What the fuck do you want?" he demanded in his most frightening voice. The figure watched him as he moved closer, an amused grin on his lips.

"Peace, love and the American way, son," answered Gabriel, laughing softly.

Jimmy, teeth clenched, growled and lunged forward, stabbing the blade towards Gabriel's neck. The big American swept his arms up, first deflecting the knife then grasping Jimmy's arm at the elbow.

"Whoopsie," said Gabriel.

He twisted his arm, suddenly pushing the elbow against the joint. There was a brutal cracking noise, and Jimmy's entire side was enveloped with pain. His face went white almost instantly, and the knife dropped harmlessly to the floor.

As he fell to his knees, Gabriel calmly walked over to him and watched as Jimmy stared at his arm, now twisted into an unnatural position.

"That's gonna smart in the morning, son," he said, before removing a pistol from his jacket and bringing the butt down sharply onto Jimmy's neck.

Jimmy collapsed, barely conscious, and he lay immobile on the parquet, watching as two expensive leather ankle boots appeared before him.

One of them kicked him full in the face and Jimmy fell into blackness.

---oOo---

"We're heading to Oxford, aren't we," I asked, as Nadir drove steadily along. "Quicker on the M40, actually."

"And easier to get followed on the M40, Mr Devenish." She smiled. "Haven't you realised we're being followed?" I half-turned to look behind me, but I could only see a stream of headlights along the road. "One lead car and a follow-up. They take turns to get closer, then drop back and swap. It's cute. Probably MI6." She kept smiling as she drove, enjoying the curves in the road. "Don't you feel comforted that they care about your wellbeing, Mr Devenish?"

"Is that not a problem to you, then? Getting followed by British spies?" She shook her head, laughing.

"Not really." She checked her phone, pulled up a speed-dial number and pressed 'call'.

"That's a driving violation right there, Nadir. Points on your licence." She raised the phone to her ear and spoke shortly.

"Two minutes out. Get ready." She put the phone down and turned to me. "Which licence? I've got about a dozen..." Ahead was a junction heading toward some country village I wasn't familiar with. Nadir flicked the indicator on, slowed, and turned up the lane toward the village, high hedgerows on either side of the narrow road. "Watch this," she said, amusement in her voice.

As she drove first one, then another, set of headlights followed us into the lane.

"See? Lead car and back-up. And they didn't have time to find an alternative route to join up with me later. Quaint." She smiled and accelerated a little down the road. After a mile or so we entered proper countryside, passing a couple of farms along the way. "Here we go," she said, slowing the car down. Behind us the tail cars slowed awkwardly as well. One flashed his lights, probably in a half-hearted attempt to convince us that they were late for an urgent appointment in the middle of nowhere, and that we were holding them back.

Suddenly, from the farm exit, a huge combine-harvester, probably as wide as the road, pulled out between us and the tail cars, and began to laboriously creep along the lane.

"That should do it," she said, and hit the accelerator. The beeping from the tail cars faded as she sped along the tiny road.

Thirty minutes later we pulled into the street behind my home, all alone, with nobody following us.

"Showtime, Mr Devenish." Nadir got out of the car but I sat still, my heart pounding. I hadn't expected to meet here. She leaned in toward me, placing a delicate hand on my shoulder. "You'll be fine. Let's end this."

There was a note of finality in her tone.

---oOo---

Chapter forty-nine

"Good to see you again, Wolf, me old mucker!" Gabriel's attempt at an English accent was dreadful, but the strength of his handshake and the flinty look in his eyes warned me not to mention it. He was immaculately dressed and smiling broadly as he stood in my lounge. "So this is where it all began, and this is where it'll all end, eh?" He motioned for me to sit.

Zara was sitting on the far side of the sofa, a loosely knitted shawl across her shoulders, which she clutched around her body tightly. I could see the strain in her eyes, but otherwise she looked okay. Beside her, snoring away and leaving fur all over my rug, was Marcellus.

"Are you alright, darling?" I asked. She looked at me, with more hope in her eyes than sadness, and nodded. "Did he hurt you?" She nodded again before speaking.

"Not much, it's fine. It's not me he hurt. Let's just get this over with, Wolf, please?" I turned to Gabriel with what I hoped was hate in my eyes, but he returned my stare with amusement.

"I barely touched her, Mr Devenish, so calm down, eh?" He gestured to the laptop bag. "Right, we don't have a lot of time, so give me the laptop." I passed it to him and he sat next to Zara, pulling the device onto the coffee table. Nadir stood close to the front hall, anxiously watching the street.

"So, no chance of coffee this time, eh?" I asked Nadir, who simply shook her head and checked her watch. Her suit jacket was hanging loose, and I noticed the bulge on her hip. I didn't think it was cellulite.

"So here it is..." Gabriel held up the drive and inspected it. "Doesn't look like much, does it?" He took a small torch from his pocket and shone a pale blue light on the device, turning it over in his hands a few times before switching off the light. "Well, I'm relieved to see you didn't just try and fob me off with Cassiel's fake drive. Of course we'd put a few UV markers on it just in case." I hadn't even thought of doing that. Christ, I'm glad Martin hadn't either. He put the hard drive in the laptop case, leaving the disembowelled machine on the coffee table.

"Time to go, Gabe. We got to run." Nadir was edgy, uptight. Somehow different to the Nadir who drove me home. It was as though she expected something bad to happen.

"Yeah, I got it," he replied, curtly. He slung the bag over his shoulder and stood, turning to Zara. "Sorry about all the unpleasantness, but I guarantee you that it was worth it." He stroked the dog on the head, Marcellus looking up at him with chocolate eyes. "Nice dog." Gabriel approached me in the centre of the room. "Well, Mr Devenish. I'd say it was a pleasure but, well, we'd both be lying. Anyway, best of luck in the future and all that shit, and thanks for doing as you were told. I've got a little going away present for you." He reached inside his jacket and I flinched back against the wall.

This was it. This was how it would end.

"Don't be an asshole, Devenish," said Gabriel as he produced a small memory stick and tossed it to me. I was frozen to the spot, and it clattered onto the floor. "Jesus, but you're useless, boy. Glad that son of yours has more *cajones*." I picked up the memory stick, aware of Nadir growing more anxious by the door.

"What's this?" I asked. The stick was unmarked.

"Well, as Ms Moore will tell you, we weren't the only visitors to your home this evening. There was another gent here, sent by someone called Lowry. Sounds like a bitch if you ask me. Anyway, my guess is he was here to cover up something for his boss and, by covering up, I mean covering you up in your own blood." He smiled. "Lucky I happened along, eh? Every cloud and all that."

"Gabe. Now. Come on!" Nadir was near to panic.

"Right, right... Jeez. You on your moons or something, Nadir? Well, whatever Lowry was trying to cover up is on that memory stick. Enjoy." I put the stick in my pocket. "Oh, your visitor is lying down for a bit on the spare bed. Seems that he had a few mishaps on the stairs. You should really check that out. They're not safe." He went to the door and Nadir opened it for him.

"One last thing, the feds will be along shortly. I'm afraid our little artifice didn't last as long as I'd hoped, so they're chasing the hard drive. Of course we'll be long gone when they arrive, but they'll probably want to ask you two a few hundred questions. I'd start by telling them about your houseguest upstairs, just in case you forget about him." He walked onto the pavement with Nadir following, and took a quick glance around before turning to me once again.

"Blame me for the rest. I couldn't care less either way." He turned to leave. "See you in another life, Devenish."

He waved shortly and walked briskly across the road to his Mondeo. Nadir jumped into her car and started the engine, while Zara came over beside me, putting her arm around me tightly. We watched numbly as Gabriel unlocked the door and turned to beam at us once more, all teeth and smiles.

On the pavement across from the house a small figure emerged from a patch of darkness beneath the neighbour's weeping willow tree, just another shadow leaving an even darker one. He strode quickly toward Gabriel's car and pointed his hand at the American. His gun glimmered in the streetlights.

"Gabriel!" I shouted, instinctively. Gabriel spun around and reached into his jacket, but the laptop strap caught in the expensive cloth, keeping the jacket closed. Suddenly there were two bright flashes followed by twin 'cracks', and Gabriel spun backwards, landing in the street.

The short figure paused a second, raised the gun toward us, then turned and dashed up the road. I could swear that I'd seen him somewhere before. As Zara and I ran from the house Nadir, her face deathly pale, spun her car onto the road and sped off. She looked horrified as she passed, her eyes wide and skin pale.

Gabriel lay on the road groaning, bloodstains growing on his sleeve and shoulder. He looked directly at me, his grey eyes glistening in the light from the street.

"Help me, Devenish. Help me finish this."

---oOo---

Chapter fifty

Parkinson and Laura stared at the bloodstains on the road, reflecting the blue lights from the myriad of police cars now blocking off the road. Along the houses, uniformed police were knocking on doors, gathering witness statements from the residents and curtain-twitchers. A few scene of crime officers were wandering around in their white body suits, looking angrily at the two MI6 officers as they contaminated their crime scene.

"Well, this is a bit embarrassing," said Parkinson, trying to ignore the phone vibrating in his pocket. Cornfeld must have arrived at the airport now, and was determined to burn up the CIA's free minutes by bothering Parkinson.

"It's certainly hard to understand, sir." Laura felt exhausted. Losing Devenish was bad enough, but not having people in place at his home sooner was a genuine error. "We really thought there was no chance he'd be taken home. It doesn't make any strategic sense. This kind of thing is done in darkened lanes, far away from prying eyes. The last place on earth I would have expected Gabriel to go was here."

"Precisely why he came here, Ms Berne." Parkinson switched his phone to silent. "What do we know about the man upstairs?"

"The uniforms say he's known to them. He's been a suspect in a variety of violent crimes. Nasty bit of work, it seems."

"Gabriel's type?" asked Parkinson.

"Gabriel wouldn't employ people who end up tied up on a bed, beaten half to death, with the words 'bad man' written on his head in permanent marker. The police think he was after Devenish. They'll be talking to him when he's safely in hospital."

"Did anyone see anything at all then, or is that too much to hope for?" asked Parkinson, wearily.

"Nobody seems to have seen the shooter, but after the shots a car was seen speeding off, the description was that of the hire car we followed earlier. A man and woman came from the house to attend to the bloke who was shot, witnesses identified the man as Devenish, and they pulled him into the backseat of another car, just another non-descript rental, and nobody saw the plates. Apparently the woman ran back to the house and came out carrying a dog before they drove away."

"To hospital? Have you checked?" Parkinson was biting his lip, the nearest thing to emotion Laura had seen him display to date.

"Of course, sir. No GSWs reported for 40 miles. A couple in London, but they're all kids. Gang-related."

"So, what do you think? I need something to tell Cornfeld and his team, as no doubt he'll arrive with half of Arkansas in tow."

"I think Devenish and Moore helped the shot man." She paused, considering her words. "I think the injured man was Gabriel."

"Why on earth would they want to help him? Stockholm syndrome?" Parkinson shook his head in amazement.

"Well, the only options I can think of, sir, are that they were under duress, which doesn't make sense since Gabriel was incapacitated. They may have been feeling sorry for him after the shooting and decided to help him. Equally they might have been sucked in by his charisma. It's possible, but very unlikely, that they were in it with him. I can only think of one other reason they helped him, sir. But it's not very helpful."
Parkinson stared at her.

"Continue."

"Well, sir. To be frank. They might just be fucking stupid."
Parkinson nodded.

"And we're meant to protect these people" he said, before taking his phone out to return some awkward calls. "Find them, Ms Berne. I want to speak to this Mr Devenish."

---oOo---

"Don't you dare let that hippy put any of her stupid potions near me, Devenish! Tell her to leave me be, she's not listening to me," moaned Gabriel in the back seat.

Gabriel had been whinging for twenty minutes now, and I spent every one of those minutes wondering why I was driving the lunatic towards Salisbury. Zara dressed the gunshot wounds using the car first aid kit, and she claimed they were just flesh wounds, although what a veggie like her knew about meat I had no idea. The bleeding had mostly stopped now which was a shame as if he had bled to death at least he would be quieter.

"She's trying to help you, Gabriel. For Christ's sake will you stop moaning?" I shouted at him over my shoulder. Zara shot me a hard glance.

"He's hurt, Wolf. Don't fill him with negative aura when he's injured." Gabriel flashed his grey eyes at me, and I sensed more than enough negative aura there already.

"Well stop the damned dog from licking me, Chrissake." Gabriel pushed Marcellus gently into the footwell using his good arm. He looked at Zara. "You need to stop giving that dog so many lentils, babe. He's fat as a Mexican mama." We continued along the road into the countryside before Gabriel spoke again. "You'll have to pull over Devenish. Something I have to do."

I pulled the car off the road into a side-lane, and onto a little verge beside a field.

"Right, help me out." Zara seemed mortified that he wanted to leave the back seat, but I opened the door and pulled Gabriel to his feet. He looked at his suit jacket, stained and torn by Zara's treatment. "That cost nine-hundred bucks, goddamit." He put a finger through the hole in his sleeve.

"What do you need help with? God, Gabriel, you should be in a hospital." I still couldn't believe I was helping this man.

"I'll be in the bed next to you if you don't zip it, son. Just 'cause you folks are helping me, it don't make us buds and don't forget it. Now open the trunk." I released the catch and pulled the boot open. He took the drive out of the laptop bag, taking care not to get blood on it as some was still dripping down his arm, then handed me a torch. "Shine it here."

I did as I was told, and he pulled another bag from the boot, a thickly padded one with Velcro closing straps. He felt carefully along the padded lining and tried pulling at it for a moment before swearing. "Look, Devenish, you've got fingers like a girl. Feel along this seam until you find a tiny tab, then pull it, okay?" Sighing I reached for the bag, but he grabbed my hand halfway, a manic grin on his pale face. "Gently..."

I stroked the inside of the padded fabric for a moment until I felt a little flap of fabric, like a tiny version of the ones you get on clothing. Pulling it gently the padding tore away from the bag liner, revealing a thin line of Velcro and some ominous looking wires.

"What's that," I asked, wondering if this night would ever end.

"Just a tracking device." Gabriel fiddled around with the bag for a moment while I held the torch for him, before carefully replacing the padding and putting the hard drive into it. "I'm a paranoid type of guy." He set the bag back in the boot, before closing it with his good arm. "Right, let's get on the road." He paused, embarrassed. "Oh... wait a second, I need to take a leak." He looked meaningfully at me. "What with my arm being out of action, what you say you give me a hand, Devenish?" he asked with a wink.

"Go fuck yourself," I replied, to which he laughed.

"Fair enough. Just goosing with you anyway, Devenish. Let's go and, on the way, you need to listen. I'm going to need your help again."

We drove off towards Salisbury, following his directions. Along the way he told me what he needed me to do.

---oOo---

Chapter fifty-one

It was full dark when Abdul-Khaliq Hassan and his men arrived at the car park, more like a little washed out gulley in the moor rather than a proper parking space. But it was far enough from the road and deep in the middle of nowhere on Salisbury Plain, so perfect for their purposes this night.

Gabriel was late.

They amused themselves in conversation while a few of his men stood around smoking and peering across the moorland. He never understood the Arab obsession with cigarettes, but he couldn't ask his men to quit just because he didn't like it. He had asked enough of some of them in the past to forgive the occasional vice.

After half an hour or so, lights appeared in the distance. A single car on the distant road. Abdul-Khaliq checked his watch, and motioned for his men to get into position. There was nowhere to take cover nearby, evidently as Gabriel had planned, but he had one man lie down in a little gulley next to the track just in case things went wrong.

The approaching car pulled into the lane, and stopped twenty or thirty metres away from his own, the lights switching off but the engine still running. A figure emerged from the driver's door, and Abdul-Khaliq told his driver to put their own lights on.

The man wasn't Gabriel.

He gestured to his colleagues to get ready, and he produced a pistol from his own pocket, quietly pulling back the action. He exited the car and walked toward the figure, keeping the pistol behind his back. The unknown man stood at the rear door, pulling it open as he approached. Perhaps he was just the driver.

"Where is Gabriel?" demanded Abdul-Khaliq. A voice from the car rang out in the still air.

"Right here, buddy!" That American twang. That condescending tone. If he wasn't so useful to them, Abdul-Khaliq would have done to him what he wanted to do to all

Americans. The driver reached inside the car. Beside him, Abdul-Khaliq's men withdrew their weapons ready for any tricks. The driver stood upright again, helping another, taller man out and to his feet.

Gabriel.

"My friend, what has happened to you?" asked Abdul-Khaliq, his voice filled with sympathy he didn't feel. He could see the blood stains even in the low light, and Gabriel's face was pale and gaunt.

"I shot myself shaving," replied Gabriel with a smile. He gingerly walked forward and shook the Arab's hand, taking care not to move his shoulder when he moved. His suit was steeped in blood.

"Should we be worried?" asked Abdul-Khaliq, noting that Gabriel's driver looked scared out of his wits, usually a sign that things were about to go wrong.

"Nah... nothing to do with you. Don't fret, Abdul." The way Gabriel used his name filled him with anger, but he restrained himself. He used his name – the name Allah had given him – like an insult. "I've got the hard drive you wanted. It's right here." Gabriel passed a padded bag across to Abdul-Khaliq, who gave it to one of his men, asking him in Arabic to check it.

The man pulled the drive from the bag, and handed the bag toward Gabriel.

"No, you keep it, bud," said Gabriel. "Can't be too careful with static electricity." The Arab looked to his boss, who nodded shortly. He walked back to the car, bag and hard-drive in his hands.

"Thank you, Mr Gabriel. As always you have come through for me." He opened his arms in embrace, his eyes saying anything other than 'thank you'.

"You don't want my blood on your shirt, Abdul. You never know where I've been," chuckled Gabriel. "So, what about the money?"

"When Hatim judges that it's all in order I'll make a call and the money will be transferred. Is that acceptable?" Gabriel nodded. "Who is this?" he asked, gesturing at Devenish, "I've not seen him before."

"He's my caddy. I'm playing golf later. Got luminous balls." Abdul-Khaliq smiled tightly. He hated this man, with his insolent wit and arrogant manner. From the Arab's car, Gabriel could see pale lights as they hooked the disk drive up to a portable computer. Abdul-Khaliq noticed the woman sitting in Gabriel's vehicle, as pale as the driver.

"And who is that? Someone to pull your trolley?" smiled the Arab.

"It's my mother. It's her birthday," said Gabriel, as Hatim re-emerged from other car. "So, what about the money? We good?" Hatim spoke to Abdul-Khaliq in Arabic, and he turned to Gabriel and nodded.

"We are good." Another quick exchange in Arabic, and Hatim took a small satellite phone from his pocket and made a call. He finished and put the phone away. "The money is transferred."

A few moments passed and a short click told Gabriel he had a text message. He checked his phone and nodded. The money had arrived in his account.

"Thanks for the business, Ab-dul..." Gabriel winced as he shook hands again, but he kept his smile nonetheless. "Look forward to working with you next time."

"You too, Mr Gabriel." He regarded Devenish once more. "And your caddy. I hope he feels better soon." He returned to the car, and the Arabs got inside.

"Let's go," said Gabriel, and Devenish helped him into the back seat again before reversing out of the lane, trying not to notice the Arab who appeared from the side of the road, a pistol in his hand. "Just keep driving, Devenish," said Gabriel, quietly.

Turning at the end of the track, Devenish switched on the headlights and accelerated slowly away.

---oOo---

"Were they terrorists," Zara asked, and I looked in the mirror to see Gabriel's response.

"Well," said Gabriel, "one man's terrorist is another man's freedom fighter, or something like that." He was grinning, although obviously in quite a bit of pain.

"Are you telling me that, after all this, you just sold a secret weapon to Arab terrorists?" I tried to keep my voice level, but my adrenaline was flowing and fuelling my anger. Gabriel nodded happily. "And we just helped you to do it?" He nodded a little more, smiling broadly.

"Well, Devenish, your journalism career wasn't working too well for you, so I figured you needed to diversify a touch. I thought that international terrorism would be a step up for you. Just think of all the excitement and glamour." He gingerly looked behind him, spotting Abdul-Khaliq's car headlights in the distance.

"I feel sick. You bastard," said Zara, her beautiful face twisted at the thought of what we'd just done. "You're a monster."

"Well, just another twenty or so miles and you can drop me off. Got a buddy from back in the day living near the ranges. He'll see me right, and you'll be rid of me."

"And what about us, then," I asked. "What's going to happen to us?"

"Nothing. Everything you did was under duress. Believe me, when they look up my name in their records, they'll know you had no choice. It's all cool, bro." Gabriel reached into his pocket for his phone, and I noted Zara eyeing his pistol beneath the jacket. I half-thought for a moment that she was going to lunge for it and shoot him, but she just stared, pale and sick to her stomach.

"One more thing to do, mind." He looked at Zara, "could you give my old pal Nadir a quick call to tell her I'm okay?" Zara paused before answering, her features softening a little from her innate kindness and desire to help.

"Okay." She took the phone, tight-lipped. "What's the number?"

Gabriel dictated the phone number, watching Zara as she keyed it in. She finished entering the phone number, and pressed the 'call' button.

"What do you want me to..."

In the rear view mirror I saw a sudden plume of flame on the road and, in the light of the explosion, I saw the shadow of Abdul-Khaliq's car lifting a few feet into the air. The sound of the blast hit us moments later, and I swerved to keep the car on track. The Arab's vehicle hit the tarmac again, its insides filled with flame, before forlornly rolling off the road and into a ditch. There was no sign of life inside as it settled, fire and black smoke billowing through the smashed windows.

"Whoops," said Gabriel. "Wrong number." He beamed and sat back in the seat, his eyes half-closed, and I continued driving along the directions he had given me, the shock making me feel nauseous.

Zara caught my eye in the mirror, her own eyes wide and bewildered. But I saw relief too. Gently she reached over to Gabriel and pulled his jacket around him as he fell asleep.

---oOo---

Chapter fifty-two

Gabriel's directions took us to a farmhouse north of the Salisbury military training grounds, a ramshackle affair boasting a few fields, some pigs in a barn, and a manky farm collie called Bess that kept trying to shag Marcellus. His contact was a furtive, twitchy bloke called Tom, all lean muscles and wandering eyes. Beyond telling us his name, he barely spoke at all except to reprimand Zara for her 'amateur first aid.'

Gabriel's breathing had become laboured during the journey and, when we got him onto the living room sofa, Tom stripped his shirt off to reveal bleeding Zara hadn't noticed, a nasty-looking wound beneath his shoulderblade.

"Exit wound." He glared at Zara. "You didn't check for an exit wound, you fuckin' muppet."

As Gabriel fell in and out of consciousness Tom gathered some impressive-looking medical supplies out of a battered old rucksack. Smoothly he inserted a drip into Gabriel's good arm, tossing an old picture off the wall and hanging the saline solution to the hook. We watched him work as he checked blood pressure and pulse, listening to Gabriel's chest occasionally with a stethoscope, before sticking a terrifyingly large needle between the American's ribs. Taping a dressing over the wound beneath his shoulder, a fancy looking thing with a thick plastic coating, he removed the body of the syringe and attached a complex plastic device to the end of the needle. There was a soft hiss as bloody fluid bubbled into the valve, and Gabriel's breathing began to ease almost immediately.

"Collapsed lung. Where'd you learn your first aid, love? Fucking girl guides?" Zara shook her head.

"Hey, she did the best she could, right?" Tom regarded me as he gave Gabriel an injection. I noticed on the wall behind him a little wooden shield, the upturned dagger wings of the SAS displayed in the centre.

"Damn near killed him, but I got it. I have to make a call. He'll need those slugs removed and stitches to sort that pneumothorax out. Sit with him. Watch his breathing. Shout if it changes." He left the living room.

Gabriel opened his eyes, misty from the morphine, and glanced in my direction. His colour was better since Tom had stabbed him with the needle.

"This is pretty shit, no?" He smiled, not in his usual wicked way, but almost kindly. Tom's drugs were calming the savage beast. "You two need to get out of here. The feds will be after you."

"What about you?" I asked. I felt sorry for this man, this threatening, unbalanced, man who had stormed into my life and likely screwed it up forever. But lying on the sofa, the one-way valve bubbling away each time he took a breath, he looked smaller somehow. Less dangerous.

I couldn't figure out exactly what I was feeling, but it seemed that there was a connection between us now. It wasn't because of what he had done to us personally this last week, nor what we'd help him to do to the Arabs. It was an understanding that for the rest of our lives, whatever they might bring, Gabriel's impact will have altered our paths forever. My conversation with Nadir floated into my train of thought, and I realised that she was right. I had glimpsed a little of the shadowy world beneath my own mundane existence and, like her, I don't think I would forget it.

My eyes had been opened.

"Ah'll be fine here for a couple days, Devenish, old pal. Tom will look after me and I'll be on my way again soon." He tried to reach his jacket, and Zara lifted it up for him, unconsciously keeping her hands away from the big pistol lying next to it in its shoulder holster.

"Check the pocket, boy," said Gabriel, pointing inside the jacket. I reached in and pulled his wallet out, offering it to him. He shook his head. "Nah... there's a bit of money in it. Take a grand or so. You folks shouldn't be using any bank cards for a day or two." I checked inside, finding a thick wad of notes, both British and American currency. I removed a handful and counted out eight or nine hundred pounds, in fifties and twenties. There was plenty left, so I didn't feel bad about leaving him short. He looked to Zara.

"Grab another two hundred for the hippy. She needs a new dress, and she needs to take that damned dog to the vet, get a stomach band or something." I passed the money to Zara, who tucked it a little pocket inside her dress. Tom came back into the room, carrying a bottle of scotch, a half-full glass already in his hand. He checked Gabriel briefly, listening to his chest, then sat opposite him, next to the little log fire crackling in the grate.

"How do you know Gabriel?" I asked him. He raised his glass to the wounded American, a smile playing on his lips.

"Oh, I've known this bastard for years, mate. Good times, shit times, and stupid times like this." He chuckled as he drank.

"Yeah, well you did your share of stupid shit back in the day too, bud, if memory serves." Gabriel raised himself up on one elbow, laughing at Tom. "You remember Shirley, you crazy English fuck?" Tom, his face straight but eyes glinting in the firelight, raised his glass in toast once again.

"Best tits in Abergavenney, Pete. Worth every second." Gabriel flicked his gaze to Zara.

"Captain fucking Cock here decided to do the dark dance one night with Shirley round the back of the pub car park. Course her husband, the landlord, saw them and put two barrels from a twelve-bore straight into his ass." Tom stood and wiggled his behind at us, and I noticed one cheek was slightly misshapen, even through his jeans. He sat down again and began rolling a cigarette.

"Nearly got kicked out over that, but Pete smoothed it over for me," said Tom, nodding gently as he lit his cigarette. "Good of him, given what a cunt he is most of the time." Gabriel laughed, his laugh turning to coughing almost immediately. When he caught his breath he turned to me.

"Right, Devenish. Take your good lady and the hire car off somewhere for a day or two. Think of it as a holiday. My thanks for helping me out. When you get home again, the feds will be all over you, so if you fancy enjoying the next few days just put the car out of the way and don't check in using your real name." He paused for second, then smiled at me again, a flash of his old venom reappearing. "Fact, I wouldn't use your real name ever, Devenish. Stupid fucking name."

He offered me his hand, a genuine smile returning. "Look. I'm not sorry about all this, don't get that idea. But you two probably saved my life. Probably saved a few thousand more lives by helping me. You're likely gonna be in the shit for a bit, but tell them the truth and it'll be okay. I forced you, right? Blame me. I don't give a fuck. That right, Tom?"

"Pete's never given a fuck, folks. Not once," said Tom, tossing the dog-end into the fire. Gabriel continued.

"No hard feelings?" I considered him for a moment before shaking his hand, feeling the cool sweat on his palm. His grip was still strong.

"No hard feelings, Mr Gabriel." I released his hand and shook Tom's. "Look after him." He nodded before returning to his whisky. Zara thought for a moment, then blew Gabriel a kiss.

"You should put some honey on those wounds when they heal up, Mr Gabriel," she said. He looked at her like she was insane.

"It's a bullet wound, darling, not a waffle." She pursed her lips before lifting Marcellus, holding him close as he panted happily, tongue hanging out. Together we left the farmhouse, driving west along dark roads in Gabriel's big hire car.

---oOo---

Epilogue

The police came for Zara and me as we were leaving Bill's funeral, the perfect ending to a truly shitty day.

We'd learned about Bill's murder the day after we left Gabriel, and decided that we had to attend the funeral even if it meant cutting our time together by half.

It was truly a bittersweet affair, and my mood flipped between deep sadness at the loss of my friend to wide-eyed amazement at the surreal funeral Bill had organised in his will. The solemn eulogy to Bill and his life was delivered by the Master of Jesus College, dressed in all his regalia. This was followed by ten burlesque dancers performing 'It's raining men', dressed in unique regalia all of their own. The rest of the funeral continued along similar lines.

The two detectives stopped us as we left the college grounds. We noticed several police cars, both marked and unmarked, along the road, but at least they were sensitive enough to the occasion not to take us during the ceremony or to have their lights and sirens blazing.

We were arrested ostensibly on terrorism charges, the upside of which was that we were held separately in an old house outside of Guildford rather than in a police station. The place was full of commotion day and night, and we both went through endless hours of questioning. 'Debriefing', as the skeletal gent in the suit called it.

After seven days of this a red-faced American got his turn, and he forced us to tell the same story again and again, his face growing redder at each retelling. Eventually he gave up, throwing his hands in the air and walking out of the debriefing room.

When the security services had finished, a Detective Inspector from Oxford arrived to discuss Bill's death. I didn't have much to tell him that he didn't already know, but related the story of how I had been looking into his sudden resignation.

He explained that the case had been closed, and prosecution charges were underway against two individuals. The man from my house was to be charged with two counts of murder when fit enough to face the magistrates, and a second suspect, a lady who worked at the college, will face several charges, including fraud and accessory to murder. The detective asked if I would be willing to testify at trial before leaving, and I agreed, happy to do what I could to avenge Bill's murder.

Finally, on the tenth day, Parkinson, the skinny man from MI6, told us that we were no longer terrorist suspects and free to leave. I asked about Martin, and Parkinson told me that his tenure at the university was at an end. He would be returning to England within the week.

Released together, we were given a lift back to my house, where I removed the police tape and we entered the lounge.

Half-expecting to hear Gabriel's sardonic voice when we walked in, instead I ploughed into a pile of mail that had built up during my enforced absence. Zara and Marcellus, returned from his own interrogation in the kennels, curled up on the sofa, both exhausted. I swear the dog had lost weight. As I lit my little gas fire and grabbed us some wine, I flicked through the mail. Scattered through the bills and adverts were a few things that caught my interest.

There was an offer from one of the local publishers suggesting a ten grand advance for my writing a book about the Sir Rodney story. I guess that was good news, but it was offset by the letter from Bill's solicitor telling me that he had left his house to me in his will. The precise wording, standing out starkly among the legalese of the letter, was simply 'every knight needs his own castle.' I started to cry, a bitter emptiness welling up within me as I thought of my friend, now gone. Zara, taking the letter from me and reading it, cried too.

The final post of interest was a simple postcard, a picture of the Eiffel tower on the front. Sent from France and addressed to me, it was written in a tight, careful hand, and had a two line message.

"Enjoy your life, Mr Devenish. It may not be black and white, but the colours are beautiful."

---oOo---

The End

Gabriel will return in "Chasing Lead", due for

release in Spring 2014.

Here's a little taster... PC.

Prologue

The still waters of the Gulf of Aden flowed off in every direction, reflected starlight scintillating on the swell, and a soft wind blew misty spray across the bow as the big ship cut through the sparkling sea.

High clouds cast faint shadows on the surface of the water as they scudded across the sky, black shapes flowing across the ripples of light. To the south a faint glow in the sky, the Somali port of Bosaso, competed with the starlight to make an artificial dawn. Scattered here and there were other craft, plying their midnight trade on the edge of the Arabian Sea, their motes of light drifting like tired fireflies caught in a desert breeze.

From the bridge, fifty feet above the water, the view in any direction was the same, a tapestry of velvet sky and silky sea sprinkled with a million pinpricks of light.

"I fucking hate this place," said Atkins, the ship's captain, as he scanned the horizon. "It's a total shithole."

He set his binoculars on a chair and walked to the radar display. There were over a hundred contacts within a twenty mile radius of the ship, some large and labelled with ship transponder codes, the majority small and unidentified. "Bet half of those bastards are pirates and smugglers," he moaned.

His white uniform shirt was a pale green from the fluorescent glow as he leaned over the screen, and his grey hair appeared silver in the light. On the port side of the room stood a slightly-built Filipino, barely nineteen, peering across the water with binoculars. Relaxing on a seat in the centre of the room, a bored expression on his face, was another man. He wore black combat trousers with a holstered automatic pistol strapped to the leg, lightweight boots and a bulky protective vest emblazoned with the words 'MAST COMMERCIAL SECURITY'. Hanging by its strap on the side of the chair was an MP5 submachine gun, magazine loaded, which swung side to side with the movement of the vessel.

"Fuck I know," he said, stifling a yawn which muffled his New York accent. Atkins stood and turned from the window, glaring at the man in the seat. A gruff northerner, with thirty years experience at sea, man and boy, he wasn't known for his patience.

"And how exactly are you helping defend us from bloody pirates sat there on your arse, you lazy shite?" he thundered. "You haven't done a damned thing since you came aboard."

The man stared calmly back at the captain, chewing his upper lip between his teeth, his eyes dark and flat. Eventually he sighed deeply, lifted the MP5 from its resting place, and slowly got to his feet. He paused to take a piece of chewing gum from his mouth then, without breaking eye contact, flicked it onto the deck.

Throwing the strap of the weapon over his shoulder he walked casually out to the little steel walkway which circled the bridge, the captain watching him with growing fury, a redness rising in his cheeks. He pulled the door shut, leaned against the window and lit a cigarette.

Atkins stood for a moment, breathing deeply, before pointing at the chewing gum.

"Jejomar," he said. The Filipino turned to his boss.

"Captain?"

"Pick that shit up, son." Jejomar put his binoculars on the windowsill and cleaned up the chewing gum, wiping the deck with a piece of cloth. The captain returned to the controls, muttering darkly to himself. The GPS showed that they were leaving the Gulf and entering the Arabian Sea proper. He felt a movement as the big ship began an easterly course correction into the open sea, further away from the troubled shores of Somalia.

The armed team, six strong, boarded a few miles off Jeddah, part of a private ship-security contract with the ship owners to ensure their expensive boats and cargoes pass safely through the hostile waters bordering the Gulf. The hostilities in this volatile region meant that he was stuck with the arrogant sods until they reached Karachi, although there would be little risk of attack once the *Ardent Spear* clears the coast of Somalia in a few hours time.

Atkins wondered if dropping chewing gum on the deck was enough of a maritime crime to warrant marooning the bastards.

Ten minutes later the door opened, and the leader of the security team, the tall American, sauntered in. His easy smile and jovial manner had done little endear him to the captain, who didn't like the way he walked around the ship as though he owned it. With greying fair hair and a lean, muscular build, he was wearing the same uniform as the guard outside. He crossed the bridge and stood next to Atkins who acknowledged him with a curt glance.

"Your man out there," the captain gestured sharply with his thumb. "He's a lazy bastard." He turned and looked up at the security man. "I'll be sure to tell that to the owner when we reach port." His face was still slightly red.

"Cassiel?" The team leader smiled. "Oh, he's from the East Coast. They're all lazy bastards there." His eyes glittered in the dim light.

"He spat chewing gum on my deck," said the captain tersely, through tight lips.

"Christ, captain, I've been with him after a night on the JD. You're lucky that's all he left on your deck, I can tell you." The American laughed and leaned over the ship's computer. He began to type quickly, his manicured fingers clicking as they struck the plastic keys. Atkins' jaw dropped.

"What the hell do you think you're doing?" he demanded, stepping forward and squaring up to him. "Get away from that machine. Now."

"Just checking your manifest, Ahab. Nothin' for you to worry about." He continued to type.

"The ship's manifest is strictly private." The captain was fully enraged now, but something about the man's demeanour frightened him. "Stop that right away or I'm going to radio your organisation. I am the captain of this ship, and you are under *my* command." He picked up the ship to shore satellite phone and held it to his ear, hand poised above the dialler. The American sighed and stood to face Atkins.

Calmly, without fuss, he pulled his pistol from its holster and levelled it at the captain's chest.

"Think you're under my command now, bud." He gestured to the computer. "Bring the manifest up, Captain." Atkins glanced to Jejomar for help, but the Filipino kid was kneeling on the deck, hands on his head. The lazy security man, Cassiel, stood beside him, MP5 at the ready. He was chewing on a fresh piece of gum and had a smug smile on his face.

"This is an act of mutiny," whispered Atkins, his face pale.

"Nah, just a bit of fun." The American gestured to the computer with his pistol. "Manifest please."

The captain went to the computer and brought up the file, page after page of listings detailing the contents of the containers on board. As he scrolled down the list the American tapped the screen with the pistol.

"Stop here. Write these container numbers down." The captain grabbed a pad and paper and started to copy down numbers and codes in a tight scribble. He recognised the consignment. Boxes of small arms and ammunition destined for India, and from there to Pakistan. It was a fairly typical cargo in this part of the world.

"Good." The American took the pad and left, pausing on the way out. "Watch them, Cassiel." The door slammed shut.

Still smiling and chewing, Cassiel gestured for Atkins to join Jejomar on the deck. The captain sat next to his crewman, hands on his head as he fought with crazed thoughts of trying to disarm the gunman.

"What is he going to do with those containers," asked Atkins, quietly.

"Fuck if I know," said Cassiel. The captain sat in silence.

After a time the American returned, beaming broadly as he peered through the windows toward the bow of the ship.

"You'll enjoy this, Captain Kidd," he chortled. "Come and have a look-see." Atkins got to his feet gingerly, his frame not used to sitting on hard surfaces for long. Following the American's urgent gestures he looked across the cargo deck, noticing the first true glint of dawn in the east.

On the port walkway next to the container deck two figures were throwing objects into the sea. Two or three at a time, they were tossing bundled rifles, still wrapped in the factory plastic, into the sea. Occasionally cases of ammunition or explosives were passed to them, and they followed the guns into the still waters.

"Fun, ain't it?" said the American.

"That's a perfectly legal consignment. What you're doing is crazy." *At least pirates keep what they steal*, thought Atkins.

"Oh, the only one crazy here will be old Jimmy Hassan when he comes to collects his containers."

"Who's Jimmy Hassan?" asked Atkins.

"Old Jimmy? He's an arms smuggler. Gets guns legally in India, guns like the ones you're carrying, and then they mysteriously leak through the borders and end up in all manner of sweaty little hands." The man laughed shortly. "Not these guns, though, Jimmy... not these ones." He glanced at Atkins, a serious look in his eyes. "Jimmy only has one nut, you know. A hooker in Thailand bit one off few years back."

"What are you trying to do here? Make a point? What difference will a few hundred guns make to the world?"

"Oh, this is just a message, buddy. Don't you worry about it." He laughed. "Just prepping the ground for the main event."

"Who the hell are you people?" said Atkins, his head spinning.

"My name is Mr Gabriel," said the American, smiling once more. "You be good and sure to tell your bosses that."

---oOo---